Horace Elisha Scudder

**Life and Letters of David Coit Scudder, Missionary in Southern India**

Horace Elisha Scudder

**Life and Letters of David Coit Scudder, Missionary in Southern India**

ISBN/EAN: 9783337135232

Printed in Europe, USA, Canada, Australia, Japan

Cover: Foto ©Raphael Reischuk / pixelio.de

More available books at **www.hansebooks.com**

# LIFE AND LETTERS

OF

# DAVID COIT SCUDDER,

## MISSIONARY IN SOUTHERN INDIA.

By HORACE E. SCUDDER.

NEW YORK:
PUBLISHED BY HURD AND HOUGHTON.
BOSTON: E. P. DUTTON AND COMPANY.
MDCCCLXIV.

RIVERSIDE, CAMBRIDGE:
STEREOTYPED AND PRINTED BY
H. O. HOUGHTON AND COMPANY.

# PREFACE.

I HAVE tried in this volume to record the life of an elder brother, who was a missionary in India of the American Board of Commissioners for Foreign Missions, and died at the beginning of his twenty-eighth year. My thanks are due to the various persons who have assisted me in this work by allowing me to examine and use the letters which they had received from my brother, and by furnishing me with recollections of their intercourse with him. Especially I would acknowledge the service rendered by Mr. Capron and Mr. Washburn, members of the Madura Mission.

It should be stated that the chapter on Cromlechs was compiled from material which had also been used in the preparation of a paper upon the subject, read before the Boston Society of Natural History by my brother, S. H. Scudder. and inserted in the published Proceedings of the Society.

The portrait which precedes the volume is engraved from a photograph by Black, enlarged from an ambrotype taken in India, a few weeks before my brother's death. It was judged to be the most satisfactory picture that could be secured of him as he appeared in

India, and I only regret that it was not practicable to insert also one which should recal the face most familiarly to those who remember him as he was at the time of leaving America.

If it had been possible I would gladly have used throughout the book the method adopted in the latter half, of giving the narrative in the missionary's own words, but a slight examination will show the reader how necessary it was that the account of the greater part of his life should be given by another: the record did not exist in his own language, except as it related to the merely incidental side of his life. There can be but little interest and less importance attaching to any mere narrative of adventure, where the life of a student is concerned, and I have followed my own kind of interest, in trying to disclose the mental growth and change in my brother, by the various means which his life afforded. It is not so much to tell what he did, as to show what he was, which I have kept before me as my aim in the biography.

In narrating his missionary experience, however, I have been fortunate in being able to give it entirely in his own words, and I hope that the acquaintance with him formed from the first part of the Life may help the reader to understand and appreciate more fully the character which lies behind the journals and letters. The account of missionary labor, although based on a short eighteen months' experience, will perhaps be found to have a special value through this very limitation, since it is freed from a confusing repetition of similar scenes, while the time is long enough to allow an exhibition of the various sides of missionary life. The freshness of the impressions which the traveller recorded was saved from the danger of error and superficiality by the previous theoretic knowledge which his study had given him, and by the companionship of older residents.

I have not thought to raise a broken shaft over my brother's grave, for I cannot think of him as one having an untimely end, but as one who was permitted to show a rarely completed life within the compass of a few years. It was the rapid, but healthy development of his nature which induced me, with perhaps too partial an interest, to be more particular in my narrative than the reputation of the subject would naturally warrant. But after all, now that the record is finished, I am oppressed with the thought how inadequate must be any biography to reflect the life of a man. To those who knew my brother, this book will doubtless bring back his image in many lights; for those who knew him not, I can only hope that it will make them wish that they had known him.

Boston, *July*, 1864.

# CONTENTS.

It is not growing like a tree
In bulk, doth make man better be;
Or standing long an oak, three hundred year,
To fall a log at last, dry, bald, and sear:
A lily of a day
Is fairer far, in May,
Although it fall and die that night;
It was the plant and flower of light.
In small proportions we just beauties see;
And in short measures life may perfect be.

*From a Pindaric Ode on the Death of Sir H. Morison.*

BEN JONSON.

# LIFE AND LETTERS

OF

# DAVID COIT SCUDDER.

## CHAPTER I.

### CHILDHOOD AND YOUTH.

[1835–1851.]

DAVID COIT, seventh child of Charles, and eldest of the children of Charles and Sarah Lathrop [Coit] Scudder, was born on the 27th of October, 1835, in Boston, Mass., U. S. A. The family was of Puritan origin, tracing its lineage on one side to Governor Winthrop, on the other, to a Scudder of the earliest days of Massachusetts Bay. Two brothers of the name, joining the young colony, had separated: one going to New Jersey, where his descendants abound, the other remaining at Barnstable on Cape Cod. For two hundred years this latter branch has kept its place on the sandy cape, and during most of the period has extended its name but a short distance from the original seat. Like most families similarly established, it has had little part in that westward emigration which removes the hearthstones from so many New-England homes. It is not the rich soil of the West, but the unplanted deep lying to the East, which entices the young men of Cape Cod. They sail over the seas to distant lands, or, if less

1

ambitious, coast to the Banks as fishermen. A more permanent removal is to Boston, where mercantile life attracts, especially that connected with the sea.

It was at the beginning of this century that our father, missing, by one of those notable seeming accidents, the vessel which was to have started him on a sailor's life, came to Boston and began the hard work of an apprentice in business. Before he was of age, he was enabled to undertake business on his own account, and for fifty years continued as a hardware and commission merchant, when he retired from active partnership. Of his business-life little need be said. He was so long identified with the city, that, without seeking distinction, he was widely known. His reputation for honor and integrity in the conduct of his business was of the highest kind, while his sound judgment made him an excellent adviser and trustee. He had lived in Boston thirty years when he married Miss Coit, who, though born and educated in New York, was of New-England parentage and ancestry. Through the Manwarings and Saltonstalls her lineage is traced to Winthrop; and the families by which she was thus connected to the Governor had centred chiefly about Norwich, Connecticut. Our father and mother were thus Puritan in origin and they preserved the principles of Puritan life, relieved of the severity which an earlier necessity had imposed upon Puritan manners. The same principles held in the conduct of the household, while the peculiar state of society in Boston at that time made more imperative that jealous ward which Puritanism is wont to exercise over its followers.

Dissent from the Trinitarian creed had resulted in

the separation of the Congregational Church into two sects, — the Orthodox, holding to the old belief, and the Unitarian. A separation in society had followed, quite radical at first, from the conviction, on the part of the Orthodox, that the matter in dispute was of vital importance and affected the dearest interests of every man : they dreaded worldly-mindedness as leading to laxity of belief, and gave their adhesion to a code of manners which they considered as witnessing to their system of doctrine. The Unitarians, as a body, conformed to an outward state, opposing that of the Orthodox, and intended as a protest against it : accusing their antagonists of an unchristian rigor of life resulting from a narrow and slavish belief, they asserted for themselves what they called a more generous life, the offspring of a more liberal faith. In 1835 the two parties had been so long separated as to have in some measure escaped from the anger which followed the open rupture ; the increased intercourse between them had disabused each of erroneous notions respecting the other, and the extension of family relations served still more to produce common feeling ; but, after all, the antagonism remained, even if robbed of its harshest features ; and a child born in a family holding decided views respecting the controversy, was likely to grow up under social influences representing and enforcing these views.

Our father was a firm supporter of the Orthodox belief, a prominent member of the Orthodox connection, and, as Deacon in Union Church, (Essex Street,) an active promoter of the interests of his church. The schools to which he sent his children were, with the exception of the public schools, under Orthodox direction ; their amusements and occupations, when touching questions of moral advantage, were made to conform to the standard of Orthodox principles; and in all parts of their education a jealous care was exercised, lest they should become lax in religious belief and worldly-minded in their habits of life. In the conduct of the household, there was recognition of some more profound meaning in life than could find expression in mere enjoyment of living, while the presence of a real religious sentiment banished that counterfeit solemnity which would hang over innocent pleasure like a cloud. Yet, while this indicates the principles which governed in our home education, the informing life which saved the principles from producing formalism, or a violent repulsion, was the personal presence of our father.

He was the sunniest-minded of men as he was physically the heartiest: throughout a long life he had scarcely a day of sickness; and with equal truth it can be said that he never suffered in mind those bilious attacks which so few escape; the sunshine within seemed to chase away morbid abstractions. He led a life of peace, which was no mere avoidance of difficulties, but a positive superiority to them; he suffered reverses and failures, he passed through grievous trials, but he kept his spirit in contentment; his mind was in perfect peace. There was a light within of holy love, which shone through the thin casement of his daily life with increasing brightness as he neared the end of his days. Life never became wearisome to him, for nothing was foreign from his concern. The generous instincts of childhood grew with the growth of his mind; and it is not easy to over-state the hearty pleasure with which he entered upon whatever engaged his attention; and these things were often the affairs of others, for he invited confidence by the readiness of his interest. No coldness, no indifference even, could last in his genial presence ; his very smile was a benediction, and strangers were drawn to him by the irresistible charm of his countenance.

It may be judged how bright he made his home. It was a Puritan home ; the " Assembly's Shorter Catechism " was learned in it; the " Sabbath was strictly observed," as the saying is ; there was no anxiety to meet the world half-way and shake hands with it ; and yet, contrary to a general prejudice, there could have been no home where a merrier laugh went up, and more unaffected, abundant, rational enjoyment prevailed. There was seriousness indeed among the elders, for life seemed no trifling matter when they looked so confidently to a divided state in the world beyond, and a graver tone existed than might have arisen had that belief received no outside assaults. The children could not but perceive this seriousness ; and if that had been the burden of their elders' lives, they would likely enough have been utterly repelled from a religion so sombre. But if they looked in the father's face, they knew that religion had not spoiled his life : as they grew older, they saw that it had renewed and enriched it.

There were four older children in the family at the time of David's birth. Within three years, two more boys were added ; and, except that the oldest two sons were shortly after married and established in Boston, the family remained quite unbroken for twenty-five years. The house in which David was born was in Temple Place, but his recollections of childhood centred chiefly about the one afterward occupied in Essex Street, near Lincoln. At that time the neighborhood

was a pleasant one ; directly opposite stood the Or-
phan Asylum with its open grounds, and the adjoining buildings, though plain, afforded decent company.
Near the head of the street, at the corner of Rowe,
stands Union Church, the ecclesiastical home of the
family. The private school, to which David was sent
when a child, was kept by Mrs. Lothrop and her
daughters in the basement of the First Congregational
Church, in the same neighborhood ; while in the opposite direction, at an equal distance from the house,
was the East-Street Grammar School, where his public
school-days were passed.

It was a simple but varied life that we led. There
was comfort, without display, in the household economy,
and pleasure was preferred when it brought the least
worry. The family contained within itself abundant
sources of enjoyment. The family connection, too, was
large, and a constant interchange of visits took place ;
so that from one year's end to the other, new faces appeared or absent old ones reappeared, creating a brisk
feeling in the house, and keeping alive that sort of
hearty cheer which seems to result from a great deal of
welcoming and shaking of hands. A city-life, under
any circumstances, furnishes a fund of novelty to citi-
zens and strangers alike ; and as we were content with
the more simple forms, *ennui* was unheard of. There
always were concerts and lectures for the elders, shows
and celebrations for the children ; there were Whig
torch-light processions, when the house was illuminated,
and Democratic ones, when all the shutters were closed
except one in the top story, where we stood huddled
together to peep at the sight of what we would by no
means countenance.

The church-relations, also, it may easily be inferred, gave character to the daily life. The children had less part here, but came in for a share of the interest. By what mysterious power was it that meetings of the Maternal Associations were exalted in our eyes to the dignity of state occasions, especially that yearly one at the minister's house when we received each an apple and a cake, invested by the ceremony with a superior nature, and eaten slowly, as if they were some exotic fruit? A more serious and thought-provoking occasion was the eventful day when we were graduated from the Maternal Association, with the diploma of book and note from the Secretary, telling us that we had now reached the limit of thoughtless childhood, and were thenceforth left somewhat to ourselves, though never beyond the reach of the circle of praying mothers. Surely, with a tender child a new feeling of responsibility is suggested by this simple ceremony, and it was desired in our Christian society to produce such a result.

If the seriousness, the habit of seeking for religious foundations in all enterprises, which held among the elders, was unconsciously transmitted to the children, whatever direction religious enthusiasm took in the church was even more quickly and more fully taken by the responsive enthusiasm of the children of the church. Thus was it with reference to the Foreign Missionary work, which at that time excited, perhaps, more lively interest from its intimate connection with the church-life in Boston. The missionaries to any point sailed from the city, and became individually known to the churches. Their visits were made the occasion for special fervor of feeling. The Scripture promise, of a multiplication of homes to those who should leave one for the gospel's sake, was fulfilled in the hospitality extended to every member of the missionary body, however humble; and when such a one went on his way, the ship which carried him was watched by hundreds of eager eyes, and remembered in hundreds of praying families. The more prominent of these missionaries, those gifted with special powers of eloquence, or who had enjoyed long experience abroad, were received with proportionate attention, and their presence would form the topic of conversation, and be turned to the increase of the missionary enthusiasm.

The enthusiasm extended, naturally enough, to the humblest and youngest. The Sunday-schools had their missionary societies; and in such day-schools for young children as were under Orthodox direction an interest in the cause was promoted. David, once enumerating in a paper the causes of his missionary purpose, named first the influence of Mrs. Lothrop, his school-teacher; and it is certain that pains were taken by the more devout Christians to give such a tendency to the thoughts of their children or pupils. These learned to associate the missionary with all that was especially heroic. They were not taught to regard him as a man who had made a sacrifice of all that was pleasant in life, and had done violence to his nature; they knew him as the highest type of an excellence which they were daily bidden to strive after, and understood that the most cherished desires of their parents, the most earnest prayers, would be fulfilled if they were to attain the same position. I have happened to read the personal experience of many young missionaries contemporary with my brother, and in almost every case there is reference to the wishes of Christian parents as strong motives for their subsequent choice. My brother gave as a second motive in his case, " My mother's wishes."

Our father's house was always open to the missionary, and none sailed from the city whose acquaintance he did not take pains to make. Most of them were visitors at the house. Certainly no one gave them a warmer welcome or a more earnest farewell. Among the most noticeable of these men was Dr. John Scudder, missionary in India, whose personal presence, more than that of any other man, I suppose, kindled the enthusiasm of the friends of missions in Boston. His name, from the first, attracted our father's interest, although the identity of the two families ceased here, since they were removed from a common origin by six generations or more. The strong bond of a common object, however, stood in the place of blood-relationship, and ever after a close attachment existed between the two families, which had frequent opportunities of expression, since Dr. Scudder was accompanied and followed to India, from time to time, by a large family of sons, the youngest of whom, years afterwards, sailed for India in the same ship with David.

Dr. Scudder was known, and is now remembered in large part, by the power which he displayed in interesting and impressing children. Whether he was the first to give special attention to this matter, I do not know; but he succeeded in leaving a vivid impression upon the minds of the children of Orthodox families. Possibly this vividness owed much to the striking person of the man. A childish recollection presents him to me as tall and commanding, with very white and erect hair, generally adorned, while he was making an address, with gold-bowed spectacles that had been pushed up from the nose; a penetrating eye that fixed attention, and a voice that could terrify as well as please. Indeed, there was considerable spice in his addresses of suttees and self-torture. Yet, despite or perhaps through this element of terror, he wrought to great effect. The fervor of his manner, which was impressively solemn at times, and the excitability of his temperament, made children listen to him, and come away with a sense of accountability to him in the matter of personal devotion to the work of missions; for it was a frequent word of the Doctor's that he should expect to meet this child and that in India, — yes, at the very landing-place in Madras; and many a one, in the simplicity of a child's reasoning, felt it incumbent upon him not to disappoint his confident friend. My brother was very susceptible to personal influence of this sort; and when Dr. Scudder, then staying at our father's house, laid his hands upon his head, and — far as his authority went — set him apart for missionary work in India, he gave implicit assent, and exhibited thereafter a child's unquestioning enthusiasm for his venerable friend and for the cause which he represented. His teacher relates that she found it easy, in those days, to check his rebellious spirit by appealing to his honor as her little missionary. And in the paper to which I have referred, he gives the third and last cause of his decision, "Dr. John Scudder's personal interest and influence over me."

If Dr. Scudder had not put in the first claim for my brother's services, perhaps he might, in after-years, have chosen the Nestorian people for his labors, so strongly was he affected by the visit to this country of

the Nestorian Bishop, Mar Yohannan, who came in
company with Dr. Justin Perkins, and stayed awhile at
our father's house. The swarthy Oriental, with his
flowing robes, entering our New-England home, was
like a story from the " Arabian Nights." Half in terror, but fascinated by his presence, the children of the
family watched the guest and followed him in his
walks. David was engrossed with this wonderful sight,
and for years always kept in his room a print of the
Bishop, with turban and robes and sweeping beard
attending a most lordly mien, and treasured up little
relics that once had belonged to him. His early interests always kept their place. It was not long before
his death, that, wishing to institute some closer connection between the native Christians of his mission and
those in other parts of the world, he induced one of
them to write a letter to Mar Yohannan, which was
answered, though my brother never saw the reply.

It is easier to state the special influences which affect
early boyhood than to lay hold of and measure those
of a by-character, which may yet be quite powerful.
If one would see what manner of man this child would
be, he must observe him not only under the school-
mistress' eye, paying his tribute to Dr. Scudder's power,
and guarded by the ordinances and habits which ruled
in the church and household-life of a conscientious
Orthodox family, he must see him also in his street-
life and in his experience at a public school. But just
this side is the most difficult to present by incidents.
One would have seen him, in those days, a white-
haired, excitable boy, brimming with life, never knowing a listless moment, hurrying from school to play,
trapping pigeons in the freight *dépôts*, acting out all

his boyish notions of Indian warfare, and going through
the whole zodiac of a boy's sports with untiring zeal;
forming warm attachments to a curiously chosen band
of school-boys and neighbors; yet, by a gentleness easily
discoverable under a sturdy exterior, shrinking from
vulgarity, and obeying fearlessly an educated instinct
of pure-toned morality. He was a troublesome boy,
heady and determined; but somehow quite as obstinate
in doing disagreeable things which he felt to be right,
as in following the bent of his will when it opposed
itself to authority. He was a little torment to his
brothers from pure love of fun, and stood in the way
of their peace provokingly; but mean and dishonorable
he never was. With a natural shrinking from inflict-
ing pain, and an almost timid nature, he never came to
blows with his comrades, and never made any enemies;
yet he was constantly getting into half-serious quarrels,
and making up in some irresistible fashion, which kept
him always a favorite and always a vexation.

His earliest associations were of the city, with a few
summer hints of country pleasures, for which he showed
a most eager relish. To the Cape, also, our family
went every year, visiting the old homestead. At first,
before the railway was built, the journey was the great
charm, when we were packed into a carriage and drove
at our own leisure, making two or three days on the
road. Cotuit Port, Hyannis Port, on the opposite side
of the Cape to Barnstable, and Chatham, nearer the
horn, were the visiting-places; and half of the pleasure was in the hearty zest with which our father returned to his boyish scenes, was welcomed by his old
friends, — he seemed to know every soul on the road, —
and pointed out to us his old work and play-grounds;

while we children tried for ourselves the edge of the ocean, and fished off the rocks, that, at low tide, lie along the shore at Hyannis like sea-monsters. David was the most venturesome, and was in perpetual excitement at wind and wave, throwing himself, after his impetuous manner, into the life of a Cape-Cod boy, as if he never had lived in Boston, and scorching his feet in a fearful manner, because he would go barefoot like his cousins, though the sand was hot and the beach-grass sharp.

When he was eleven years of age, the family removed from the city. Some change was necessary, for the neighborhood of the house had become changed by the approach of the foreign population, that, with business, turns so many families out of their old homes. The purity of the childrens' lives, however, formed the strongest reason for moving to a place then on the country side of the city of Roxbury, three miles from Boston. The house was a large brick one, on Warren Street, standing high enough to command, from its upper windows, a noble view of the harbor, and surrounded by thirty acres of land, partially under cultivation. A half-dozen acres only were attached to the house; but no visible boundaries separated the remainder, while there adjoined the place quite an extensive piece of wood and pasture land, since reclaimed, together with the grounds, for building purposes, but then affording an excellent play and roving field. Beyond was pretty open country, with half-wild patches of woodland and small ponds; so that, with the city at handy distance on one side, and the country on the other, abundant variety of scenery and occupation was furnished. It was no great distance either to the water-

side, where the harbor **pushes** its way to the border of
**Roxbury and Dorchester,** affording a capital swimming-
place.

The restless activity which, with David, had spent
**itself in street sports and on** such pets as a city yard
**would permit, found in** the country unlimited range ;
**and as he had a** healthy practical side to his **nature,**
all possible **pleasure** and good seemed contained in a
**farmer's life. He** became instantly all **alive to such**
pursuits, **and was** by no means a play-farmer boy, but
one **in good** earnest. He had his plot, where he made
**vegetables** grow whether they would or not, watching
**them** with untiring vigilance ; **he** kept **hens and** pigs,
which always throve under his care ; and in the larger
**cattle** he seemed to claim an ownership by the interest
which he showed in them ; while to his collection of
**pets, rabbits, pigeons, and fancy fowl,** he gave the
**most** zealous attention. **His** generous **and simple na-**
**ture** showed itself in the intense interest **which** he felt
in the tribe of animals about him ; he loved them
almost as **if they were** children, not **with** any foolish
sentimentalism, but with a wholesome, hearty affection.
**I remember an** instance of that steadfast, unflinching
affection with which David held to anybody or anything once finding a place in his heart, **in the persist-**
ence with which he clung to a house-dog when it grew
old and was **afflicted with a** loathsome **disease.** Nep
had some horrible ulcer in his head, and spent his days
flapping his ears and howling and **rolling** over and over,
**but** David stood stoutly by his shaggy and disgraced
**friend,** walked with him, played with him, defended
him against all the reproaches of those unable to find
Nep endurable, and never bated one jot of his affec-

tionate care to the end. The end was the drowning of the poor animal, after David had entered college, and he writes home, upon hearing of it, "I had a real crying spell over Nep. However, I am glad he is dead."

The same strong attachment took hold of the place itself. He scoured all the country about in his walks and sports, knew the wood-paths and the depths of the ponds; and afterward, when he had left college and the family had returned to the city, he took many an excursion to the place and lingered about his old haunts. May-day became a sort of anniversary to him, when he would walk out to Roxbury, lie down in the woods overlooking the pond where he had skated and fished, or sent Nep in on errands after sticks and stones, and mingle these recollections with ardent anticipations. It was a most hearty and natural life which he led in those days, entering with such contagious zest into all his pursuits, and finding in the free air which bore his shouts a spirit akin to his own, in his dog bounding beside him a companion that could respond to his exuberance better even than his playfellows.

Of playfellows he had an abundance, both because he was so popular and because his father's place afforded such a capital rendezvous. Something always was going on. Up early in the morning, he was out feeding his dependants in the barn-yard; rushing off to his plot with Nep at his heels; riding the horse bareback or chasing his rabbits; running to school across fields at the last moment, and coming in out of breath with just enough surplusage of spirits to keep him on the verge of disgrace or difficulty; rushing for the bats or the football at recess, and going home on the same fast run which never fell off into a saunter; using every spare

moment at noon for farm-work; repeating the morning
in the afternoon, and ending the day in a race with
his dog up or down street, or across the pasture. In
short, one remembers him in those days as half intoxicated with life, wilful in his love of freedom, and
impatient of all restraint. His wilfulness frequently was
obstinacy; he was a hard boy to manage, but down at
the bottom of his heart, beneath the rough exterior,
was a strong love, and in all his actions one could read
the manly stuff of which he was made.

Shortly after the removal to Roxbury he was sent
to the Latin School of the town, and spent four years
in immediate preparation for college. Mr. Charles
Short, now President of Kenyon College, was the
master of the school, and under his instruction David
formed a more thorough, and at the same time more
genial acquaintance with the classics than falls to the
lot of most lads not living in the city. He always was
extremely apt at acquiring language, and indeed so
glib in his use of a tongue as to be obliged to guard
against the superficiality of ready linguists. His taste
for pure nonsense took the form of a liking for out-
landish vocables, and kept him not only airing his new
languages at odd moments, but also contriving new
combinations and discoursing in tongues unknown even
to himself. When he came to exercise himself upon
the Tamil speech, he found his organs of utterance in
a tractile condition which may have owed something
to these boyish practices. For mathematics he had no
inclination, while letter-writing and composition of
any kind were very distasteful. This was natural
enough, for he had not yet begun to think; he was
thoroughly a boy in his entire freedom from speculative

habits; he did not know what an abstraction was, and indeed pure meditation never was very natural to him; his mind seized most firmly upon what was presented in some concrete form. His early letters, few enough in number, are amusing for the *naiveté* with which this outness of life is displayed; he begins with what he has last seen, and if, before he has finished the account, something comes to interrupt it, down goes a notice of that in a parenthesis, and then he resumes his thread. I think that he went through his preparatory course with very little intellectual excitement; his quickness and habit of obeying, rather than any fondness for study, carried him through with credit.

It was this habit of attending to what was right at hand which gave him so tenacious a hold of life, and induced such hearty concern for all his interests and associations. Thus in school he studied hard; in play-time he played with a will; and as for all the drudgery of farm-work, he entered into it with a spirit which never flagged. It was not strange, therefore, that places and animals and friends to whom he had given so much of himself should have a strong hold upon his affections. Toward his school-comrades he never grew cool. In after-years he would come home delighted at having met in the street some one of them whom perhaps he had not seen for years; he sought them out and cared for their spiritual interest when that became the chief thing in his mind; and in his letters from India, would sometimes break out into a naming of one after another of his playmates, with whom school connection was quite all that he had ever had, and ask a remembrance of them should his brothers ever chance upon them.

2

He was as true to his nature when in the church as when in the school-room or the playground. His religious training, both at home and abroad, was of that kind which looks to firm foundations of religious belief. It was taught him that nothing short of a radical change of heart would answer the requirements of God's word. All the ordinances of religion acknowledged the necessity, and there was no room left for the satisfaction of conscience short of this complete change. David's naturalness and love of truth would have revolted at any suggestion of assuming a concern which he did not feel, while his Puritan instinct and education made him accept without question the religious observances which were required of him. He had no liking for these, but he kept to them with particular obstinacy when they happened to be rather disagreeable or unpopular, and was wholly indifferent to ridicule. I remember how, when he saw one coming whom he disliked and whom he knew to be seeking him for the sake of giving advice upon matters of religion, he jumped behind a stone wall and mischievously watched him through the chinks as he went by, looking about in astonishment at the sudden disappearance of the boy; and I remember also how, wishing to complete a reading of the Bible within some appointed time, and finding himself in arrears, he read the book at every spare moment with a ludicrous energy, — in the barn, on the school-house steps in recess-time, or wherever opportunity occurred, quite regardless of quip or remonstrance. The missionary zeal which had possessed the child found in the boy no outward expression at least, for he understood very well that missionary life was conditioned on a religious character which he did not pretend to have.

He regarded going to college as a matter which he could not very well avoid, and he did not therefore worry himself much about it, though he thought it rather an unnecessary measure for one who was to be a farmer. It was the height of his ambition now to emigrate West in a covered wagon, containing his goods and chattels, while he walked beside in a smock, and a dog ran beneath the wagon with that studied precision of gait which always astonished him. The summer before he entered college he spent upon the large farm of a relation in Wethersfield, Connecticut, where he was thoroughly in his element, working with a zeal and steadiness which won the praises of the farmer himself, generally incredulous of the agricultural fever of city-boys. "To-day," he writes, after recounting the glories of his life there, "I am going to study, although I do hate to. I do not want to go to college, but should like to stay here all the time. If I stay here much longer I shall be a decided farmer." His father, always ready to humor the taste of his sons, knew that he was too young to decide for himself, so he required at least a year or two of college-life before letting him have his way in this. David's habit of obedience had more force than his mere inclination, and he entered on college-life with his customary heartiness, which never permitted any "might have beens" to interfere with the business at hand. His parents, solicitous first of all for his spiritual welfare, indicated a preference for Williams College, where education was under guard of Orthodox principles, and where a man was the head whose name, besides its renown in philosophic inquiry, was a security for the maintenance of those principles in their integrity. David joined the Freshman Class of the college in September, 1851, just before the close of his sixteenth year.

## CHAPTER II.

COLLEGE LIFE — FRESHMAN YEAR.

[1851–1852.]

" My earliest recollections of Dave," writes one of his classmates, " is of seeing a white-haired boy in short jacket dart out of the house next above mine, at recitation-time, and move up the street on a keen run. That was his usual street-gait ; indeed I cannot seem to associate him with a sober walk at all." His boyishness at the first marked him, for though there were some in the class younger in years, these were every one more mature, and at any rate concealed much of their youth under the cloak of college dignity. David was a boy in mind and in manner, — wholly unconventional in his habits, with an instinct of freedom which at home sent him roaming over the fields, and showed itself also in a determined will, a capricious impatience of restraint. The change in his outward life brought influences which acted upon his growth with great force, and produced a more rapid development than would have seemed possible under other circumstances. At home his love for nature, which was one manifestation of his instinct of freedom, had fed upon the decorous forms of suburban beauty ; now he came suddenly upon the mountains and rushing streams and untamed tracts of northern Berkshire. He knew not why, but he knew how much this wildness and unshorn strength responded to his instinctive desires, and at once threw himself

eagerly into out-door life, without a thought of anything beyond a natural liking for it, and yet surely
receiving in return the fullest reward.

To those unfamiliar with this district, it would be
hard to convey a notion of its impressive character.
The town itself rests upon the uneven surface of a valley surrounded by hills, which rise in several instances
to the dignity of mountains as regards height, and in
almost all cases have the gullied declivities characteristic of the mountain formation.   The valley through
which the Hoosac River flows is cultivated, and contains many spots of tender beauty; especially is this
tenderness discovered when looked at from East Mountain which banks the river, but the prevailing impression made by the scenery is of a ruder, wilder force.
The roads which lead in various directions, connecting
the town with North Adams, with Pittsfield, with Ben-
nington, and with Troy, either follow the winding course
of streams or climb and descend successive hills, so that
by no one of the travelled ways can one fail to find
variety of scenery, sudden surprises, and often pretty
rough passage.   But the roads do not reveal the chief
wonders of the country.   Only one who climbs the
mountain-paths, and strikes off from the rocky roads to
follow a brook or reach some remote patch of wood or
pasture land, learns the secrets of this wild and glorious
spot.

The tops of the surrounding mountains were the
goals which my brother, with his restless eagerness, from
the first desired to reach.   He seized the opportunity
of every holiday to climb Greylock or West or East
Mountain, and cast his straining look to the horizon,
sweeping an arc which embraced, sometimes the scarred

sides of other mountains, and sometimes the quiet farms and still life of the valley. Part of his satisfaction was in the rough ascent, before which he was undaunted and in which he never faltered, in the bracing air of the heights, and in the sensation of animal vigor; part in the wide range of vision and the fuller life which seems to flow about one on those solitary summits. I can see him now, upon the top of Greylock, as he describes himself in an early letter, going away from the smoky tower and the groups of uproarious students, to a lonely rock looking off upon the broad view, and shouting forth, in the exultation of his spirits, the morning song which Milton puts into Adam's mouth, beginning, —

> "These are Thy glorious works, Parent of Good,
> Almighty. Thine this universal frame."

It always did him good to shout. I never was with him under similar circumstances but that he would give expression to his excitement in one or two prodigious yells, after which the quieter thoughts and emotions would have their turn in a pertinacious silence. This shouting or singing aloud by himself was a favorite occupation; it was, to use a common simile, a way of letting off steam. I remember how, once in his Senior year, walking alone upon one of the Williamstown roads, no one in sight, he was bawling at the top of his voice, when suddenly, upon turning a corner, he came full upon the college President, who was as much entertained as David was confused at the encounter.

From the very first he entered upon this hearty outdoor life. Indeed, he was so fresh in his enjoyment of it, so boyish in his way of engaging in it, that his friends were all the while kept amused by his freaks.

The longer walks could only be taken on holidays; but
the hills, which were at an easy distance from the college, afforded an opportunity for numerous short excursions.   Flora's Glen, a wild ravine, and Stone Hill
were his favorite haunts.   On the latter he began to
set rabbit and squirrel traps as soon as he had become
fairly domiciled.   He had rather meagre success, considering the pains he took; but that made no difference.   Almost every day, alone or with a comrade, he
would trudge up the steep hill to look after his traps;
and when he did catch an animal, he made his friends
nearly as much interested as himself, by the contagion
of his enthusiasm.   His early letters always contain
some notice of a hunt after rabbits, apples, or nuts,
what new style of trap he meant to contrive, and how
he had learned to skin his captives.   He joined the
Lyceum of Natural History, then in a most impover-
ished and unsteady condition; and although he never
brought much scientific learning into the meetings, he
had such a healthy enthusiasm that he was a valuable
member of the society.

His first winter in Williamstown quite intoxicated
him, one might think.   The long, blustering, and
stormy season which shrivels up a good many students,
and makes Williams' graduates shiver as they recal it,
seemed to bring out all the glow of his nature.   In
those early days, with a sort of stubborn hardihood, he
disdained great-coats, and never would wear them until
the severity of two or three Williamstown winters and
the sensitiveness of a changing *physique* forced him into
them; he always displayed a ludicrous horror of them,
as if they would make him effeminate.   His classmates
remember his grotesque appearance that Freshman win-

ter, as, wearing his boyish roundabout, but no coat, his feet encased in enormous India-rubber boots, his hands in great fur gloves, and his head smothered under a fur cap, he would clatter down West College staircase, dragging at his heels the sled of which he was so proud.

His growth in character was favored not only by the wild and fascinating country, which called forth his instincts of freedom and gave force and direction to his nature, but also by separation from home and the consequent necessity for self-dependence. He was much younger in mind and experience than most boys of his age, and, in common with all who lead an instinctive life, had accepted with implicit confidence the guidance of his superiors. He was slow in assuming responsibility, even in minor matters of college experience; he felt no disposition to release himself from his accustomed dependence. In nothing was his inexperience more noticeable than in his absolute freedom from " knowingness." I take the word of one of the most observing of his classmates when I say that it was a thing rare and quite unexampled to find one who, like David, had spent his early days in the streets of Boston, and all of his youth in public schools, with almost unrestrained choice of associates, so incredibly ignorant of what is called " the world." Not long after entering college, some allusion was made, in the chat of a knot of students, when David was present, to a classmate who had been drunk the night before. Nothing so very astonishing to them in this, however else they might regard it; but David was aghast. " Drunk ! " said he; " a fellow in college, and in our class, drunk ! Why, I did not know that any one in college ever was

drunk!'" His incredulity must have been matched by
that of his companions at his unheard-of simplicity.
This is but a single example of his ignorance of evil,
and also of his *naïve* frankness in admitting the ignorance.

How much his home education and how much his
semi-country life had served as safeguards against a
familiarity with forms of evil, it is impossible to say;
but it is most natural to refer his ignorance of the
world to his own straightforward and transparent character, under the favoring influence of a religious training. His simplicity of nature would not invite, but
rather check solicitations of evil; an education based
upon firm principles of the highest morality fortified
his natural security against gross temptation; and,
finally, his whole-souled absorption in out-door life
furnished an escape for his animal vigor. The same
causes conspired to protect him, now that he was
brought into more immediate contact with evil, and
was also left more to his own control. Danger there
was, and he drew a long breath in after-years as he
considered what he had escaped. What he might have
been, he could see in the wrecks about him of boys
who had come up to college with much the same freshness that belonged to him, but who had not withstood
the shock of evil communications.

The students at Williams then numbered about two
hundred and forty, distributed pretty equally among
the four classes. The college formed a community by
itself distinct from the village; and since it was so
small a community, and so dependent upon its internal
resources for comfort and pleasure, there was more
mutual acquaintance than holds in larger colleges and

in those near cities. Many knew not only their own class well, but a large portion of the upper or lower classes. The societies brought men together, and it was consequently a pretty compact community, in which each individual with difficulty remained aloof. The country element was dominant, and served to give a certain tone to the society there which it is hard exactly to describe. In part, a sturdy independence belonged to many of the countrymen, the result perhaps of an early necessity of self-reliance; a high estimate of the value of education; and a determination to make the most of college, giving a healthy tone to the life there. With this frequently was associated a pettiness and narrowness of conduct, a ridiculous eagerness for small distinction, an incorrect understanding of what college could do for them, and a ludicrous exaggeration of the grandeur of the college equipments. All this was tempered by a certain infusion of city civilization, in the form of a generosity running too often into recklessness; a courtesy which is bred of intercourse with cultivated men and women, but which, in the weaker sort, became mere foppishness; an acquaintance, moreover, with the refinement of learning, a side rarely exposed to the country seeker after wisdom. Though a city-boy, David was strongly countryish in his inclinations. His taste, which led him to take pleasure in the worth of men, unaffected by their social culture, was confirmed here, and a habit induced of measuring men generally by a more liberal standard than refined society is apt to adopt.

His intercourse with his college-mates threw him among those who were older and more accustomed to self-management. They were wonders of wisdom and

experience in his eyes, and he looked up to some even
in his own class with a real veneration. He accepted
implicitly the lead of these, transferring to them the
faith which he had reposed in his superiors at home.
Yet every new experience added to his self-reliance, and,
after the novelty of college-life had worn off a little, he
began quite unconsciously to live less instinctively, and
to bring some reflection to bear upon his position. One
can hardly speak too positively of the absence hitherto
of any exercise of thought as directed toward himself;
he lived freely and outwardly as a child. The new
atmosphere of college, however, where he found his fellows engaged upon subjects of thought quite beyond
his wondering mind, and the stimulus which a community of students supplies, did awaken thought in him.
The separation from home, too, brought an old influence in new shape, — his father's counsel, — which
would now be given through letters more systemati-
cally, and with the weight both of fatherly affection
and of remoteness. There began a kind of intercourse
which was impossible in earlier days. The entrance
of the son upon a regular educational course, away
from home, elevated him to a more independent position, and it was easy and natural for the father to address him, not in the tone of parental authority, but in
that of a wise man talking familiarly with his junior
whom he takes into his counsels, treating him as almost
an equal. How happily his father could use this tone
is instanced by the following extract from a letter written at this time : —

ROXBURY, Oct. 6, 1851.

MY DEAR SON DAVID : — You made us all very
happy by so long and so nice a letter, and particularly

because we found by it that you were happy and contented at Williamstown, both in respect to your college duties and your boarding-place. I have no doubt that the more you think of the duties that now devolve upon you, the more you will think of the responsibility that attaches to those duties. We have placed you in college from the conviction, after much thought and prayer, that your ultimate happiness and success in life would be promoted by it. I have long felt that I never would consent, if I could avoid it, to place any more of my sons in the commercial life, because my own experience is decidedly averse to it ; and as to any mechanical business, unless there is a predilection that way, or a bent of mind decidedly in favor of such pursuits, I have not thought it desirable to have any of my sons go to a mechanical trade ; but it has been the height of my ambition to give to all my dear boys a good education, because I have seen, in the experience of many years, that boys, when well educated, make men, and men that can make their way in the world somehow ; that is, if they do not abuse their privileges by neglecting them, and giving themselves over to the Evil One. Now if you would continue to make me happy, you will persevere in your studies, conquer all the obstacles that come in your way, and if you do not gain the eminence you aim at, be careful to deserve it by your diligence and good conduct in all respects, so as to gain the love and good-will of your teachers and your fellow-students. . . . .

Your affectionate father,

CHARLES SCUDDER.

While he was in the full tide of his hearty enjoy-

ment, engaging with zest in all his pursuits, setting
rabbit-traps on Stone Hill and exploring the country
about, there came news to him of severe losses in business which his father had suffered, involving the necessity of greater economy in the mode of life at home,
and possibly the removal from the country place to
which all had become so attached. In the simplicity
of his heart, he went straightway to the Professor of
Mathematics, as the authority most competent to explain to him the true nature of a failure in business,
and one also of whose good feeling and sympathy he
felt assured. After getting all the light he could, he
made up his mind promptly as to his duty.

He wrote home begging to be permitted to stay only
through the rest of the term, and then to resume his
old and cherished pursuit as a laborer upon some farm,
where he could at least relieve his father of expense,
and support himself. "You know," he says, "that it
has long been my wish to be a farmer, and it has not in
the least abated." Meanwhile, since, at the best, this
was a measure of economy which could not be put
into execution for several weeks, he immediately made
arrangements for cutting down his already moderate
expenses. He was rooming out of the colleges, as most
Freshmen did who preferred the increased cost to the
perils and discomforts of life in the buildings. Almost
before he could get an answer to his proposition, he
had vacated his rooms and gone into West College,
taking a great barn-like room at the top of the building; besides, he applied for and obtained the position
of janitor to the recitation-room, — a position taken by
one of the poorest of each class, requiring most vexa-
tious attention, and standing him in some trivial sum or

freedom from certain college taxes. All this was unnecessary : it was not recommended by his father ; but it was just what he could not help doing. He did not trouble himself to reason much about it ; he only considered that there must be retrenchment in the household, and that it was his business to cut down his own expenses immediately to the very lowest point.

This occasion, so characteristically met, was important for the impulse which it gave to his thought. At the bottom of his letter home concerning the failure, he writes with a Freshman's ardor and confidence : " I am studying hard for the first place." He was aware of the little likelihood there was that his father would listen to his proposal, though he had made it in good faith ; since he must stay, he applied himself with zeal to the task of making as much of college as he could. He gave as an object of study the one which was prominent in college, not that he cared particularly for it, but because he could not easily give a proper reason. Really he had an excellent reason, namely, that it was his business just now to study hard : but then he had hardly begun to state to himself reasons for doing anything. He did things for reasons, but not much for stated reasons.

His usual life went on much as ever. The present and the visible were too engrossing with him to admit of much reflection, in his untutored mind, on the uncomprehended difficulties of his father's position, or much anticipation as to what he himself meant to do. He continued to set his traps and to write home directions about his old pets and small stock, entering with animation into all measures talked of at home. His letters contained messages to every soul about the

house.   This college-life was not near so much to him
as his home ; it was more remote from his sympathy,
and he would sit for hours with some friend, telling of
his little world with the most simple enthusiasm.   His
studies gave him no great trouble, since they were
chiefly in the classics, where he was best qualified and
where the majority of the class were most deficient.
Mathematics caused him to groan inwardly, but he
found most delight in his manifold out-door occupations ; then his labors in the recitation-room kept him
busy.   He was up early on the cold mornings, sweeping the room, kindling the fire, and lighting the lamps
for the barbarous dawn recitations.   It was Freshman
recitation-room, and he found a horrible state of things
in it on some days.   His class will recollect the scene
one afternoon in February, when, in the middle of the
recitation, a log of wood, flung through the window of
the adjoining wood-closet, burst the door open, and let
into the room a bewildered sheep, which David, as
janitor, proceeded to eject by catching his hind-legs
and walking him out wheelbarrow-fashion.

It was on his return to college, at the close of the
long winter vacation, that the thought which had been
working in his mind took a more fixed character, and
he began to feel within himself the stirring of conscience, demanding that he should decide the question
of personal religious duty.   Ever since his connection
with the college, in accordance with his home education, he had been a frequent attendant upon the op-
tional as well as upon the prescribed religious services
of the college.   He had an unquestioning conviction
of the truth of religious doctrines, as set forth in the
Orthodox creed, without ever making any systematic

inquiry. Such an inquiry would have been impossible to his unthinking mind; and now, when awakened to thought, his difficulty was not in the way of intellectual belief. The formulas of Orthodox theology, compassing the way of salvation, were familiar to him, and the common religious talk and appeals in the prayer-meeting were based upon an acceptation of the doctrines of evangelical belief. The question with him, free from all difficulty in theology, was one of simple submission to the Divine will. He struggled long in darkness, seeming to himself ready to submit, and yet, through his meagre power of introspection, unable apparently to discover the obstacle which stood between his desire and its fulfilment. There was a conscientious perseverance and honesty in his character, which refused to be content with anything short of full satisfaction on this point; nor was it possible that a will so stubborn and determined as his should accept, without severe struggle, the entire self-renunciation required of it. Thus the period of his contest extended over several weeks. His room-mate, for he had taken one at the beginning of the term, speaking of this time, says: "I had noticed there was something serious on his mind, and my interest was excited by the singular circumstance of his repeating the same verse for several days in the noon meeting: 'So foolish was I and ignorant. I was as a beast before thee.' (Ps. lxxiii. 22.) I have no remembrance of dates; but one day he came into the room, threw himself on the floor, and began to weep and moan and roll about, seemingly in great agony. I went to him and talked for a while, when he became calmer. It was that night, I think, that the struggle was over."

The difficulty which lay in the way of his peace, and which for a while he seemed not to recognize in thought, became plain when it was stated to him by another. One cherished purpose stood as the representative of self, endeavoring to maintain a supremacy. A few years afterward he wrote as follows to Professor Hopkins : " I well remember the day on which in anxiety of mind I called upon you, not knowing why I did not find peace in believing. You asked me if I had no cherished purpose which stood in the way. That question at once let in a flood of light, and was the most weighty question which I ever was called upon to answer. I saw then that the alternative was before me, — to be a farmer and a sinner, or a missionary and a Christian. My boyish inclination for a farmer's life appeared in its right light, and I was helped, I believe, to give it up and to give myself to Christ and his Church."

This then was the crucial test. I am confident that he had never failed to regard the question of becoming a Christian and that of becoming a missionary as inseparably connected for him ; his decision of the latter was a test of sincerity in deciding the former. So also he stated it to the ecclesiastical council which ordained him. Every way the act was characteristic. He had early and always associated the missionary with the most advanced stage of Christian profession. He could not be half-way in anything he undertook, and in assuming the vows of a Christian, his whole nature hurried him on to what he regarded as the most complete fulfilment of those vows. His being, like the cloud which

" — moveth all together, if it move at all,"

carried him undoubting and with whole-heartedness into the missionary idea. Henceforth he had this ruling purpose, and eight years afterward he could say, in the letter to Professor Hopkins just now quoted: "Inseparable as these two acts appeared then, they have been no less so in my feelings since that day. I have never made any other formal committal of myself to the work, and have never seriously wavered in my decision. Having this definite end before me so constantly has been of immense service to me as a Christian, and I thank God for it."

Nor was there absent the influence of personal association always strongly moving him. From the day when old Doctor Scudder laid his hand on his head and claimed him for the India Mission, he had felt the touch, and when now he had decided, without recal, to enter the missionary field, it would have been almost as impossible to choose any other country than India, as to have chosen any other work than the missionary. Just before leaving college, he makes the brief entry in his journal, "Heard of Doctor Scudder's death at Cape of Good Hope. I can never have my desire gratified of seeing him in India;" and eleven years afterward, when he had closed his short career in that distant land, a brother-missionary, arranging his library for transmission to America, found a little paper-covered book well worn by use, but tenderly preserved. It bore the title, "Letters to Sabbath School Children, by Rev. John Scudder, M. D., Missionary at Madras," and written broadly across the fly-leaf, "Master David Scudder, from his affectionate friend, J. Scudder, New York, Aug. 8, 1843." This, with one or two pale letters, the young missionary had treasured since childhood;

they were to him dear signs of the affection of his revered predecessor, and he carried them to the shores where he had hoped to be welcomed by him. It was not thus to be; yet surely our faith may warrant the imagination which pictures, when the two did meet, a holier greeting than Madras beach would have witnessed.

The period of his conversion was every way the most important epoch of his life, for it was the dividing point between the old, impulsive, unthinking life, with no aim beyond the nearest object, and the new life of thought, of loyalty to an idea, — a life having a purpose comprehensive enough to bind together all his manifold interests, and so far-reaching as never to fail him. No sooner had he got the clue to his existence than he followed it. A great impulse was given to his intellectual faculties. The awakening which his thought had undergone and which had begun to reveal to him something of himself, was aided by a powerful agent in the sense of its being his duty to think. His letters, both before this and for some time to come, are faithful exponents of the outward life which he habitually led; consequently they have very little other worth, being occupied chiefly with the commonplace news of college. A single example will stand for all, and I select one in which he communicates to his parents the fact of his conversion, — it is so transparent in its display of his character. The intelligence in the latter part is of course wholly unimportant in itself; the significance is in the naturalness with which he passed from religion to rabbit-traps, and back to religion again : —

WILLIAMSTOWN, Feb. 21, 1852.

MY DEAR FATHER AND MOTHER : — I have just returned with chum from the lecture by Professor Hopkins. The President is not very well, so he took his place. But I attended to him with far different feelings from what I have been accustomed to, for, dear parents, I hope that I am a Christian. Yes, I hope that I have made my peace with God. I can hardly realize it. It has always seemed so far off. But how simple a thing it is. The great trouble with me was, I think, unwillingness to give the world up. I went to Professor Hopkins's house the other day to talk with him. I came home and talked with chum some time, and then consecrated myself to God. I felt willing to say, 'Lord, what wilt Thou have me to do?' I felt at peace after that. It is nearly time to go to the office, so I must close with some things of great importance to us. First. The Gymnasium is burnt down to the ground. I will tell you more about it in a letter soon to be written. I want to know how much I may put down my name for, to go toward erecting a new one. A subscription is being taken up. Our class have subscribed one hundred and twenty dollars, so far; ten dollars apiece for twelve students. Can I subscribe? It is not to be paid till next term. Second. (My chum has had a very bad stye on his eye.) That last was written by my chum's gold pen. I made a trap to catch rabbits with this afternoon. They are very plenty. I saw three partridges to-day. But I must close. With much love to all, I remain your affectionate son in Christ, DAVID.

His letters, and indeed all kinds of writing, were for a long time extremely incomplete expressions of his character. He was a great deal more than he could

write down of himself, or than one could discover through
his writing of any matters. It was both interesting and
amusing to watch the first efforts which he made to
train his reflective powers; the necessity of their use
had become apparent along with a sense of his deficiency, and the moral duty of using them was an irresistible plea. He felt keenly the inability to write out
his thought, which, of course, was chiefly the result of
an inability to think; so he set himself painfully, but
most doggedly to work, mastering the difficulty. He
had a composition to write as a college exercise, and
long before the dreaded day came he began his task.
One of his friends, I know not with what evil intent,
supplied him with the subject — "Independence must
have limits." David addressed himself to the task, first,
of discovering the meaning of this oracular saying, and
then of proving the assertion so positively made. Day
after day did he turn the apophthegm over in his mind;
with a ludicrous persistence he battered it with all his
mental force; at all manner of odd moments, when his
attention was detached from some more immediate matter, he would return to this, and assert stoutly to himself — "Independence must have limits;" then he
would ask himself, why it must have limits and what
limits, and where were any instances of limited and
unlimited independence. He had no sort of shame in
his helplessness, but with a comical bewilderment would
apply to his friends, startling them with the assertion,
and waiting to see what effect it had on them; whether
they might not even deny the fact, and so bring on a
discussion which would throw light upon the matter.
A vacation intervened, and I remember with what
gravity and apparent pride at possessing a piece of

wisdom of great value, he took an early opportunity to deliver the oracle to the younger members of the family, who, he was glad to see, felt the full mystery of the saying. "Dear chum," he writes at this time, "I have written ten lines of my composition 'Independence must have limits.'" Somehow or other he managed, at last, to defend the thesis, but it was severe work for him.

In his new and honest desire for improvement he was the victim, like many before and since, to the systems recommended by well-meaning, but injudicious advisers. Method he found everywhere inculcated as the prime condition of effective mental labor. Of course he read many "Letters to a Young Student," and of course immediately, after the pattern of such books, made piecemeal of a day already quite minutely broken up by the regularly recurring college exercises. The effects of this systematic dosing of himself were so natural that I quote a part of a letter in which he unconsciously betrays his sense of the artificiality of the plan.

[TO HIS MOTHER.]

It is now my time, dear mother, that I devote to writing, or the improvement of my intellectual faculties, and I intend to devote it to the former at this time. —— lent me a book, entitled "Letters to a Young Student," the author of which I do not know about, but the recommendation of which is by N. Lord, of Dartmouth College. It is a very instructive book, and I trust that I have already gained some good from it. Advised by it, I yesterday made out a schedule of the manner in which I propose to spend the day. I allotted to each study a particular time, and that

part of the day not taken up in studying, I assigned to
reading, writing, or some other intellectual pursuit. I
have just finished my Latin, and have now an opportunity to answer your nice long letter. I would say, in
the first place, that you must not always expect a letter
from me Wednesday, since I cannot promise to write
invariably on Monday. Nevertheless, I shall always
endeavor to write home either on Monday or Tuesday.
I have been reading the allegory of Cheever, called
" The Two Ways and the Two Ends." It is well worth
the reading. It contains very many beautiful thoughts
and sentiments, some of which I purpose to write down
in a book, according to another suggestion of that book.
Somehow or other I feel just like an old man ; at least
I hope that I shall be more of a man than hitherto.

As his desire for improvement had mainly a religious
basis, so it was to religion that he naturally looked for
aid, and in religious exercises that he felt his deficiency
most. Entering the number of Christians, he found
them engaged in mental processes unfamiliar to him.
He heard them describe their spiritual conflicts, and
discovered in many a rigorous self-examination, which
aimed at a daily inspection of such thoughts and feelings as could be marshalled by memory. He also was
fighting daily to overcome the evil nature within him,
but he was conscious of an almost total inability to get
at and express the nature of his spiritual difficulties, or
to make any thorough inquiry into the causes of his
irregular emotions. The difficulties he had and the
irregular emotions, but, wanting the power to put into
correct and natural language all this experience, he
adopted the current phraseology with the most honest

purpose, while to common ears his use of it bore an
artificial sound. His letters show this most markedly,
for it was chiefly through religious topics that his pen
was first diverted from its ordinary occupation of chron-
icling the events in his small college-world. There is
a strained character to the religious portion of his letters at this period, not wholly lost for some time afterward, quite at variance with his customary naturalness
when speaking of common matters ; yet the fault is not
in intention, but in an inability adequately to interpret
his thought and emotion. Through all the conventional language, one must discern the glowing nature
of the young Christian, longing after perfection, making
constant discovery of his own failings, and ardent with
love for the souls of those who had not yet shared his
gift, leading him to plead with some friend in language
of unquestioned earnestness, however forced might seem
its terms.

I think this is a just explanation of a phase of religious life often displayed in young converts. With
those who never grow in mind beyond this period, such
phraseology becomes the prevailing order of the exposition of their faith ; they continue to exhort and pray
in the same terms as at first, exaggerating the tone of
their address, as it loses force by repetition, until unawares they reach a habit of speaking upon religious
topics, which shocks and repels men by its apparent
insincere use of the most awful terms. They are not
themselves, nor are those like them, aware of the wide
distance which exists between the primal meaning of
the Scripture phrases which they employ, and that
which their short intellect after dull iteration gives to
them. Like many others, my brother outgrew this

unformed state, and whilst he preserved his warm feelings and tender solicitude for others, he reached also
a juster understanding of the relation between thought
and language, learning to express his ideas in a manner
more natural and simple and thus more effective.

But his intellectual inexperience betrayed him into
graver errors than a temporary resort to conventional
phrases for the expression of his poorly-worded thoughts.
With the sensitiveness of his frank nature, made more
tender by his new knowledge, he was peculiarly open
to influence from without; when he heard his fellows
relating experience in religious matters quite out of
the reach of his mind, he reproached himself for the
absence of what was impossible to him; his use of
common forms of religious sentiment to cover his deficiency of expression, if they corresponded to no distinct experience within himself, served to harass him,
since he felt that he ought in sincerity to have the feelings which a strict interpretation of his language would
presume. Perhaps also he came into contact with men
inclined to morbidness by temperament or education;
he also began to watch the thermometer of his emo-
tional nature, with fear lest he should not maintain that
warmth of feeling which seemed to him so surely in-
dicative of high spiritual attainment. He always had
been subject to waywardness; his mercurial temper
suffered from all the variations of the atmosphere in
which he lived; now his moods were heightened and
deepened by an infusion of religious feeling. To what
was a constitutional fitfulness he gave a religious character; if he were depressed he accepted the mood as
necessary to one so aware of his spiritual deformity,
and grew to have a sort of pride at what he fancied an

excessive degree of self-abasement; if his animal nature chanced to be exuberant, he connected with it his religious aspirations, and gave thanks for a return to the early glow of Christian purpose. Bewildered by the vagrancy of his sensational nature, and by the painful incompleteness of his thinking powers, he stumbled toward the light, and while he did at last receive the reward of those that seek, he retained for a long while the signs of this disordered period.

There was however so simple a directness in his nature, that, despite these evil tendencies to which his untutored mind exposed him, he did make decided progress in Christian life, obeying those instinctive calls of duty which he could not miss understanding, and through this obedience gaining the power to comprehend those demands upon him which were more abstruse. Nor could his passionate attachment to free life in the open air fail to correct a good many mistakes which he might make over his air-tight stove. He struggled manfully with the tyranny which his nature had set up over him; with the imperious will, venting itself in caprice; with the strong prejudices which seized him so readily, and with all the turbulent force of his passions; and if he wasted some of his blows on imaginary tyrants, the largest share went to real ones. The struggle was carried on with intermittent force even to the end of life, but his repeated victories over evil had rendered it so feeble that even in his youth he had received his reward in a spirit docile, calm and equable.

Coupled with this self-discipline, in its influence upon his character, was the zeal with which he tried to win others to the peace which he had obtained. As happens in the case of most young converts, he sealed the confession of his faith with an immediate endeavor after the spiritual good of others. A revival of religion began in college simultaneously with his own conversion, and there was great activity among the Christian students. David's friends were in the habit of meeting together for prayer and talk, in his room in West College; and David, impetuous yet timid, would resolutely shut down the disagreeable sensations in his mind, go into his neighbors' rooms, choosing those least familiar with such gatherings, and deliver an invitation to his meeting as frankly and innocently as if to an oyster supper. His letters contain disclosures of his interest in his classmates, and in those still more dear to him. He could not, perhaps, answer with wise care the objections which hesitating minds proposed, but he could meet them more effectively by his unassumed earnestness, and by the sincerity of his faith; pleading personally with those whom he loved, and praying for them with ardent desire, he brought to bear upon them after all a more powerful and lively influence, it may be, than mere judicious counsel would have exerted, since in a large number of instances the objections which the intellect opposes are only the hiding-place of an unwilling heart, which is drawn from its refuge by the affectionate solicitations of a kindred spirit. Not that David's zeal was without knowledge, but that its force lay in its contagious fervor.

I have dwelt at some length upon this epoch in my brother's life, and its immediate results in his character and purpose, because it is so prominent as the beginning with him of positive growth. He did not, he could not suffer any violence in his individuality; but while before the force of his nature, so wide in its range, and yet so concentrated in all its movements, had thrown itself into the purpose of the moment, so that his progress was blind and vagrant, henceforth this same force, intensified by being hemmed in, was set steadily in one direction, from which it never swerved. He still gave himself up with wonted eagerness to an undivided care for that which was actually before him, following his active impulses which called him in so many different directions; but these momentary purposes, hitherto his sole guides, now became subordinate to one comprehensive, ruling purpose, which forbade his life ever to become disjointed or capriciously vagrant. The fulness of his nature, supplying him with so many and such varied objects of interest, was not long held in by false or narrow opinions respecting duty; it overrode the captious criticisms of a disordered conscience. He kept his naturalness, and that, in turn, kept him.

He continued to make daily excursions to his rabbit-traps, and to coast, while snow lasted, down the long hills; he wrote long, loose, hap-hazard letters, mingling incidents of college-life with earnest regrets of his own coldness of heart, affectionate expostulations, and eager inquiries after the small tribes of the barn-yard. In college he was known for his unaffected heartiness; he was singular enough to excite universal interest. It did men good to hear his peculiar laugh, so clear and above suspicion; to be pounced upon, as they were walking gravely to prayers, by this frolicking boy, whose exuberance of spirits seemed to run over into oddness. No one could tell what he would do next. If others were walking soberly, he was most likely running backward and displaying his antics. As in his school-days, he was perpetually falling into half-serious quarrels which never weakened the lightest friendship; nothing seemed to delight him more than to confound some one by the appearance of a sudden revulsion of feeling. He had an incorrigible propensity for making people stare, and was led by it into all sorts of harmless jests. His room-mate relates an example : —

" We had been together but a few days, when an incident occurred which was characteristic of him in his earlier college-days, and, from what David told me, I should infer of his boyhood also. We were carrying up wood, and both of us in very lively mood, when suddenly he broke out into what seemed to me a most violent passion. He seemed uncontrollably vexed with me, and I thought he was about to tear himself in pieces. After he saw I was sufficiently astonished and alarmed, which was not a little, he burst out into a loud laugh. Nothing occurred equalling this trick in violence, but most of his succeeding odd fits were more a reality."

Pleasant as residence at college was, there always remained the keener delight of going home in vacation. The ushering in of the holidays was attended by so much circumstance that an excitable mind was kept in constant motion. Examinations and exhibitions closed the last days of the term. Lucky students, who had contrived to anticipate the breaking-up, went off singly or in small squads, envied by the rest, like the raven from the ark; then the bustle of getting in readiness, and finally the morning of departure, when there was some anxiety lest the stout stage-driver should not have coaches enough for all. It was a picturesque sight when the college broke up at the end of the spring or summer term. The train from North Adams, the nearest railway station, — these were days when the Troy and Greenfield Railroad was only talked of, — started at a very early hour, in order to connect with the trains on the Western Road, at Pittsfield. This was the usual mode of exit from the town, though slow stages did crawl west, north, and south, if any chose to use them. To take this train at North Adams, the stage-coaches had to leave Williamstown at a still earlier hour, and at the end of the term a margin was allowed for the inevitable confusion and delay attending such an *hegira*. Thus long before the sun rose, and while the dawn showed only the coldest light, one could see, up and down the street that ran through the town, little piles of trunks surrounded or surmounted by sleepy students. The stages would come slowly along, zigzagging to pick up one load after another on either side of the way, the driver pounding at the door of some house where he had been ordered to stop, but where no trunk was to be seen, and where, at the last moment, the half-clad student would tumble out, just in time but very cross. The students on the last hill by East College would be waiting impatiently and with some anxiety; then the clambering up and in, the sometimes surly, sometimes brisk salutations, until all were packed, and the stages would roll down the hill to the rendezvous at the foot, where the driver-in-chief, stout to the fullest requirements of stage-drivers, would go about among the stages, with a lantern in his hand, collecting the passage-money. It was a sleepy set that he used to carry over, but those who had their wits were well repaid for the loss of sleep by the sight of the kindling dawn, though the sun would hardly be risen by the end of the drive.

David's favorite method of going home however was to give no warning of his approach, but to take the noon-train, reaching the house in Roxbury after midnight, steal through the cellar-door, all a-prickle with excitement, and lie *perdu* in the darkness till morning, when he would come up into the house, swear secrecy on any servant that might happen in sight, hide in the closet, in a fever lest somebody should open the door and discover *him*, till the family were seated at breakfast, when he would burst forth to the astonishment of all, and his own extreme delight.

## CHAPTER III.

### COLLEGE–LIFE — LAST THREE YEARS.

[1852–1855.]

SOPHOMORE year showed David in much the same light as the last two terms of Freshman year; his character gained in stability and the ruling purpose held, but the growth of his mind was slow and marked by few noticeable efforts. Life at Williamstown does not present many salient points apart from those already intimated. The town is so insignificant that it supplies very little to interest the student. His return to college, at the beginning of a new term, brings him once more into the routine of college-life, and so he continues until released by another vacation. Indeed, everything about the return to Williams, with a city boy at least, seems to remind him of his separation from the busy world. He arrives at the railway terminus, hilarious over the comrades he has met on the way, and mounts again the rocking stage-coach which travels the road winding among the hills into the secluded valley. For a day or two there is the bustle of settling down, and then all goes on as before. He passes his days very much alike, varying the course of study with sallies in the literary societies, and for recreation joins in the college-games, or tramps, rides, and drives about the country. Every Wednesday and Saturday afternoon one may find students scattered over the neighborhood, seeking the Sand-Springs which bubble up a mile

4

or two from the town, — mineral springs of the same
temperature the year round, and confined in tanks for
bathers; or the Weeping Rocks on the Pownal Road;
the Natural Bridge near Adams; the Cascade, and all
the many curious spots.  Most however walk for the
pleasure of it and for the mountain-views; or, likely
enough, are incipient naturalists, with tin trunks slung
at the side for botanizing, or maybe with long butterfly
nets which they flourish about in a frantic fashion,
while sportsmen with guns and rods disappear in the
woods.

Everything in fact that the student wants for occupation he has to find close at hand; the nearest town
amusements are twenty miles off, and are hardly attractive enough then to draw many.  Such circumstances
serve to crowd the students together, and fierce little
revolutions are excited, so that generally every class
has suffered in its course some violent rupture.  The
younger members of college, transported from a society
in which they were minors to one where they enjoy the
rights of citizenship, are greatly elated with their new
consequence, and prate of college as if it were the central sun in the social system.

> " They take the rustic murmur of their bourg
>   For the great wave that echoes round the world."

The world itself comes to them once a day by the help
of the stage-driver, who enters at night, galloping his
horses through the village, and blowing his horn to call
the students to the little post-office.  For the quiet
pleasures of student-life the place is wonderfully fit.
In those days there was a barbarous custom of holding
morning prayers before sunrise sometimes; but after
all there was, to those who were not too sleepy, an

exhilaration in this early summons to labor, and an inspiration to be drawn from the clear morning air. More than once has the crowd of students, filing out of the chapel, stood still instinctively to look off upon some sunrise when the eastern sky hung in gorgeous show over the long mountain.

In such a life as this did David rejoice. He had no restless discontent luring him away to forbidden pleasures and more showy entertainments than this valley and its circle of hills could afford. He loved his friends, and after the first, each new year brought one of his brothers, with whom he could share his pleasant life. As for study, his new convictions of duty forbade him ever to be negligent, but his immaturity of mind prevented him from a full comprehension of the studies in the college course; so that, while his scholarship was always respectable and his faithfulness unimpeached, he fell just below the " honor men " of the class. He was a quick student and had received a schooling in the classics more thorough than had most of the country boys who formed the majority of his class. One accomplishment especially he possessed, upon which he plumed himself a good deal, the art of scanning Latin and Greek verse fluently and correctly. His native glibness of tongue and his liking for rattle conspired to give him a fondness for the art; and the class would listen with amusement, sometimes with applause, when as, at the given signal, he would stand in his place and let slip from his tongue the Homeric hexameters. Mathematics he found as ever a sore burden, but a sense of deficiency led him to make an effort at mastering the difficulties of a science so alien from his mental cast; and after he had been a year in college, he took up

arithmetic with a fellow-student, resolutely going back
to elementary knowledge.

Composition and all logical processes were still formidable, though his persistent efforts and his general
growth robbed them of some terror.   One plan for
acquiring a habit of thought was certainly straightforward enough, and showed him in earnest.   Getting up
a half-hour earlier than even the very early prayer-
time required, it was his custom to pace the hall upon
which his room abutted for the express purpose of
*thinking*.   He would take some subject which he was
expecting to use in composition ; I believe " Independence must have limits " attended some of his pacings ;
or the last debate in the society hall, or some topic
which had been suggested in conversation or reading,
and for the half-hour conscientiously, as well as his
poor, untutored head would allow, discuss the matter
with himself, arguing back and forth as he walked, —
very much relieved, no doubt, when the prayer-bell
released him.

The course of study for Sophomore year presented
little difficulty to him except in these points, and he
fell under the influence of the prevalent mood among
Sophomores, catching a little of the indifferentism
and self-conceit which marks that stage of a student's
career.   He even so far fell into a comfortable and
complacent mood as to congratulate himself upon being
popular, and to take some pains to increase the good-
will of his comrades.   His letters were somewhat
bombastic and wordy, and he assumed a sort of conse-
quential air which ill became him.   Yet this was after
all exceptional ; he caught the way from others ; his
own rightful nature asserted itself more strongly, and

he made real progress, despite occasional fits of waywardness.

The Greek drama to be read this year was the
" Electra " of Sophocles. The class, with Sophomoric
wisdom, decided that the drama was too difficult for
their unaided intellects, and agreed, as a body, to obtain
translations, — by which piece of mutual transgression
the weak in will or conscience might have the moral
support of their fellows. David, who, from his residence in Boston, was constantly made an agent for the
class, was appointed commissioner to procure the copies
during the next vacation. The only translation he
could find was one included in a complete translation
of Sophocles, published in Bohn's " Classical Library."
It seemed foolish to buy the whole book for the sake
of forty odd pages; and after some embarrassment it
occurred to him to get the " Electra " printed by itself.
He had a reckless disregard of common sense in business affairs, and the unlucky measure resulted in obtaining a quantity of unbound " Electras," which cost
more than if he had bought the entire volumes. The
class had a good-natured laugh at him for his simplicity, but relieved his mind by paying the bill.
Meanwhile his room was full of the translations, lying
about everywhere for any who chose to call and obtain
their copies. Nearly every one used the help; and
it was considered wholly justifiable, first because the
Greek was so hard, and then because where all went
astray, the responsibility was equally distributed; but
not once did David ever glance at the English " Electra "; he labored through the unadulterated Greek
alone.

He began this year to read outside of the college

studies, with no very clear notion of what he wanted,
following the suggestion of the time; but even then
there was indication of a preference for a class of reading which afterward engaged his attention, — the suggestive writings of essayists, like John Foster, which
treat of morals in the broader relations, and yet give a
practical turn to the results reached.   There was a
catholicity about David's mind which, so early as this,
made him best pleased with truth when presented in its
sphericity, while he was so practical in his application
of truth that he wished the sphere, in conclusion, to
become a wedge.   There is plenty of time in the idle
hours of Sophomore year for reading, and many students become diverted by it from study, persuading
themselves that one may fairly choose between discur-
sive reading and close study, getting about equal advantage from either.   Sophomore wisdom fails frequently
when tested on this point.   David's diversion from
study by reading was very slight; he kept at his books
as much as seemed necessary; the by-hours he preferred to spend on excursions, and in dabbling in Natural
History.   There was, besides, the traditional initiation
of Freshmen in the trials of college-life; but where this
was neither illegal nor mean, there was little to recommend it to any one's notice, so that he kept clear of
such folly.   Back and forth between Williamstown and
Boston, he kept up outwardly an uneventful life, unless
there be excepted the long excursions which he planned
so profusely whenever summer approached, and some one
of which he carried out each vacation, — taking long
pedestrian tours through New England, or, with his father, ever desirous of anticipating his pleasures, travelling into Canada.   He was restless with schemes, going

just as far as the tether of circumstances would allow, and taking the keenest delight in the fulfilment of his plans.

When he returned to college, at the beginning of his third or Junior year, he found a necessity for most resolute exertion. The classics were dropped out of the course of study after a portion of Demosthenes and of Tacitus had been read; the prominent study of the year was Physics and higher Mathematics, together with an increased amount of composition work. His youth and unmethodical habits of mind made all this hard for him; besides, the Junior dignity is rather ashamed of the flippancy and laziness of Sophomore year, so that he entered with resolution and industry upon his tasks. He never achieved any honor in the performance, but he had the greater gain in a more capable mind and readier pen. Surely and rapidly, by vigorous application to work, he was adding to his mental stature. A certain extreme confidence in other men's opinions gave way to more careful judgment and self-reliance. He stood higher, took in a wider reach in all his observations, and moved unresistingly forward in his proposed career.

As his mind became more analytical, he understood himself better, and could detect the true character of his unhealthy moods. The corrective measures which formerly he had instinctively adopted, were now employed at the suggestion also of his thought. The morbidness clung to him, since by his injudicious, ignorant yielding it had become a habit, only to be worn away by constant attrition with his will, and by the severe letting alone which he learned to practise. The beginning of this unhealthy state of mind has been indicated;

the disease was at its height during this year, and the
following extracts from two letters, written in immediate
succession, give pretty fully the form which his self-
torture assumed.   A frankness is used which we should
call unmerciful to himself, were it not in part one of the
very symptoms of the disease, that it hides itself for
a time only to pour its horrors more fully into the most
sympathetic ear; some momentary relief is thus gained,
but such a confidence, by its outward expression of
vague experience, rarely fails to give body and long
life to the diseased fancy.   I have hesitated whether it
be right to disclose such a revelation of himself, but the
mastery which he obtained over this strong evil cannot
adequately be indicated unless the strength of the evil
be first shown.   The extracts show the workings of his
mind better than any mere description of mine could.

WILLIAMS COLLEGE, May, 1854.

. . . . Different circumstances conspire to render
me perfectly miserable; a very agreeable condition, I
assure you.   I don't know as you are aware of it, but
I am very often subject to fits of the *indigoes*, as some
would term them.   At all events, whatever may be the
causes, I am altogether in despair at such times. . . . .
For the last three years nearly, I have seldom been happy for any length of time, — all last vacation I was
wretched; to-day I have almost wished to die.   My
prayers seem like mockeries, heartless, cold, and ineffect-
ual.   I can and usually do appear lighthearted, but
within a continual fire is burning.   I see what I ought
to be as a Christian, but not having motives to exertion
sufficiently heavenly, I make but little true progress.
. . . . I have harbored these feelings for so long that

they have become a kind of monomania, which I love to gloat over, and thus they continually react upon me. Instead of building castles in the air, I dig dungeons in the earth. I continually think of myself as of no ability, having no decision of character, no originality, no judgment, no perseverance, no taste in regard to any matter, no conversational powers, no power in writing, no agreeable companionship, and, in fine, no anything which I ought to have. I seem to have lost all true self-esteem; and to crown all, and that which causes me most to despair, is my want of patience in well-doing, my having a name to live when I am dead.

. . . . As regards my religious feelings, if I wanted to be better I could, but there is a kind of dogged, sullen determination to continue as I am, moping and fretting; and the only cure is to let myself alone until I see what a fool I am. You seem to think that I have deep sorrow for sin. I differ from you. I don't know what true, sincere, heartfelt sorrow is — no *godly* sorrow, for godly sorrow worketh repentance unto salvation, not to be repented of. My sorrow produces no such results. Vanity of the lowest stamp here comes in, and I delight in feeling miserable, and would rejoice if others knew it and would *pity* me. I know perfectly well that I ought to forget myself and look to Christ, but I don't want to, for that would be depriving my mind of one source of its delight, morbid self-contemplation. . . . . The least sign in any particular that I am low in piety is magnified and construed into a sort of invincible sin. For instance, when prayer is offered, no matter where, I *cannot* follow, but instinctively my mind goes hop, skip, jump. I have tried a little to overcome this propensity, but in vain. I think I see pretty clearly what a Christian character is, and if I am to be a missionary, I must be a *holier* man.

. . . . Here is another source of discouragement, — I cannot write decently. Behind all lies the cause, — entering college too early. I did not know what I was to study for, and failing once, I have been gradually falling backward, and am now a meagre student. This fact is impressed upon me every day. I went on to Greylock Monday : coming down, the conversation turned on saw-mills, thence to water principles, which we have studied, and with which we should be acquainted, but I could only be silent from ignorance, and so on ; when anything was talked about I had to remain *mum*. I kept busily punning until I became disgusted with myself ; and so it is at any little meeting of students, — I cannot engage in general conversation. In my reading I am very superficial, — remember nothing scarcely of importance, and the quicker through the better. I am exceedingly barren on common topics and general information, so that I am very seldom of use to anybody. I am conscious that I am boring you, and doing myself harm, perhaps, but I am through in this letter.

It must be observed that though he was so open in this letter, his ordinary comrades saw little evidence of his morbidness ; he wore an outward cheeriness even when depressed at heart, for he revolted from that form of self-tormenting indulgence which leads one to seek compassion by the exhibition of a doleful face in public. How he dealt with the evil may be seen from a few words addressed to one who disclosed very much the same experience to him a year afterward. " You

seem to think," he writes, " that I should be able to
offer some remedy for ' blues,' as I have been so subject
to them. . . . . One thing I *know*, that if a person
gives himself wholly to the work of good, if one em-
ploys all the energies of body and mind, whether the
result of one talent or of ten, if, forgetting self as
much as possible, we labor for our Saviour, we shall
lack *no good thing*. I believe that the secret lies in
dethroning self entirely, and living altogether in accordance with the great law of benefaction. That
must be it."

It was work and a spirit of beneficence which brought
for him a deliverance, in large measure, from unhappy
moods; as these were closely connected with his religious convictions, so it was Christian activity that supplied the regulative power. Constantly, spite of failure, pressing toward a higher tone of life, the ultimate
motive with him was loyalty to the Saviour. This was
no occasional, fitful incentive to a better life, a more
energetic service; it was deep in his being, occupying
the very heart, and issuing forth through all the channels of his nature. The hearty affection which held
him so firmly to friends was rendered more catholic by
his love for the Saviour of men. In this spirit, and not
under the thraldom of an unloved conscience, though
duty ever stood ready to press its claims, he tried to
bring others into the kingdom of God. There was
such a transparency about his motives, such a winning
power in his artlessness, that he was able to reach some
who would have repelled religion coming in the un-
lovely guise which it not unfrequently wears in college.

Whilst he was bewailing, and honestly, his own slack-
ness and timidity, the record of his brief note-book

shows him going to one and another, for what purpose one may easily see who knew their characters. Nor did he do this with incautious zeal, but rather with earnest prayer, and with judgment correct, because instinctive. These men loved **David.** They saw in him not only a good fellow, but one who was staunch in his loyalty to his Lord, struggling after purity; they were sure he worshipped at the cross. Thus writes one of his classmates: — " He did not shut himself away from men's hearts because they believed as he did not, or because they had not yet proven themselves worthy and Christian. He was not afraid of being soiled by publicans and sinners; he could sit at meat with them. He did not pour on the ground the humanities in him, when he resolved to serve the Lord Jesus as a missionary in India. . . . . Men were not repelled from him by any conventional manners, nor any assumed frigidity. He put constraint on no company when he entered it, nor did he leave his principles at home, either, for any fear. He was willing to show what he was, a friend of Jesus, and he was not willing to seem what he was not."

The missionary purpose, which had its birth simultaneously with his Christian life, remained unshaken, and in the last two years of his college course was set in constant motion. There existed at Williams, then as now, the Mills Theological Society, — an association of such students as designed entering the ministry. It was chiefly a literary society, holding its meetings on Sunday evening, one week giving the time to theological discussion and essays, the next to missionary intelligence and essays upon kindred topics. It held its own better, and was subject to less fluctuation of interest in those days than any other of the societies; there was little of that hustling for places of honor which worked evil in the secular societies; a well-defined purpose regulated the conduct of the meetings, and some of the worthiest efforts in college were made in the Mills. David joined the society early, but it was not till his class had come forward into Junior year that he took any active part; then and thereafter he was a leading member. As a debater and essayist, he made little show; but as far as spirited interest and unwearied labor were concerned, he was extremely efficient. He was not content with performing his allotted duties, but engaged in new enterprises in behalf of the society, and was continually plotting how he should advance its interest. He entered into correspondence with individual missionaries all over the world, especially those who were graduates of the college, enlisting their sympathy, obtaining fresh intelligence, and what was better, connecting the idea of missions in the minds of the members with personal associations. He sought out Christians in the lower classes, bringing them into the meetings, and by his ardor generally giving a warmer tone to the proceedings of the society.

"I shall never forget," writes one of a lower class, "the first time I saw David. It was one Sabbath afternoon shortly after I entered college. He came to my room in New Street, to find out whether my chum and I were Christians. H. had filled the room with tobacco-smoke, and we were reading. David, I fear, thought it rather a murky atmosphere for very vigorous piety, though he said nothing of the kind. But his earnest, enthusiastic tone when he spoke of the Mills Society, (of whose existence I was then for the first time informed, and which I joined at his invitation,) and his entire manner, was a severe rebuke to my lifeless piety. I felt, when he left, that I had met with a *living* Christian, and this, I think, was the impression he always made. There was no ostentation, no thrusting the fact upon you; but his spiritual life seemed as natural as the fragrance of a rose, or the activity of a healthy, animal life."

The library of the society had been growing by slow accretions for several years, but had received no careful attention until he busied himself about it. He laid aside his constitutional shyness, and addressed himself to all manner of people who were likely to be of any service; in vacation he was constantly on the hunt for books and money, and showed such unfeigned pleasure when he got what he wanted, that his possessions increased rapidly. In this way he secured several hundred volumes of worth, and when during Senior year he occupied the room of the society containing its library, he had the most fond affection for the cases of books which had so increased under his administration. The whole library, indeed, he inspected carefully, rearranged, and catalogued.

The society took its name from Samuel J. Mills, whose place in the history of American missions is so notable, and whose memory is one of the sacred traditions which those of like mind at Williams love to preserve. David, always ready to be impressed by Christian heroism, felt a personal enthusiasm for the man and all relating to him, as a labor of love applying himself to the recovery of what stray, unrecorded . facts there might be about him, which he afterward wove into an address before the society. He was particularly anxious to get some likeness of Mills, with the intention, I think, of securing a satisfactory painting for the society. His search was unsuccessful, but it deserved success. He wrote letters and took long journeys on foot, visiting the places where Mills had lived, hunted for his relations and friends, and did not give over till he had tried all possible measures. In all of these labors he seemed wholly absorbed in the immediate ends proposed, singularly forgetful either of good or of honor for himself. He was surprised when elected president of the society, pleased chiefly because of the appreciation manifest in the election, and anxious lest the feelings of others should be hurt by his promotion. Indeed, it was the same in all the societies which he served in college; he never seemed to seek office or personal distinction. His labors had no concealed end in his own glory.

Nor was his zeal for missions confined to the Mills Society. He recognized then, as more fully afterward, the value of personal influence in these matters. He did not leave the truth to find its way to the hearts of men; he carried it himself and presented it to them. His own plans were so definitely formed, his conviction of duty so firm, that he was somewhat impatient of the slower decisions of others. It was so plain to him — he would make it plain to them. Although several of his class and associates afterward became foreign missionaries, yet he was the only one I am told, of those who then expressed an intention to engage in this occupation, who ever entered a foreign field. He was toasted at the farewell class-supper as the missionary to India: that was his distinction. Indeed, it was impossible for him to conceal a purpose so mastering; any one who liked could see how much he meant.

With all this active zeal for the missionary cause, there was kept up a careful preparation of himself for the work which he had undertaken. Aside from his regular studies, the pursuit of which received also an impulse from a consideration of their bearing upon his profession, his elective study and reading looked in this direction; yet, from the outset, his catholicity of nature led him to take a wide and profound view of what constituted intellectual preparation for his work. His desire for a positive object had led him to choose not merely serving Christ, but serving him as a missionary; not as a missionary merely, but as a missionary in India; nor even there did he pause, but he chose the very district of India in which he should establish himself; thus only could he satisfy his nature. So also in study, his guiding thought was not for improvement of his mind as a disciple of Christ, but running through general purposes, he came quickly to the special purpose of becoming acquainted with India, and minutely of that section which was to be his home. But as his instinct for special ends in life did not belittle his more comprehensive purpose of serving the Lord with body, mind, and soul, so neither did his demand for special preparation induce a narrow estimate of what constituted that preparation. He believed in the largest culture as essential to the most effective minute labor of the missionary. His tastes and interests were of so wide a range, that he could not become narrow-minded so long as he permitted them to indicate the direction of his studies. He governed the extent rather than the kind of his pursuits, displaying good judgment in knowing where to stop. He never forgot his purpose, but he did not force all studies and plans to do the bidding of that ruling purpose; rather that purpose was so much his entire life, and he was so hearty and natural, that all effort was inspired by his Christian and missionary zeal.

The Rev. H. R. Hoisington, formerly at the head of the Batticotta School in Ceylon, was at this time occupying the pulpit at Williamstown, having been compelled to return to this country on account of ill health. It was a most fortunate thing for David that, at the beginning of his missionary studies, he should have had the advice and assistance of one so calculated every way to assist him. Mr. Hoisington was an admirable Tamil scholar, and, at his suggestion, David commenced the study of the language as by-work, at first only familiarizing himself with the vocables, and then going further and further, with an untiring zeal which seemed in no way to be weakened by the unavoidable breaks in the course of study. I do not think that the difficulty of the language ever seriously disconcerted him. He took it as a matter of course that he would have to master it; he must learn Tamil at some time, it were better if he could know something of it before going to India; and here was the opportunity. After he had begun upon it, there was no thought of relinquishing it; he was not in the habit of torturing himself with the objections which one may so easily call up, after he has made a decision. His ease in acquiring language and his humor for airing strange words gave some zest to the pursuit.

"While it certainly was amusing," writes a classmate, "to see his enthusiasm, and the facility with which his

rapid tongue adapted itself to the speech, it was also
more than amusing: it showed how cordially he had
taken in hand the business of his life, and how practical
were all his conceptions of it.  I don't believe he really
found any sympathy among his companions with what
he was doing.  I surely never stopped to consider much
what he was at — why he cared to bother with a Tamil
lesson two or three times a week, and what relation it
had to the great interests of man.  Probably most of
us laughed at him, — thought it was one of his queer
freaks, an easy way of letting off some of his superflu-
ous energy, — would have been wholly incredulous if
any had told us that this was the thing that lay nearest
his heart, and that was really proving him a hero.  As he
jabbered to us the final syllables he learned, — a thing
he often loved to do, — we did not see at all how directly the whole force of his being was pressing toward
the one desire of his life."

India was always near to him, never far off.  This
was the secret of the ease with which his mind adapted
itself to apparently remote enterprises.  To a mind
seeking near objects upon which to exert itself, it is not
so much distance in time or space, which constitutes
remoteness, as abstraction from the realms of practical
effort; thus metaphysics David could not bring within
the range of his vision, yet there were some minds in
his class to whom the "oversoul" was far nearer than
the profession which they may have anticipated entering
a few years hence.  A year before he graduated, David
wrote: — "Father! you can have no idea how much I
think of India.  It is almost my first thought in the
morning, and is present during the day.  You talk
about my studying two years before entering the semi-

nary. Impossible! I should pine for 'India's coral strands.' India! is my watchword. I know the Tamil alphabet, two hundred and twenty-eight letters. It is quite simple, but such words! whew! enough to take the breath out of your body before you finish. For instance, ŭyirmeyyĕrlŭttu, one word, which is much harder to pronounce than it looks to be on paper. The letters of that word are these in Tamil. (Here follow a dozen of the Tamil characters, which were freely sprinkled in his letters.) Before long I shall read, and before long preach *the everlasting Gospel.*"

I have been forced, in illustrating the growth of his mind, to anticipate any account of the closing year of his college course. Little remains to be said, since this year did not differ materially, in its outward character, from the preceding. More leisure, indeed, is allowed, as the student becomes able to be trusted with it, and this is turned to the advantage of reading, especially on subjects collateral to the investigations in philosophy which form the basis of Senior studies. This year at Williams enjoys some reputation from the tuition given by Dr. Mark Hopkins, the President of the college: many fancy that the advantage, apart from his personal power, lies in a more philosophical arrangement of the subjects discussed; but they seize upon only one part of a system which unifies the entire course of education in the college, a system under which the student works, unawares, but which, at the beginning of the last year, is explained to him. This system has for its informing idea the doctrine, that the student is to work out his own education and is not to be overlaid by any merely applied knowledge. I do not hesitate to say that the one value which attaches preëminently to Williams, spite of the many weaknesses in the college appointments, is the power which belongs to it of inducing independent, vigorous thought. Culture, in its ordinary sense, there is none; men leave the college frequently with as little grace as they entered; of acquaintance with general literature there is scarcely anything; the libraries are scantily supplied; thorough scholarship in the classics is quite unknown, (I speak of the days when my brothers and I were there,) but after all there remains a substantial success, of which the college may justly be proud, in the ability which has been given to the graduates to use themselves.

The same immaturity which previously had prevented David from getting the full value of the college *curriculum* existed still to much greater disadvantage, yet he grew rapidly, although far from comprehending the studies in which he was engaged. His previous vague and uncertain intellections were fast giving way to more careful and definite reasonings. In his reading he grew more methodical and judicious. He enjoyed most heartily the life he led. He could feel the satisfaction of being employed upon studies most valuable to him, which were daily setting in order his willing mind; the abundant leisure was grateful, as it afforded such opportunity for carrying out his prolific schemes. His friends were fast, and two brothers, in different classes, gave him companionship beside. My first year at college was David's last, and I cannot forget the manner of his life so full to overflowing: his days flying by under the pressure of occupation, and even his nights contributing to his draught of life; for there was a passage from his room in the upper story of East College to the flat roof of the building; there on starlight

nights he would carry up his blankets, and rolling himself up in them, fall asleep with thoughts of India, and
of the more distant land unseen by mortal eyes. Such
nights had their surprises too, when his dreams would
become grotesque, and his waking consciousness would
be puzzled at the quick drops of rain which at last
drove him headlong through the trap-door, dragging
his blankets after him.

In August, 1855, when lacking a few months of
completing his twentieth year, he graduated with his
class, taking a creditable position, and carrying away
at any rate the entire respect of officers and students;
more, bearing with him the personal affection of many,
and the genial remembrances of all who had been associated with him. Surely he had no enemy, notwith-
standing his strong prejudices and the difficulty he
found in concealing his opinion of whatever was mean
and dishonorable. With great charity for the weak
and ignorant, always glad if he could favorably interpret ambiguous incidents or characteristics, he could
not bear what was mean, or indeed what was unnatural. It was amusing to see the vehemence with which
he would express his disgust at the ridiculous affectation
of a child that crossed his path very often, as if his
whole nature revolted at such a twist of childhood.
In his class there was one for whom he had an almost
ungovernable distaste, on account of a silly arrogance,
poorly borne out by the person's position and attainments. But when Commencement Day came, he did
not like to part with any of his class except on the
kindest terms; he was aware that he had failed to
conceal his contempt for this person, so, swallowing the
disagreeable sensations that arose, he sought him out,

and said in his cheerful, hearty way, "Come, ———,
we must part friends," and held out the hand of recon-
ciliation.    All that he got in return, he told me with
amusement, was two fingers, by which he was to cling
to this man's good-will.

It was with unfeigned reluctance that he left his four
years' home.   His last letter from Williamstown, written when the bustle of Commencement was over, ends
thus : — "All over, David C. Scudder, A. B.!   Oh,
how I shall long to come back here again.   C. M. has
just come to bid me good-bye, and soon the last good-
bye will be said, and I shall be left to myself, lonesome
enough.   I did and do love my classmates, and these
noble old hills, and college-life.   But I 've got to be a
man like all the rest."   The mountains to which he
bade good-bye with sorrowful feeling, giving them each
a personal farewell, had witnessed a great change from
the headlong, unthinking boy, who scoured them with
all the eagerness of a wild nature.   They had seen his
awaking to thought, his hard struggle with an unruly
spirit, his gropings after clearer light and more peaceful
air ; they had been his friends when, to his mind, all
others seemed in vain, and he had fled to them, wearied
with labor.   His ardent purposes and strong resolves
had gained in firmness as he climbed the rugged hills,
and his eye, looking off from the heights of Greylock,
had been outrun by his vision of more distant lands
which he longed to reach.   He associated with them
his inner life, and they were almost a part of himself.
Once, at midnight, at the beginning of a new year, he
entered the town in company with a brother, who was
making his first visit.   The moon was shining, giving
a wonderful character to the silent hills.   To any one

it was a scene of bewitching beauty, but for David it was illumined by

> " The light that never was, on sea or land,
>   The consecration."

" This," said he, turning to his brother, " this is my home.   Here I was born."   So did he ever regard the place ; and if the mountains had known him as he knew them, they would have seen him leaving this spiritual home, not soiled by college associations, but ennobled, and rising to the estate of manhood ; all that was generous and right in his character confirmed, and a power obtained over evil which gained in strength at each conflict.

# CHAPTER IV.

### A YEAR IN THEOLOGICAL SEMINARY AT ANDOVER.

[1855–1856.]

It is the wont of many American collegians to intermit systematic study for a year or more after graduation,
occupying themselves with teaching or travel, before
beginning the special study which prepares for profes-
sional life. David had expected to observe such an
intermission, from a consciousness of immaturity, although his eagerness to conquer time, as well as other
obstacles, made him impatient of delay. He finally
decided to pass directly from college to the Theological
Seminary, and take the first year of the course before
interrupting regular study. In September, 1855, he
entered the seminary at Andover, Massachusetts, with
an older brother who had graduated from college a
year previous; others whom he knew had been in the
seminary a year or more; some of his own college class
entered with him, and while pursuing the course, he
welcomed friends from classes succeeding his. In fact,
when transplanted to Andover, he carried with him a
good deal of the Williams soil; it never was easy for
him to detach himself from friendly associations, and he
retained the liveliest interest in all the concerns of his
Alma Mater. But he was quite differently situated
now. Instead of being in the seclusion of Williamstown, a day's journey from home, he was but an hour's
ride by rail from Boston, living in a town which, from

its nearness to the city, has caught enough of city civilization to have rubbed off something of its rusticity,
and yet is surrounded by a pleasing country, tenanted
by country folk. The land about Andover is varied,
affording delightful walks and rides, without requiring
the severe toil which frequently is necessary in Williamstown; within a circuit of five miles, one may find
the most diversified scenery; the roads branch off in
every direction, and one following them indifferently
will be led to woods and ponds, and round, bald hills.
One may trace the windings of the Shawshin, walk
along Indian Ridge, lie on the gentle slope which overlooks Pomp's Pond, with its setting of forest-trees, so
many-hued in autumn days; while Sunset Rock, on
the edge of a tangled wood-lot, above a valley, gives a
noble view of the western sky.

Hither upon pleasant evenings straggle small parties
and solitaries, bound like sun-worshippers to their evening devotions. The transient population of the town is
so large that there always are some to try the pleasant
walks, or make excursions for so unworldly an object
as to see the sun set. In ordinary country villages of
New England, it is only the children or occasional visitors that take a walk for the pleasure of it; the busy
villagers, when they find leisure, seek their entertainment in some other form. Andover is an exceptional
town; a pretty large share of its population is of those
who come to be taught and those who come to teach,
while the regular inhabitants find a good deal to do in
providing for the wants of the shifting school-class.
The Theological Seminary, Phillips Academy, enjoying
some celebrity under Dr. S. H. Taylor's charge, as a
school preparatory for college, a large girls' school,

called a Female Seminary, smaller boarding-schools for girls, and Punchard Free School for the towns-people, serve to give an educational character to the town, while the constant introduction of new classes of students, and the large supply of young people, keep the face of society changeable.

At Williamstown David had seen nothing of society except that of collegians, which was not likely to teach manners, whatever else it might teach; at home, he had been impatient of the restraint imposed upon him by society; it made him fidgety, and he used to escape formal company when he could. Much of this was owing to a half-tamed boyishness and a natural diffidence, so that when he went to Andover, he seemed to regard his aversion from society as a serious matter. Accordingly, he began faithfully to attend the regular social gatherings, held at the professors' houses, where he did his best to enjoy himself, with tolerable success; only tolerable, however, for he often rebelled. He was so unconventional that he was restless amongst conventional people, and felt the light restraints of formal etiquette as if they were fetters. Sometimes, when our own house was the scene of his misery, he would steal out into the back-yard for a whiff of freedom, and come back meekly to his bondage. It made him wretched to go into a room full of people, to smile and smile for an hour or two, talking in driblets with various acquaintances, and, in fine, conducting himself with propriety. He rebelled against propriety; it was hot within him to do something startling, and then his feeling of being *de trop* made him out of humor with himself. It seemed to him that he could give nothing to society; he thought much worse of himself in this respect than did others, who found him a fresh talker, with so much whimsicality about him, that, on the shortest acquaintance, he was likely to say or do something extremely original and mirth-provoking. In less formal society, and among friends, he talked well, though at first with a somewhat limited vocabulary. His own purposes and topics kindred he did not push forward, but was ready to kindle on the theme when encouraged. He did not seek a great deal of society; he was quite content with the stated seminary levees and occasional parties, and with calling upon the members of his Sunday-school class; having done his duty, he dismissed the matter for more congenial pursuits.

A new place and a new set of friends seemed to bring out afresh his boyishness. He was rather more unique when contrasted with students in Theology than when among collegians. The prevailing sobriety made him more intemperate; he would come out of his room at the close of study-hours, and the first taste of fresh air would send him frolicking among his staid fellows, till they could not resist the contagion. His fondness for startling people was as strong as ever, but if he found his motives misconstrued he was ready at once to explain himself, for he could not bear that any one should suffer through his escapades. The students looked on with amusement; they could not help making friends with him at once. One of those, who was afterward an intimate acquaintance, Rev. Charles Newman, thus gives his impressions of David at this time: —

"My first acquaintance with your brother was in the fall of 1855. On my return to Andover, I found him at my boarding-place. I was favorably impressed

by his evident activity of mind. He seemed always
on the alert, never sitting down in reverie or abstraction. It was his habit, when waiting for meals, to seat
himself upon a stool, or perhaps the floor, attract at
once the interest of the children, and engage them in
some conversation or play; or he would take a book,
or something else into his hand — his manner expressing
an incessant activity. One evening, as I was walking somewhat in advance of the others, he came up
with me on the other side of the walk, and by most
irresistible grimaces drew my attention; in such a
strange way as this was formed an acquaintance which
became very intimate. He was full of frolics and
gambols, continually surprising one by some outburst
of his excessive vitality and glee. I walked much,
and he offered himself as my companion; through the
winter and summer it became a regular thing, until
every object on the route became familiar. He would
address apostrophes now to a dog, now to a peacock,
and now to a wood-chopper, whom we passed on our
way; he would climb a bank, and with wild, extravagant gesticulation recite some passage of poetry. I
never saw in any one else that combination of exuberant, gleeful, animal spirits, and such single-eyed devotion and earnestness."

His old habits evidently had not deserted him; even
the rabbit-traps were set when the winter came, and
the old story was repeated, of something getting in and
something gnawing out. He wanted the same out-of-
door life to carry off his exuberance, and besides, if
the truth must be told, his dyspepsia. His college diet
was bearing its fruit, and for the first time in his life
he began to suffer from physical weakness and disor-

derly system. Other ailments appeared, and it was interesting to see the decision with which he set about recovering robustness ; he held himself strictly account-able for any failure of his body to do the bidding of his mind. The friend just quoted adds that he wore no great-coat this winter, for which he gave the whimsical reason, that he was fitting himself to go as missionary to Greenland, if it should be thought advisable. Really, he wanted to force his system into obedience, and took this for one means.

The routine of seminary life is somewhat similar to that of college. Recitations and lectures succeed each other at regular intervals, and the methodical bell tells off the hours with precision. The student, however, is allowed larger liberty, compulsory exercises are fewer, though a pretty careful watch is kept that no erratic student shall have his own way too much. The char-acter of the studies and the object of the student give a religious tone to the exercises, and produce, indeed, an atmosphere somewhat different from that of col-lege. The tendency frequently is to harden the re-ligious life, to exalt the intellectual above the spiritual, to create a too curious and irreverent attitude toward the divine mysteries. This is the direction in which human weakness thus placed is liable to err, but the inhering advantages of the system are no doubt supe-rior. At first, the change from reckless college associ-ations to the quiet, serious way in which seminary exercises are conducted, touches the heart of a Chris-tian, till he thinks nothing could be more favorable to religious growth.

So it seemed to David, when he began his course there. He liked the custom of opening the recitations and lectures with prayer; it seemed to sanctify mental labor, to keep alive the remembrance of a consecration of all powers to holy service. He liked the social prayer-meeting, where a freedom of expression, a fulness of sympathy prevailed; he enjoyed study which brought him so close to the divine wisdom; the cast of his mind was reverential, and I do not think that he fell much into the intellectual snare set for young theologians. The chief delight, however, which he found, was in an association with those in the seminary who were expecting to become foreign missionaries. To such he needed no other commendation; they were his brethren, and he gave them unstintingly of his generous affection. If there were any amongst them with whom, otherwise, he might have little in common, yet, for the sake of the Cause, he loved them heartily, while he gave his warmest affection to such as were after his own heart.

A week or two after his entrance of the seminary, he was asked to join a society of "Christian Brethren," which was composed exclusively of those who had devoted themselves to the foreign missionary work, and whose object was mutual encouragement and the promotion of a missionary spirit in the seminary. The society had been founded by Mills, in Williamstown, had been removed to Andover, and maintained ever since, not obtruding itself upon notice, and, indeed, so private in nature, as to be unknown in name or existence to most of the students. Each week, on Tuesday evening, the little band met, and in the most informal manner carried on their meetings, chatting over personal matters, while beneath the surface flowed the deep current of an earnest purpose which needed no conventional propriety to make it known. Here they prayed with one another, conferred as to the best manner of awaking an interest in missions, and when one of their number sailed, he was bidden Godspeed, by that circle of young men, with deeper earnestness than by the church at large. To this gathering did David go weekly, for there he could give out the ardor of his purpose without fear of its falling upon listless or sceptical ears. The personal companionship of the individual members was much to him, but I feel sure that he looked to the Brethren for the largest measure of inspiration. The purpose which had been growing in his soul had been, in large part, nurtured in solitude ; none of his college friends, dear as they were, could give him that perfect sympathy which he craved ; the encouragement from his own family and from Christian friends was sincere, but it was far off. Doubtless, he had been made more self-reliant by such a discipline, but what he now needed was intercourse with kindred minds, who had common purpose and interests with him. This was granted him. In the Brethren he had those who meant what he did, and to whom he could freely declare himself. They were brothers, and he gave them a brother's affection.

The effect upon him was most generous ; there was a roundness to his life never before seen ; delicately sensitive to outward influences, though often he seemed roughly to overbear them, the warm atmosphere about him was favorable to his growth. The enthusiasm with which hitherto he had pursued his studies had been subject to fluctuations, now it was more steady, more full of hopeful power. He started afresh in work. India seemed nearer than ever, there were fewer years to look across, and having about him those who were bound on the same errand, a briskness was imparted to his energies, an unhasting diligence. The regular studies of the course he took hold of energetically. With characteristic interest he seized upon Hebrew and twisted the forms round his flexile tongue, adding new words to his *patois* of languages. More noticeable, however, is the industry which he showed in private reading. There is a long list of books read by him during this year, in which, among numerous works in general literature, one can trace the beginning of a tolerably close investigation of his favorite subject, which hardly has a distinct name, unless it be the Natural History of Man. The unity and diversity of races, types of mankind, the philological interpretation of history received his attention, and a foundation was laid for more careful researches, as we shall see hereafter. In the ardor of a young philosopher, he began to write his views upon these subjects, and discoursed upon " Language," and " one Primeval Language," in the " Williams Quarterly," the magazine of his college. These essays are written with care, though by a pen not yet very facile ; he follows his authorities, but with open eyes, and attempts some little theorizing himself. The papers are nothing in themselves, but how wide an interval there is, in intellectual culture, between them and his maiden compositions, — " Ambition," and " Independence must have limits ; " nay, between them and recent efforts of Senior year at college there is a wide difference, indicating the impetus that has been given to his mind, and showing promise of a full and rapid growth.

The long term in Andover is a very long one, lasting

from the middle of September to the middle of March, when a vacation of six weeks follows. David had enjoyed this stretch of study, and had worked with hearty interest, keeping his heart warm by intercourse with zealous men, and interesting himself with a class in the Sunday-school. It was a quiet winter, unbroken by any more exciting events than two or three holidays spent at home, infrequent visits from some of the family, and the social gatherings in Andover, to be taken once in a month, with as few grimaces as possible.

He remembered his college in those days. Two brothers were still there, and he insisted upon knowing all the gossip, and above all kept in mind the spiritual welfare of his Alma Mater. He begged for news of any increase of religious interest. "You say nothing about the state of religion," he writes; "now remember, never write a letter again without [speaking of it], whether affairs are dark or bright. All here look for news with deep interest." In concert with his fellows from Williams at the seminary, he prayed earnestly and affectionately for the college. Often did he press upon his brothers' minds the warning that never again would they find men so impressionable. "Boys," he would write in his eager way, "I want to urge upon you to bear constantly in mind that you never again will be placed in such a favorable situation for affecting the souls of your fellows. You will regret when you leave college and look back upon the opportunities for doing good lost, I tell you." When the spring vacation came, he took a journey to Williamstown, going unannounced, as he always delighted to go, surprising his brothers and friends by suddenly appearing at the 'Logian meeting. He spent a fortnight there, for the

6

sake of Mr. Hoisington's aid in his Tamil studies, which he had kept up through the year, and enjoyed exceedingly a return to his old haunts. Once more he took his favorite walks, went into the college exercises, and showed the attachment of a son to his old home. He had for some time been considering the project of spending a year or two years in teaching at the South, and was rather perplexed, partly from the difficulty of obtaining a desirable situation, partly from the strong aversion which he felt from postponing too long his departure for India. He visited New York after his stay in Williamstown, but found little satisfaction, and returned to Andover to reside for the short term, still undecided in his plans.

The beauty of this gentle country captivated him, and he was light-hearted as he studied by his open window, or sought for early flowers along Indian Ridge. " Dingy, dark Myrtle Street!" he writes to his sister, " what misery to be shut up there this charming day. Andover is coming out in all its gayety and loveliness ; and our room — just as pleasant as it can be, looking out on the old orthodox green, so very orthodox that all the paths are at right angles, and no cuts across. I could wish for no better days for study. The rigor of winter not yet departed : just at that temperature where a fire is not needed, and where heat is not felt. I am in perfect trim for study. And I am happy — God be blessed for happiness." His perplexity regarding the coming year kept him, however, unsettled, and liable to returns of his old enemy, — morbidness, not yet wholly overcome. The one strong desire in his heart was to get to India ; some of his friends in the Senior class were making their preparations for departure, and every sound quickened his own desire. Often in his brief diary of events and books read, he breaks out — "Shall I ever be in India? Can it be?" and one could not fail to see that this was the desire of his heart, driving him willingly forward. Yet his judgment assured him that the right course was to wait. Friends wished him to intermit two years, but he would consent only to leave the seminary for one. Whilst he was thus hasting, as if he had intimation that his time was short, one can easily imagine that different feelings prevailed in the hearts of his home: they are best expressed by the following passage from a letter of his father's: —

BOSTON, July 15, 1856.

MY DEAR SON: — I do not wonder that you begin to feel some solicitude, as to what disposition you should make of yourself for the coming year, if you do not pursue your theological studies, for a state of uncertainty is anything but pleasant. . . . . I have thought a good deal of late about you, particularly since I received your letter which you sent to me just before you last came down. I have prayed much for you, and feel much for you, more than I have ever expressed. When you made known to us your intention to become a missionary of the cross, and to devote yourself to your Saviour in a foreign field, I felt that you had done so from a conviction of duty, and from love to our dear Redeemer, and I could not throw any obstacles in the way, however painful the thought might be that after a season we should be separated from you, perhaps for this life: in respect to myself, it will only be for a short time. I have almost arrived at the common age of man, and if you remained in this country, I should be quite as likely to be deprived of your society, as God might have employment for you in some distant portion of our own land; so that, on the whole, I could feel to rejoice that God had inclined your heart to enter upon the field of duty you have chosen. And now, my dear son, if you are convinced that God in his providence points out to you this way to glorify Him, let nothing hinder you from prosecuting your design: do what you can to qualify yourself for the work, but deliberately, and with no undue haste. I do not want you to hasten away before you are fully prepared: while this work of preparation is going on, you will undoubtedly have some trying seasons, — a sense of duty and inclination may come into conflict, — you will have temptations, but look away from yourself to Him who redeemed you with His blood, and who will reward you for every act of self-denial you may make for Him, by imparting to you more of His grace, and giving you sweet peace, in the consciousness that, though you leave father, mother, brothers and sister, for His sake and the Gospel's, you will receive a hundred-fold in this life, and in the world to come life everlasting. . . . . .

Affectionately yours,

CHARLES SCUDDER.

At the close of the year, in August, 1856, he went to Williamstown again, to be present at a Mission Jubilee, held in connection with the College Commencement, to celebrate the fiftieth year since Mills and his associates inaugurated the Mission movement beneath a haystack, in Sloan's Meadows. The ground where the haystack stood had been purchased for a Mission Park of ten acres, by the friends of the college, and it was intended to hold the jubilee there; it was even proposed by the enthusiastic professor who was the chief mover, to have a Bungalow on the grounds, for the accommodation of the visitors. That, however, was given up, and the day proving stormy, the exercises were held in the church. Regular addresses were given, a number of missionaries spoke, and David, who had taken a lively interest in the affair, appeared with some ancient letters of Mills, together with the original constitution, in cypher, of the society formed by him. In a letter to a friend just sailing for India, he gives this brief account of his share in the proceedings: —

"It rained all the time, — hence the haystack was not resorted to, and we did not meet in the Bungalow as was expected. But the church was comfortable, and we enjoyed the occasion highly. It really passed off finely. Professor Hopkins's was the main address, and an able production. He brought in two of his hobbies, which limped slightly, — a Mission Seminary in this country, as preparatory for a foreign field, where languages could be taught by returned missionaries, and lectures on the philosophy and character of different countries be delivered. Also his colonization plan, of sending out Christian farmers, mechanics, and so on, to work religion into the pagans. In the Alumni meeting next morning, a resolution was passed that proper measures be taken for the establishment of a Mission School as soon as thought advisable. So that may amount to something yet. In the midst of his speech, he said — 'Let Mills speak for himself,' and sung out at the top of his voice, 'And we've a young brother from Andover come up to help us!' Whereupon, with stately step and solemn, I marched upon the stage and delivered the constitution into the hands of the chairman. He handed it to Dr. Cox to decipher, when we had quite an interesting colloquy. I then read a portion of the letters, and retired — a lion."

He visited New York again, when he found an opportunity to act as Bible colporteur in the neighborhood of Orange, New Jersey, whither he went, after a short visit home, in September, 1856.

## CHAPTER V.

### A YEAR OF EXPERIMENT.

#### [1856–1857.]

THE Bible agency was only intended to occupy a couple of months. The advantage which he anticipated from it was an increased facility of converse with the world, knowledge of men, and knowledge of himself. The life which he had led had brought him very little into contact with persons holding religious views different from his own, or with persons in a different order of society; he had in fact seldom been thrown among strangers. If he was to be an efficient missionary, it was essential that he should learn, by practical experiment, how to deal with men; besides, the life which a student leads has a tendency to withdraw him from that sympathy with unintellectual people which is a requisite of successful ministry; many a theological student, brought face to face with a sleepy parish, has then to take his first lesson in the art of discovering men, — a lesson which ends usually in the equally valuable discovery of his own strength and weakness.

David had a special disability for such work as he undertook, in a shyness which made him retreat from the presence of a stranger; in a sensitive dread of contact with rudeness; in a stubborn, and somewhat surly moodiness, which, when on him, kept his mouth closed as if it were locked and the key thrown away; in an

unready speech, moreover, which want of practice had
rendered still more broken and stammering. The work
of peddling Bibles, accompanied with religious teaching, was as uncongenial as it well could be; it was,
perhaps, the most violent method that he could have
adopted for breaking through the crust of reserve
which idiosyncrasies and student-life had formed over
his nature. The Bible Society had contemplated a canvass of the entire country, in order to offer the Bible to
every soul that could be reached; accordingly the separate districts were circumscribed. David's embraced
Orange, New Jersey, and the villages lying near. How
he managed to get through with the task, for such it
ever was, will best be learned by the following chronicle, drawn up from his diary and letters of the time.
His diary, as before intimated, never was anything but
the briefest memorandum of daily doings, with occasional breaths of desire or regret; he had a repugnance
to formal statements of religious feeling in it, believing
that momentary sensations thus imprisoned were very
unnatural, and very untruthful indications of religious
progress. I have selected such entries in his diary,
and such passages from his letters, as show the general
course of his colportage: —

*Sep.* 11. I am to proceed to Orange, and commence
in the village on foot; when done with neighboring
houses, to go to another town, say Bloomfield, and so
on to several in the thickest parts; then take a horse
and wagon, and go through the different outskirts.
Here I am, and soon to be at work. I try to think as
little about it as possible till I commence. How my
arms will ache!

*Sep.* 13. Books came at nine o'clock. Worked two hours in morning, but almost every one is supplied.

*Sep.* 15. A very pleasant day indeed. Had a long talk with a shoemaker on English Catholicism. He quoted English history at a great rate. Must learn to present the gospel boldly. Be not ashamed of Christ and his word. Another had never had a Bible, and when I gave him one, let go his work and commenced reading just where he opened, and became so absorbed that he noticed me no longer. Such men I am to learn from.

*Sep.* 16. Talked a long time with a man who was a general unbeliever: hope with a right spirit. A Catholic shut the door in my face. I wonder that Catholics usually are so polite.

*Sep.* 17. Had a curious talk to-day with a man who professed to doubt the genuineness of the Scriptures. He paraded his learning at a great rate. Also talked about a half an hour with a Catholic woman, comparing Bibles, King James and Douay. 'T is of no use whatever to combat their errors by argument, they are so wedded to them. How can we reach them but by long-continued, patient labor? Don't think I make a very efficient colporteur.

*Sep.* 19. A week already spent in Orange at work, and finished almost all of my work for first visit. To-day have been in the worst hole of all, Reeves's Row: quantities of Irish huddled together. But I found them remarkably ready to receive Bibles, and I gave them about fifteen.

*Sep.* 25. Spent the day in Bloomfield: finished. What is the reason? I was told that I should visit about forty families in a day, but to-day I have seen eighty: very little destitution.

*Sep.* 29. In Belleville. **A man berated** me soundly, but I laughed at him, and soon made him laugh himself. He was in good humor when I left, — did n't think I was a bigot, and hoped that some day I would bring around Bibles for Bishop Bailey. I think it is wrong for distributors to throw tracts into a house, where they refuse to receive them; it only incenses them.

*Sep.* 30. Last day of September. Good-bye. **Next** month may I do some good. [He had an odd way, throughout his diary, of bidding good-bye to each month and year.]

*Oct.* 2. **Have visited** ninety-four families to-day in upper Belleville. **Left Orange** at 7.30 A. M. Walked to Bloomfield; took horse to Belleville, and worked till 12.30 ; got dinner for horse and self at a small farmer's ; worked from 1.30 to 5.30 P. M., and ended with losing my way, so that I did not quite finish Belleville. **Rode to Bloomfield, and walked and ran** back to Orange.

*Oct.* 3. Worked in Belleville. Irish funeral made some confusion. One woman was " rather light in her head, and I 'd better not be bothering her ! "

*Oct.* 7. Every morning regularly I 'm blue; toward dusk I grow happy, and when trotting home I hum tunes, interspersed pretty thickly with " Go 'long ! " " Get up ! " and think of all sorts of nice things, with a beautiful Orange sky right in front, and a happy circle in prospect. I feel good regularly in the evenings, and decidedly bad when I get up. I decided to-day that I would read on Catholicism when at home, and take a tract district and talk. I meet many an intelligent Catholic. I meet too the most odd of remarks and arguments. I was talking with a woman to-day about our sins. " Yes," said she, " I 'm a right bad Catholic, thank God ! "

*Oct.* 10. I suppose I ought to leave a practical exhortation at every house, but most of mine are expended on my horse, and appear to have so much greater effect upon him than upon the human kind that I think of confining my remarks to him in future. I ask if they have a supply of Bibles ? they say, " Oh yes, we have more Bibles than we make good use of." It strikes me that that phrase must have been in some shorter catechism, or an example in penmanship, — people know it so well. I am heartily tired and sick of hearing it. Once in a while I meet a poor family where I give a Bible, and try to say something, but it usually amounts to no more than a general remark of about as much significance as " Fine day to-day." *You* does n't figure enough in my talk. If success in the work is gauged by despatch and number of Bibles left, I have done pretty well. Yesterday I made a hundred and nine calls, working hard nine hours. This morning I met a nice old man, and had a real good chat. As I left he gave me his blessing and said : — " Pray much. Look up, not down. Burn inwardly ! Said Dr. Duff, ' A man of fire is worth three men frozen.' Mark that ! ' A man of fire ! ' "

*Oct.* 11. Coming home in P. M. met a little Polish boy, a peddler. Asked him if his basket was heavy. " 'T is n't that," said he, " but I have n't sold a cent's worth to-day, and have lost a dollar's worth." The poor

fellow cried heartily.  He said his father would lick him.
I gave him a dollar and quarter: he kissed my hand.
I felt happy.  A cup of cold water.

*Oct.* 13.  I asked one woman why Christ died.  "My
dear boy," said she, "that's a very simple question, and
very easily solved, very;" and after saying that from
a child she had known the Scriptures, asked if Nicode-
mus was n't the man born blind, and Moses the ruler of
the Pharisees.

*Oct.* 27.  In New York.  I am twenty-one to-day,
and ought to put away childish things.  Had a talk
with Woodin to-day.  He means to be a missionary.
Can it be that India will ever see me?  May God prepare me.

His work was interrupted at this time by the Annual
Meeting of the American Board of Foreign Missions,
at Newark; after the week he returned for a few days
to his colportage, when he completed the canvass of his
district, and returned to Boston, rather out of sorts
with himself at what he considered an unfaithful service.
Such he always afterward regarded it, and certainly
whatever success he had was won by patient contin-
uance in an unloved work.  At the beginning of November he was again at home, just too late to cast his
one Presidential vote for Fremont.  It was a disappointment to him, both because he thought that he
would never again be in America at such an election,
and because he had taken an unusual interest in that
spirited campaign.  "It would be pleasant to us as it
would to you," writes his father, "to have you throw
one vote for the President of the United States, but so
far as the vote of Massachusetts is concerned, that is

sure for Fremont, by many thousands; if it were a closely contested vote, as that of Pennsylvania is likely to be, I should say come home at all hazard or expense."

When he came home it was decided that he should remain at his father's house for the remainder of the year, extend his studies more widely, and busy himself with such religious work as was at hand. The consciousness that he had failed to do all that he might have done in his Bible agency, made him more anxious now, when established at home, to resume the same kind of work, and in accordance with a plan formed in New Jersey, he took a district in the city, High Street and neighborhood, in which to distribute tracts. Under the system in vogue, it is the custom for each visitor to receive monthly a package containing perhaps fifty copies of a single tract, which he is to distribute among the families of his district, using the opportunity afforded by the offer of the tract, to make the acquaintance of the poor, with a view to giving Christian instruction and learning their temporal wants. The efficacy of the system depends upon the chance of the tract being appropriate, and upon the patience and tact of the visitor; but it is at best a bungling system, and the visitor is constantly entangled by it. There are few persons indeed, who do not go their monthly round with disagreeable anticipations; they are heartily glad when it is over, and likely enough reproach themselves for being unwilling to take up this cross, when they would cheerfully seek the same end of instructing and aiding the poor in some less artificial manner. Their sense of delicacy is shocked, not so much by the contact they are forced into with rudeness, as by the feeling

that they are assuming a position ᴠtoward the poor
which they themselves would resent if the tables were
turned.

Perhaps the discipline was needed by David, but discipline it was to him. He made a pretty wry face at
the middle of each month as he began his rounds,
which occupied two or three afternoons, but he worried
through the work with occasional pleasant reliefs. He
dreaded the appearance of being thought proud, and
offered his unloved missives to a poor man with much
more sensitiveness than he would have felt toward one
his equal in rank. He had a feeling that these ignorant
poor men ought to be angry with him, and took their
graciousness, when it was shown, as a great favor. He
had no consciousness of superiority to them, would enter
a room blushing, and if allowed, sit down for a pleasant
talk on many things, stammer forth his message of
good tidings, then leave hurriedly, glad at heart if he
could say something, and submitting cheerfully to be
driven out of the next room by an enraged tailor with
his scissors. One adventure which he had afforded
him great amusement. He wrote of it, both briefly in
his diary and more fully to two of his brothers, so that
I give the narrative in his own words :—

Knocking at a door in High Street, it was slowly
opened by an Irishwoman, who beckoned me in mys-
teriously with her finger, waved me to a seat, muttering,
" I want to spake wid ye." I entered, thinking that a
tract might have been working.

" Perhaps ye a'n't a-knowin' me." Dim visions of
cooks and housemaids passed before me, but none to
respond, and I answered, —

" Well, I 'm not aware of the fact. Where did you know me?"

" An' whar did ye lave yer father?"

" My father! I left him over in the other part of the city. I have just dined with him."

" Och! ye tell me so! D'ye think I'm not a-knowin ye?"

" And where?"

" In Ireland, sure!"

" You did! Why, I never was there in my life."

" Out upon ye, are n't ye knowin' better than that? Did n't I know ye well, and did n't ye run away down to Cork with the provisions and get thirty shillin', and come back wid the small-pox, an' away to Ameriky, and send back to yer father for the thirty shillin', an' he send them on to ye, eh?"

I took several long breaths. And am I thus?

" And what part of Ireland was I born in?"

" County Cork."

" What town?"

" Bonny O'Clagh."

" And what was my father's name?"

" Sure yer mither's name was Sweeny, and yer father's name O'Burke!"

I took out my note-book to help my memory in case I should be called to make deposition at any time respecting my right to lands in said town.

" Oh, now," said she, " as if ye did n't know yer own name and all this!"

" What is my name?" I asked, persisting in ignorance.

" Neddy O'Burke." I took a long breath, — at last thought to ask, —

" But how do you know I am he ? "

" Sure, an' ye have yer father's hair ! "

" And is my mother yet alive ? "

" Oh, no, dear soul. Did n't ye have a sister, — swate little thing she was too, — and did n't we sit up to the wake two days and two nights when she died, and yer poor mither took on so about it, — an' she died too, och hone ! "

I almost dropped a tear.

" Had I any brothers ? "

" To be sure: there's Dan, he's the oldest, an' you're the youngest, an' there's two betwane, but I don't jist remember them now."

" How old is my father ? "

" I don' no."

" As old as you ? "

" Yes, indade. I was at his weddin', and was only about so high at the time."

" But how did you know about me ? "

" Now, ye're mighty innocent, a'n't ye ? Sure, the last time ye was round, I thought an' it was you, an' I told my daughter, an' I had a mind to spake wid ye, whin ye come round again. An' did n't I hearn tell of ye by my son, as workin' out in Dorchister, thegither wid Tom Lane ? "

A pause ensued, when she offered me a pinch of snuff, saying, —

" An' perhaps ye did n't know I was related to ye ? "

" Well, no, I was not aware of it," declining the snuff. " What relation are you ? "

" Second cousin to yer mither."

As I rose to go, after more words, I said, —

" Won't you take a tract for sake of old times ? "

" Indade an' I won't. Out upon ye! What are ye bringing round those dirty papers for? What would yer father be doin' to yer if he knowed it?"

I thereupon took my leave, decidedly in a cloud, but as I was walking along I thought that here at last was a solution of many a strange freak of my childhood, and my pride arose as I bethought myself of what noble blood I was, — the Burkes being able to hold up their heads with any one. I went again to see my "cousin," but she remained positive. "Sure, there's not another man in Ameriky has such fair hair as ye!" she insisted.

What he wanted of this tract distribution was to acquire the art of presenting the Gospel simply; he knew that most of his work was to be with uncultivated minds, and he desired to learn how to address such. If he had shrunk from this task or given it up in discouragement, doubtless he would have found his after experience in India very much more trying than it was. Besides, he loved the poor, especially poor children; in his walks he would stop to play with them, and give them sweetmeats; he wished to be brought into a connection with them which implied some sort of equality, the true equality of rank which is measured by divine rules. He found what he asked in two ways more natural and more congenial to his feelings than distributing tracts.

One was the care of a Bible-class of poor Swedes in a Mission Sunday-school. They were rough men and women, but possessed the affectionate and docile nature so characteristic of the Swedish people. The teaching was an admirable exercise for him; his class could speak

7

English but indifferently, and were very ignorant, so that he was compelled to present truth in its simplest form and most intelligible language ; this in fact was just the sort of instruction, though not so difficult, as that which he was to attempt in India. It was a fine sight to see this ruddy boy, surrounded by the uncouth crowd, looking, he used to say, as if they would devour him, and putting his whole soul into the effort to make them understand the Gospel. He visited them in their homes, and got them to sing Swedish songs to him ; he helped the needy, and they all learned to look upon him as one of their best friends. Once, one of them lay dying in the Hospital, and David was sent for. " How that man loved me ! " said he afterward with unaffected humility ; " he could not speak, but he pressed my hand to his heart. It made me feel so guilty. How little I have done for these poor men, and yet they love me so."

The other help which he found in converse with the poor was through attendance upon what in Boston are called " Neighborhood Meetings." The city mission- aries in their regular ministry arrange to have weekly an evening prayer-meeting, held in the room of some poor Christian, where the neighbors are invited, the missionary with outside help conducting the service. To the educated Christian such meetings frequently afford greater spiritual nutriment than the more formal ones attended by his own class ; there is a homely fresh- ness about them which animates his soul, and he finds himself often nearer the Divine presence, when among the lowly, than if surrounded by those who might, through his consciousness of their unspoken criticism, impose restraint upon his freedom of utterance. David conducted one of these meetings regularly and attended others. He found a rare enjoyment in bringing to these humble people the results of his own Biblical research and Christian experience; he learned of them and kept the lamp of love burning steadily, because he fed it with the oil there to be purchased. So he would climb the rickety stairs or stumble into the cellar, entering a room hot and close, with dim candles sputtering on the table, where rested a Bible and stack of hymn-books; chairs of every sort ranged about the room and filled by men, women, and children, who were likewise distributed upon every other available piece of furniture, while babies crawled about the floor, breaking out into unseemly noises at the most inopportune moment. Here would he stand, his heart kindling as he looked upon his audience, and in the simplest language try to teach them the law of God, or to direct their sight to the Divine love shining in upon the assembly.

Children of all ages were brought to the meeting, and he soon began to turn his attention to them; it was in these meetings that he acquired the facility, afterward so noticeable, of suiting his thought to the capacity of children. He had some power of imagination, perhaps no unusual endowment, but he cultivated it with such industry that soon it became exceedingly fertile. His life in Roxbury, his walks among the mountains of Berkshire and New Hampshire, were laid under contribution to supply apt illustration, and the necessity for fresh material made him very observant in his daily walks, so that he would come to his meeting with quite a store of illustration, gathered in a ramble through the streets. His reading also gave of its abundance, and he began to draw upon India for fund of anecdote. It is an illustration of the thoroughness with which he pursued whatever commended itself to his heart and judgment. Every week he was becoming more proficient in this art of addressing plain people and children, an art which was to be of inestimable value to him in his missionary labors. That, however, as an end was not so moving in his mind as the nearer one of success in this undertaking. He loved the work and the people whom he met; especially the children attracted him, and they on their part were drawn to him. "This afternoon," he writes in his diary, " took two little boys, Cassitye by name, to ride ; they belong to my meeting. We went out to Brookline and West Roxbury, and into the woods. They enjoyed themselves highly ; are nice boys." Our father at this time was President of the City Missionary Society, and it was one part of the pleasure which he took in David's residence at home that they were in such complete sympathy in these matters. By every interest they were united : so young was the father, so growing the son, that they were companions ; the father enjoyed his boy's mirth and enthusiasm, so accordant with his own sunny temper and unselfish interest, and it was a happy life that the household spent that winter.

This mission-work amongst the poor did not withdraw him from his own church, in which he was ever ready to spend his labor. He was faithful as a member, and did not forget that the advantages of education which he had received called for a return ; so he was ready with his suggestive comments upon the Bible, bringing to the evening prayer-meeting, for the pleasure of others, some bit of exegesis which had struck his attention in study. His name however was that of a missionary

student, and he did what he could to excite an interest
in missions at his church, devising a plan for making
the monthly concert of prayer more systematic and
comprehensive. He was much concerned about the
best form of presenting missionary operations. "We
want," he said, "general facts and principles forced
upon our attention by means of life-like illustration."
He found this most to his mind in the English periodicals, and for this reason, as well as from a desire to
induce a more catholic interest in missions than that
confined merely to the workings of the American Board,
he used these periodicals very freely at the meetings of
the church.

His own spirit needed no prompting; if he should
become forgetful, his Tamil grammar and reader stood
upon his table, furnishing both reminder and an excellent means for conveying increased ardor into practical
channels. Once or twice he went up to Andover on a
Tuesday and surprised the "Brethren," who gave him
a most hearty welcome, while those of the number who
had already entered upon missionary life furnished him
with occasions for correspondence. But the letters
which he wrote to the Brethren generally are based
on so intimate an acquaintance as to be too private for
publication. He spoke and wrote to them very freely;
especially when wide seas separated, he was emboldened
to a more frank disclosure of his mind than was likely
to be made where a face-to-face meeting might produce
the consciousness of an extreme openness; writing to a
friend upon the opposite side of the world, whom we
scarcely expect to meet again, is like whispering secrets
in the dark. The following extract is from a letter
written to Mr. Dean, of the Mahratta Mission : —

BOSTON, April 11, 1857.

I often sigh for Andover influences, but still am very glad I remained at home. I long to be a missionary, yet feel more and more my unfitness. I seem to see pretty clearly what a Christian ought to be, and yet approach no nearer that desired state. Every missionary I am sure should feel an ardent love to the Saviour in his own soul, for else how can he love others? Do you feel your love deepened as you go on? I know you must. I feel myself like a man standing on the borders of some fair land open to him, who yet is satisfied with but an occasional glance. The riches of Christ's grace I know are free to all who seek them, still I stand reluctant to apply.

What sort of a place is Seroor? By the map it appears to be on the Kokasee River. What sort of a river is that? anything like the Shawshin? How that name brings back old times! I seem to see you and Capron, as you met Newman and me day after day, always with the same benignant smiles, gracefully doffing your hats as we passed. Do you suppose we shall ever all meet again this side heaven? What a blessed, blessed hope it is that we may and shall surely meet there at last. Oh, we are not thankful enough for the many kindly emotions and peaceful expectations which Christianity affords us.

With the exception of a short interval, when he gave private tuition to the ward of a friend, his whole time this year was his own, and was spent after his own mind, in diligent study and in such occupations as I have intimated. He gave most attention to a more complete acquaintance with the Biblical studies of the previous year, especially Hebrew, and to his Tamil; but the more marked characteristic of his taste was the extent of his general reading. He seemed to devour books, reading with great rapidity, — too fast as he knew for mental digestion, — and extending his inquiries in many directions. It is, of course, no criterion of a man's scholarship how many books he reads. Attention is drawn to this phase of his mental growth, as indicating how rapidly he had outgrown the earlier stage of indifferentism toward a student's occupation, for even up to graduation from college, active life had received his first attention. It was his missionary purpose which had started his mind; the same purpose governed the growth. At first, under the conviction that a liberal education was essential to the efficiency of a missionary, he had begun to read upon subjects of which he was ignorant; now, without any careful calculation of the value of his reading for the special end first proposed, he was led by interest in his pursuits to a far more varied course of reading than ever he would have been likely to pursue, unprompted at the outset by some such special end. One would have said in his boyhood, and even in his college days, that the last character in which he would appear would be that of a bookish man, and yet he had now become so much of a book-lover as to be touched with the fever of making a perfect library in his special department of India; so much of a book-fancier, indeed, as to treat his books as playmates, take them from the shelves to dandle and to feast his eyes upon their forms and dress.

Two writers may be singled out, from the many whose acquaintance he now made or continued, as

especially his favorites, — Thomas Arnold and Isaac
Taylor. He knew Arnold, as he is known to most
Americans, chiefly through the medium of Stanley's
admirable Life. So far as he was conversant with the
accidents of Arnold's position, with the movement in
the Church of England, its action upon Arnold's mind,
and the reaction of his earnest spirit upon it, he could
appreciate more perfectly the character thus revealed;
but an interest in the man himself existed, and always
may exist apart from a full comprehension of the man's
surroundings. Such an interest David felt in Arnold;
it was in fact what he would have felt in himself, could
he have been separable from himself, for he was attracted by just such a character as his friends discovered
in him. It has been noted that in earlier days he had
read John Foster; the difference between these two
men indicates to some extent the difference in David's
spiritual affinities at the two stages of his growth. Then,
in the maze of his self-inquiry, led astray into gloomy
introspection, he was drawn to the meditative seriousness which characterizes Foster ; such words of sombre
thought as met him gave voice to his own unspoken
emotions, and he even began to covet the life of a
recluse. Now, escaped from the entanglement of a
disordered conscience, and yet honest in his dealings
with his own heart, hasting to the fulfilment of the
great work which enlarged his soul, he found in the
earnestness of Arnold a counterpart of his own ideal
excellence. Just these two classes, the serious and the
earnest, seem to divide thoughtful men, and we have to
thank Arnold for making current the word *earnest*, and
for stamping the coin with his own image.

The writings of Isaac Taylor had a somewhat similar

charm for him, since they corresponded with his own natural treatment of religious topics. The catholicity of his mind induced an exercise of charity toward all forms of belief and disinclined him to prejudgment, while his habits as a student led him to a search for fundamental principles in any system. This temper had been confirmed under the admirable tuition of Dr. Hopkins, who, charged by some with an over-cautiousness of mind, showed the real nature of his caution in dismissing class after class, impressed with his habit of careful examination, but not impressed with his private opinions upon the subjects to be examined. David found in Taylor a method of inquiry, agreeing with his own less ambitious method, and he turned to the writings of that author for a completion of the lines of thought upon which he had begun, but which his youth and lack of erudition forbade him to follow to great lengths. He had a confidence in Taylor's writings, which was no doubt in great measure the result of their agreeing so totally, both in subject and manner of treatment, with all that he had himself applied his mind to finding out. Hence he read with pleasure anything that he could lay hold of, and used to show an enthusiastic delight as he discovered one after another half-forgotten work of that voluminous writer, too careless of his own reputation.

Though more of a student, he kept his old love for Nature, and daily took his excursions out of town or about the city. He revisited old haunts. " Roxbury Neck was my walk," he writes, " where I brought up on Tommy's Rocks. Such a time as I did have! How old Nep came back! Remember that pond on Akron Street, just before you enter St. James from Warren,

with steep rocks on one side? and how Nep one day
ran right down their face? I do. And don't you remember how there used to be springs on the sidewalk,
opposite the Warren House on the right as you go up
the street? they bubble still! and that pump which used
to be chained? chained still! and the reservoir on the
Rocks with a ball on top? there still!" He explored
Boston, with a companion if possible, but generally
alone. He loved the old place which had grown so
familiar to him; he never could fairly live in a place
without carrying off in his memory the very shapes of
houses and shops, of sign-boards and street-turnings.
"You must always be ready to give me street-gossip,"
he writes from India. "Are any new buildings going
up? How does the block in Winthrop Place look?
It was half done when we left."

He closed this year of intermission by a summer
jaunt in Connecticut, and went as usual to the farm in
Wethersfield where he had worked so enthusiastically
just before entering college. He resumed his old employment, but now he writes: — "Finishing our 'home
lot' is quite an affair, though it may look small on paper. They began the day I came, and have been at it
ever since. Next week we begin on the meadow hay,
which will be finished in about two weeks. By that
time I shall throw up my hat and shoes, used up decidedly, and give three cheers for Wethersfield, but
nine most hearty ones for good old Boston and for
home. After all I was n't made to be a farmer. I have
had as pleasant a time as I could ask for here, but . . .
I am glad I was not called to this life, but to another."

## CHAPTER VI.

### COMPLETION OF THEOLOGICAL STUDY.

#### [1857-1859.]

IN September 1857 he returned to Andover, resuming his studies where he had left off a year before. Two years remained for the completion of systematic study, and he entered on his work with increased enthusiasm, for India seemed to be only waiting for these two years to be finished. I am indebted to Rev. Charles Ray Palmer, of Salem, Mass., for an account of David's life during this time, — an account which is more valuable since it comes from one previously unacquainted with him, and able to note afresh the characteristics which marked him. It is not always easy to know how far one's estimate of a brother's character or attainments is free from a too partial consideration, and I gladly avail myself of this friendly testimony to fill out the sketch of David's life : —

" My acquaintance with your brother commenced in September, 1857. He at that date joined my class in Andover Theological Seminary, which was then beginning its Middle Year. We had known one another by name before, through mutual friends, and were soon familiarly associated, I believe with mutual regard. Nothing ever happened to disturb the relations so established between us, and my satisfaction with him as a friend, as a fellow-student, and as a Christian brother,

was never less than complete.  His genial fellowship in
the pursuits which we had in common, his talents, good
sense, and scholarship, his energy and thorough enthusiasm, — partly a matter of temperament and partly a
result of the habit of self-concentration, — and above
all his humble, devout, and spiritual piety, marked him
at once in my estimation as no ordinary man, and speedily commanded my hearty admiration and esteem.

"I confess to a feeling of doubtfulness whether any
description of David Scudder can be written, which
would give to those who never saw him a conception
of him at all adequate.  He was truly a man of genius,
and a man of genius never can be ranked or estimated.
How great such a man will be, if he lives, none can
affirm beforehand: how great he is, is vaguely compre-
hended by his contemporaries: how great he was, the
world that comes after looks back with wonder to see.
There were men in Scudder's class who in particular
powers excelled him ; but every one by this time knows
that to have particular powers in excellence is not necessarily to be a remarkable man.  There were others
who, upon a tutor's books, would rank as more uniformly successful in reciting ; but every one knows by
this time that it is not in the tutor's books that we are
to look for the *data* to determine who is the most of a
man in a class.  Of just that peculiar constitution by
temperament, by mental qualities, by what happy influences have wrought upon natural susceptibility, and by
what are immanent of the results of rapid and easy
acquisition from manifold sources — which you recognize at once as rendering the person in whom you see
it certain to be *something* in the world — of just *that*
which for the want of a better name we call *genius*,

David Scudder had far more than any of his class. I do not hesitate at all to say this. Looking back from this point of time, I feel more confident than I did when we were together that he was the man of whom all discerning observers would predict success more positively than of any other.

"It is a remark of Francis Jeffrey that men of truly great powers have generally been cheerful, social, indulgent; while a tendency to sentimental whining or fierce intolerance may be ranked among the surest symptoms of little souls and inferior intellects. No one will ever recal Scudder but as the very embodiment of sunny good-nature, so free and abundant in its manifestations of itself as to be almost mirthfulness. He had indeed not only 'the habit of being pleased,' but a habit of being amused. A characteristic passage in a letter of his occurs to me: speaking of the first impressions made upon him by sights and sounds of India, he says, — 'The first morning that I walked out in this new land I fairly ached that I might have some one like you to nudge and have a good laugh with.' It was an evidence of the healthfulness of his whole being, that while he keenly entered into all the wrongs and miseries of the world of men, and was burdened with a true sympathy with the suffering from any cause, he was at the same time — and that without any painful lack of dignity — as keenly alive to all the fun that could be found in men's follies and mistakes, always appreciating with great zest everything whimsical or humorous.

"Yet with all he did not lack that part of the temperament of genius which renders it 'soft as the air to receive impressions.' He was sensitive, he was even

tender, and liable, like other intense natures, to periods
of depression.   This was at any rate true of him in
college and in the seminary; I know both from testimony and from observation.   As he matured in Christian living, he may have gained a greater equanimity.
I remember times when he seemed to be entirely overcome of the 'blues'; they were short times, but while
they lasted he was exceedingly melancholy.   Few I
think will be surprised at this.   It is the inevitable for-
tune of persons who are the most of the time wrought
up to the pitch of enthusiasm, to suffer periodic reac-
tions from a physical or psychologic necessity — reac-
tions which moral treatment will not reach.   Rest and
diversion are the only restoratives.   I recollect that
David was greatly comforted once by my telling him
something like this, because he was disposed to blame
himself for ever being anything but cheerful.

"I do not recal anything to be spoken of as striking
in David's student-life.   I mean in the restricted sense
of the term.   He was a thorough and systematic student, regular in his attendance upon all exercises.   He
was a conscientious member of the seminary — which
all students are not.   He never manifested that contempt for regulations or defiance of authority which
some seem to consider essential to their manliness ; I
believe he despised it.   In the recitation-room he was
always well prepared.   In the mutual examinations of
Middle Year, under the Moderation of the Professor,
he could maintain himself under the sharpest cross-
firing, as many able men cannot.   In the exercises of
criticism in Senior Year, he showed good appreciative
powers.   He was a diligent learner, a candid and vigorous thinker, and though steadfast in his opinions, a

tolerant opponent. He had none of the affectation of independence which disgraces some Divinity students, but he had the real independence which too many lack. His course with respect to the seminary *curriculum* was most characteristic. He never forgot what he was to be — a pioneer missionary in India, and this fact determined his attitude with respect to the different departments of study. In the study of the sacred languages he was zealous as might be expected. He acquired languages readily, and was an excellent linguist. Systematic Theology he gave sufficient attention to, but evidently did not make it a specialty. He was much more anxious to obtain a systematic view of truth which he could defend against Heathenism, than to learn the shibboleths of schools, or attract notice as a champion of superexcellent orthodoxy. He showed no keenness to enter into the polemics of Theology, and no disposition to identify himself with a Theological party. But he did desire and labor to attain a clear understanding of what was essential to *a* Theological system, and what was the substance of the faith once delivered to the saints. In the Rhetorical exercises of the seminary he had comparatively little interest, perhaps too little; indeed, after graduation he confessed as much to me. The explanation was, that he judged that for the science and the art of public speaking he should have no use in India whither his face was set. It was a fixed purpose, therefore, that with the Rhetorical Society he had little or nothing to do, laughingly refusing the solicitations of 'the embodiment of Rhetoric,' as he jocosely called the President of the society, and in the department of Sacred Rhetoric he bestowed comparatively little effort. He was content to do no more than necessary to sat-

isfy the claims of the Professor.  On the other hand,
Ecclesiastical and Dogmatic History had a closer connection with his future work, and in that department
he was a very diligent student."

It must be added to this statement that aside from
David's judgment as to the comparative value of his
studies, his own mental bias furnished the reason for
much of his choice.  Abstract truth and systems of
truth were not in themselves attractive subjects of
thought with him ; it was when they were embodied in
some concrete form, as the historical for instance, that
he preferred to consider them.  One of his friends, once
meeting him on a walk in Andover, noticed that he
wore a very lugubrious expression, and stopped him
with — " What makes your face so long, David ? "
" Oh," he sighed, " I am thinking up my creed."  With
him this was both a difficult and an uncongenial task ; his
belief was positive and had its seal in earnest operation,
but he disliked setting his belief forth in its dogmatic
form.  Thought found its expression more aptly in
practical effort than in rhetoric.  Even his letters show
this : they read smoothly where he is dealing with incident, but the moment he comes to any statement of
feeling or of opinion, there is an abruptness as if he
only began what he had to say and left the remainder
to be inferred : for this reason there are few letters
written by him in America which I have thought it
worth while to print ; while once in India, his letters
become most admirable interpreters both of his outer
and of his inner life.  He had thought, clear and determinate, but he lived rather than wrote it.

The studies peculiar to his own work were prosecuted

during these two years with as much energy as his accumulating tasks would allow. He foresaw that Hindû philosophy would demand his attention, and before any very close research into its mysteries, he aimed at as thorough a comprehension of the history of Occidental philosophy as his limited time would permit, while with Orientalism in its outward form he grew daily more familiar. The Tamil language he continued to acquire, and in connection with that study entered upon more careful inquiry into the philosophy of language, studying some of the more attainable results of Comparative Philology. He was fortunate in beginning Tamil when the grammar had to be his chief mode of access to the language, since it insured a more thorough foundation to his knowledge of the tongue, and by the kind of study which it required gave a more philosophical character to his early intimacy with the movements of the Hindû mind. To make the acquaintance of any language through familiar practice alone may give one a readier use of the vernacular, but is very likely to operate as a barrier against an acquaintance with the thought that underlies the foundation of the speech. David had besides the valuable aid of Mr. Hoisington, who was able to be his guide both in the familiar use and in the more scientific treatment of Tamil. To his home in Connecticut David took a journey as often as was practicable, and found in him something more than a guide in scholarship: he formed a warm friendship with him and his family, so that when in the spring of 1858 Mr. Hoisington died, David could mourn with the family the loss of a noble Christian friend, who had been of inestimable worth to him.

8

If when connected with the seminary before he had been marked for his missionary zeal, he took now a still more prominent position, and was at once identified most closely with the cause of missions. Of course he was in his place among the Brethren, and was the soul of that little company. " He projected himself also," continues Mr. Palmer in his letter, " with characteristic energy into the Society of Inquiry, and ultimately the Monthly Concert. The society meetings very quickly showed the power of his influence, in the increasing attractiveness to all earnest men in the Institution, and in the greater numbers attending them. By the end of the Middle Year of his class, so entirely was he recognized as the leading spirit in all matters connected with the objects of that society, that he was elected its President for the year following. Besides this public working in behalf of the cause of missions in the seminary, he labored incessantly in the opportunities offering to reach individual consciences with what he believed to be the call of the Master. If I am not mistaken, he privately labored with every member of the class, striving by every means to interest them to the point of feeling personally drawn to missionary life, and with respect to several he was entirely successful. To-day, though he sleeps in an Indian grave, he preaches Christ through more mouths than one or two in dark places of the earth. Thus ' his works do follow him.' Nor were such efforts confined to his own class. By similar methods he reached others to whom he gained access in the classes below him ; and when he had done all in the way of solicitation that he could, he planned still another method. By means of his official position in the Society of Inquiry, he made arrangements for a discussion, at one of the monthly meetings of that society, of the question, — ' On what principles should a Christian student decide to what field of labor he is called?' or something to that effect. To take the parts of this discussion he selected two who had decided to be missionaries abroad, one who had devoted himself to the West, another whom he believed to have conscientiously decided that his duty was to be a pastor at home, and two others who were still undecided. (I give the details as I recollect them and may not be exact.) When he had perfected these arrangements, prayerfully and somewhat anxiously he awaited the result. It was a most interesting discussion, and satisfied his expectations in itself considered; whether it accomplished its design in awakening consciences which he believed to be slumbering, I have no means of knowing. The personal influence which he exerted by all these methods could hardly be overstated.

" One thing must still be added, or this feature of his life at Andover will not be appreciated. The seminary classes are very unequally constituted. There are men fresh from college, and men who have been for years teachers in various positions, and men from other avocations in life. There is a good measure of friendliness between these widely differing individuals, and more and more of sympathy grows up between every two, through the influence of their association in prayer and study, but as a rule, the younger men are never appreciated by the older ones, the men of twenty-two or twenty-three by those of twenty-eight, thirty, and thirty-five, and are often made keenly to feel that they are not appreciated. But Scudder was the youngest of all, and ever conducted himself as if remembering the fact ; and yet he commanded the respect of all, and was himself a power over all, as I have shown above."

If the testimony of his comrades could be taken, I think that additional force would be given to the above statement. David was the last person to allude to his own success, and his modest bearing forbade any impression of that pragmatic importance which we sometimes attach to efficient workers in a confined sphere. Yet the fact remains that whereas when he reëntered the seminary, Middle Year, the number of the Brethren was but five, that number increased steadily until at his graduation it was twenty. These were men who had definitely decided to enter the missionary work, but the missionary spirit may justly be supposed to have been more widely extended, entering into the character and work of those who never left their own land. It is not intended to refer this remarkable increase solely to the power of David's personal influence, but Professors and students alike knew and testified that he was the moving cause, prominent above all others. He believed in individual preaching, and applied himself with great tact and industry to the art of finding out the best method of reaching men. One of his brother missionaries gives an instance : — " One morning he told me of his plans to interest one of his class, — a musician and noted lover of music, — by drawing his attention to the intricate system of Arabic music, knowing that this would open a door to frequent conversations. It was his custom on three or four days of each week to select some one of his own or another class, whom he thought he might influence, and make him a companion on a long walk, in which the subject of personal consecration to missionary work was one of the topics."

His fertile mind conceived another mode of creating a general interest in missions, which with three other of his classmates at Andover he carried into execution, — a series of papers in the " New York Independent," intended to present principles as the most valuable form of appeal. The subjects of his contributions to the series were " Reform in Missions," " Return to the Principles of the Early Church," " Christian Missions and Christian Beneficence," and " The Family a Missionary Nursery." This last paper contained his favorite views, then occupying much of his attention, upon the matter of interesting and educating children in the mission cause, a matter which will more fully be treated of hereafter. It need hardly be added that he continued his correspondence with such of the missionary brethren as had entered upon their fields of labor. He wrote gladly to them for the love he bore them, and because thus only could he most fervently give expression to his pent-up desires. " Dear Capron," he writes, " how I could cry for very longing to see you and have a good talk like old times. When discouraged, I go back of the cemetery where you told me that your throat was so bad that you feared you could not go. God was better to you than your fears. He will be to me." The following are extracts from a letter to Mr. Dean, of Satara :

ANDOVER, June 7, 1859.

" We have just had one of our delightful meetings of the Brethren here in my room, the room where Obookiah once lived, and where, tradition says, he first began to live the new life. We number now some

twenty members, and good substantial ones too. To-
night we are feeling that we have not been doing
enough for our brethren outside, and I hope we may
the rest of the term pray and labor more assiduously to
interest them in missions. . . . . Dear Dean, by the
time this letter reaches you, I shall be about leaving
this sacred place, which has become endeared to me by
so many precious associations. As I look back, how
the thoughts do whirr around me. You and C. walking side by side around Indian Ridge ; all those little
meetings in C.'s room and that little company of ' believers.' Precious days they were, were n't they? And
they are all gone, and days of equal joy since known
will soon follow in their train. How the future does
look ; bright, yet not wholly so, for many a dark river
must be crossed before we reach the end of our way.
As I write these words, the remembrance of your calm,
quiet confidence comes before me and really does refresh my mind. Yes, as I was saying to a dear missionary brother to-day who had met with a sad cross in
his path, — as we were walking back of the cemetery, —
here is the hill that I like to visit when despondent, for
here one day C. talked with me, and said he feared his
throat might prevent his going to India ; and now he
is there, fairly at work. Begone dull doubt and welcome faith. You in India. Capron too. Winchester
in Turkey ; but —— at home. . . . . Is it a year
since I wrote you last! Another year would God I
might write you from Madura ! "

During these two years he was in the habit of spending Sunday at home, for the sake of his Swedish class
and his neighborhood meeting. It was a new life in

the household when Saturday noon came and brought with it David, bustling with the glow of return, full of questions and anecdotes, and hurrying away after dinner to libraries and bookstores on his many errands. Monday morning he was off again with his bundles, returning to seminary with a similar eagerness, making everybody who came in contact with him partake of his good-natured cheeriness. I close this chapter, which I have intended chiefly to contain the testimony of his friends, with a letter from his classmate, Rev. J. M. Sturtevant, Jr., of Hannibal, Missouri, premising that it anticipates mention of a journey taken to the West, a year later: —

"To me the most striking trait in David's character was his earnestness, and it was not only that earnestness of voice and manner, that enthusiasm about trifles which made him seem rough and eccentric to me when I first met him, but which afterward became one great charm of his society, — he was in earnest about everything he turned his attention to, but not equally in earnest on all subjects. His feelings increased in depth while they grew more quiet in their manifestations as the theme rose in dignity. This peculiarity of his character made him an enigma to many. He seemed so full of life and enthusiasm on ordinary themes, and so quiet when the most sacred themes were touched, that few suspected the depth of his religious feelings. I can truly say that I never saw a man who had more of what Dr. Arnold calls moral earnestness. His morbid habit of introspection made him often distrust the sincerity of his own religious emotions, but no one who had an intimate acquaintance with him could doubt for a moment that they were of the deepest and most fervent character. His intense individuality made direct personal appeal to others a hard undertaking for him. Perhaps most persons who have long been in the habit of thinking and judging for themselves find something of the same troubles. Personal appeal does not seem to them best calculated to be useful to them, and they doubt their power to make it useful to others. But while he shrank from it, he longed to seize this and all other means of promoting the kingdom of Christ. If any one had called at the room of a fellow-student for personal religious conversation and he knew it, no matter how late it was, he never would retire to rest until he had heard the result of the conversation.

" Perhaps my most vivid recollections of him cluster around two conversations. One occurred one Sabbath at Andover. There was quite a revival of religion in Phillips Academy. Our meetings all day had been full of interest; until very late I had an inquiry-meeting in my room to which God in his mercy had sent several members of my Bible-class to ask the way of life. At last quite exhausted I was left alone. In my sense of weariness and helplessness my thoughts turned at once to David. I seemed almost too tired to pray more, but I would go to his room, quite sure to find him still up, and he would calm me with one of his earnest, heartfelt prayers, and then I would return to my own room to sleep. Often had I felt amid the storms of a very uneven, a very inconsistent Christian life, that I would give everything to possess that simplicity and straightforwardness which so pervaded David's religion. Guess my surprise when, on my asking him to pray with me, he replied with a burst of emotion such as I had never before known him to exhibit, 'I can't! you must pray for me.' And then he went on to lament his lack of sincere religious emotion, almost wishing that he had been a more wicked man that he might know greater heights and depths of religious feeling. His humility humbled me more than many reproofs could have done, and though he knew it not, he certainly was the best teacher for me that night.

"The other conversation was impressive chiefly for the circumstances under which it took place. I can hardly give you an idea of its details in this short compass. He was just about to leave me, after a short visit at this place, and we never expected to meet again in this world. We were walking upon the bold bluff just below the town, about two hundred feet above the river which ran at our feet. We talked of old times, pleasant scenes never to return, but bright in our memories as the sunshine of that fair summer day; and then our thoughts went forward into the future, and we laughed with almost boyish glee over some of his funny fancies as to what might be, and then we grew more sober as we thought of that world-wide separation, and talked of the mystery of that Providence which had destined us to such remote positions, and had probably appointed us equally dissimilar experiences. Then we talked of that eternity beyond, to which, by whatever path, we were both bound as surely as the waters at our feet were gliding toward the ocean. We reasoned thus until all our earthly life which, while we talked of its varied possibilities and all its depths of feeling, seemed like a great sea before us, was like the Mississippi at our feet, narrowed to our vision, by the height from which we looked, to a mere belt across the landscape, and the heavenly land seemed as real and as near as the bluffs gleaming in the sunshine miles away across the river, where we could just catch on their summits the signs of an inhabited country, and on the very horizon, faintly drawn, the spires of a distant city. So we parted, but I never shall forget that glimpse of the heavenly land. The narrow belt was narrower for him than I thought; crossing the river and entering the city of God came sooner than I expected. I pray that even as we talked that morning we may meet ere long in that land whose rivers will not always make us think of death, and whose hills will dwell in everlasting sunshine."

# CHAPTER VII.

## ORIENTAL STUDIES.

[1859–1861.]

WHEN David left the seminary, it was with the expectation of sailing for India in the autumn of the year following; this expectation was not realized, various unforeseen delays occurring which kept him in the country till the early spring of 1861. He remained during this interval in Boston, at his father's house, occupied with work which by degrees came to look almost exclusively Indiaward. In the seminary and previously he had followed various lines of study bearing upon India, and the result was a growing familiarity with Hindû speech, literature, philosophy, history, and manners, but — except in his study of Tamil — he had not investigated any subject with that strictness which he desired; his prescribed tasks and various occupations forbade him to give more than his spare hours to India. Now, master of his own time, he turned with avidity to the books which he had been collecting, and made the study of them his chief employment. The eighteen months, which elapsed between his leaving Andover and his departure for India, found him going deeper and deeper into the mysteries of Hindûism; his interest thus concentrated impelled him to more thorough research into a few subjects than would have been possible had many occupied his time. His own library and the library of the Oriental Society at New Haven, together with the public and private collections in Boston and Cambridge, furnished him with material, and in the confined department of Hindû literature, as introduced by English, French, and German scholars, he thought that he had used pretty much all to which he could gain access.

It is an example of the educating power inhering in a great purpose, once possessing the soul, that my brother should at last have been brought to a kind of work so foreign from his mental constitution. It is an example also of the broad foundation upon which the very purpose rested in his mind, that his habit of measuring study by its practical value in his career did not lead him to set aside the investigation of the abstruse philosophy of India as not germane to his work. The abstruseness did not attract him, although his active mind found pleasure in such alien speculations to a degree that never would have been predicated from quite recent observations; it was the bearing of the work upon his future labors which gave it a hold upon his interest. He found it not always easy to pursue this course, since he was not always sustained in it by the judgment of his missionary friends. Yet the predilection of Mr. Hoisington for these studies had influenced him quite strongly in his choice of them.

He gave increased attention also to the study of Tamil, and had the valuable assistance of Rev. Edward Webb, a missionary of the Madura District, who was at the time in America. During this period his letters to missionary friends give some insight into the character of his studies. One of these friends, Rev. George T. Washburn, of Battalagundu, Madura District, India, had been a college and for a while a seminary classmate; a common purpose and destination had brought them together, and their intercourse at Andover had been characterized by a very full interchange of sentiment upon matters relating to their expected labors in India; and Mr. Washburn preceding David, correspondence followed upon the same topics, until they were reunited in India; from David's share in this correspondence I am able to give a more familiar statement of his opinions upon his Oriental studies than could be gained otherwise.

He found it most easy, natural, and agreeable to his purpose to throw the results of his study into some written form, and accordingly there remain three or four essays and series of essays, containing proofs of his industry and indications of his attainments. The first of these was the series of papers to which he alludes at the close of the following extract: —

[TO REV. GEORGE F. HERRICK.]

BOSTON, Oct. 28, 1859.

. . . . By the time you receive this, you will I presume have found your way about the great city [Constantinople]. What a dream you must be in — for what amazing feelings will such a city force upon a student of church history. I feel as if in thought I could share the excitement with which you draw near your future home. But I don't much like to think of it, nor of any of our fellows who are favored like you. It makes me discontented. I burn to be off, and feel that only the grace of God can keep me from unworthy chafing. But I am sure that my post is here for the present, and I do really praise God when I see any one take his leave of home. Blessed privilege! God grant that I may soon share it.

You have long pronounced me incorrigible. Everybody must now coincide in your view. My morning is spent on Tamil grammar, my afternoon on Ancient Hindû history, my evening on British Indian history. The first I mean to work steadily at; I love it and it loves me. The last I must finish this winter, and as to the other, I may as well tell one of the four that I am getting ready to write a set of papers on Ancient Indian Literature, as illustrative of Hindû character in general, hoping to show the noble capacity of the race.

These papers were published in the " Boston Recorder," a weekly religious journal. They were twelve in number, and limited of course to a very brief and — from the manner of the publication — disjointed exposition of the subject, but well adapted to the object for which they were written, to give an interesting summary of Hindû literature in its chronological order, for the purpose of indicating the capacity of the race. It may be observed, too, that the ability to present the subject so concisely, and yet in so lively a fashion, supposes a power of mastering the study, higher in character than that which merely undertakes to record at length the same results of investigation.

In the two following letters he alludes to his study of Tamil, indicating the sort of interest which he continued to take in linguistics apart from the practical value of which the Tamil speech was to be to him : —

[TO REV. GEORGE F. HERRICK.]

ESSEX, CONN., June 11, 1860.

. . . . It has afforded me not a little pleasant thought of late to see how closely you and I are to be connected

in our missionary labors. Whilst you are attempting to
stammer out the message from above in a speech which
laughs at all order, after the English sort, and which
calls upon a man to *deglottize* himself, so I, in my poor
way, shall attempt the same after the same fashion.
For if you will notice, Tamil alike with Turkish belongs to that class of Agglutinative languages so utterly
at variance with Indo-European speech. I have been
studying a South Indian Comparative grammar of late,
and have been struck with the remarkable analogies
therein drawn out between two languages, geographi-
cally so separate. But poor fellow! to think of you
sweltering not merely under the load of one tongue, so
diametrically opposed to inborn notions of what speech
should be, but even forced to hoist on to your aching
back another language, belonging to still another class.
And what can I say for the poor unfortunates of the
Persian hills, who, as Dr. Perkins tells me, if they
would learn Persian well, must also dig out Arabic and
Turkish? It seems like attempting to obliterate the
traces of Babel thus to shoulder three languages, the
types of the three great families of tongues. I with
my simple Tamil, may well flatter myself.

[TO REV. GEORGE T. WASHBURN.]

BOSTON, July 27, 1860.

. . . . Perhaps you remember that when you left
I was at work about the Hill Tribes of India, as the
remnant of the aborigines. The essay is done. . . . .
I trace the earliest notices of aboriginal races in the
Hindû books, then give a sketch of all that now seem
allied to them, gathered from Travels and Oriental Magazines, closing with a brief statement of the present

opinion respecting their affinities, judged from their
speech. Its novelty at least will not be denied. So
you have read " Ancient Sanskrit Literature " (Müller). I need not ask you whether you enjoyed it, for
so rich a treat you could not but enjoy. Since you left,
the Boden Professorship at Oxford has been made vacant by the death of Wilson. Three rivals compete
for the chair, Müller, Monier Williams, the author of a
Sanskrit Grammar and English and Sanskrit Lexicon,
and Dr. Ballantyne, of Benares. I trust Müller will
get it, for then we may count upon his more undivided
attention to the study. Jos. Mullens has published
a book which shares a prize with a similar treatise by
Ballantyne, called " Christian Aspects of Hindû Philosophy." I do not however set a very high value
upon it. I take it that while Mullens may be a good
statistician, he can be but an indifferent metaphysician.
Moreover he is not a student at first hand, I judge,
whereas Ballantyne is. . . . . I have laid out a course
of study upon Hindû Philosophy ; have got a host of
little books, aphorisms of the different schools, and begin to-morrow on the Sankya Philosophy. Whether
my courage will endure to the end I dare not predict,
but I question much. Any study in that direction,
after leaving the country, must of course be limited
and what I do must be done now. . . . . Tell it not in
Madura, I have begun Sanskrit. I got Oppert's grammar in French, commendable for its brevity at least,
and am now at work scratching unsightly marks supposed to represent sounds. I do not expect, at present
at least, to more than peep into it, but I thought that a
slight acquaintance with the principles of its grammar
might aid me in studying Tamil, and especially in the

use of such works as " Caldwell's Comparative Grammar," where Sanskrit is ever referred to for illustration. Perhaps I may carry it on at intervals hereafter. It will be a pleasing diversion.

The essay referred to in the last letter appeared in the " Bibliotheca Sacra " for October, 1860, under the title " Aborigines of India." When that was completed and published, the day of departure, which he had been anticipating might be earlier, was set for the following February or March, and the question arose in his mind, how the intervening time should be occupied. The necessary preparations for departure, a proposed jaunt to the West, and his various plans for interesting the churches in the missionary enterprise, seemed to him insufficient for fully occupying his time, and thus warding off that impatience and worry which he knew would get hold of him. He decided to give more close attention to a subject which he had long been engaged upon in a fragmentary way, — a systematic view of Hindû Philosophy. He wished for his own sake to reach a more determinate knowledge, and no work of which he knew covered the ground which he proposed to occupy; the prospect of producing a work, really worthy as a matter of scholarship, and supplying a desideratum in Oriental studies, gave zest to his intention, and though harassed with numberless calls upon his time, he worked diligently and perseveringly, completing his task but a short time before sailing. The essay was published in the " Bibliotheca Sacra," under the title of " A Sketch of Hindû Philosophy," appearing in two parts in the numbers for July and October, 1861. The following letter is in reference partly to this essay, and

9

in reply to certain **doubts** expressed by his correspondent, whether it were worth while to devote unusual attention to subjects that after all had little direct bearing upon the missionary work, which was to be bestowed almost exclusively upon the degraded classes. " I hope you will keep on studying," he writes; " I don't think we know too much about Hindûism in its higher forms. Only don't expect that such knowledge is going to be any great direct missionary agency to the people."

[TO REV. GEORGE T. WASHBURN.]

BOSTON, Nov. 23, 1860.

. . . . One would hardly think perhaps that I was following the suggestion of your letter, could one see me, day after day, poring over Yoga, Nyaya, and Vaiseshika schemes of thinking. But do not think I misunderstand you. I liked your remarks; they fell in with and gave expression to thoughts which had been floating in my own mind in the shape of questions. I do not like to speak too strongly. I am not inclined to be over-confident as to my success as a missionary. Still, I have a tolerably correct conception of what a missionary life *should* be. If I come short of reaching my ideal, that is another matter. I do feel this, — a longing desire to get my general, wishy-washy notions of Hindûism some substantial bottom. I don't believe there is another system of faith, or rather congeries of discordant systems, to be found under heaven that will compare with that of India. An inane jumble of fact and fiction, myth and history, religious, metaphysical and superstitious notions. Such Hindûism certainly appears to a novice. I feel uneasy until I grasp some few principles or facts which may serve to attract about

them the varied phases of faith that India presents. I
think the chaos is becoming less "*voidic*" to me. We
need to bear in mind the great ethnological fact of the
presence in India of at least two, and most likely three
separate races or classes of race, and the relative position they hold to one another. We need further to
bear in mind the radical difference between the two,
that one is a savage, the other a cultivated people;
that the latter exhibits not one phase, but several phases
or stages of growth, and that while these have risen
and fallen away in succession, many of their results
are undoubtedly existing in the civilization of to-day;
the religious history of the latter race we may be able
to trace, but that of the former is a wellnigh hopeless
mass of inconsistencies.

Now the Philosophical period was a most important
one, and cannot be passed over in a study of Hindûism.
Indeed, next to the Vedic, it is the most important, and
with reference to this era has no rival. As a student
of general history, aside from all questions of missionary life, I should be justified in studying it; as a student of India life, of course I must. I fully believe that
I am denying myself much gratification in the pursuit
of this theme by going to India. Were I to remain
here, I should expect to do far more in this and cognate
studies than I can possibly do at home [*i. e.* India
home]. I agree with you that the brunt of the work
for us is of a different sort. Still I flatter myself that
I may be able to bring to light some data for others'
investigation while I am in India, and what acquaintance I have now with these topics may prove of advantage in preventing me from throwing away time in
directions which would be valueless.

I have a notion that I shall be interested in gathering together customs and beliefs of the lower castes whom we meet, to see if I can trace any systematic belief which will serve to stand as an outline of faith held previous to Arian immigration. What do you think? As to philosophy, you know enough of me to know that I am in no sort of danger of making or trying to make use of my knowledge of systems in meeting a Hindû. I hardly know enough to wield an English or an Aristotelian syllogism, — to say nothing of the Hindû Nyaya's five-membered conceit. The fact is patent, however, that five hours a day do I plod my weary way through Sankya, Yoga, and Nyaya; not weary way either, for I enjoy it. I am now running through the six systems and giving a syllabus of each. Next I am to study the historical connection of all, and weave them into an essay in chronological order, stating the occasion of their rise, progress, and present position. I hope to get ready a couple of long essays for the "Bibliotheca Sacra" before I leave. I have all the material nearly that is to be had in English. You say you have sent for Mullens's book. I have it. I have a dim idea that you have Ballantyne. Mullens as a philosopher is not worth a straw; but his book is worth having, as it gives the best general compend of the different systems. He is much more full than Ballantyne in stating the facts, and draws almost wholly from Ballantyne's little translations. Ballantyne makes the Nyaya philosophy his standpoint of logic in his duties as preceptor of Hindûs. And we Westerners certainly have more sympathy with Gotama than with any other Hindû sage. In his conception of God he is nearer the Christian than any of his fellows.

A rich and rare book is out, — No. II. of Muir's " Original Sanskrit Texts." His object is to convince the Hindûs that their fathers came from beyond the Indus and are connected with Persians, Greeks, &c. The argument is no new one to us, but in his rigid discussion of it, he marshals a host of facts on the dialects of North India, the course which the Arians took in entering India, and their relation to their kindred and to the aboriginal tribes. His first part meets the Hindû on his own ground and shows from the contradictions in his own books that caste is a modern invention; that the Brahmans are not divine, and so forth. Two more volumes are promised: one, historical proof of origin of caste; the other, illustrations of earliest life and religion. Hurrah!

This evening I propose to visit the Public Library. In the " Journal de Savants " is a review by M. Barthelemy St. Hilaire of Max Müller's " History of Sanskrit Literature." St. Hilaire is a sort of general Hindû scholar, who has distinguished himself by his *memoirs* on the Sankya Philosophy, the very sight of which is enough to make one vow never to be a philosopher, if so much paper is to be spent in his dissection. But I want to see what the Frenchman has to say upon Müller. You know I presume that Müller and Monier Williams are rival candidates for the vacant Boden Professorship. The contest will soon be decided, and most likely in favor of Müller.* He surely is the more learned man of the two. I have however a high respect for Williams. I have just bought and begun his Sanskrit grammar. I want to get hold of the grammar, not expecting to do any more. I like his

* It was so decided.

far better than the French grammar of Oppert which Professor ——— suggested to me. Oppert is too brief and condensed: Williams does not presume upon any previous familiarity. He is fond also of tracing evident analogies between Sanskrit and western languages.

Do you know what you are asking for when you request me to buy Bopp? Have you ever seen it? if not, you are an innocent child. The sight of its learning is to me appalling; if you have, I wonder at your self-confidence at presuming to wish you had it now. However I shall get it on the strength of your word, and because I should have got it without that too, — as a book of reference at some future day. I presume one can with dainty fingers pick out a morsel here and there, Jack-Horner-like. You speak of works on Comparative Philology in general. The best book undoubtedly, of such a cast, is Müller's "Languages of the Seat of War." Have you it? I forget. Its comparison of Turkish and Tamil is very striking and pleasing. You speak of Bunsen.* I have hesitated long about that book. I have read and reread it. Müller you know contributes the portion on the Turanian Researches. That includes Tamil, but M. M. does n't know *boo* about Tamil. Professor ——— told me that he would n't give a snap for the essay, but even he is inclined to derive Dravidian languages from Sanskrit! Yet he and any one could see that Müller's theorizing was upon a very rickety foundation, and some of his erroneous results Caldwell points out. What I think the essay most valuable for is the history of researches in this direction, and his original and valuable remarks

* Philosophy of Universal History.

upon the Sanskrit portion of his theme. Perhaps for this object the essay is worth having, but the book is costly. The other essays in the volume (always excepting Brother Bunsen's vagaries) are valuable. I wish we could get the one volume of linguistics separate, and leave off the baseless applications to the Philosophy of History by the doughty chevalier.

The discoveries which he had begun to make for himself in this field served to stimulate search and to make him desirous of more thorough inquiry into many questions which his work suggested. He looked with a half-regret to the departure which was to bring to a close this extended study ; he felt that his scholarly instincts were growing keener, and that if permitted to follow their lead he might achieve worthy results. It was but a half-regret, nor would he have been easily content, if circumstances had required him to remain longer in America, even though the stay were to give him unbounded opportunity of study. It was work of another sort which lay nearer his heart, and to this he looked with more ardent desire.

[TO A CLASSMATE IN GERMANY.]

BOSTON, once more, Feb. 4, 1861.

Your letter has long lain on my table, pressed down by many another and sighing for relief. The time has come at last, — the time of doing the last things, of winding up affairs, of putting one's house in order. I have kept you waiting purposely, determined to write you when I knew somewhat certainly when I should leave this semi-barbarous land for the professedly savage country of my choice. Answering letters is my job for a week to come and yours comes first, first in time and first in worth. Let me thank you for it most heartily. I enjoyed it hugely, and so has many another, D. included, and W. shall. How these names link together the wide world! You toasting your mental limbs by German hearths, G. W. cooling himself off by copious draughts of Brahmanic philosophy, D. lazily drinking in Chitty and Coke in Cambridge, and your penman absorbed in saucepans, boxes, bedsteads, and all the appurtenances of tropical housekeeping.

. . . . Oh, how I should like to sit by you in your snuggery, and have a wholesome chat over men and things. I rarely have such nowadays; and to think of sending you such a scribble as this. Well, I shall soon, please God, be in my place in the breach and trying to do my part. I dread it of course, and the more, as so novel to me. In my better hours I rejoice, and I daily pray for a long life for me and mine. I love India with all my heart, and long to do somewhat for her regeneration. . . . . I think often of you in Germany, and wish I might be with you, though I fear I should desert Tholuck and Müller for Bopp, Weber, Lassur, and Roth, and dive into philology and Indian archæology rather than theology and church history. How delightful it is to study. I have begun Sanskrit, and shall work hard at Tamil on shipboard.

## CHAPTER VIII.

### ENTERPRISES — LAST MONTHS IN AMERICA.

[1859–1861.]

DURING the last year of the seminary course David had occasionally preached, after the custom of theological students, and while at home awaiting his departure, he took what opportunities offered for practice in this labor. He did not regard sermonizing as of much importance in his case, since work abroad would admit so little of the sort of preaching employed at home; the half dozen sermons which he wrote are characterized by the philosophical element, so frequent in students' discourses, and pervaded with his spirit of moral earnestness; he added to the force of his sermons by his impressive delivery, which borrowed little from the rules of oratory, but was instinct with his personality, tender, solemn, whole-hearted. One sermon received unusual attention from him as embodying his views respecting the missionary work, and containing the grounds of his own confident belief that it was the highest form of Christian activity. The character of the sermon is indicated in the following letter: —

[TO REV. J. M. STURTEVANT, JR.]

FALMOUTH, MASS., Feb. 23, 1860.

. . . . I have just written up to the conclusion of a missionary sermon, my first one. It is a missionary sermon, but not exclusively a *foreign* missionary one.

Indeed I fancy that I have hit upon a way of presenting Christian duty, which is somewhat new to me
and seems also plausible and fair; my sermon would,
I am sure, suit you, at least as regards its catholic
spirit; it is not much more foreign than home. My
text is, — "As my Father hath sent me, even so send
I you," one which I long since chose. The one thing
which marks it is the position that all such divisions
of the field as Home and Foreign are really nothing
more than convenient geographical distinctions; that
the Scriptures and Christ recognize but one grand divis-
ion, — "the world" and "not of the world"; that all
Christian work either is self-culture or aggressive enterprise, and that the latter aims at the whole field,
called in Scripture "the world," all which is not Christ's
by actual possession; so that *all* work which is aggressive is by its very idea *foreign* and essentially *one*,
whether labor for unconverted neighbors, western missions, or labor in heathen lands. The argument of the
sermon is, that there is no reason, either in Scripture
or common sense, why a man should cease his labor
at any given point in this one field, but on the other
hand everything points him to the duty of laboring in
all his work for the evangelization of the whole. I try
to show it by appealing to Christian instinct as corrob-
orated by the idea of a Christian life, — self-sacrifice, —
and to History which shows that the church has pros-
pered according as it has admitted this or not. What
do you think? I wish I could read it to you in number seventeen, Phillips Hall.

. . . . Do you remember Thompson's anniversary
address before the Porter Rhetorical Society? You
have seen it though, I presume, in the last "Congrega-

tional Quarterly." He is called missionary to Persia, which he requested them not to mention. I might be an advocate for Congregationalism if in the West, but as you say you accept it because it is needed at the West, so I imagine if you were to be in India you might feel that some other form than pure Congregationalism would better fit into the present phase of society. At least so I theorize; how I shall think when I get there I don't know, but I believe that no Procrustean bed should be received as the bed for all Christians to repose upon. I did not agree with Thompson at the time, but for Persia I can believe it may better suit, as more manliness and independence of thought can there be found.

The chief advantage which he sought from preaching was the opportunity it afforded him of visiting new places. Wherever he went he was known as one soon to enter upon the foreign field, and he threw all the weight of his personal presence and influence into the enterprise of awaking new interest in the work of missions. He always appreciated the value of personal association, and knew that every one whom he interested in himself, he interested likewise, to various extent, in the cause which he represented. It is with children that this personal association is most weighty, and with them David employed it most. Reference has been made to his habit in the seminary of talking to Sunday-schools and to juvenile missionary societies. He began in a small way, carrying a few images of Hindû gods and telling stories out of the sacred books about them, connecting his talk with the effort which the children were making to send the truth to the wor-

shippers of these very idols. He repeated his stories
in different places, and as he gained in familiarity with
the work, he studied more carefully the structure of his
discourse. He had attained a confidence in addressing
children, and was now able to make experiments ; what
had been a simple talk, suggested by the images, began
to assume the shape of a speech, studiously contrived
with reference to the working of a child's mind, was
altered and remodelled as new experience supplied him
with better forms. All this was for the simple and
general purpose of awaking a vivid interest among
children, and of providing them with a more correct
understanding of the object at which they were aiming.

This latter purpose soon showed him that the children were at a disadvantage from the want of some
specific end ; when they gave their contributions it was
to objects too large for the grasp of their minds. He
felt this, and the result was a scheme for turning the
contributions of children into a special channel, — the
support of schools connected with missions. The Board
of Missions had taken up the matter with care, making
inquiry of those best qualified to advise, and David
eagerly entered the same field ; he wrote for suggestions to missionaries and to Sunday-school officers, and
became absorbed in the subject which ever afterward,
as indeed it had previously, held a large place in his
mind. His share in the work consisted in addressing
schools wherever he could, inducing them to pledge
themselves each to a yearly subscription, adequate to the
support of a school in the Madura mission, in return
for which he promised a quarterly letter, having special
reference to the schools thus supported. His plan also
embraced the occasional support of a native preacher

by some school desirous of making larger contributions. To maintain a school required a yearly outlay of twenty-five dollars; to provide a pastor, one of eighty dollars; in the latter case he promised a special letter.

In consequence of this plan he modified his address to children, introducing considerable matter respecting native schools in India, and after repeated delivery he moulded his address into a form from which he found no reason to deviate, excepting that he always introduced it in a novel manner, catching his inspiration most happily from the occasion. Long familiarity with Hindû life gained by research and by reading, by intercourse with missionaries and by correspondence, made him perfectly at home upon the subject, so that the effect upon his hearers could hardly have been different if he had really been in India; so at least it seemed when he was speaking, though doubtless had he ever returned to America after a stay in India, he would have brought a new element into his address; his manner was so confident and his utterance so rapid and fervid that many were astonished to find a " returned missionary " so very young. I am sorry that no notes remain by which the address which he finally came to deliver could be reproduced, since I feel sure that even separate from the force which his personal presence gave to it, there existed a real power in the admirable adaptation of its matter and language both to the comprehension of children and to the excitement of permanent interest. Still the moving force was in the person himself, standing on the platform, ruddy with youth and glowing with earnestness, which kindled as he went on, flushing his cheek and making his voice to grow more eager and impetuous. I think the impression left was of a most happy sort; his words were free from any appeal to a morbid horror or sympathy, always healthy and cheerful. There was a directness about them, an honesty which children like, establishing at once a personal friendship between him and them, as they would crowd around him afterward to examine the palm-leaf book, stylic knife, and Tamil Gospel of John which he used to illustrate his speech; the idols he had given up.

The appreciable result of these efforts was the securing of forty schools, increased afterward to sixty, pledged to maintain the same number of schools abroad, besides the support of a native pastor. But the result in the wide-spread interest which he created in himself and in his work cannot be estimated. Often was he touched with the simple expressions of affectionate interest which his words drew from children. Like himself when a child, little boys came forward and said they were going to India. Wherever he went he left behind witnesses to his power in children who could not forget his zeal, and whom he animated with a similar purpose. It was not a mere momentary interest which he excited, because his appeal was not one to the emotions alone; he furnished children with plans of work and lasting incentives, so that the natural result of his addresses was active enterprise and not mere sympathetic interest. In the days when he was thus engaged instances of this effect of his speaking were constantly coming to notice, too simple perhaps to be recorded, but affording the strongest evidence of his power. May it be that years hence some will be found who shall remember his personal presence and find in it an impulse to missionary labor, even as he ever kept in mind the few words and more forcible image of the aged Doctor Scudder.

In connection with this labor among the children should be mentioned a package of children's tracts, — "Tales about the Heathen," — published for him by the Tract Society in Boston, containing several of the stories which he used to weave into his address. They afford an excellent illustration of his manner of treating such subjects. The following passage from a letter shows another favorite project which he always hoped to carry out : —

[TO REV GEORGE T. WASHBURN.]

BOSTON, Nov. 23, 1860.

. . . . Now about your proposal of a history of each mission. I like it. I thought of it awhile and almost made up my mind to write a history of Bombay, Madura, and Ceylon Missions, but upon second thought, I concluded that such a sketch, to be good for anything, must be something more than bare, skeleton history, and would necessarily include descriptions of places, scenes, people, and customs; and that such a sketch prepared by a stranger would be jejune and materially defective. I have accordingly dropped Bombay and Ceylon from my plan, and have put it down in my memorandum-book as something to be done in India, — to prepare such a story of Madura. I know well that my hands will be full of business, but I am so convinced of the thorough need of such a work, I love the task so much, and it is so comparatively facile work to me, that I shall indulge the hope of being able to accomplish the design. Mr. Dulles's book certainly does not cover the same ground, while it will give me aid.

. . . . I think there might be prepared a history of missions which could be studied just as the Acts of the

Apostles is studied. No inspired man, to be sure, would pen the narrative, the narrative itself would lack the divine sanction in any special form, and lack the power of the divine mind; yet the acts of our modern apostles are in a sense equally important with those of early days. We should be familiar with them, and they ought to be studied in the Sunday-schools.

It is hard to enumerate the manifold forms of his unceasing activity. He was not only keenly alive himself, but he inspired all with whom he came into contact with something of the same energy. His father's house during those eighteen months was the scene of constant excitement. David shared his plans so freely with the family, that it might be said they spent their time in hearing or in telling some new thing. He set others to work, and indeed it was hard to stand idle when one was present who worked so incessantly. From week to week he was about his business, — preaching, planning, scheming to interest people in missions, holding neighborhood meetings, talking to children, inquiring into educational systems with reference to his future labors, attending medical lectures, for he took a partial course in Medicine though with no liking for it, reading, writing, sending long letters to correspondents and letters to religious journals on missionary topics, on the watch for everything likely to increase knowledge or interest in missions, so that at the outbreak of the Druses he prepared and delivered an admirable address on the subject, and in the midst of his multiform labors, finding time to explore the mystery of the six systems of Hindû Philosophy, and to reduce to order his accumulated knowledge.

But though busily occupied while thus detained in America, his thoughts flew across the sea to the land which he longed to reach. His very occupations constantly reminded him whither he was bound, and more than once did he give way to despondency as the day of his departure was still kept distant. His friends, some of whom perhaps were leaving under his influence, sailed one after another to different parts of the world; he entertained them at his home, — indeed, scarcely was one sent on his way before another's approach was heralded; he helped them in their preparation and watched them from the wharf as they sailed off on their errand, while he turned away reluctantly; with a melancholy jest he would liken himself to the captain who saw all on board before he himself made ready to follow, and so he gave vent often to his longing in impassioned words to brother missionaries who had been blessed as he had not been.

[TO REV. GEORGE T. WASHBURN.]

ESSEX, CONN., Jan. 20, 1860.

So you are at last fairly staggering on India's coral strand! How do things look? Did you have a pleasing time on those Masullah boats? Are the natives oily? Did they come out to you on their catamarans? Were you wet? How does Madras look? What kind of a place is Popham's Broadway? Fairly ashore! Oh for the fancy of a De Quincey, the pen of a Macaulay, both of whom are dead, that I might indulge myself. I can but say — fairly ashore! and such phrases as are fit I must leave to others less in earnest, less interested. For would n't I give a small sum, could I but be trudging by your side, gazing, like a raw Yankee, as I am, at

sights and *sounds!* Is it hot? I don't know what to
write. What sort of a mood are you in and how shall I
suit it? You must let me into all the changes of feeling possible, so that I shall know how to feel one of
these days, because you see if I don't have some rule
to go by, I fear I shall get unmanageable. George, I
was walking out this morning, and my feelings, my
longings for a sight and a touch of India were such as
could find comfort only in outspoken prayer to God.
I lay upon the rocks and thought of you — away off on
the blue sea — and my whole being leaped — impatient.
I prayed aloud to God that he would not detain me
long in *this* foreign land. . . . . And you are really
there! Do you feel the crowds around you? Are you
impressed with the fact of your being in a land whose
history is so dark? that these swarthy ones love not
God? or do they pass, come and go, with no more impression upon you than the throngs in our cities? I
can't bring myself to feel that this letter is to be read
by one greedy for news rather than sentiment.

[TO THE SAME.]

BOSTON, April 2, 1860.

. . . . And so I am to imagine you just now, where?
that big blot which so disfigures the page expresses my
ideas on the subject, although I presume you are by
this beating up to Madras. I have a chart of Madras,
so that Mr. Hunt will not need to come down to escort
me to his house. I can find Popham's Broadway without him. Do they have any ice-cream saloons? on
Mount Road? Even if you could not get a veritable
piece of ice, why would it not be a good plan to prom-
enade up and down the Ice-House Road and snuff the

fancied breezes? The very name of the road has something refreshing, like the clinking of ice against the pitcher on a hot day.

. . . . I preached in Nantucket a few Sundays since and had a pleasant visit. I went over to the south shore, where there was nothing but water between me and the other side, and scratched my name in Tamil on the sand and thought of you in India. . . . . I have bought a set of the Asiatic Researches which I hope to place in the Madura library. I find myself in danger of being much absorbed in these pursuits. Were I to remain here, I should delight in nothing more than in such study; but as it is, I am weary of this and feel the need for spiritual sake of shutting up my books and shipping for Home as soon as possible. I feel it impossible to maintain a live Christian character, when one is not engaged in practical work for God. . . . . How did you bear your voyage? What a blessed thing your first letter will be, but how much more the next shake of your hand. Blessed day! pray that it may come soon. With love to all I know, to all I don't know, to Dindigal Rock, to Madura Walls, and to the first glossy Hindû that you see, and wishing I were never to write you from America again, I actually am

D. C. S.

In the autumn of 1860, when he could look more definitely to an early departure, he took a journey to the West, going as far as to cross the Missouri River at St. Joseph's to say he had stood on Kanzas soil, and returning home by St. Louis, Louisville, Mammoth Cave, Cincinnati, and New York. The following extracts are from a series of letters produced by the journey out: —

NIAGARA FALLS, Oct. 11, 1860.

I have seen it! I am now ready to depart home. I have seen It, and what else is worth looking at? As I write, weary from constant walking, the roar of the cataract is ever present, like the rolling of ocean-surf, only less inconstant. Many travellers aver that at first sight they are disappointed. Whether from being on my guard against such an undesirable impression or not, the contrary was the case with me; one thing is certain, that my first feeling was of higher grade than my previous imagination, and the impression deepened as I looked and looked.

Upon first seeing the tower which overlooks a portion of the Fall, I had the same feeling that I had many years since when first looking upon Connecticut River from Mount Holyoke. How much it looks like the picture! So thought I this morning. I think the familiarity, which we derive from pictures, with the main features of the scene is rather a disadvantage. The scene is not altogether new, and the littleness of the impression obtained from pictures tends to cramp the magnitude of the actual thing. One thing my previous conception was at fault in: I had supposed Goat Island to be a little spot of perhaps half an acre in extent. Instead of that it is nearly a mile in circumference, and separates the whole Fall into the two main divisions, the American and the Horse Shoe Falls.

However true a picture of the Falls may be in outline and general color, the best picture fails and must fail in at all adequately representing the thing itself. No pencil can paint the ceaseless crushing, deafening roar of the cataract, the sweeping spray rushing wildly up from the seething caldron below, or the immense volume of water falling or pouring over the rock, breaking in its descent into myriads of drops of water glittering in the sunlight. No picture can give you, for one thing, the Horse Shoe Falls embosoming in its arms a great gulf, which you can't help imagining bottomless and Tartaric.

I have wandered all about and seen everything to be seen and now can't say what view I like best. You cannot take your eyes off whatever point may chance to catch them. The first thing of special interest which attracted me was the Cave of the Winds, hollowed out of the precipitous cliff over which a portion of the sheet falls. You stand at the base of the Fall and the entrance of the cave, and look and look till your legs tire, for your eyes never can. I seemed to be in a kind of dream. The tremendous sheet of water came thundering down by my feet, crashing on to the rocks, and as I stood it seemed to grow louder and louder and louder, till it fairly seemed as if the whole creation was coming over that cliff. . . . . But I am foolish in attempting to give any sort of idea of this wonder. . . . .

CHICAGO, Oct. 16.

. . . . I think I wrote you last from Niagara, after having taken my first look. Next morning I took a fresh gaze before breakfast and after, and tried to look so hard that four months' wetting of the salt sea and twelve years of blazing sun might not obliterate the impression. . . . . I made my way to the cars, which bore me slowly over the fearful Suspension Bridge. . . . . A custom-house officer amused a crowd by digging into a negro's box for suspected contraband goods, and hauling out nothing but Newcomb's Question-Books and iron kettles! We finally got under way, and after a dreary ride through a desolate country, found ourselves at Detroit. Three Douglas men by me had quite a discussion, and all along supposed me to be one of their clique. I kept quite mum, until one man came out with the notion that the blackness of our negro brother was the curse of God upon Ham! upon which your clerical correspondent thought the credit of his cloth impeached, fell in, and of course annihilated his adversary. To Chicago Saturday.

Como, ILL., Oct. 18.

. . . . I'm having a capital time. A. is a student of the true stamp; can quote Schelling, Lessing, Hegel, and all the German fry; will discuss Theology, Metaphysics, Religion, or Hindûism with me to my heart's content. So you can easily understand that I am up to my head in bliss, to find any one who does n't brand me as a fool for looking up a little harmless Orientalism, and is willing to draw me out on the heights and depths of blessed Brahmanism. This is my joy and delight, and A. has been reading Hegel and Schelling on India to me, while I have taken the liberty to question some of their statements, and find some judicious suggestions in their weighty thoughts; so we have been talking nothing else ever since I came here.

Cameron, ILL., Oct. 20.

It is seven o'clock A. M., and I am standing at the desk in the store of C. Waste, Esq., who is advertised to sell Sanative Pills and Bibles. In Cameron there may be at the outside fifty dwelling-houses and a new

Campbellite church. I have been in Cameron about
an hour before any Cameronite has stirred, having been
ejected from the cars in company with another traveller. Ah! tell it not in Myrtle Street. Instead of wast-
ing Mr. Waste's writing materials, I should about this
time be steaming away toward Quincy. Allow me then
to present a scientific statement of the causes which
have produced the present mishap, — which tale must
condemn me.

If my recollection serves me right, I left Como at
nine o'clock last night, — though night and day are
sadly commingled in my head. I rode fifteen miles to
Dixon, on the Illinois Central Road. I had then two
interesting and delightful hours, from ten to twelve P. M.,
in the hospitable Wachusa House of that inland city.
My companions resorted for relief to billiards, oysters,
and hotter drinks ; I settled myself in a chair, munched
a huge apple, and gave myself up to concocting articles
of faith and meditating upon the grounds of moral obligation. At 12.13 I again entered the cars, which in
another hour brought me to Mendota, on the Chicago
and Quincy Road. There I rechanged my seat at 1.30
A. M., entered a sleeping-car, got a berth, pulled off my
boots, began to wind up my watch, and thanking my
stars that good comfort was in store for me, was upon
the point of committing myself to the graces of the
King of Nod, when the steward called for my ticket,
and then calmly informed me that I was in the wrong
train. Imagine my feelings and the rapidity with which
boots and hat went on, and I went off just in time to
get into the right train. Fairly in and safe I clambered
up into a top berth, and endeavored to make myself
indulge the fond feeling that I was abed. I was hardly

conscious of having slept at all when the steward called the sleepers up, announcing Galesburg, a change of cars, and time for breakfast. So I stretched, rubbed my eyes, found it was about five o'clock, and stumbled into the breakfast-room. I swallowed a beefsteak, when, "Cars ready!" "Where?" said I. "Burlington Road?" "Yes." "There!" So in I went, choking with corn-cake. Settled at last, thought I; but alas for human hopes! the remorseless conductor came round, took my ticket, read "Galesburg to Quincy." "You're wrong!" said he. The next station was Cameron, — Cameron, Ill., — and ill-luck prevailing, here am I. Moreover, and besides to-day is Saturday, the only other train leaves Galesburg so as to reach Quincy at ten P. M. Hannibal is twenty miles down the river, and the only boat from Quincy leaves at ten A. M., on the arrival of the morning train, which I should now be in, and does not leave Sunday morning. Am I not dished? most positively and effectually dished? One only expedient remains, and that I am resolved to try.

It is to swim. It is only twenty miles. The Hellespont has been crossed, and why may not the Father of Waters be swam down? I propose to mount a snag and go swaying down, arriving in time to preach, which I am engaged to do. Professor Hopkins gave me as his sentiment in my college-book, — "Some resign themselves but with some exceptions." I never saw the special significance of the words nor their application to me. Now I understand and receive them as words peculiarly appropriate to my present forlorn lot.

MACOMB, 4 P. M.

In confusion worse confounded I begin to write this.

A political mass-meeting is going on, with all its attendants of rum, show, and sin. Macomb is on the way to Quincy, and hearing that Tom Corwin was to speak I concluded to hear him and see a unique phase of Western life. I am all tired out with standing full two hours, and rest myself by opening your letter, which cannot go before Monday, and adding to it. After vainly trying to find some rest in a deserted tavern at Cameron, I wrote to you, and then went out to view the country. The only visible eminence was a Virginia rail-fence. So I made for that and mounted it. From it I could see miles and miles of dead level prairie, cultivated with corn. I rode afterward along five or six miles of one continuous cornfield. On the fence, and away from anybody, I essayed to try my lungs. I succeeded. I rehearsed my missionary sermon at the top of my voice, and just as I was in the midst of one of my most stirring passages, a man appeared coming across the prairie, riding on a mule. He came up to me and accosted me with "What's up? What's up?" I informed him that I was up, on a fence. He said he thought I was sick, and rode off. Cameron, I take it, was slightly disturbed; but what care I? my neckcloth was not white.

. . . . I find that my mistake has put me into a tight place. I shall reach Quincy at ten P. M. Possibly a chance boat may go down during the night, and I may be summoned out of bed to board it. Possibly I may persuade some one to drive me down to Hannibal in the night. I find too that a boat goes on Sunday at 11.30. Now what shall I do? My conscience is not so clear that I at once decide not to take the Sunday boat or get some one to drive me down Sunday morn-

ing.  I am expected to preach and talk to the children.
Personally I should have no hesitation in going on Sunday under the circumstances, but what effect will my
talks have upon persons who may know the facts and
not reason as I do? . . . . I think I shall probably be
at Hannibal to-morrow by some way, right or *wrong!*  I
forgot to tell you how I made my mistake, and that I
ought to do, for honor's sake, you know.  The road
from Chicago is called the Chicago, Burlington, and
Quincy Railroad.  But it forks at Galesburg, having two *termini*, one at Burlington and the other at
Quincy.  I had not so understood it, and in my five
o'clock state hardly had my wits about me, and accordingly when pointed to the Burlington cars thought myself all right, — but it was all, all wrong, as my present
state beareth witness.

ST. JOSEPH, MISSOURI, Oct. 23.

Here I am on the muddy Missouri, writing with none
to molest, on slave-soil, but with suffering Kanzas in
full view. . . . . I must for your sake take up the
thread of my chronicle where last broken off, and that
I believe was in the interesting town of Macomb, where
the din of a Western Republican meeting was thundering in my ears.  Well, I managed at last to escape
from the Wide-awakes, who gathered in great numbers
to escort me to the train (Tom Corwin was also abcard)
at about seven P. M.  We arrived at Quincy at ten, and
I gained my first peep at the Father of Waters by
moonlight. . . . . The keeper of the hotel promised to
wake me if a night boat, down, chanced along, but
none came, or rather I was not waked up.  Sunday
morning came.  I rose early and at once ferreted out a

livery-stable and woke the keeper with the question of how much he would charge to take me to Hannibal, twenty-one miles. After some chaffing we struck a bargain, and I told him to hurry round to the hotel; so by seven A. M. we were off for Hannibal, — and Sunday morning. What do you think? It was my first experience of the thing, and I by no means felt at ease. The noon boat down would not reach Hannibal until afternoon. I did not know how much S. might be depending upon me, and the only real doubt was as to the keeping of the livery-man at work. Concluding that I would strike hands with conscience by agreeing to preach to the man on the way down, I decided to go. If it had been any other day I should have enjoyed the drive hugely. I could easily have fancied myself in the far South. The road took us down the river, but the river itself we left some four miles away. A broad belt of meadow, skirted on the river side by a timber-growth, lay on our right, and quite a high bluff just at our left, sometimes wooded, sometimes cultivated, and delighting one with its graceful curves and green slopes. As for houses and inhabitants we saw but few, and the fewer the more pleasing was the prospect. We met quite a number of folk riding, apparently to meeting, but where the meeting-house was I couldn't divine. Once in a while some urchin would come out of the woods on one side and cross over on his bony horse to the opposite thicket, and again a scowling man with a savage-looking rifle would make his appearance. We passed an opening where an emigrant train was halting, perhaps for the day. It was a rough-looking set, and rather threw dust upon the picture of such life that I used to draw when a boy. We finally reached the ferry as the bells were ringing for church in **Han-nibal** on the other side. The boat was on the other side, too, and I had to wait some time before it crossed, and then had to pacify the man for being the only one wishing to cross by paying double ferriage. Arrived in Missouri, my first thought was, I am on slave-ground. I had nothing incendiary with me, however, so I pushed boldly up the street and entered the Plant-ers' House.

I deposited my bundle, brushed off the dust, and in-quired at once for the new Congregational church. I found it at the other end of the city, and entered just as S. was giving out notices with no reference to me. He saw me just as he was reading his text, and though rather disconcerted, went on with his sermon. It was as I supposed. He had been depending upon me, and was giving for the morning an old sermon, hastily dressed up. I sent a card to him offering to preach and talk, and at the close of service he announced that I would address the Sunday-school at noon, which I did, and also preached in the evening.

In the morning S. proposed that I should take a trip to Kanzas, offering me a free pass there and back. So you see I thought it too good an offer to let go unused, and accepted it. S. could not come with me, but I came, and here is thy servant in a tip-top house, as much at home as if in New York. I am content. I have at last reached the goal, — I am at the West. My room looks out upon the Missouri as I saw dimly last night. So I left my blinds and windows open for an early look this morning. When I awoke I rubbed my eyes, and raising myself in bed looked out. The very first thing that greeted my expectant vision was an enormous sign right before me, on which was painted in huge letters — THE WEST. It needs no sign however to prove to me that I am West. A walk soon does that. Mules parade the streets. Queer-looking covered wagons are seen. Mail-bags turn out of the post-office, marked Denver City, and so on. Pike's Peak stores and Pike's Peak hotels stare at one at every turn. Every other man you meet, almost, has a gun in his hands, and a four-mule mail-wagon passes you with ominous-looking muskets peering out from beneath the seats. The city itself is an admirable example of a Western city. You can see it grow.

While on his return he heard of the death in Persia of the Rev. Amherst L. Thompson, who had been a classmate at Andover, a member of the Brethren, and from his congeniality of temperament a warm friend of David. There was so much in common between these two, — so much of the same fire and eager expectation, — that the sudden death of the missionary just entered on his work sounded like a clear bell in the atmosphere of David's life. He listened and was impressed as never before. There are few witnesses to the struggle which then passed through his mind, — only a few written words, a Sabbath of silent meditation in New York when no preacher drew him forth from the solitude of his room, for Thompson's death was speaking, — but certain it is that thereafter he was conscious of other, deeper feeling respecting his work than the eager, almost boyish enthusiasm which hitherto had possessed him. At his conversion he had once and for all given himself up to the missionary work; years afterward he could write — "Since that time I have never made any formal committal of myself to the work." Now he did consecrate himself with a holier purpose to a service which he was willing never to perform if God should so require of him. As one who once seeing Death now sees Life newly revealed to him, so David from this moment kept steadfastly before him the revelation; the voice which spoke through Thompson's death never grew faint.

[TO REV. BENJAMIN LABAREE, JR.]

BOSTON, Nov. 10, 1860.

Delay in answering your two last letters seems unpardonable, but I have been full of business, having just returned from the West. I was away four weeks, and stopped at Cincinnati on my way back. Whilst there I bought a copy of "The World." In it was Washburn's Turkey letter, and at the close a brief sentence weightier than all the rest to me. I was all alone, and in a state to have the sad news weigh upon me in its full power. Arriving at New York a few hours later, I found your letters awaiting me at H.'s room. I hardly knew what to think. My first feeling was an indefinable one of insecurity, as if I myself were standing in some perilous position, in momentary danger of death. You know my own circle of friends has seldom been broken in upon, and I think this bereavement has come nearer to me than any previous one. Our little company all seem like brothers more than "Brethren," and Thompson was a near brother. I thought of our class-meeting and its final scene: Thompson leading us, and speaking of his prospects as cheerfully and hopefully as any one of us. . . . . So even in the first moments of dismay, I felt that his death was proving a blessing to me in opening my eyes. He with his firm health, his high aspirations, his full plans was not proof against the Destroyer, and was I? I found that I had been looking to the future with unwarranted presumption; that I had not so much lived in the spirit of the prayer — "Take me not away in the midst of my days," as taken it for granted that these past days of preparation, this clear sailing toward my goal, were surety to me that I could presume confidently upon at least a few *years*' lease of life. My eyes were opened, and though I rode homeward saddened by the event, yet I could not but feel thankful that I was led by it to look upon life in a more truthful aspect.

The day of sailing was at length set for the 11th of March, 1861, and the bustle of immediate preparation began. It was well for all that so much was required to be done. David was busier than ever, attending to a thousand things, and still working perseveringly at Sankya and Yoga; but all his business could not keep his thoughts off the day so near at hand. It has been shown how eagerly he looked forward to this day, how impatient he was of the repeated delays, and how hard he found it to be content to remain at home. The one purpose of his life impelled him and there was little looking back; forward he always had looked by the very cast of his nature. It was all changed now. The deep home affection which had found abundant expression was intensified by the coming separation; it was India still to which he was going, but — it was home that he was leaving. These things cannot be written, perhaps his own words are too sacred to be here set forth; but I am writing of one who left home,

brothers, sister, father and mother for the sake of
Christ, and the fulness of the sacrifice can only be
shown by what it cost him to make it. To Mr. Labaree he writes : —

"I write you once more from these shores, that I
may call to mind a dear old acquaintance and remember
that Persia has a special hold upon my love. A long,
long time it seems since I bade you good-bye, but at
last my turn has come. Leaving home is not a fancy,
but a living fact which strikes me hard. I did n't know
I loved my home so much. But He giveth me grace.
To-night I bid good-bye to ——. So they go, one by
one. How full these days; how one's heart sinks. But
let us put a cheerful courage on and look up. Well, I
am as near to you in India as here, — and as near
heaven. Good-bye, Ben, and good-bye to the others
with you. When I pray for you I still unconsciously
whisper Thompson's name. He needs not our prayers.
Pray for me."

To Mr. Washburn he writes : — "I am off. We expect to sail on Monday next. I write only to hail you,
though I must say I am not in a hailing mood. . . . . .
But I must go. Duty, work, — Christ calls me hence
and I must obey. But I must *obey*, not go because I
have made up my mind. These sacrifices I must make
for Christ. I think I wish to. I cannot write more
now. I am to leave for India, *dear* India. I may not
live long there, — indeed I cannot drive away the feeling that I shall not, but let me be faithful while I live.
And you will meet me and welcome me? Do, — and
help me to be faithful on the ship — that I may be in
India. And I will always love you. Love to the Brethren, *my* brethren, now at last, — an unworthy one am
I, your old friend David."

He was ordained as a missionary on Monday, February 25th, in the church in which he was educated; his pastor, Rev. Dr. Nehemiah Adams, preached the sermon. Rev. Edward Webb, of the Madura Mission, gave the charge, and his brother, Rev. Evarts Scudder, gave him the Right Hand of Fellowship; the other parts in the ordination were taken by Rev. Drs. Fisk, of Newburyport, Thompson, of Roxbury, and Hooker, of Boston. On the Wednesday following he was married to Miss Harriet L. Dutton, daughter of George D. Dutton, Esq., of Boston, who was associated as deacon in Union Church with David's father. Monday, March 11th, was the day appointed for the company to sail, and the following extract from a letter written to an absent member of the family presents the scene of the embarkation : —

" The people began to come by nine o'clock, and every one must see the state-room. There was a terrible jam, and persons would stand and stand in the passage-ways. The day was perfect, a good westerly breeze, bright sky, and fleecy clouds, a little bit cool, so that the religious exercises were held in the cabin instead of on the deck. Those outside joined in the singing, but were half a line behind the others at one time. After it was through the missionaries stood outside and bade all good-bye. Father was off in the forecastle talking with the sailors, and knew nothing of the persons leaving the ship, and was one of the last to go. David had to go ashore once or twice to bid some one good-bye who in the hurry had passed him by, and there was in general some little hurry. The exercises were at ten, and the tug started after eleven. The end of Devens's Wharf and the whole sidewalk of the bridge

11

were packed with persons, though many had gone away
unable to wait so long; they waved their handkerchiefs
till the very last, a mass of moving white, and sang
' Coronation ' as the vessel started fairly from the bridge.
It sounded most beautifully on the ship.   J. said that
they started very loudly, but that as they went on singing and the faces began to become undistinguishable,
one voice after another dropped away uncontrollable.
We rounded the point at the north end of the city, and
gave our handkerchiefs a last wave, till David said
' There, they are gone out of sight,' and I turned and
saw the big tears stand on David's eager, joyful face.

" . . . . We who were with them went out to the
outer light; they told us it was time to get into the tug,
and put a ladder down the side for us to get in by.   It
was pretty hard work, for the little tug was pitching
and rolling at a fearful rate.   Dave had gone down
into the cabin and I had to rush around in a great
hurry.   I bade him good-bye and hurried down the
ladder, — pretty difficult work, for it was grinding on
the side of the ship to the danger of crushing fingers
and toes in our descent.   It was well we hurried, for
scarcely were we all aboard than one of the hawsers
parted with a snap.   We got on top of the deck of the
tug and gave them three hearty cheers, which they returned lustily, but we soon found that we had not yet
parted company, but were putting to sea with them,
dragging them after us by a long rope; after two or
three miles, the rope was heaved overboard and we gave
them six glorious cheers which they again returned,
David's clear voice ringing above them all : there stood
Dave, as I last saw him, waving hat and handkerchief,
which we returned as we could with our only free hand.

Just at the end of hailing-distance I shouted, 'Good-bye, Dave,' — up went the sails, away they sped, a no-ble-looking sight. We kept our handkerchiefs going as long as we could see them, not knowing how long they might distinguish us with their marine glass, but as we were going against a strong wind, it was pretty cold, and so we held our handkerchiefs between our teeth and buried our hands in our pockets. So we stayed till half-past two, when she was obscured by the horizon."

So the ship sailed away; the crowd that watched it and sent up prayers for its safe passage separated; the two families who had been bereft in the sailing of the ship turned homeward, the father of the young mission-ary to record in his brief diary : — " Thus have we parted with our beloved son and his wife, after contem-plating it for many years; he is followed by the prayers and good wishes of numerous friends, and we trust the sacrifice we make in thus parting with him is well-pleas-ing to Jesus Christ, the great Head of the Church, our Saviour and Friend."

## CHAPTER IX.

### THE VOYAGE AND THE LANDING.

#### [11 MARCH–26 JUNE, 1861.]

THE company on the "National Eagle," Captain George Matthews, consisted, besides my brother and his wife, of the captain's wife and young son; Rev. Edward Webb, Mrs Webb, child, and infant, returning to the Madura Mission; Rev. John Scudder and wife, on their way to join the Arcot Mission; Mr. Gould, an invalid gentleman of Boston, in quest of health; and the wife of an Indian civil officer, returning to her husband, whom she had been compelled to leave in the revolt of 1857. There was scarcely a drawback to the pleasure of the voyage; sometimes it was tediously slow, and it was remarked that where they expected trade-winds they had calms, and steady winds where they did not look for them. The passage was a little longer than the average, one hundred and seven days from Devens's Wharf to Madras, but it was a welcome interval, bringing rest from continued labor and preparation for coming scenes. How the days were passed will be learned from the following letter: —

[TO REV. J. M. STURTEVANT, JR.]

. . . . One day here is like another. Let me give you a specimen brick. At 5.30, I am awaked by the slushing of water upon the deck overhead, which is washed every day; descend from my shelf, don my garments, rush out and souse into the big salt water tub. At 6, gaze at the gorgeous sunrise, — never equalled even your way, — and read till prayers at 8.30. Prayers in the cabin, when all passengers attend, conducted by us three in turn. Breakfast, always ending with the hominy or mush, and always accompanied by the onion-hash. 9–10, Tamil, when ladies appear and study; I go into Comparative Grammar. 12, men have dinner; in hot weather cool ice-water is drawn from the tank and we refresh ourselves. 12–2, I write, and the ladies recite to Mr. Webb. At two we dine, recite from three to four, and I read aloud to H. till half-past five. Till six, bean-bags, exercise and sunset. Supper and prayers, then moonrise and chat on deck, and to bed.

Sunday alone is different. At half-past ten the ensign is wrapped about a low ventilator on the poop-deck, which serves for a pulpit, seats are brought, and the watch above ordered aft for service. The crew is divided into two watches of four hours each, day and night, and at ten and a half the watch from four o'clock to eight has turned in. One of us preaches, taking turns, and I tell you it is not an unpleasing sight to see a company sitting thus under a clear sky about you, singing praises, listening to God's word, and praying to Him. The crew are quite attentive: they are mostly foreigners, Swedes, Danes, Dutch, Prussians, Italian, German, English, and Nova-Scotian. I brought with me enough Bibles for all, and all are eager to learn English. A few Sundays out, when over sea-sickness, I made my first attempt at reaching them. I saw a number reading and went forward; found them reading the Bible, and talked with them about their country, &c., helped them read, and finally proposed that after dinner we should have a Bible-class. They said yes, and so with some trepidation, when dinner was over, I visited the forecastle. Soon after entering, one man remarked that he came from hell last; true, doubtless, but I told him it was a better place to come from than to go to, and as the others did not countenance him he kept still. We read in John about an hour. The next Sunday I attempted the same, but found only one there and sat down with two or three outside, and read. So I have done every Sunday since, thinking it hardly worth the while to attempt a formal class where so few could understand me. I enjoy reading with them and have better chances for talk. . . . . John Scudder has a Bible-class with the boys and two mates, who bunk separately forward. One of these I had a long chat with one night on the lookout. But it seems almost impossible to get *into* these foreigners, so wrapped up are they in the educational trammels of a State religion.

"Yesterday," he writes in his journal, "I read a couple of hours, one with the carpenter, a Swede, who seems to have taken a liking to me, and calls me Master David, just like Mr. Bookland of old. I like him for his simplicity and earnestness, and good shelves too, — he has just put me up a shelf over the foot of my berth. The other hour I read with Hans Peter Andersen, or Peter as he is known. He is a sail-maker, and a quite superior fellow, a Dane. Both of these I had Testaments for. I spend pretty much all of Sunday among the men forward, and like it; they are a clever set."

Later in the voyage he adds, "One thing presses upon me as we go on: two weeks may close our voyage, and for aught I know, no one on board is the better for our presence, certainly none has yet changed the purpose of his heart. This ought not to be, it seems to me, and I chide myself. Last night I had a pleasant conversation with ——, and my first upon personal religion. My feeling afterward was — why did I not begin earlier? Is this to be the way through life, a neglect of duty until the startling view of the next world wakes me up to effort for my fellow-men now? I am too much inclined to preface direct Christian work by a host of preliminaries, instead of marching straight to the mark and doing at once that which I am called to do."

So even a life admits of little excitement beyond the speaking of a ship or the sight of a whale, but the company was large enough to admit of variety in society, and the days went by evenly and full of simple enjoyment. There was a deal of pleasurable occupation also in watching the varied moods of the sea. David made friends with all, frolicked with the captain's boy, and kept the interest of the crew throughout, and often too he turned away from the present company to the home friends whom he had left, journalizing for their benefit, hoarding up the scanty bits of ship news and holding more familiar intercourse with separate friends. His father had begun his correspondence already with a long and minute account of his life, written for David's entertainment and intended as a pleasant surprise. "How much we enjoyed father's long letter," he writes. "But it is too good a joke not to tell, how well he was

blinded about my supreme unconsciousness as to any
such thing being done. Did n't I believe that father
would write it when I asked him, and did n't I think
something was in the wind when I saw him writing so
industriously at the back-parlor window, day after day?
Did n't mother cough to father when certain loose
sheets were lying about on the centre-table, and was I
not very good never to notice that mysterious bundle
shuffled so adroitly into the box in the dining-room?
And did n't I wonder who on earth it could be who had
written what would be worth more than all the rest
together, as mother averred?"

[TO HIS SISTER.]

I wish you could board us one of these bright moonlight nights and see how delightful everything appears.
Just sit down in the stern of the ship and look down
into the foaming waters, as we rush along, ten knots an
hour, — and off into the wake of the moon dancing up
and down, and to the sails all set and glistening in the
bright beams. Such nights are the cream of our enjoyment. . . . . We are fast passing out of our last
cool weather, — are now off Madagascar with its cruel
queen and Christian king. But oh, could you see these
tremendous swells! When the ship is going right before the wind and the wind blowing just as the swell,
then you have it! You can hardly believe that the
huge swell will not walk right over you; and then,
when on the crest I can compare it to nothing so well
as to the scene from West Mountain, Williamstown,
looking down on to a sea of lesser hills, stretching on as
far as the eye can reach, — and so up and down, the
birds sailing about you, gigantic albatrosses sweeping

about in graceful awkwardness, and the frisky Mother
Carey chickens tripping lightly about from wave to
wave, daintily touching their toes on the water, or tipping now one wing and now another. Oh! we never
tire of looking.

The quiet period, after the bustle of preparation and
the eager expectation of years, was sure to bring many
thoughts of his future work, many strong recollections
of what he had parted from; indeed, so painful was
much of this recollection that he would not suffer himself to give way to it nor to speak with the freedom
which his longing for expression prompted. Some
signs of what he felt, looking behind and before, are
shown in individual letters. Thus in his letter to Mr.
Sturtevant he writes further: —

". . . . I have just re-read your letter of March 2,
which reached me in time. You say that it will be but
a few days before we all reach home. I say Amen.
Do you know that since leaving home I have felt as
never before that the true home is after this life, and
seem to feel that this separation is but momentary?
Indeed I have suffered more in parting with friends
than I anticipated, and I humbly hope that I am reaching some of the missionary blessings. I am beginning,
I think, now that India draws nigh, to see my needs.
I long sometimes to do a good work for Christ, but all
my reading and conversation lead me to see that the
self must be dropped from sight, the real aim of the
worker kept full in view, and I be willing to meet the
severest want, not as a disappointment, but as another
step in the appointed course which, as unforeseen, shall
offer fresh food for study."

To a brother also he writes: — "It is a sore, sore trial to be away from home, I tell you, and what is worse, to feel that there is no recal. How privileged are they who are called of God to labor where they may *see the living faces* and hear the tones of voice of those they love. But I believe a dearer joy is reserved for us, when the work against sin shall be finished, and the reunion above be effected. I am beginning to believe in heaven as a fact, ever before us to cheer. I seldom thus far in life have longed to be there, — since leaving home I have."

[TO REV. S. B. TREAT.]

A sea-voyage is a good place for sober thinking. How often, in looking out upon this sea and these changing heavens, have my thoughts wandered over the past and peered into the future. This is a good place to form resolves in, over a fresh study of God's word. Most heartily I thank God for this opportunity that I do not plunge thoughtlessly into the work. Paul's stay in Arabia — may it not have been of great value to him in his after-course? I have been led especially to study Paul's epistles during the last month, and have been stirred up as never before. What am I going to India for? How am I to live there? I firmly believe that for me the isolation from Christian society will, by God's help, prove of real worth to my religious character. I experienced a deal of spurious religious exhilaration, and did much that *looked* like active work for Christ in America. Now, I feel that the true test of my Christian spirit is to come in India. It is comparatively an easy thing to go about the country and talk fervently on missions, gaining the credit of a heart

fully in the work; but how will it be, when the voice
of praise will be but dimly heard and dark night be all
about me? Paul answers, and I can see in a measure
what the true missionary spirit is, even though it has
not yet possessed me, — "I glory in my infirmities that
the power of Christ may rest on me." I wonder at
his willingness to abnegate, disregard self. It must to
the world appear to border upon pusillanimity. "I will
very gladly spend and be spent for you, though the
more abundantly I love you the less I be loved." I
can see the Christian heroism of the man, but I look
on such a spirit as almost unapproachable. I am sure
that I could not say that now. Still I believe that I
long to be able to say as truly that I care not for self,
and take pleasure in infirmities. Paul could not have
reached that height at one step, but only by constant
struggle. I foresee many positions where I shall be
called to sink private preferences at others' wish, and
where I should be guilty did I not do it. But it will
come hard. And then to preach the word night and
day with tears to an unsympathizing, sneering crowd;
— where is my sufficiency? I believe I see it in this
— let me be fully possessed with a sense of the wonderful depth and fulness of power in the message of
life. Here was Paul's stand if I read him aright. I
never noticed before how his naturally national mind
stretched out to reach all nations, how he burned as he
wrote of the mystery hitherto hid, now made known,
that the Gentiles were to be fellow-heirs and partakers
of the promise with the Jews. A strait Pharisee rejoicing over this! Now is not this my word? Though
men revile and turn their backs, yet may I not gain
such a sense of this ineffable grace of God, His love

which would seek to reconcile His haters to Himself,
that I shall always be cheerful? I feel that to be truly
successful as a missionary, counting success not by the
number of converts, but as Paul did, according to the
faithfulness with which I testify of the grace of God, I
need to stay myself on the true, the firmest ground,
allowing secondary and subordinate motives to help me
on, but grasping with my might the cardinal principles
of the kingdom of heaven. I do long, yearn at times,
to be Christ's. Yet I am not weak enough now. I
have not proved my weakness as I shall some day.
Then Christ will be prepared to show his power in me.
I have felt however my insufficiency on shipboard.
Here we are, within a fortnight of Madras, and not
a soul here has become a Christian. We have had
preaching service and a little Biblical instruction, and
private instruction has not been wholly neglected. Yet
I have not been as faithful as I might have been. I
have been pleased to find true Christians as I believe
among the foreigners.

The following entry in his diary shows the result
of his study on shipboard: — "I have been through
Pope's 'Tamil Hand-Book,' Pope's 'Third Grammar,'
a part of Galatians, have written two or three prayers
and a good part of a sermon in Tamil. I have read a
good part of Caldwell's 'Dravidian Grammar,' one
volume of Bopp's 'Comparative Grammar,' Renan
on 'L'Origine du Langage' twice, Farrar on 'Origin
of Language,' part of Renan on 'Semitic Languages,'
Weber's 'Littérature Indienne' (in part), Kaye's 'Administration of East India Company,' Kaye's 'Christianity in India,' 'Life of Carey Marshman and Ward,'

part of Maury's 'Physical Geography of the Sea,' 'Adam Bede,' 'Memoirs of Lobdell,' 'Weitbrecht,' 'Fox,' 'Knill,' Gibson's account of 'Revival in Ireland'; I have written a long journal home and about twenty letters."

On June 25th they sighted Friar's Hood, a peak on the Island of Ceylon. The next day they saw plainly the coast south of Madras, and David bringing his sea-journal to a close writes: — "Our voyage is over, all full of goodness from the hand of God as it has been. My home is at hand. My work is before me. India is to be the Lord's. How soon?" The quiet of the voyage was followed by the bustle of landing, and the next day, in Madras, he finishes his sea-journal with the following account of the close of the voyage, and his first excitement upon fairly standing on the shores of India: —

In a dream, in a dream. Here we are at last fairly tossed out into an Oriental jumble. Haw! haw! croak the crows, and all about chimes in, dinning into one's eyes as well as ears, — "You 're a Griffin," as they call new-comers here. But lest I jumble up you as well, let me begin at my last break and run as far as I can, telling tidbits, letting big facts go. The first living thing we sighted was a *dhorey* or native sloop. Soon we spied a black, triangular-looking thing which turned out to be the black sail of a *catamaran* going out to fish. *Catamaran* means "tied-trees" and is nothing but three logs bound together. Squatted on these boats when at anchor, standing up when going, were some sable natives who gave us our first introduction to India. When at anchor they squat, throwing their

lines out and putting the fish into date-leaf baskets.
Pretty soon the sea became alive with this style of
craft.   One came near us and a man held up a fish.
I used my first Tamil, and shouted out " Come here ! "
but he could not catch us.   Thicker and thicker they
came, till we could hear them chattering to one another.
They had none too much raiment on them, and one
wonders how they can bear the hot sun on their bare
heads and naked backs.   Soon one chap came alongside
and crawled over ; a scrawny-looking fellow enough
and stupid withal.   We could make nothing of him,
but if my alcohol had been at hand I should have got
some prawns and fish for S. [a Naturalist brother.]
I hope to yet.

Just as this catamaran came up, a Masullah boat
appeared in sight.   On it came, bearing several gay-
turbaned individuals in the stern.   As soon as alongside,
all hands scrambled on deck, and here were Hindûs
indeed.   The rowers, about a dozen or eighteen, were
mostly fine athletic men.   The turbaned fellows were
sent by the consignees.   They were large in their own
eyes, especially one fellow who, like all Hindûs, considered that an aldermanic protuberance was the highest
ornament to the person.   He strutted about with folded
arms and high mien, looking as if he would not refuse
a good slasher of beef.   One or two were really hand-
some.   Several had the mark of the beast on their
forehead, — Siva's three marks.

Pretty soon another big boat-load of the same sort
came alongside with turbaned individuals, carrying their
characters in their pockets and offering their services.
We were busy now, for letters and papers had come
for the captain, and all gathered round while we read

extracts from Boston papers and the telegraphic news
from a Madras paper, extracts which let us at once
into the midst of your tossings and fever. We feared the
worst and it had nearly come. This mixed up matters
most provokingly. News of Tammany sachems, becoming wise at last, was jumbled with Tamil chattering
and orders about the ship. We had by this time rat-
tled out our anchor. The deck was a perfect Babel,
naked humanities running about and poking their chaffing English into people's faces, while the new sailors
stared at the queer sight. The custom-house officer
too had come, and was consulting with the captain.
But suddenly our maze was disentangled by the coming of another boat, in which we made out John Scudder's brothers. He hurrahed, they shouted back, and
soon the brothers were embracing and laughing, and
playing their jokes in a most brotherly fashion.

Another boat! This makes for the forward part.
I run and peer over and see two men. " Mr. Bancroft," says one. I rush back and tell the captain that
the ice-agent has come. Mr. Webb looks over and
sees his old friend, my new one, Mr Hunt,* who clam-
bers up and greets us all in his quiet, affectionate way.
Hurrah! Home letters! Down we sit on our tied-up
mattresses and cut open the fat packages. No one
missing. H. is at hers and I at mine, letting all other
sights and sounds go now. But I only read enough to
find that all are well, and that blessings unsupposed
though not unprayed for had come upon ours, — and
then we put up our last bundles ready for shore. F.
is let down into one boat by a chair, H. on the other
side of the ship descends in an Occidental fashion. I

* The Printer and Agent at Madras for the American Mission.

rush about, shake hands with all the sailors, say a final
" Come along! " to Polly, the parrot, and down I go.

Now for Madras and the surf! We are in a Masullah boat, a big trough of a thing made of boards tied
together and the seams stopped up with grass, so that it
may give when going over the rollers. The seats are
nothing but bars three inches square and four feet apart,
that is, those for the rowers. A little raised platform,
decidedly rickety, holds with squeezing Mr. Webb's
party, Mr. Hunt, Mr. Bancroft, H. and me. *Ava!* here
we go! and now we have done forever with Stars and
Stripes and Western ways. Down go the oars, long
poles with teakettle-covers at the end, and with grunt-
ings from the men and *pos!* from us we are off. As
the men pull, they sing out in a low tone, not opening
their mouths, for the other organ suffices, *Annán! Annán!* helping it out with an occasional *Vadáh! Vadáh!*
In five minutes we are upon the rollers. It is a calm
day and the rollers are lower than usual; we row on to
the first swell. The men lay by, and as soon as fairly
over, *Jéldi! Jéldi!* shout the men, and away we go to
the next; so on and on, for six or seven times until
we ground on the beach. It is raining hard, and the
water rushes in upon us somewhat from behind. Here
we lie till some black chaps, who need not be afraid of
wetting their clothes, came out to us and carried us to
the land in chairs.

Mr. Winslow's carriage is waiting and in we crawl.
Mr. Webb goes with Mr. Hunt, and John with his
brothers. Here I try my Tamil again and manage to
get my things on board. (There! we are lands-folk
now.) Now for a drive in this *bandy,* better looking
than most others, which remind me of our Boston

House of Correction carts that we boys used to be so mortally afraid of. Away Po! The horse-keeper runs ahead to keep people out of the way, but as the drive is out of the business parts, we meet few carts. We have a jolly time. "Nothing looks natural," says H., "but the surf." That's a fact! Scrawny palm-trees half withered up; crows cawing at you with the most brazen impudence; clumps of queer-looking grass; cactus growing on the beach, no flowers though, except a little purple one nodding cheerily to us as we pass. I try my Tamil again, solely in the form of "Is this so and so?" and get the very flattering answer "*Am*," — Yes. I feel fine, but come down when I find that the driver was wrong, and that the natives will always say "Yes," when they think it will please you. We pass some fine houses and come out at last into a native neighborhood. Here is a cluster of low-roofed, thatched houses, quite respectable for the kind, and men, women, and young brats doing all sorts of things and all in a queer way. The young ones kick up and have a jolly time here just as we young ones used to.

But we go too fast to see much, and speedily rein up before Mr. Winslow's spacious house. Mr. Winslow comes down the steps and greets us both. Mrs. W. follows and we are at home, — in India. Everything looks roomy. We are shown to our room, and I walk back and forth and touch the walls to assure myself that I have over six feet of spare room. The room is higher than it is broad, and everything bears the appearance of airiness. I come out after looking over some letters and walk up and down the veranda (*alias* piazza) with Mr. Winslow. We chat about everything, especially about the war at home. Before

long Mr. Webb comes with Mr. Hunt, as this is the
evening for a prayer-meeting.

Soon after Mr. Webb came, Abraham Alleine, a
Christian *mûnshi*, that is, teacher, came in to greet him.
He had been ten years with Mr. Webb at Dindigal.
He gave me a pleasing idea of the Christian, " for,"
said he, in English, " I cannot stop.  I must do God's
work first; I am on my way to our prayer-meeting,"
a native meeting. . . . . We had a hearty meeting,
praying especially for our own land; the spirit was
most refreshing, so natural and rich.  After they had
gone we opened a budget of letters from Madura and
found a hearty All hail! from the missionaries there.
It fairly made us cry to get such a warm greeting
from strangers; but we are strangers no more.

To one of the letters referred to in the last paragraph
he replied as follows : —

MADRAS, June 28, 1861.

Nothing, my dear brother Burnell, has affected us
so deeply as the receipt of words of hail from those
unknown to us, save by name.  Let me return your
greeting, and try to join you in thankfulness to God that
He has counted me worthy to touch India.  As a new-
comer, let me ask peculiar interest in your supplications
for me that I may be fitted, by a personal acquaintance
with Christ, to testify of the Gospel of God.  I am
more impressed as I walk about, with my own lack
than with the heathen's misery.

Hoping to see you all in peace, I remain
Yours sincerely,
DAVID C. SCUDDER.

## CHAPTER X.

### STAY IN MADRAS.

#### [27 June—16 July, 1861.]

[From the time of leaving home until his death, my brother kept a full journal, in the form of a letter to his father and mother, which was regularly mailed once a fortnight. This contained the record of his daily life, and was intended for the circle of friends at home, around which it passed ; to separate friends also he wrote, and to those who had access to his journal his letters were frequently more personal. From both these sources, his journal and his letters, I am able to give the narrative of his life in India in his own words. The occasional editorial notes which may be required will be indicated in this part by brackets.]

[JOURNAL LETTER.]

THURSDAY, June 27.

. . . . This morning I was up and out and oh, ——, how I did pine for you just to have you by to laugh with me. As it was I had to ha! ha! right out: I could not help it, if I was a missionary. To see a little tot strutting about free as the air, unfettered by civilization, cunning and nimble as Puck'! The first thing that stopped me was the sight of three bits of ebony dabbling in the mud, for all the world like white youngsters. The oldest, a little girl, had a necklace on, and all had bright chirk faces. I grinned and they grinned.

I said in Tamil, " Are you well? " They only grinned, and so ended my first attempt at trying the children. I like them though, and take back what I once said in our Sabbath-school, on authority, that all the little children in India were old men. They are not; they are *bonâ fide* children. They romp and look demure and smile at you, and dig in the dirt just as they ought to.

But how can I tell what I saw? Patterns or else the originals of all vehicles, from the " carriages " of the Acts, rather hard! to the go-carts of nowadays; bullocks with stiff and crumpled horns; gaunt sons of Arabs trotting by; bandies of all sorts and shapes. There comes one: two bullocks jog along, with a rope through their nostrils, the driver sitting upon the pole; inside — a space of four feet square — sit four or five swarthy sons of this land in hot contiguity, looking as if going to be sold in the shambles, chattering like apes. Here comes a woman, modestly apparelled, as all are, with a young brat puss-back, or rather puss-hip; some ride puss-shoulder, always one leg behind, one in front. Here is a fat and oily Brahman with his cord about his neck. Here is a man carrying two earthen pots full of something, slung by a stick over his shoulder. *Peons*, that is, policemen, walk about with their brass badges, and here is a Mussulman woman covered from head to foot with a white cloth, so that nothing can be seen.

I walked as far as the stone statue of Sir Thomas Munroe, a former Governor, and turned back. It occurred to me that I had seen no temple, so I looked out on my return, and found one close by a wretched collection of huts, which brought to mind a picture of an African kraal. I saw what looked like a temple,

and would you believe it, it was one of Pilliyar which
I had so often described in America. I really could
not but feel amused. There it was, a stone or clay
building, about twelve feet cube, crumbling to decay,
with a low portico, under which was Siva's stone. On
the outside, in a small niche about two feet square, sat
Pilliyar nearly filling the space and made, I judge, of
black stone. The niche had two doors which I suppose
are shut at night. There I stood and looked and
thought and prayed. Inside I could hear the mutter-
ings of the poor priests or worshippers, and as I stood
there, a man passing by on his way to work raised his
hands and bowed his head and went on. Here was
idolatry ; it is marked too on the foreheads of men, in
the sectarian signs of chalk and ashes. Turning into
the compound or enclosure of Mr. Winslow's house, I
met a Christian teacher and passed a few words in
English. I said, " This is my first day in India."
" Yes," said he, " and I am the first person to meet
you, which will be pleasant in your memory." A
small bit of Orientalism I suppose.

After breakfast I went to Popham's Broadway in a
*palkee.* A *palkee*, short for palanquin, is about six
feet by three, and four feet high, lined with chintz ; the
bottom of cane, covered with a cushion or bed ; two
sliding doors on each side ; a shelf with drawers in
front, and a back of pad, something like a coach-strap,
to lean on as you half sit up ; a pole is fixed for four
men, two at each end. One end is raised, you com-
pose your members properly and then the other end
rises. Grunt! off we are, slow at first, then fast and
faster. Eh! says one in front, Ay! says one behind,
and so it runs from back to front and back again, as the

four men make their way in a dog-trot style, swinging their free arms as if to strike their breasts, and writhing their swarthy bodies very oddly.    They sing in a low, monotonous, nasal, and half-pitiful way, eh! oh! ah! eh! oho! ay-ai! the man behind breaking out now and then into a hi! or ho! and something that sounds like pass po! pass po! as if in his last gasp.    Every five minutes they change their shoulders, without however setting you down, and begin their grunt again, but always on a different key.    I like the way of getting about and the chant is rather soothing.

.    .    .    .    In the late afternoon we drove out to the beach where everybody goes and which was lively enough.    The surf rolls in finely and thus we have Nature's anthem.    The band gives us art.    The whole road is lined with carriages of all sorts, and horses of every kind galloping about.    The horse-keeper always runs ahead of the carriage, shouting to folks to clear the track.    Fine turn-outs have two runners, who keep a wisp made from the tail of a *yâk*, a kind of goat from the north.    But this is civilization and you don't care about that.

.    .    .    .    I like the affectionate way that the natives have toward each other.    You often see two men walking along with their fingers joined, not the whole hand, but swinging their hands by their fingers.    Then at night when all are on their way from work, it is common to see one leaning with one or both hands on another's shoulders in a very brotherly way.

FRIDAY, June 28.

.    .    .    .    I started at five and a half P. M, and made my way to the native bazaar.    A bazaar is much like a Fourth-of-July or Fair-Day booth strung out. There were whole streets of them. Everybody saluted me in broken English, but I let my eyes alone do duty. I walked where I chose, and it was not long before I got lost. All the streets look exactly alike and all queer. I did not much care what happened for a while, bound to see all I could. I came across many little temples, as I suppose, though I fancy most were only private dwellings, with niches in the walls for household deities. I have as yet seen none but the most innocent paintings on temples or house walls, nothing indecent, in all my ramblings. Black Town, the native part, is only about a mile in diameter, and I have wandered over a good portion of it.

But what amazed me most completely was a school that I happened upon. All my previous ideas were tame enough. It was gathered on the low mud veranda of a native house, and on the ground, sheltered from the road by a cane screen. I knew it at once by the din of voices, but oh the sight! The whole set of thirty or so were yelling out their lessons from blackboards. At one end sat the teacher, a man of about sixty, with silver-bowed goggles, and a piece of green leaf against his face to keep them from chafing, I judge. By his side stood a boy of about twelve, almost naked, his hair tied in a queue behind, reading out of a native printed book. As he saw me stop, he went at it with unusual energy, yelling so as to be heard a half a mile away. He stuck out his thick lips, drew in a tremendous breath and then let it out: it was perfectly deafening. His voice grew lower and lower till it sunk into a whisper, while he writhed his head and body to squeeze out the last bit. Then he began again, singing off the words. Once in a while the old man would stop him, and show him how, in exactly the same style, only his toothless mouth contrasted queerly with the shining ivories of his pupil. I stepped up and looked over. The old man was very polite and showed me the book, which turned out to be in Telegu. He grunted and I grunted back. Finding that I could get off a little Tamil, he sang out to somebody inside to come out, but I feared the consequences and beat a sudden retreat.

SATURDAY, June 29.

. . . . This evening I took a walk on Mount Road, leading to St. Thomas's Mount, the favorite drive. The English shops here are decidedly unique and are fine establishments. Many look like palaces, having long sweeping avenues leading up to them, with beautiful grounds about, containing twenty acres or more. The roads too are well macadamized and broad, so that an evening drive here along the sea-side, where the surf beats up ceaselessly, is decidedly refreshing after a hot day. The picturesque garb of the natives makes a pleasing addition to the scene. As I sat on a parapet by the road-side, a young girl came by and seeing me stopped, stooped and made a gesture as if scooping up sand and putting it on her head ; all gracefully done, and she went on her way. It is often done to you and strikes one very unpleasantly. The ordinary and only salutation that I have seen is touching the forehead and slightly bowing. At first I did not like it, but I think now it is nothing more than equivalent to our lifting or touching our hats. It seems humiliating, though, to pass as I did yesterday between two long lines of beggars, and have them bow their heads to the dust.

MONDAY, July 1.

Yesterday morning at seven o'clock I went to preach before breakfast in the Baptist chapel. There were about eighty present, mostly Anglo-Indians or Eurasians, as they are called, half foreign, half native. I preached *extempore* on the words, " Freely ye have received, freely give," — a good text for me and my favorite. The audience was very attentive. One thing was Asian : *punkahs* were swinging everywhere. I used to have a very indefinite idea of what a punkah was. It is simply a narrow strip of board covered with cloth or painted, from which hangs, on the edge, a fringe of thick cloth. It is hung by long cords from the ceiling, and is pulled by a cord passing over a pulley in the opposite wall. In the church two long ones were swaying back and forth across the body of the church ; four or five swung to and from me on each side-aisle, and one small one over my head. After service I came home, ate a hurried breakfast and went into Mr. Winslow's Tamil service. He preached on the fall of Jericho, and I made out to understand considerably well what was said. In this chapel the natives generally sit on seats like Europeans, but most of the children squat on the floor with two or three female teachers. The teachers are Christian, and it was a pleasant sight to see them, as they first sat down, bow with their faces to the ground toward the pulpit in silent prayer. Their quiet, pleasing faces bore the mark of Christian intelligence. But the little ones ! They were disposed in two semicircular rows in front and looked demure enough, but some of the uncurbed ones rolled about, chuckled, kicked up their shiny feet and had a good time evidently. One little fellow, about four years old, had a check jacket, but he clearly considered it an encumbrance, and was not satisfied till he had disrobed himself and crumpled up his jacket between his clenched fists. Several times during service a crow would perch on the window and haw! haw! most saucily. The singing is fully equal to the most orthodox music in New England. The only organ used was the nasal, and that was played on to perfection.

We had Monthly Concert at four P. M. Mr. Winslow asked me to speak — in Tamil, which I declined ; by an interpreter, which I agreed to. But afterward I asked myself, Why not begin in Tamil to-day? It will do to tell of at least! So at meeting when Mr. Winslow introduced me, and Abraham came forward to interpret, I began in Tamil ; he gave an involuntary oh! and retreated. I told them where I had come from and why I had come to them. A large part of my discourse consisted of the text of my morning sermon. I was rather flurried and hardly "raked an X," as we should say at Williams. But I made a beginning and mean to keep it up. By the way, in what I said was a good illustration of the liability to mistake and egregious blunders under which a novice labors : after meeting I asked Mr. Winslow's servant if he understood me. "Yes," said he, "but what is *kodai?*" "A gift," said I, or tried to say, but he could not quite comprehend. There is no good single word for *gift;* *kodai* is used and I took it when saying, "God has given me a gift." It is not a common word, but another, similar in sound, is common, viz: *kudai*, where the *u* is pronounced almost precisely like *o*, and which word means *umbrella*. He thought I said "God has given me an umbrella," and naturally was puzzled.

However he told me, laughing, that he was not going to talk English any more to me, and he does not. I heard of a more ludicrous mistake. A missionary in Bombay was discoursing most eloquently to a native assembly, and in the course of his speech hoped that the Lord would give them all an understanding; unfortunately the term for understanding closely resembles another of different meaning; and, blundering, he hoped that the Lord would give to all of them an old woman!

. . . . This morning I went to a book-store kept by an Englishman, where was a very good assortment of books, but, much to my relief, I found nothing which strongly tempted me. Coming to India gives me grace, I fancy, father. Down-town I bought a pith hat, covered with white cloth; when appearing in this, you might easily imagine that Robinson Crusoe stood before you. It is shaped like a washbowl, and fits to your head by a band, connected with the hat only by four supports, thus allowing a free circulation inside. Indeed the wind fairly howls about my head. . . . . I paid my palkee-bearers yesterday more than the usual price. When the chief man took it — a half-rupee — he began to expostulate with me on the wretched pay. I marched off, whereupon, with a most contemptuous look, he flung the money on the ground. I paid no heed, but left him, and presume that he condescended to pick it up finally. Not long ago, a man bet with a new-comer that the latter would not pay his bearers enough to satisfy them. The man went to ride, and afterward paid the bearers four or five times the usual sum. With most profound bowings, the head-man begged of his honor to have compassion upon them, so

poor, and give them enough to buy a sheep! It is of
no use to try to satisfy them.  Yesterday, when coming back, a new set bore me, and waited an hour on
the veranda in hope of more pay.  Every time I
looked out, I could see them with their hands to their
foreheads.

JULY 10.

I see some new sights nearly every morning as I
take my walk.  A few days since, I was wandering
about among native streets, when I came across a
mosque.  There are many Mohammedans throughout
Southern India, and many are very rich.  They were
the rulers of the country before the English, and ill
brook the English supremacy.  This mosque was a
broad, white building, with two tall minarets, one at
each end.  A large yard was all about it, and I only
ventured to look in.  I could see on the pavement
before the mosque men bowing and prostrating, first
one way and then another.  I made my way about,
and through a noisy bazaar, stopping to look and laugh
at two boys who were lugging off another brat bodily,
and at last turned into what seemed a burial-ground.
The people stopped to look at me, and I to look at a
man dressed in gay colors, who was seated on a slab,
with an old manuscript before him.  There he sat,
swaying his body, and chanting through his nose some
religious sayings, — perhaps the Korân.  It was a picture of desolation — that Mohammedan poring over his
books in the midst of decaying tombstones and tumbled-
down sepulchres.

JULY 11.

As I was riding alone to-day I passed a man in the
road, who was, I suppose, performing some vow.  He

had in his hands a little basket, adorned with flowers. Keeping it in his hand, he rolled over and over on the ground, muttering something to himself, looking the very picture of deluded superstition. Poor fellow! And oh, these beggars! that ah! ah! at you from the corners of the streets, and the horrid cripples and lepers that hold out stumps of arms and awful deformities for you to see — they haunt one!

[TO REV. EVARTS SCUDDER.]

. . . . Madras is a city of magnificent distances; one can go ten miles in most any direction. Royapuram is a suburb where Mr. Hunt lives. It is a beautiful place, full of nice green gardens and cocoa-nut forests. Walk half a mile from his house, and you are in a wood that reminds you at once of pictures of South American forests. Magnificent cocoa-nut palms wave their spreading heads, tamarind-trees cast their thick shadows about, bamboos bend and bow so easily, and occasionally you see the long, pendent shoots of the banian, — all giving an air of gloom. In the trees you can see men climbing about, getting the sap, and at short distances are native villages, with mud-walled, thatch-roof houses. Did I write about a visit here on Sunday? I will now, at any rate. About four in the afternoon Mr. Hunt and I rode out, sending the cate-chist before us. We stopped on the border of this forest, and walked a little way to the preaching-place. This is a mud house, whitewashed, only one bare room. The windows are grated with thick iron bars. One door forms a sure protection, as —— once found to his comfort when set on by an excited mob. We went in and sat down on a bench. Two young men then sang a Tamil hymn, and people began to come and look in. Before long we had quite an audience, marks on their foreheads showing them to be heathen. The catechist preached; the men listened well, often nodding their heads in approval. Two boys making some noise in play, a queer-looking man got up, caught them by the little knot of hair on their heads, and hauled them out-doors. Outside, close by the preacher, were crowded a dozen people, — men, women, and babies, — standing off, or pressing their faces against the iron bars, seemingly eager to catch every word, and caring nothing for the strangers. A capital audience; and how know we but that a seed dropped into good soil?

In about half an hour we walked out, and pursued our way to the Tinnevelly Settlement in the Forest, boys and men pressing eagerly about, asking for tracts. The catechist came with us, and pointed out a good place to preach in. So we stopped, and the catechist, standing at the root of a tree, began to read a "proclamation." Several people were about and stopped to listen. Others passing turned aside, — men with big burdens on their backs, women carrying water. Before long a large audience, perhaps thirty, were standing in quiet attention, when a man bearing a brass pot came up, elbowed his way through the people, put down his pot, and stood looking at the catechist with folded arms. Pretty soon he began to look excited, and in a few moments broke out into a perfect storm of passionate words, fierce gesticulation, and scowling looks. I never in my life saw such a picture of satanic rage and fury. He fumed and fretted as if actually possessed of the devil; his face was most fiendish. I could hardly understand a word, but could easily guess the purport of what he said. He declaimed for a long while, without paying the slightest heed to the catechist. At last he lost his breath, and gave others a chance to speak. Who should oppose him and defend the truth? Not a single Christian was present save us three. Who should step forward, right in front of the man, and take up the gauntlet, but a bright boy, about fifteen years old! Manly fellow, he was not a member of any church, but in some of the mission schools he had learned enough of Christ and Christianity to know that this man was an ignorant defamer, and he meant to defend the truth against him. So he did; and, I tell you, I got as excited as could be, fairly trembling as I stood and looked on. Then a man with a huge bundle loosed his load and put in a word, well, too, for he got the laugh on the man from the whole crowd. It was soon clear that the man met with no favor from those present, who knew him to be a pestilent intermeddler. The catechist himself was known in the village, and respected even by the heathen. Mr. Hunt closed the dispute by stepping up to the man and handing him a tract on repentance, when the company, now fifty or more, dispersed. The whole scene was very impressive. So the gospel fares.

[It will be remembered that my brother had engaged to correspond with such schools as should contribute to the support of native schools in the Madura Mission. The following is the first of a series of letters written under this plan; and while of later date, it relates to scenes in Madras, so that it properly belongs in this chapter. I give it entire, although there is sometimes repetition of what has appeared in the journal. With this letter closes the account of the stay in Madras.]

DINDIGAL, INDIA, Aug. 6, 1861.

MY DEAR YOUNG FRIENDS, — Here I am at last, on the opposite side of the globe from you, under a different sky, and among strange faces. Before I left home I promised you that I would try to write you a letter about my voyage to India, and the things I first saw there. I am spared to reach India, but how, what shall I write? Did you ever try to pour water out of a small narrow-necked bottle? what a rattling and gurgling it makes! Just such a bottle am I, — full enough of things to say, but so very full that they roll ever one another in great confusion if I try to pour them out. So this time you must let me gurgle a little.

I have so much to say about India that I shall have to leave out all about the oceans that we crossed, the ships we met and bowed to, the big whales we saw, the birds we caught with fish-hooks, the stormy winds, when the great waves rushed in over the ship, and the hot, still days, when the great ocean was as smooth as a mill-pond. Read the 107th Psalm, and you will have a good picture of life at sea. Through all God kept us. For more than one hundred days we sailed along without once seeing green grass, or even barren sand, until, one fine morning, the cry came down to us from the mast-head, Land ho! How we did cheer and rush to get a sight! We strained our eyes, and there, away off over the water, was a dim blue line — land at last, hills in India. The wind was blowing us quickly

toward it, and soon we could catch the form of other
hills, and then the beach, the white sand glistening in
the sun, and there were trees — yes, living trees — tall
cocoa-nut palms waving their feathery leaves in the
morning breeze. There's a village! "What! that?
how muddy it looks." Yes, and well it may, for all
houses in India are built of mud. "But see those
black things all around us on the water; why, there's
a man on them, on every one! what can they be?"
Those are boats, made of three logs tied together; they
are called *catamarans*, which means "tied trees."
They are fishing-boats, and those men who look as if
they were dressed in black, but are really dressed in
nothing, are the fishermen. Here they come alongside, with fish to sell. But we can't stop to look at
them, for there, just coming in sight, is Madras, where
we are to land. We can see plainly the ships lying at
anchor, the flag flying in the fort, the tall towers of
Mohammedan mosques, and, what is still more pleasing, the steeples of Christian churches. Soon the captain gives orders to cast anchor, we hear a tremendous
rattling of chain, down goes the anchor to the bottom
of the sea, and our long voyage is over.

Soon other larger but very odd-looking boats row up
to us, and in one of them comes Mr. Hunt, the missionary printer; we are glad to see him, for he brings
us letters from home, which we left four months ago.
If you want to know how blessed a thing it is to get
good news from a far country, come to India and see.
We sat down at once, tore open our letters, found all
were well at home, and then made ready to go ashore.
We pack up our last bundle, bid good-bye to the captain and all the sailors, climb down into the boat, push

13

off, turn back to look once more at the good ship which has borne us safely so long, wave our handkerchiefs, and in fifteen minutes are standing on " India's coral strand." Then we are glad. Now, let us have a good night's sleep, rocked to rest, not by tossing waves but by happy thoughts, and to-morrow we will take our first walk in India, to see what we shall see.

Well, morning comes in India just as it does in America. We wake up, dreaming that all the crows in India are having a grand meeting right outside the house, — such a terrible cawing! We get up and look out, and there, perched on top of houses and walls, and wheeling about in the air, are hundreds of noisy crows; they are as plenty here as doves at home, very tame and very troublesome. The natives call them " *Ka-ka ;* " a good name, is n't it? After scolding at the crows, which only makes them scold back, we set out for a walk.

The first thing we notice is four little children playing in the sand, — little nut-brown bodies, how oddly they look. I wonder whether they know how to smile. I 'll stop and try. Yes, sure enough, they all smile back, showing their clear white teeth. That 's a good sign ; for if a boy or girl knows how to smile, there must be some good in them — don't you think so? Well, walk on. Here come some women carrying their babies ; and how, do you think? In their arms? no. Do they ride puss-back? no; they ride astride of their mother's hips, or else across their father's shoulders. And what a queer dress the people wear : the men all dress in white, though some have only a cloth tied around their waist. The women like gay colors, and if they can have a red cloth, feel quite grand.

Then they wear ornaments : bracelets of wax or of glass or brass, rings on their fingers and toes, bracelets on their ankles, rings in their noses and in their ears. You see little girls going about with a great hole in their ears, kept open by a roll of leaf as large as a quarter of a dollar. Nearly all the men shave their heads ; some leave a little tuft on top, others on the sides ; most all go bareheaded, and look very droll, with their smooth heads shining in the sun.

But what is this strange-looking cart coming ? It is called a bandy, and looks for all the world like a little girl's Quaker bonnet on two wheels. It is drawn by two oxen, or bullocks as they are called. Some of you boys would laugh to see the way the natives drive. The driver sits on the pole of the cart, and holds in his hands the reins, which pass through the nostrils of the bullock. He keeps his hands on the bullocks' backs, and if he wants to go fast, kicks them with his naked feet ; if faster still, twists their tails, all the while talking to them in a queer way.

We are on the opposite of the world from America, so we must expect that many things will be different here from things at home. I might tell you of many strange ways of working the people have. While I am writing, a tailor is sitting close by ; if you watch him, you will see that he sews by pushing the needle from him instead of towards him, as you girls do. When the people milk the cows, they always sit on the left-hand side, not on the right. It is not thought wrong to walk into a gentleman's house with your hat on, but it would never do to go in without taking off your shoes ; nor must you ever go away from a house before you are told to. Which of you boys or

girls is number one at school? If you should tell a
Hindû scholar that you are number one, he would
think you were at the foot of the class. If there are
twenty boys in a class, number twenty is at the head.
So, when the Bible tells us that Elisha was ploughing
with twelve yoke of oxen, himself with the twelfth, it
means, in our way of counting, that he was with the
first.

But I forget; we are taking a walk. Do you notice how all the people you meet have marks on their
foreheads? here are some who have three marks of
yellow and white, up and down. Here are others,
that have a broad mark across their foreheads, and
even on their breasts and arms; others have a spot as
large as a five-cent piece just above their noses, and
others a blue line running down their noses. What
are they for? They are sacred marks, showing what
god the people who wear them worship. They are
made with ashes or chalk, and are rubbed on every
morning; but some of the marks are rubbed in so deep
that no washing can take them out; so I have seen
some Christians here, who were once heathen, wearing
these marks still. They are the old marks, and as
those can never be washed away till death, so many
spots on their soul shall not be clean gone till they pass
to where the pure live, and have on their foreheads a
new name written. There are no marks on your foreheads; are there any on your souls? The Roman
Catholics here mark their foreheads with the cross,
and well show by that how like the heathen they
still are.

But we have taken a long walk, and the sun is up;
it will not do to stay out late in this hot country, for

the sun is scorching. We have seen no temple as yet;
let us look out for one on the way back. Just before
you turn into the missionary house, on the left-hand
side of the road, you see a man turning round and
round, bowing and muttering over something. What
is he about? Go a little nearer, and there, hidden behind some trees, you see a small whitewashed house.
In front of where the man is standing is a hole in the
wall, about two feet square, and inside it sits a great
black dirty - looking image, with a garland of red
flowers around its neck. Look carefully and see if you
can tell the name of the image. Do you remember
the story I told you about the god with an elephant's
head? this is the one, for you can see his trunk as he
holds it in his hand. Was n't it strange that it should
be the first idol I saw in India? It made me think of
the many Sunday-schools to which I had told the story,
but here really was that idol; yes, and here was a real
man praying to it. Of course, I knew before that real
men did such things, yet I had never seen one till now.
There he was, joining his hands together, bowing down
and saying his prayers to that black stone. Poor man!
do you truly believe that such a thing as that can hear
you or do you good? I could not talk to him, for I
did not know his language; so I stood and looked and
wondered. Pretty soon he walked around to the front
side, where was another stone image. He bowed to
that with his face to the ground, turned round five or
six times, and bowed again, and was doing so when I
left him and went into the house.

How do you suppose that temple happened to be in
just that place? Some years ago there was a large well
on the spot; some priests spread a report that at the bot-

tom of that well was a god, and that he wanted to be brought up and worshipped. So they called a great crowd of people together, had a feast, said prayers, and then sent some one down into the well. Down he went, and after a time came back, bringing, to be sure, the god with him. Then the people shouted out, and said that the god must have a temple on that very spot. So they set to work, the people giving money ; and the building I saw was the temple which they put up for this god.

Since I began this letter, I have been out with some other missionaries, to preach to the heathen in another place. On the way back I saw what was a new sight to me. Under a large tree were some idols ; all around the tree were swings made of wood, hung upon wooden frames about six feet high. What, think you, were they for? they were put there for the gods to swing on! Every dark night, say the people, when the wind blows high, the gods come out and have a swing ; we can't see them, because it is dark, but we can hear the swings creak as they sway back and forth.

Now I must stop ; but what have I written this long letter to you for ? can you answer ? Because you promised me that if I would write you three or four times a year, you would give enough money to keep a Christian school. In these schools the children will be taught not to bow down to stones, but to the living God. Do you not think that they need to be taught this ?

I have not told you about these schools yet, because I had so much else to write about. In my next letter I shall try to. And now don't forget your pennies, and when you drop them into the contribution-box, wrap each one up in a prayer to God that He will make them do good for the little heathen children in India.

Your affectionate friend,<br>DAVID C. SCUDDER.

# CHAPTER XI.

## JOURNEY FROM MADRAS TO MADURA.

### [16 JULY—10 AUGUST, 1861.]

[THE district in which the missionaries were to be established was that of Madura, farther down the peninsula, and whose chief city with the name of the district is about three hundred miles distant from Madras. By taking a route somewhat circuitous they could avail themselves of the railway as far as Salem, about a hundred and seventy miles from Madras, and visit on the way the Vellore Mission. Mr. Webb and family travelled with them as far as his own station at Dindigal. The narrative of the journey is contained as usual in his journal. The first date is the fourth day from Madras.]

### [JOURNAL LETTER.]

MALLUR, GOVERNMENT BUNGALOW, July 19.

. . . . We set off on Tuesday the 16th for Madura *viâ* the Scudders at the Arcot Mission. Of course this involved a temporary surrender of our Orientalism, as the only way to get there is by rail; we left at 3 P. M. and reached Vellore at 8.30 P. M.; the distance is about eighty miles over a flat tame country, the only thing noticeable being the occasional rice-fields and the more frequent temples. Vellore is well known in Anglo-Indian history as the seat of what is called the Vellore Mutiny of 1808, when the garrison was murdered. We reached Silas Scudder's at ten, had supper and went to bed. The Scudders all have a punkah pulled over them during the nights of the hot season, and so the man began on us. It was really so cool that we did n't need the new breeze, so I went out and said to the man, *Vendâm. Po!* Most invaluable words are these, which I would advise every new-comer in India to commit to memory as his first lesson in Tamil. *Vendâm. Po!* — that is, "Don't want. Go!" So I said "Don't want. Go!" to the punkah-man. He looked rather disconcerted, but I turned in. Soon I heard the grunt which every native uses when he wants your notice. The punkah-man was back and said, "Master hired punkah for the night." Not wishing to have a bother and cheat the man out of his wages I let him pull, and pull he did all night. Think of it, what an intellectual operation. It was really too cold, and waking every once in a while, there was the punkah swinging over our heads ; — it was oppressive to think of that man.

About eight o'clock in the morning I made out to take a breath and a walk, my first walk in the country. The garden, or compound, as they call it here, is full of large mango-trees, somewhat like our apple-trees, but larger and more beautiful. I wandered about breathing in huge mouthfuls of the delicious morning air. Butterflies flitted about ; bugs of every color crawled ; lizards kept dodging round the trees. As I was going along a path I was stopped by a crowd of black ants ; they were travelling back and forth on an ant-road as if on some matter of life and death. I watched them awhile and then tried to trace their way. One end I could not find, the other I found in a hole. It looked

as if a big colony were migrating.  I amused myself
a long while in stopping up the hole, laughing at their
bewilderment and wondering at their pertinacity.

. . . . The next day we took the cars again at 10.-
30 A. M.   The ride was delightful, through a country
that reminded us of Vermont, the way lying between
ranges of high hills, giving us now and then beautiful
reaches of rice-fields of varying shades and growth and
rich foliage.   Salem we reached at last; Salem is a
pure Tamil word.   I jumped out, and the first thing
that caught my eye was what I thought must be my
bandy.   It proved to be, and as I am in a favorable
position, sitting with my feet on the wheels, let me
describe it.   It is called a box-bandy, and well called so.
H. says it looks most like the " Black Maria " [prison-
cart, so called, in Boston].   You enter by a step behind,
cab-like.   Inside, it is arranged nicely: the blinds let
down all around, above the wheels; there are two
seats, one at each end; the sides are lined with cane;
a cane seat, movable, also falls down from each side, so
as wholly to cover the empty space, thus making a good
place for a mattress.   The bandy is about five feet
ten inches, by three feet six inches.   A slide lifts up so
as to give the space under the driver's seat to stow away
your feet in.   All the room is well taken up with boxes,
leather cups and straps; a side-board outside keeps off
mud and dirt.   The color is dark brown, and the whole
affair is well finished off.   With a good pair of little
bullocks I can hold up my head with anybody.   To
be sure it jolts and jerks, very much like a chaise of
home make, but it is decidedly comfortable, comparatively.

We found bullocks awaiting at the station, which is

some distance from the town, but through a mistake no
cart except mine. We took tea at the depot, and finally
started off for the town. All but Mrs. Webb and the
baby were in my bandy; they went in the palanquin,
which had been provided as an easier mode of travel.
It is picturesque enough in a moonlight night to see the
palanquin pass along, — the men chanting and a bearer
swinging his flaming torch. At Salem we found carts,
and disposed ourselves for the night. Mrs. Webb and
baby went in the palkee. H., Sarah Webb, and I arranged ourselves in the bandy. Mr. Webb took a
common cart, but did n't start until after the rest had
left. Oh that ride! We put our mattress in, but
little sleep had we, though it was after eight P. M. when
we started, and after one when we reached Mallûr, eight
miles! The novelty was enough to keep one wakeful,
but the ruts and rocks were added. Just as I was
about " losing myself," H. remarked that the oxen were
stopping very often. I thought they were tired, but on
looking out we soon saw the reason. We seemed to be
in the midst of a mud-hole. The driver flung his Tamil
about profusely, he could talk no English. So I had a
chance to try my Tamil again, and I did my best. I
made out to discover that it would be well to get out
of the bandy. So I got my shoes and jumped out. I
saw what looked like a road mending and walked on a
little way. I soon satisfied myself and came back, got
H. and Sarah out, and we tramped on over rocks and
through mud, till we reached the road again, the bandy
in the mean while nearly upsetting in the same endeavor. It was midnight, and what a fix we were in!
Who knew where we were? I did n't even know the
name of the place to which we were going, and we were

nearly three hours already, and only eight miles in all
to go.  But the man said he knew, so in we got again,
and after an hour's jolting we found ourselves at the
bungalow.

NÂMKAL, Sunday, July 21.

We are fourteen miles from our yesterday's station,
Mûnsavadi, which was ten miles distant from Mallûr.
This morning I walked out with Mr. Webb and he
found two congregations to preach to.  I believe that I
can do no better Sabbath work than to have a sort of
monthly concert talk, as I used to in the old vestry,
only based on a little better knowledge.  We reached
this bungalow about seven o'clock last evening.  Perhaps I have not said that a bungalow is a house provided by the English Government for the accommodation of travellers.  We find an empty hotel open to us,
for which we pay about twenty-five cents a day; of
course we do our own cooking, and bring our own beds,
chairs, tables, cots; sometimes crockery and cooking
utensils are furnished.  As we enter this place the first
thing we see is a huge rock, four hundred feet high,
topped with an old fortress built by Hyder Ali, now
deserted.  At the base of the rock is a large tank of
water, and in the centre of the tank a sort of temple,
which is nearly covered when the tank is full.  Half-
way down the rock is another temple, which looked
quite prettily as we drove by in the early moonlight,
while a band was playing in its neighborhood.  The
village lies on one side and is quite populous, straw-
thatched houses appearing on all sides.  The bungalow
is a little distance off from the village to insure quiet,
and quiet it is as on any Sabbath-day in New England.

At about half-past six this morning Mr. Webb and

I sauntered out toward the village, looking for a chance to preach. In a minute or two we came upon a large enclosure, where we had seen a great number of native carts the night previous. Most of them had left, — there is no weekly rest in this land, — but a few men were about, bringing straw for the oxen and preparing to start; some boys were idling around, while a little girl sitting on the ground was feeding a still smaller body with some wild berries. Here we stopped, and Mr. Webb, taking his little pocket Tamil Testament, read a verse or two and talked to them. I could only catch a word or two, such as Jesus Christ, Saviour, the Son of God, and Gospel. The word *gospel* in Tamil is not understood by the common people, and so Mr. Webb had to explain it, telling the men that it meant "good news," and then sketching what the good news was. I wish you could have seen the crowd, or rather little gathering; there were only about a dozen; one rather sinister-looking man acted as a sort of spokesman, or, better, echo, for it is quite characteristic of the people of the country to echo what you say. If you say to them, " We are all sinners," in response they do not express their assent as we should by a special phrase, but catch the very words and repeat them after you. So did this man, while the others nodded their assent to what was said. This nodding, I might say, would perhaps disconcert a stranger, for universally here an affirmative nod is a shake of the head sideways, which looks very much like a disapproval.

After talking about fifteen minutes we passed on. We came soon to a cluster of idols. Hard by the roadside, on a raised platform of earth and stones, not more than two feet high, were five or six black, oily stone images. Most conspicuous among them was Pilliyar, with his elephant head, whose story I have so often told at home. In front and facing him was the rat which he is said to ride; on either side were three or four images of the hooded snake, or cobra, one five-headed, others double, twisted together. Even such a little spot as that, usually under a tree, is called a temple. I have seen them all along the road since leaving Madras; I had not heard about them at home. Unsightly looking things they are. A little beyond was a huge car of some idol. It was about thirty feet high, borne on four enormous wooden wheels and figured all over with representations of gods. In front was a heap of chain with which the people drag it. Close by was another car. Indeed, this must be a holy place. Near by was a native cutchery or court and the post-office. This is a low whitewashed house with pleasant porch. Here was quite a gathering, and we went and greeted the men. They rose and made way for us. Two or three were busy arranging the mail, the rest were looking on. We sat down and asked the others to. They did so, squatting on the floor; others, seeing the white men, came up and joined the crowd, and we soon had an audience of fifty or more. This time, Mr. Webb did not exactly preach to them, but told them the story of a man who was converted on board the ship which took him from India to England. Orientals love stories, and all paid good attention, echoing his words and nodding, for half an hour. We did not wish to stay long at a public place in business-hours, and left after a profusion of salaams and interchange of courteous words, with the intention of going again this afternoon. As Mr. Webb closed his talk, he told the men that just as they scattered the rice-seed, so he was sowing the truth by grains, hoping that some would bring forth fruit.

Indeed it is scattering. Look on the map and find Salem which we have left, and Dindigal, to which we go. This is a distance of one hundred miles, and we are now about forty miles south of Salem ; in all this extent of one hundred miles not a single missionary or native catechist is to be found, not a word of gospel truth is preached to the people, unless it be by some stray passer-by, who like us spends a Sabbath on the way. Does it not require a living faith in that word of God which abideth forever, to look for the regeneration of a land so sparsely supplied with the heralds of the truth ? One Christian woman we found here. As I write this, she comes up to the bungalow, for we are to have a little meeting now, — twelve o'clock. She has gone to call more. — Meeting is over. There were four women and three men present. One poor woman was stupid enough, and I suppose never before had a thought of anything but how to cook her rice.

DINDIGAL, Tuesday, July 23.

Well here I am at last, fairly within the boundaries of the mission-field where my India-life is to be spent. We arrived at eight this morning, after a night ride of forty-five miles. I did n't sleep a wink all night, spent six miles of the way in beating the bullocks, running alongside to break their idea of the respectability of a walk. I have tried to sleep, but don't succeed, and write to put me in the way of it. . . . . Sunday toward dusk, I strolled out of the bungalow-yard. As hill air is always bracing, my legs soon carried me up the steep rock and into the fortress which I have spoken of.

It is rather a formidable-looking affair, but wholly desolate, or nearly so; the gods alone hold it. A sculptured
griffin, cut in the rock doorway, stands guard. Passing
in, you turn several corners, and soon are in the enclosure; crumbling buildings are all around, a green water-
tank collects the frogs, lizards crawl about, bugs wink
at you, and the only pleasant thing that greets you is a
pretty little wild flower, which still clings in fondness to
the decaying fortress. A magnificent view of a well-
cultivated country is sufficient reward for the climb,
and I hoped to enjoy it, as a good sight of the plains of
India that now knew no Sabbath, but should erelong.
But as I was walking about I was surprised at suddenly
seeing a crowd of people coming out of a building,
close by which some flags were flying. They saw me;
some ran back, the rest came forward, salaaming at a
great rate. I salaamed back, and the leader came forward and stood waiting. What could I do but bring
forward a little Tamil for their edification? I showed
them what I had and they seemed pleased and showed
me theirs. We were soon good friends. They were
all boys, and the oldest, about seventeen, was a fine,
pleasing-looking boy whom I took a fancy to at once.
He offered to show me about, so I followed him, asking
all sorts of questions, as well as I could. In the middle of the fort stood an old temple fast tumbling down;
at the entrance was a pillar, mounted by a frame for a
lamp. On two opposite sides were figures of some idol.
It being probably a Mohammedan fort, I thought that
the mark upon the other sides must be the hand, which
makes so large a show in Mohammedan symbols; so I
asked the boy. The only reply was a most contemptuous look and a kick of his foot against the carving.

It was really the mark — a trident — which all followers of Siva wear on their foreheads. He took me inside,
where as usual elephant-headed Pilliyar was enthroned,
and others by his side. All greasy and disgusting
enough. The boy was a Mussulman and he and I
could agree on the first article of our creed, — one God.

We walked about, and after a while I sat down and
tried to talk a little with him. The whole company
stood about me, except when sent off by the sober
ones for snickering out, as most all did. I made out
to get at some of his belief; one thing he said was,
" Jesus is your God, Mohammed our God." I knew
that all true Mohammedans hated the title Son of God,
as applied to Christ, and so purposely used it. He at
once caught me up, and holding up a finger said, —
" Only one God ; how is Christ the Son of God?"
My Tamil was not free enough, nor my purpose such
as to lead me to reply, so I turned the subject. He
was studying English, and as I walked off with him,
expressed a wish to have a book. So I invited him to
go to the bungalow with me. Down we went, the
whole troop of us, he keeping all the boys from stepping ahead of me as we walked on. People stopped to
look at us, and it did look not a little droll to see me
heading a company of some dozen little boys or more
into the bungalow-yard. Mr. Webb had come back
from another street-talk, and I brought him my congregation. He had another talk with them. One thing
the boy told him I never had heard of before. He said
that Jesus, the prophet, had promised a Comforter, and
that the Comforter was Mohammed. Mr. Webb gave
the boy a Testament and he left us, pleasing us all by
his frank and kindly ways.

14

Time is precious, and at midnight we were all called up to start on a trip of twenty-one miles to a place called Karûr. The first stage was twelve miles to the Câvery River, which we must cross. We poked along, enjoying the jolts, trying in vain to coax a little sleep, until 3.30 A. M., when we reached the bank of the river. Now for a good touch of Orientalism. How do you suppose we were to cross? Rubbing our eyes, all we could see that looked like boats were four concerns — the most definite term I know — modelled most closely after that well-known conveyance in which the wise men of Gotham once sailed. They were four mammoth saucers, made of slit bamboo wicker-work, twelve feet in diameter, three feet deep. This wicker-work was covered with thick tough leather, making them almost completely water-proof. The first to enter this novel boat was Mrs. Webb, in her palanquin; with many groans the bowl was tipped up on end, and the palkee walked in. Next came our bandies. How they could be accommodated seemed a problem. The wind was very high, and the river swollen, and the head boatman said that the tops must be taken off the common carts. So they stripped off the mats, and, tipping up the next boat, backed Mr. Webb in, leaving out the bullocks. He presented a most laughable appearance, sitting in his cart, the bare framework looking like a big cage, and the whole bobbing up and down. Our turn came next. We stayed in the bandy, though the matter of boarding was so peculiar. Our spirits kept up, as we could see no difference in the boat-level, and we began to have a more favorable impression of Hindû navigation. The baggage-cart came next, and when all were safely in, the men climbed in, three into each.

The Webbs' boat soon disappeared in the dusk. Our turn came, but we did not fare so well. Three times, at least, after pushing off, we were driven back by the wind and current,—as I believe, partly because the men were unwilling to go. I did n't know any words for managing such tubs, so I relieved my mind by driving at them in English. I did not at all relish the idea of spending the day there, as we had eight miles to go upon the other side before reaching a bungalow. I cried out to the cook to help off, but he said the wind was too high. But at last we started again, this time the men wading and pushing more by hand than by pole. The river was two miles wide, and we were three long hours getting over, working up-stream, and then poling across, shallow enough all the way. We spun around like tops, and at last reached the other side.

They landed us in a beautiful grove of cocoa-nut trees, and Mr. Webb hailed us with a bunch of plantains and a young cocoa-nut, the young milk of which was delightfully refreshing. Leaving the other carts to come when they could, we pushed ahead in our bandy, and before long were at the bungalow, Karûr, a wretchedly furnished place. We stayed through the day, and at four in the afternoon again set out for a night ride of forty-five miles to Dindigal. In five minutes we came to a river which we had good fun in crossing. I went in Mr. Webb's cart to try it, and my bandy went before with Mr. Webb, H., and Sarah. We left Mrs. Webb to come later. In went the bandy and bullocks, and twenty men about it, some hauling the bullocks, some tugging at the wheels, some pushing behind, and all yelling and screaming and

hurrahing like mad.  Such a droll sight!  I just looked on and roared with laughter.  The river is narrow
and shallow, but very swift.  With the help of our
friends we crossed safely, not wetting the bottoms of
the carts.  We were cheated about our bullocks, and
had miserable sets.  I rode in Mr. Webb's cart the
first twelve miles.  That is, I pretended to, but we got
worked up about the lazy bullocks; so I got out and
found a bamboo, with which I belabored the beasts,
till I showed them that they could run if they chose,
and for four miles I ran beside them, beating and yelling like any bandy-man.  They sobered down again
when I got in, so that toward the end I got out and
ran another mile, and got away out of sight of my own
bandy.  The next stage we arranged ourselves for
sleep, Mr. Webb and Sarah in his cart, H. and I in
mine.  But I could not sleep, and these bullocks were
still more stupid.  Mr. Webb went ahead, and was
soon out of sight.  So I got out about midnight, and
ran along barefoot looking for a stick, and looking out
for snakes.  I got in and beat and cried out, but scared
the driver more than the bullocks, and finally gave up.
At four o'clock we came up with the relay, and this
time had good bullocks and a good driver.  Four miles
from Dindigal we met Mr. White's bandy come to help
us ; soon a man came along to meet us, and, after the
custom of the country, brought us each a lime : if we
receive it we are friends.  The native pastor and catechists had been out to meet us, but were going back.
Pretty soon we drove up to the Dindigal house, and
received the welcome of Mr. and Mrs. White.  We
had been a few minutes here, when the Christians began to come in, each with a lot of limes, and then they

brought in garlands of fragrant flowers, which they put around our necks, so that we were soon decked out like kings and queens of May. Mrs. Webb came by twelve, the bearers having given out ten miles back, after a steady tramp of thirty-five miles. And now we are all here, the Webbs at home, rejoicing and praising God that our journey in a strange land is over.

[Dindigal is the station formerly occupied by the Webbs, now returning to it. Here the others remained a little more than a fortnight, detained awhile by the non-appearance of the train of bandies containing their goods. Mr. Washburn, whom the reader will remember as an old and intimate friend of David's, welcomed them at Dindigal, and David returned with him to his station at Battalagundu, twenty miles distant, and spent a few days, talking, as he says, "over old and new days, discussing points in mission work and Tamil orthoepy and pronunciation." Once at work in India, the studies which had occupied his mind previously were carried on by observation and practical acquaintance with the Hindû mind, rather than through much reading. The results, also, in the views which he formed, found little expression save in familiar discussion with brother missionaries. He took the opportunity while in Dindigal to make a short preaching tour with two of the missionaries; but first let him give an account of the somewhat noted Dindigal rock.]

[JOURNAL LETTER.]

DINDIGAL, July 31.

Dindi-gal means *round rock*, so named from the enormous rock that stands in the middle of the valley.

Mr. Webb, Mr. White, and I went up it this morning
about half-past five. The rock, from its size and precipi-
tancy, is an admirable natural fortress, very like the one
at Karûr. But the old rajahs built a large and massive fort upon it, and held it for a long time against
the English. The latter captured it from Tippoo Saib,
and have held it as a garrison until lately ; now it is
dismantled, and is utterly desolate. You pass through
a gate which was once the entrance to the " lower fort,"
enclosing a limited area around the rock, and soon begin to ascend the rock by the stone steps cut in it.
The ascent on this side is very gradual, but on all
others exceedingly abrupt. I should say it was about
as high as Bunker Hill Monument, though that is a
droll comparison. [It is the comparison of a Boston
boy, with whom the monument is always the standard
by which he measures height; it is two hundred and
twenty-eight feet high.] A great wall is all around
the summit, and inside are barracks and magazines
and temples, for it was a heathen fort once. Indeed,
we have here a good illustration of Scripture. One of
the temples is utterly robbed of its idols, and nothing is
in it but clouds of bats, which make the air so foul
that no one can enter. But there is little worth seeing
in the fort, except one temple where some fine carving
in granite was pointed out. When the fort was deserted, all the unworthy cannon were hurled off the
precipice to be broken. It must have been a rare
sight to see them crashing down these rocks. The
view from the rock is charming. The hills bound the
view everywhere, some of them only a thousand feet
lower than Mount Washington [6200 feet high]. Right
below are the green rice-fields, checkered by ridges,

arranged for irrigation. As we sat on the rock, we could hear the peculiar chant of the water-drawer, as he walked up and down the well-sweep, while the smoke curled up to the sky from little villages which dotted the plain all about.

DINDIGAL, Monday, Aug. 5.

I have been on a tour with Mr. Webb and Mr. White, leaving on Saturday at 3 P. M. . . . . We visited Smoke-leaf village [a place where tobacco is raised extensively]. . . . . It was nearly dark, but we found the road filled with people who had come to greet Mr. Webb. We made our way through them, salaaming on all sides, into the church. The people crowded in after us, and stayed there, I might say, until we left this morning. We managed to get them out while we ate supper, [for the church serves as resting-place to the missionary, when there is no bungalow,] but every grated window was full of black faces, grinning with wonder at our queer proceedings. . . . . At night I retreated into my box-bandy, but was awaked from sleep by a confused hum. Listening, I found that the bandy was surrounded by women and children, who had given themselves to searching into the construction of every part. Not caring to be myself fingered over, I speedily shut myself up, by pulling up the shades, and then let them look and feel to their hearts' content. I amused myself by now and then shaking the blinds, and hearing the young folk scamper away.

. . . . I talked in English, and Mr. Webb interpreted. I told the villagers about the houses which were built in Mammoth Cave for some people sick with consumption, in the hope that the even temperature of

the place might benefit them; how, instead, it proved
their ruin, and how I had heard that many people in
India had been led to do just such a foolish thing in
Satan's den, and we had come to bring them a light
and a looking-glass, that they might see for themselves
how badly off they were.   I did not see but what they
were as interested as children at home used to appear
at like stories. . . . . These common people speak so
in figures and pithy sentences that it is difficult to understand their drift.   Upon Mr. Webb's urging that
he receive the true faith, a man replied, "How can we
know which to follow?   Sometimes you put the bandy
into the boat, sometimes the boat into the bandy,"—
a saying which can mean almost anything, I suppose.

. . . . In another village, on Sunday at 4 P. M., we
gathered about us some thirty people, the entire population.   Among them was an old, old man, skin and
bones, hardly able to sit upright.   It was a painful
sight, for he sat leaning forward to catch every word
uttered.   He heard; can any have done him good?
An old woman, too, was very intent on Mr. Webb's
talk, — a rare thing here.   It was a simple gathering,
a few men and women seated on the ground before
three foreigners, away in that poor hamlet, yet in such
ways is mission labor expending.   Mr. Webb and Mr.
White spoke, and the catechist examined the people on
the Lord's Prayer.   One man, out of four of the congregation, could stumble through it.   It began to rain
as we started home, and forced us finally to spend half
an hour under a cluster of cactus-trees.   Tea was ready
on our arrival at the little church, and plenty of spectators.

. . . . When the service of preaching was over, the

work of the day was not. The missionary must now
doff the surplice, and put on the wig. A court is
speedily formed, and the judge calls for the first case:
it is a quarrel between two members of the congregation about some land. After half an hour's debate,
helped out by anybody and everybody, the judge gives
his decision, which is a complicated one, but apparently
satisfactory to all parties. One of them is to receive
six rupees as indemnity, and he at once says that he
will give half of it toward a new church in a neighboring village. Mr. Webb makes them join hands,
and all say *Santosham,* — Joy, and congratulate one another. . . . . Other cases followed, but I was tired
and moved into my box-bandy. This was a good specimen of the work which a missionary has to do on his
tours. The people are all children, and they are
poorly brought up too, quarrelsome and unprincipled.
I never in my life felt so strongly the utter inefficiency
of human means toward the accomplishment of the
object of our coming here. Put where I could see for
myself the surface appearance, the first impression was
one of utter despair. I can't convey the grounds of my
feeling ; but look at a crowd of native men and women,
— see their dull, passionless faces, their staring, stupid,
blank looks, with the marks of devotion to a false faith
patent, — and you ask yourself unconsciously, Can
these stones speak ? But I believe a Christian cannot
long remain in this mood ; at least I did not, and it was
with a positive sense of exhilaration that I looked upon
them. There was the massive wall, built by the prime
wisdom of the wicked one, appearing to grow larger
and more portentous as I gazed upon it. I felt indeed
my impotence as never before, but there came over me

such an exalted view of the simple might of God that
the obstacle seemed already gone. " Who art thou, O
great mountain? before Zerubbabel thou shalt become
a plain." I believe this is the natural feeling of one
placed as I was; certainly I felt thankful for it, and
the hour passed pleasantly as I thought how the bare
word of God, if accompanied by the Spirit, could pre-
vail against the whole force of Satan. I thought of my
future field, and how the success of the truth there de-
pended primarily upon our faith in prayer, and I determined to send home for help in this one thing, — help
which you can render us as well as any Christians upon
this side of the globe. We must have it. It will be
long before the India Church reaches the strength of
manhood. But why should we be discouraged ? Can
the labor of fifty years produce in India what the
work of eighteen hundred and fifty years has effected
in western lands ? We are wonderfully blessed, when
we think of the paltry means at command. Increase
the agency if you are dissatisfied with present results,
but be not dissatisfied. No missionary thinks of anything else than of giving thanks to God for His wonderful workings.

MADURA, Aug. 12.

. . . . At last I am at Madura, the king of cities
and city of kings. It is the finest city in South India,
and the seat of an ancient and powerful dynasty. But
I must tell you, first, not what the city is, but how I got
here. We left Dindigal on Friday afternoon, August
9, having been detained by the non-arrival of the carts
containing our goods. I went in my bandy. H. tried
the palanquin, as the road was bad, and a palanquin
was at Dindigal which belonged at Madura. I left at

5.30 for a drive of thirty-eight miles; bullocks had
been posted every seven miles.  H. was to go with one
set of men as far as Vadapatti, sixteen miles from
Madura, and to leave an hour after me.  I got along
very well as far as Vadapatti.  There Savarimuttu,
(*Xavier* Tamilized,) our faithful *maty* or head-servant,
[who had been engaged at Dindigal,] had gone the day
before to see his family, and I found him with the bullocks.  I had told him to wait and accompany H. to
Madura.  But I got there first, and what was I to do?
The relay-bearers that I had sent for from Madura
were not there, and H. could not go on without them.
It was midnight.  I hesitated awhile, but, confident
that they would come in time, I went on, telling Savarimuttu to take good care of *Ammâl*, (mistress,) and that
I should send bearers on if I did not meet them on the
road.  So, with no little misgivings, I drove ahead.

Nine miles more and we should come to the river
which runs by Madura, and is sometimes quite full.  I
should have had bullocks half-way to Madura, but by a
blunder failed to post them.  The bullocks were soon
fagged out, and by the time we reached the river were
really ready to drop.  It was about half-past three in
the morning, and never a wink had I slept thus far
over this horrible road.  The river certainly did not
look very formidable, not more than quarter of a mile
wide, and half of that dry.  After a good deal of
shouting and tail-twisting and beating, the bandy-man
made out to get about ten feet forward.  The bullocks
then seemed very much inclined to lie down.  Not
relishing such an episode in my trip, I thought it high
time to use my powers of persuasion; so I climbed
through the front window on to the driver's seat, and

took the whip, the driver taking the reins and pulling.
I shouted and yelled, punched and flogged, (I am not
yet an adept in tail-twisting,) while the driver tugged
and tried to cajole the yoke into proper practices;
then he gave me the reins, and I jerked so hard that
something gave way. Was it the bullock's nostril?
fortunately not. Then I whipped off the lash, and
sent the driver fumbling for it in the bottom of the
river, in vain; then I broke the bamboo stock, and
took the reins again. Finally, in despair, I rolled up
my trousers, jumped in, and put my shoulder to the
wheel. This was successful, and we reached the shore
in safety, with the loss of the driver's whip and my
voice. But in the midst of the river I had time
enough to chuckle over the droll figure I cut, and
to think of you orderly people at home.

The bullocks, after that, made out occasionally to
get into a walk, but at daybreak I became discouraged,
and got out, bound to walk into Madura, and scare up
some bearers for poor H. So I walked ahead, looking
at the tall towers of the great temple here, as they
loomed up boldly in front, pointing out where the city
lay. But a mile on I was met by a man driving a pair
of bullocks. He bowed to the ground, and, guessing
his business, I asked him, and found that Mr. Rendall
had sent on these bullocks to meet me. So I walked
back to my bandy, and then drove into Madura in fine
style, reaching it a little after six. The first thing to
do was to inquire about bearers. I found that no
bearers were to be had, as the Rajah of Puthucotta, an
independent prince, was on a royal pilgrimage to the
famous shrines of Southern India, to have his little
girl's hair cut by the temple Brahmans, and he had

engaged all the bearers for his suite. The only thing to be done was to send back the bandy and post bullocks for H.; this we did, and she finally arrived. So we are safely here.

[The new missionaries were most cordially welcomed by the mission circle here. With some David was already acquainted, Mr. Capron, his Andover friend, residing in Madura at that time; and with all they were soon at home. "Indeed," he writes, "it is a most blessed thing this companionship here. You love everybody, and feel at home wherever you are." Here they were to spend the remainder of the year; and accordingly, as soon as arrangements could be made, they took possession of a portion of one of the mission houses, and settled down at housekeeping. It seemed somewhat like a new beginning of missionary life; how he looked forward to that life is seen in the following extract from a letter written during the journey to Madura.]

[TO REV. S. C. DEAN.]

DINDIGAL, Aug.7, 1861.

In India at last! . . . . The prayers and hopes of nine years are fulfilled: is there anything to bring a shadow over my face? India I tread upon; I see these false gods; I see men bowing to them. I have the whole, pure word of God in my hand, and the capacity of speech in my head. My work is plain and full in sight. Onward! . . . . I went upon a tour last Sunday with Mr. White and Mr. Webb, and so had a look into a new phase of mission life and work. I enjoyed it, and it profited me, I hope, for I was brought to look so closely upon this massive wall that Hindûism fronts us with, that I felt as never before how utterly a necessity in our work, to any successful issue, is the Holy Spirit. But do you never leap at the sight of towering obstacles, when you see in their presence a new and glorious opportunity for the arm of the Lord to be raised up? I have felt it somewhat; now I want it part of my ordinary current of thought and feeling, never to forget it, and ever thus to pray.

# CHAPTER XII.

## RESIDENCE IN MADURA.

### [AUGUST, 1861–FEBRUARY, 1862.]

[THE seven months spent in Madura were occupied with immediate preparation for the care of a separate station. The best portion of the day was devoted to study, and almost every side of a missionary's life was learned through practical effort, alone or with the older members of the mission. The time passed quickly and most pleasantly. Madura is the centre of missionary operations in that district, and beside the acquaintance which the new missionaries formed with other workers, the regular meetings of the mission gave an opportunity to acquire a knowledge of missionary organization. Their life in the city is so variously described in the following letters, that scarcely any explanation is needed, and if the reader misses some details of Oriental life, it is because the final establishment at Periakulam seemed the best occasion for introducing them.]

### [JOURNAL LETTER.]

SEPT. 16.

Since last Tuesday, one week, the mission meeting has been held here. It is held once a year, to bring together all the missionary helpers, hear reports of stations and recitation of lessons learned during the year. It is an important and interesting meeting, for the natives more than for the missionaries. All the

exercises have been interesting, but one above all, and
of this I must write. By the last mail I received a
letter from Labaree, giving an account of the remarkable outburst of a benevolent spirit in the Nestorian
community. I read the letter at the monthly concert.
By the same mail came a printed letter from Deacon
Moses, Nestorian, which, I suppose, you have seen.
This letter was read at a religious service, early in the
course of the meeting, and evidently produced a great
impression upon the natives. Its results were soon
felt. Day before yesterday, Saturday, the meeting was
at Pasumalie, three miles from here. I rode out as
early as possible, but was late at the introductory
prayer-meeting. When I entered I found that something peculiar was passing, and it was not long before
I found out what it was. One of the first things I saw
on entering was a man stooping down and having his
ear-rings pulled out by another; he then brought them
and said he would give them to the American Board.
In fact the scene at Oroomiah was enacting here in
Madura. One man after another rose in rapid succession, spoke a few earnest words, and laid down his
offering. One catechist took off a silver chain and
gave it. Thereupon one of the missionaries took off
his chain and gave that. The people are poor, and
have little to live on, but they gave nobly. One with
a monthly salary of two dollars gave four dollars. One
man rose, said he had pots and vessels and cloths to
buy, and had only been a month in employ, he would
give twenty-five cents; one just married gave his wedding-ring. The people, you must know, carry a good
deal of their property on their persons, and wear ornaments profusely. One man said he would sell his hen

and give the price, which he stated to the meeting, but afterwards got up and said he had valued it a cent and a half too low, and must add the difference now. Another gave some chickens, another a handkerchief; another gave for his congregation a dollar, but said that was only a nest-egg, and he hoped that it would bring one hundred dollars before long with it. One man, who had been up four times before, giving money and jewels, got up again, and taking his cloth off, said, " It has only been to the washerman's twice; I'll give that." Another gave a lamp, another a leathern pillow which he had been making as a specimen of his handiwork.

These are but a few instances of those who gave. Over a hundred catechists and teachers were present, and hardly one failed to add something. Above the interest from giving was that from the feeling manifested. The giving was interrupted by constant and hearty prayers. This was but a half-hour prayer-meeting, and an examination was to follow; but they all said, " We would rather pray than recite, — this is not a common day. Let us defer the lessons." How could the missionaries refuse? This was clearly the presence of the Spirit; leave was granted, and a young man arose, the same who had given his wedding-ring, and said: " God, by Joel, promised to pour out his Spirit in the latter days; these are the latter days. Has not the Spirit come?" Many were weeping over the house, and missionaries themselves were overcome. The chairman called for a prayer; two broke out together, and we did not rise before five had poured out their thanksgiving and supplication most fervently. Such emotion and such earnestness in prayer are not often noticeable here. There was no undue excite-

15

ment; all was orderly and quiet. One man said, " Money is no great thing to give, we must offer our health and strength and praise." Another rose and with tears began to confess a wrong of which he had been guilty to his brother. Prayers and offerings were following each other fast; we had been nearly four hours together, and dinner-time had come. So we must stop. We came from the church feeling that this was a remarkable day indeed, such as has rarely been known here. Of course the missionaries have to follow the good example given them, and I know, for the first time, what it costs a poor minister to give. One man gave a cow and a calf, though the calf was not yet actually existing. One said, " We must not despise those who give much, for the Lord Jesus has done this."

The meeting brought about three hundred and fifty dollars, but this has since been raised to about five hundred, for the people all wanted another meeting when the women could come. Saturday we had it: all the school-girls came in, and young and old women and babies. The meeting began by a nice-looking woman stepping up and laying down twenty-five dollars for her husband. This is the largest sum given by any of the natives, and exceeded only by what some of the missionaries gave. A man got up and began to read selections from the Bible; they doubtless were good, but I fear were unheard, for men, women, and children were pressing up to the table, and laying down their offerings. Little tots, that could hardly walk, came up, and old women, who seldom had a cent in their pockets, came, and gave something so small that your currency does not recognize it, but which I doubt not has a value in the kingdom of heaven.

I fear I have made poor work of this most exciting event, in my narrative of it; let me give you some idea of this meeting as a whole. I told you the general object. It is the most stirring scene : one hundred and fifty catechists, teachers, and pastors come together to meet the missionaries for mutual help and instruction, — a visible fruit of thirty years' labor. Some of these men would appear well anywhere, strong characters, zealous Christians, intelligent, quick, well-pleasing. Dressed in their clean white clothes, with their bright faces and winning ways, you can't help loving them ; set them to singing one of the Tamil lyrics, and see if you don't feel that their souls are truly quick with a new life. All the catechists have a course of study laid out for them for each year, in Church History, Bible Exegesis, Theology, and Mental Philosophy ; the teachers have simpler studies. At this meeting they are examined as to their proficiency in the several branches. Each station, too, is reported through the catechist. They have also a Native Evangelical Society, whose object is the support of the pastors in the mission, and its establishment and successful progress are an indication that the piety of the native church is advancing.

The missionaries have also their meetings for business. To-day it was voted that no missionary be sent to a station before he pass a certain examination. He cannot, I mean, have charge of any station as his own till then. Accordingly I cannot have a station assigned me yet. The examination is to be held by the close of the first year, but as much sooner as the individual chooses. Mr. Noyes is anxious to have me share his field by January next ; so I shall try to be ready in

three months.  The course is as follows: written examination and oral; Tamil letter, sermon, and prayer;
translation of a chapter in a Tamil story-book; translation from the Tamil gospels; translation from Todd's
" Lectures to Children " into Tamil; conversation with
a native; exposition of some passage, oral.  The sermon
will be the hardest, and I shall have to study hard to
get through.  There is little doubt that I shall be stationed at Periakulam, and, indeed, the station was divided to-day.

[TO HORACE E. SCUDDER.]

MADURA, Sept. 19, 1861.

. . . . Mission meeting is just over.  You would
have been interested in the business meetings.  I can
see how residence in a mission may tend to educate one
into a man.  You are among equals, and must at once
be independent and yielding.  Important questions
constantly arise, affecting radically the future of the
church in India.  Moreover, you are placed in quite
absolute control of a dozen or twenty men and their
congregations, whom you are to oversee, care for, and
train.  No slight matter this, and a new-comer would,
I think, be impressed with the soberness which seems to
be the natural atmosphere of a mission meeting.  Grave
questions come up, and you cannot possibly shirk them.
I shrink from assuming these responsibilities, and the
mission has put off the day for three months by the
new resolve that no new missionary shall have a station assigned him until he has passed a certain examination, satisfactorily to two examiners.  He is allowed a year to study up.  The examination is difficult,
but I am preparing for a trial in December next.  I

like the plan, it will raise the grade of qualification. For one thing I am to be able to translate any of Todd's stories. I like this part; indeed, it was entered at my suggestion. I begin to look forward to the preparation of some simple Biblical work for children. My history of Madura Mission too is on my mind. . . . Oh, H. ! do step in and chat, won't you ? You hear nothing but confused native songs, and better, chirps of crickets. My fluid lamp burns brightly; it is n't so very different from home, save the wild song of natives passing by. I never knew such singers: they sing perpetually. Tell me all criticisms of " Bib. Sacra " articles. Few enough they will be, and I presume I should be better critic myself than any of them. But do come in. How I wish you would. Come, and I 'll show you heaps of " Types." Do come. Oh that I could *see* you !

[JOURNAL LETTER.]

SEPT. 20.

I have been to see a temple of Pilliyar at the foot of Secanda-malie (Iskander — Alexander, or else Scanda, a Hindû deity — mountain). It lies at the foot of this enormous rock, well called a mountain. Rising sheer out of a wide plain, it is a striking feature in the scenery here. It was dark when we went there, and I have not time to describe what we did see, but it seemed wild to be groping our way about in this old building, which the priests were lighting with dim lamps. The tall pillars, lofty roof, uncouth and fantastic sculpture, and an elephant or two close by your side, all impress one most peculiarly. But my first feelings of curiosity, at the sight of temples and worship of idols, are fast giving place to a sentiment of disgust and aversion. You cannot ride a quarter of a mile in any direction without coming upon some unsightly, dirty, filthy image, and to associate that with any sort of religious worship of human beings is to the last degree offensive to one's feelings. But I am impressed more with the deep, unfathomably deep degradation of the people than with their criminality. Criminal they undoubtedly are ; but if we compare them with the masses at home, we cannot, I think, deny that the great condemnation rests upon the latter. According to Christ, the great fault of men, that of which they are to be convinced by the Holy Spirit, is unbelief in Him. Certainly then the strength of unbelief is to be measured by the weight of opposing evidence, in spite of which the unbelief is persisted in. Weighed by this test, the Hindûs are not as culpable as merely nominal Christians at home. They will be condemned, if condemned at all, on account of unbelief in a God who is to the great body but dimly revealed. People of Christian lands, if condemned, will be so on the ground that they believe neither the Father nor the Son, though all evidence possible, consistent with moral discipline, has been granted.

SEPT. 24.

I have been more than usually saddened to-day by what I have seen of heathenism. I sauntered out for a walk about the great temple. I cannot tell you how I went, or take you with me, without being too minute now. But entering through the great portico, under a pagoda which towers up more than a hundred feet, passing through rows of the goddesses of plenty, before whom were bazaar-men selling their commodities, I stopped to look awhile at the huge holy elephants

which were fanning themselves with banian-branches.
They trumpeted for me, and I left, stepping by a poor
woman who was bowing her head to the stone floor,
and teaching her little child to do likewise ; walked by
one side of a famous tank in which men were washing
their clothes, looked at the absurd paintings on the
walls of the covered way, illustrations of local history,
magnified by myth, until I had gone as far within the
temple as unbelievers are permitted to go. When I
reached the spot there was a fearful din of drums and
shrill fifes and noisy conch-shells. In this part of the
temple sunshine never falls, and as it was now dusk,
all that could be seen was by the aid of dim lights. I
had entered by a narrow passage to a broader one leading in the opposite direction, while directly in front
was the passage to the most sacred place, which profane
feet must not pollute. As I turned the corner my eye
fell on a double line of people, thirty in number, standing by twos quite across the passage, with hands
stretched over their hearts, worshipping. Slipping
into the shadow of a huge pillar I watched them.
They were in front of a little closet-like place in the
opposite wall, — a shrine, large enough to hold three or
four persons ; in a sort of *sanctum sanctorum* was the
image, a rude figure, dressed in flowers. Before it
were two or three persons who were passing and re-
passing lamps, doing what I could not see. As they
moved the lamps, the people bowed their heads, and
at last, after a grand flourish of lights, the din and
clangor, which were perfectly deafening, ceased, and
the line of people facing about fell flat on their faces
upon the pavements and then dispersed. A like
transaction soon after took place in front of the en-

trance to the grand shrine of the goddess of the temple hard by.

As I stood thus gazing, close by the worshippers, yet apart from them, I seemed to have been carried into the very heart of heathenism. By my side was a stone bull sacred to Siva, back of me and opposite, two gigantic statues of deities, smeared with incense offered, while along the gloomy corridor were figures carved out of the stone pillars, casting their unsightly shadows around. I turned and walked along a dingy pathway, where no sunlight ever comes except in feeble glimmerings, and which was hardly passable, lighted by a few dim oil lamps, groping my way before me. A man dogged my footsteps. I was safe enough; yet the whole impression of the place, and the knowledge that many a deed of darkness had doubtless been perpetrated here before now, made me breathe more freely when I gained the open air, and after a few minutes' walk caught sight of our Christian church, embosomed in trees, a silent witness to the truth that there is but one living and true God.

[A few weeks later, the following incident occurred.] I took a stroll this afternoon, and walked into the temple. A crowd followed me as usual, but I did n't mind it, only not feeling very talkative I kept mum. Coming to a high place, and standing awhile, I jumped off, — about six feet, — and left the crowd behind, much to my relief. I had gone but a rod or two, however, before I was brought face about by a brick-bat breaking on my back. I caught up the pieces, and my first impulse was to let drive right at the crowd; but I checked myself, pocketed the insult and the pieces, and walked back to the crowd, which scattered fast. I said nothing, but contented myself with taking a cool survey of all the faces. They slunk away, and I walked back again home. I did not even offer them a piece of advice, but let the whole thing pass, not caring overmuch, except that I did feel like flooring the whole cowardly set, as I might easily have done. I don't know but I was even too pacific. I had said not a word, — indeed this was my fault, for words always put these people in good humor. And I take this as a lesson, for I might have preached a little to them had I chosen. But the fellow who flung the brick must have done it with a will, judging from the effects, for I am quite sore, and only grateful that my head was not struck, which I doubt not is contrary to the wish of the one who threw. Well, I suppose that the people as a whole would be glad to see us all stoned dead.

[TO HIS NIECE, A CHILD.]

OCT. 1.

DEAR BESSIE, — What makes me think of you on your birthday, away here on the other side of this round world? When I left home, your mamma gave me a little book to read every day. There is one page for each day in the year. When I opened it, I found written on the border of many pages the names of different people. What were they? they were the birthdays of all our family. So to-day, when I open this little book, on the side of the page I read, " Little Bessie, 1853." That tells a simple story, and says to me, To-day Bessie is eight years old. Now, why mustn't I write her a birthday letter, as well as to my brothers and sisters and nephews who haven't any " little " before their name? Do you see? I don't.

Another thing makes me think of you very often
indeed, almost as often as I use my pen ; for what is a
pen good for without a pen-wiper, and how should I
have had a pen-wiper if you had n't made me one ?
Here it always lies, right before my eyes, the stars and
stripes, with a Faber's pencil holding them up.    I
never thought before why you put a lead-pencil for the
flag-staff, but now I guess.    Was it not so that when I
should lose all my pens and have no need of a pen-
wiper, I might have a lead-pencil all ready ?

Bessie, do you remember the morning we sailed
from Charlestown, how you bade me good-bye, as if
you were sorry to see me go ?   I do, and I like to think
of it, for it makes me feel you love me and will not
willingly forget me.    You can still be my little Bessie
if you are so far away, and you can still do me good.
You know that when men go deep down into the
earth, in a coal or iron mine, they have to be let down
by other men, who hold a rope that passes over a
windlass, and then goes straight down to the bottom
of the mine.    We have come down into this dark
mine to dig out gold and silver and precious stones
for Christ.    We have been let down here by Christians at home.    They hold a chain which passes up to
God's throne, and then comes straight here.    Each link
in this chain is made up of the prayers which one
Christian prays.    Now, Bessie, if you pray, you will
add one more link, and that will make the chain
longer, so that we can go farther in, and perhaps find
some very precious jewels for the Saviour.    You won't
forget that you have a link to make, will you ? and
don't ever let it get broken.

How I wish that you could drop down upon us from

the skies, or just stop a moment and let the earth
whiz under you till we came to where you were, and
then hop on. I would take you to one famous place
here : it is a temple, and a very large one, larger than
any building you ever saw. I would take you in the
evening, when the priests were lighting the lamps
before the idols. We pass in through the great gates,
and on each side can just see in the dim light the huge
forms of enormous elephants. These are sacred elephants ; and if it were daylight, you could see their
big foreheads all marked with ashes, which the men
put on their own heads as a mark of religion. Step on
a little way, and all at once you come near stumbling
over something on the ground. What is it? it is a
mother and little girl. The mother is flat on her face,
with her hands joined, palms flat against each other,
and she is worshipping a dirty idol in front of her.
Every once in a while she stops and makes the little
girl do just as she does. That little girl, Bessie, is not
as old as you, and yet its mother is teaching it to bow
its little head to an idol. One night, when I was
walking in this temple, I saw quite a number of little
children doing just so, their mothers teaching them.
And so we might walk on through all these dark, dismal rooms and halls, where dozens of idols sit with
lamps burning before them, and all covered with
flowers and oil offered to them. But it is a fearful
place, and we are glad when we get out of doors once
more.

I told you that the people put ashes on their foreheads. It is like the " mark of the beast " which we
read of in Revelation, for it is the sign that the man
who wears them is a heathen ; and so, when sometimes

a man goes back from attending church, instead of saying that he has joined the heathen, we say, " He has
rubbed ashes." One day I was thirty miles away
from here on a visit. Some women were at work
there, pounding mortar, — for women do such work in
India. They stood in a ring around a hole, where
the mortar was, and pounded away as if they were
playing, singing a song all the while. Lots of boys and
girls, some not older than you, were bringing sand
from the river, half a mile off, in baskets on the top of
their heads. There was a brick-kiln close by, where
brick had been burnt, and which was tearing down.
A little girl spied some ashes in the pile; she picked
up about a spoonful, and in great glee ran to one of the
women with it, who rubbed it over the little girl's
forehead, so that it was all white. She ran and
brought some more, and some of the other girls and
women had ashes rubbed on in the same way. Poor
girls! they knew no better, for their mothers taught
them to do just so. I think you would feel badly,
could you see the little boys and girls here.

I wish I could send you a picture of my horse-
keeper's little daughter. Her name is Kali, which is
the name of a very cruel goddess, who is said by the
people to eat up little children. But she is a nice,
bright-eyed thing. She is just about as old as you are,
but I fancy can do some things that you cannot do.
She has been living here all alone with her father, and
has done all the cooking for him! How you would
laugh to see the little girls here, with their odd dresses
and the holes cut in their ears for rings! And I am
sure you would like to go to church, and see the rows
of school-girls, with Bibles and hymn-books in their

laps, looking neat and happy, showing their shiny teeth, that look so brightly from their black faces. But you must really come, if you want to see all the sights, for I can't begin to put them on paper. . . . . .

[JOURNAL LETTER.]

OCT. 5.

. . . . This afternoon I went to the temple where the money-changers and bazaar-men generally resort, as in Solomon's of old. I was desirous of looking at certain books on philosophy. . . . . On the way I saw a game which some boys were playing, which really was very ingenious. A famous festival is close at hand, and these were training for that. A dozen boys were dancing in three concentric rings, each having two sticks, which he alternately beat together and upon the stick of his next neighbor. The outward ring danced round the fastest, so that a boy in the middle ring had three boys in the outer one to play with. They took three or four steps, and then back again. This is quite common; but they played another game for my pleasure: it was in two parts, a war-dance and a hunt. Each boy was armed with a sword in a sheath and a shield. They danced in three lines, dancing two and then back, brandishing their swords, beating them now on their own, now on the next one's shield, who turned round to receive it, backward and forward, spinning on their heels, bobbing down and springing up; then drawing their swords and each choosing his opponent, round and round they whirled, singing a song and keeping music all the while to bells ringing. It was really a pretty sight.

[TO HORACE E. SCUDDER.]

MADURA, Oct. 16, 1861.

. . . . The last mail fairly stuck out with good things ; but what gave the cream to the letters was the appendices, announcing that the communication between America — no, Home and India was perfect. [The letters were written upon receipt of the first letters from India.] I can't put on paper the quick feelings of that hour ; it was almost as blessed a gift to us as our first letters must have been to you. I read and re-read mother's and S.'s notes, and laughed and cried, paced our veranda, feeling that I was indeed in India : no more hopes or fears : we were here, everything about me spoke of it, and fixed for life. Oh, I did long for one look in upon you ! I craved fuller description of the scenes when the letters came.

[TO SAMUEL H. SCUDDER.]

MADURA, Oct. 19, 1861.

. . . . You must let me know what special books you are studying, what particular insect you are cocking your microscopic eye at. India does not come up to my idea in the way of Nature. There are very few birds within the limits of my observation, very little beautiful foliage or bloom, very few insects. I certainly have been struck rather by the absence even of the latter than by their presence. I have bottled and canned a few things. To-day I put in a tiny squirrel to rest lovingly upon the body of a big snake. A pretty mess you will find. But if you wish, I can get any quantity of fish from the rivers. These tanks are marvellous. In the hot season most are completely dry ; but in a very few weeks after the rain falls, you

can get fish for the table. Go out any morning, and
you see the brooks and tanks lined and covered with
fishermen casting their queer little nets, and fumbling
along in the mud with their hands to catch the diminu-
tives. At night you meet the same coming home,
dressed up in their nets, their baskets on their heads,
and their nets hanging from the baskets, making a
fringe all round their bodies, — a droll sight.

[JOURNAL LETTER.]

OCT. 25.

. . . . I have commenced street-preaching. Now
this sounds important and looks bold, but it is less of
both, or both in a different way from what you fancy.
I have been feeling for some time that I might be doing
more than I was for the heathen. I knew that I could
not do much, but the assurance that it was not the
multitude of words or fluency of utterance that achieved
the result in view has been often before me, and I determined to break the ice and to do it alone. So a few
mornings since, armed with a pocket full of tracts and
my pocket Tamil Testament, with a mark at the story
of the Prodigal Son, I sallied forth, I will confess, with
some uneasiness. I chose a little village that I had noticed one day aside from the main road. By the way,
there are plenty of such places in and about the city;
if you step just outside of city limits, you can turn into
almost any footpath which will bring up in a village.
I waded over a brook on my horse, walked into a village and through it, adding at each step another to the
train of followers. At the other end was a little open
space with a raised platform. I halted and the people
stood about, looking at me as if I had been Cortez and

they Indians of the West.' I began by asking the name
of the village; receiving a satisfactory reply, I asked
them if they would like to hear a story. You see I
could n't enlarge much upon any topic, and my transi-
tion from one to another was necessarily abrupt. However they assented, and I, pulling my Testament out,
read to them the parable.

This I could do tolerably well, and they all listened
quite attentively. After that was over I told them that
God was our father; that we had all sinned against
Him. "We are all sinners," said I. "Yes," said a
man, "you are a sinner." This was meant for a sally
of wit I suppose, but I of course said a hearty Amen
to it. Then several burst in with — "If we worship
your God, will he give us clothes and corn?" to which
I could only reply, stammering, that the right heart
was better than food or clothing. I was about exhausted as to available material for conversation, so
taking out my tracts I distributed to those who could
read, and turned toward home with a light heart, not
because of my success in talking, but because I had
tried to do some good; that cheered me.

The next day I went in another direction, but found
no village. However, as I was examining a deserted
temple, some men came near and I asked them what
idol was worshipped there. They told me it was Pilliyar; and I then asked why they prayed to such
an idol. "Oh," they replied, "our fathers and mothers did and so must we; it is custom." I replied
that if their parents had a bad custom they ought not
to follow it. "If they were thieves must you be?"
and then asked them why they prayed to a god which
could not hear. To that they answered nothing;

whether the question struck them or my poor Tamil posed them I cannot say, but I fear the latter. I gave them some tracts and rode home.

Now these two occurrences are not specially remarkable, but they are interesting to me. One great part of my work ought to be to go out into the highways and hedges and compel these people to come in. It is not in itself a very pleasant thing, yet if one is willing to be a laughing-stock for his awkward speech and his unloved doctrines, it is not difficult; and when we think how much more fitting pity is than anger, it seems an easy thing thus to speak. The word of the Lord is to be preached as a witness, — the field is to be sown, dropping one seed at a time, — if my ungrammatical words are vain, yet I can read, and I hope to keep the practice up. Moreover it is a decided benefit to my Tamil. The two objections which I met are characteristic ones, ones most potent with the people: Custom rules everything, and the Belly is the God.

[LETTER TO SUNDAY-SCHOOLS.]

MADURA, SOUTH INDIA, Oct. 29, 1861.

MY DEAR YOUNG FRIENDS, — My first letter to you from India was dated "Dindigal." This was the first missionary station which we reached in coming from Madras. This second letter I write to you from Madura, which we will call the capital of our missionary country. Please look this place out on the map, so that you may know exactly where it is. It is quite a large city. But all the missionaries do not live here, any more than all the ministers of Massachusetts live in Boston. There are twelve of us, but only one

16

lives in Madura. The others are in towns around this, twelve or sixteen, or thirty or fifty miles away.

If we would preach to the heathen, we must go to them, for they will not come to us; and as some of them live a good way off, we go in carts, or on horse-back, to see them. Last night I came home from a trip of three days, which I took with an older missionary; as I was riding back on my little pony I thought I must write you a letter about some of the strange things which I had seen; and here it is.

Bright and early on Saturday morning I started off on my pony, and after losing my way among the rice-fields, at last found the village I was looking for, about eight miles from Madura, and there met Mr. Burnell, who had come from his home, ten miles in the other direction, to preach to the people in this village. We went into one of the school-houses, where is a school for boys and girls, such as you pay for. There we sat down in some chairs that were brought to us, the only chairs, I suppose, in the village; for, you know, all the school-children and teachers sit right down in the sand which is the floor. The school-house, like all others, had mud walls and a straw roof. We heard the little boys recite their lessons in geography, Bible questions, and other studies. One lesson they had which you will think a strange one. They have to learn the diction-ary by heart! They say off the words and give the meaning to them just as fast as they can talk; they sing them off, for their books are written in a sort of rhyme.

After we had heard the lessons, we had a meeting for the old people; for this mud house was the church, as well as the school-room. As the people were com-

ing in, I saw a poor-looking woman, with a baby in her
arms, climbing over a high wall and taking a seat outside the house on the ground. What do you suppose
she was climbing over the wall for, when there was a
wide door and plenty of room inside? It so happened
that there were three or four men, not richer perhaps,
but of a higher " caste " than herself, and she was afraid
that if she passed near them they would be angry, and
scold at her, or beat her. In this heathen land all men
are not equal, as we say they are in America ; but
there are a great many different classes or castes. It
is thought a sin for any two people of two different
castes to eat together.

After preaching in this place we went to visit some
of the people in their houses. While we were in one
of them, we heard a dull, heavy, drum-like sound.
" There," said Mr. Burnell, "there is a *Kodangki;*
shall we go and see him ? " A Kodangki ; what is that?
He is a soothsayer, or magician, or prophet who tells
fortunes and professes to tell where anything is which
has been lost, — to be able to cure sick people, — to
drive the devil out of them, — to make it rain, and to
do many other things for a little money. The poor
heathen believe he can do all these things, and many
are the pennies that they place before him. As I had
never seen one I was glad to go. We found the wise
man sitting by the door of a devil-temple next to his
own house. He was a young man and fine looking.
He had white ashes rubbed on his forehead. In his
hand was a drum, shaped like an hour-glass, and from
this little drum hung a belt, and on this belt dangled
lots of glass beads and sweet-smelling seeds of fruit.
It has not rained here enough to make the rice grow,

and he was singing to the god to bring the water. He stopped a little while after we came in ; and then Mr. Burnell, after talking to him, took out a dollar from his pocket and said, " I will give you this if you can tell me what I write on this paper." He wrote my name in Tamil and put the paper away. The man looked rather ashamed, but began to call on his gods. He thumped on the drum, and sucking in his breath till he grew red in the face, sang in a loud voice, crying out to the gods to tell him the secret. After puffing and singing about a quarter of an hour, he gave the answer : " You have written," he said, "about a man that people in America are disputing about." When he found how wrong he was, he did n't seem to care much, for he knew that the people, who were around him, would believe him, even if he did guess wrong. And sure enough, we had only just left the house when we heard him thumping his drum again, as some one had come to get him to bring the rain down.

The next day was the Sabbath, and it was my first birthday in this heathen land. In the cool of the morning I went away from the noise of the village, and lay down on the grass, with the sky above, which looks the same all over the earth, and in full view of the mountains, which made me think of the mountains I knew at home. Then I thought of my far-off friends, my father and mother and brothers and sisters, and I knew that they would think of me too this day. I tried to pray that God would make me a faithful servant of His, in this land to which I had come to preach His word. Will any of you ever spend a birthday in a heathen land ?

That day we preached and talked to the people, as

all missionaries do every Sabbath-day. I must not
forget to tell you that a poor woman, who had no
money, brought in, as her weekly contribution, a
wooden bowl of grain. So the next morning we had
a little auction and sold it. It brought just one cent,
a small sum, but large, I doubt not, in the eyes of the
Saviour.

Monday morning we rose before daybreak, so as to
go to a famous temple. After riding about an hour
we came to it. We were not sorry to see that many
of the buildings around it were tumbling down. Do
you remember hearing how the little banian-seed, lodg-
ing between the stones of a temple, takes root and
grows, till it splits the rocks and one by one they fall
to the ground? Just so it was here; great temples had
crumbled into ruins, looking far more pleasing to us
than when they were all whole with a greasy idol
within. But there was one temple still in use, and it
is a famous one. We were walking in to see what was
inside, when a man, and then three or four others,
rushed to us, saying, "Go back; go back; you can't
come here." "Why not?" "Oh, this is a holy place!"
So we went back. We then went into another place,
swinging open two enormous doors, over thirty feet
high and a foot thick. A man tried to keep us from
going in, but we pushed ahead. What do you suppose
his reason was? "Why," said he, "you are white
people, and can do anything; but if a black man
should go in there without leave, he would never come
out alive." It is a sacred place. There the people go
who want to make vows. They take an oath, and
throw sandal-wood up against the doors, and then
never dare to tell a lie.

We went up into a high tower of the temple, where we could see a long way off. Mr. Burnell shouted out to the people below, " Christ's kingdom shall come; and all the idols he shall destroy." So it shall come, we believe, if we do what our Saviour commands us to do. But we must work hard. " I would rather have my throat cut than be a Christian," said a man a few days ago.

Pray much, children of the Sabbath-school; and if God permit you, come out to this or to some other heathen land, to tell the people yourself of Christ. Now when people write letters they expect answers. Won't you answer this and cheer up your friend?

DAVID C. SCUDDER.

[TO D. T. FISK, D. D., NEWBURYPORT, MASS.]

MADURA, Nov. 5, 1861.

. . . . I am indeed in India, and somewhat better acquainted with it than when my ship-letter started off in search of you. And I am in Madura, the metropolis of this missionary kingdom. It is already a home to me. I thread the narrow passages of this Oriental city with as much familiarity and nearly as much indifference as you would Boston. The queer capers of naked urchins kicking up the dust, lines of men, women, and children, all bearing the mark of the devil emblazoned on their foreheads, idols, shops, temples, have all lost their novelty, while if you could be set down here directly from Newburyport, without stirring a step you would find food enough for a long day's wonderment. I was thinking to-day of a commonly accepted idea among missionary circles at home, and which I once often broached, viz: that it was well that new-comers could not open their mouths for a while, since thus they were not in danger of hurting people's feelings unintentionally.  Now this may be true of other countries, but nobody need fear, on the first day of his arrival, speaking boldly of Christ if he is able to. Common sense is enough ; a few weeks' stay gives one a reasonable acquaintance with native character.

There are some phases of native character which I think one does not anticipate.  Such, for instance, is their utter deadness of spirit, and sensuousness.  Go out and meet any company of heathen, urge upon them the duty of worshipping God.  "Who has seen him? Will he fill our belly?  We do as our fathers did," are the three stock answers, always at hand, satisfactory to them, unblushingly presented.  What special part of our theologic training has fitted us to meet such objections?  They are so utterly *low* that it is. hard to get down low enough to meet them on their own ground. The country has been suffering much from lack of rain.  I don't know how many times I have been met by the question, — "Will he give us rain?" while the processions that pass our door with sheaves of grain to be offered to the river-goddess show where the heart of this people is.

I wish you could mount your pony and ride out with me some morning about sunrise, to see whom we might meet, drop a tract and attempt a little advice.  It is a motley group that gathers around you when you stop, all respectful, but none sympathizing.  They meet your words with an incredulous smile and always have some reply at hand.  You may talk on and they will listen ; they hear as if they listened to a story or talk about crops ; rarely can you feel that one is moved a whit by any sayings of yours. Such is the work that lies before us: to proclaim the truth whether men will hear or whether they will forbear. Discouraging as it is, you find people who have many pleasing traits about them, who are ready to assist you in any way, always pleasant, quiet in their demeanor, amiable, lacking only the one thing. I can't help loving them. The children I like, particularly the boys. Bright-eyed little chaps, they are as fond of frolic as any Christian children, and their sports always please me.

A thorough missionary's work here is, indeed, different from pastoral labor at home. He has a church to care for, but his time is occupied with petty troubles. Four-fifths of his time often, or nearly that, he is away from home, living in mud school-houses, sleeping in his cart, or in a native rest-house, preaching morning and evening in the wretched villages, and having the day occupied with calls; no retirement, no leisure. A faithful missionary leads a roving life. It is self-denying. One of our most zealous tourists has travelled incessantly in his field for four years past with scarcely appreciable result; result, I mean, in conversions. It surely is a result that almost all the villagers in his district know in a measure the leading features of Christianity. The sowing of the seed alone is our duty.

. . . . How many lines of study I should delight to pursue, were I in America. Here one has precious little spare time for reading, and it is next to impossible to study upon sermons, as you would for a New England audience, when you have to preach in the most simple style possible. It is really painful to visit any of the villages where people have put themselves under instruction, and see how sadly ignorant they are of even cardinal points of the faith. Then again you have occasion to rejoice when a candidate for the pastoral office presents himself, as one did at the last general meeting, who has come directly from among the heathen, and merely by his private study of the Bible has attained views of the truth surprisingly clear and mature, even discriminating between faith and works as neatly as a practised theologian. Such preachers we want, taught of God as they clearly are.

[TO REV. CHARLES R. PALMER, SALEM, MASS.]

MADURA, Nov. 13, 1861.

. . . . Here is this great, heathenish city, where idolatry and every crime flaunt you in the face. When will it be overpowered and made a city of the Great King? The question forces itself repeatedly upon you as you listen to a missionary address a crowd in the streets, and see the unmoved or scornful faces of the people who stop to hear this doctrine. Slow work, and what we need above all things is more faith in the might of God that is to conquer. I am as comfortable and happy as if I were at home, though I do so long at times to have a good long look at the dear faces left behind. I am surprised at the climate : I suffer more from chilliness than from heat; at the water, too cool to need ice ; at the people, amiable, obliging, interesting; at all, in fact, which affects one's happiness here. One can enjoy life with as little sacrifice of personal feeling, if he choose, as at home, or nearly so. Perhaps, however, I should feel less contented had I no object beyond *living*. But you must not think of me as a martyr at all, or as necessarily very *good* for staying here. But there is the fact of the terrible degradation of this people that does oppress one, — such hovels as some of them do live in, and so far removed do they appear from the possibility of renovation.

[TO SAMUEL H. SCUDDER.]

MADURA, Nov. 15, 1861.

. . . . What a dear old man father is! Somehow or other he is losing his paternity, to me in particular, in my thoughts; he is gradually looming up as the impersonation of the true Father, always venerable, yet always endowed with the gift of youth, benignant, and constantly wearing a face full of sweet content and quiet joy. I believe I am *sort* of deifying him. Now, that's nonsense, I suppose, but the more I think of it, the more I wonder at father. . . . . But, dear me! I must stop; I can't say anything, and it makes me almost cry to write anything.

[TO HIS SISTER.]

MADURA, Nov. 16, 1861.

. . . . Though I am in India, I have not run away from all my troubles. I still have fits of blues much as of old. I might as well give up attempting to excuse myself, and say that I am both a sinner and a fool. I am afraid to go out in the morning and talk, though there is nothing which should deter a really zealous man. I find, too, that I am not so quick at catching by ear as I hoped I might be. I may possibly not judge myself fairly, but at any rate I feel a reluctance toward engaging in conversation with any one, which acts directly as a hindrance against my learning to talk. It requires a strong resolve to set me at talking. When once in my own station, may God help me to be faithful! Grace can do what nothing else can, and I feel deeply that I need, more than aught else, a thorough hold on Christ, and the possession of all the animating thoughts connected with such faith as shall naturally quicken me in work.

[TO HIS FATHER.]

MADURA, Nov. 28, 1861.

Is it Thanksgiving-day at home? It is here, for the mail is in, and your letter has come. Let me with all my heart applaud that determination of which this letter from you is the earnest, of keeping a sort of journal for us to read. It is exactly the thing, — the one of all others that we need, — a connected account of affairs, into which all other private special notes, however long, shall fall and find their place. . . . . Dear father, it does make us very happy to think of you as happy too. I certainly feel it matter of devout thankfulness that your peace of mind has not been broken by losses. There is no picture in the whole home group that is so bright and blessed to me as that of you, and mother with you. You know I am no hand to put down or speak out all I feel, but your mere existence is a joy to me that I can't possibly express. There seems to be absolutely nothing in my lot to detract from my perfect happiness. . . . . I don't know of a single privation that we suffer, which we feel, except such as are incidental to being away from home. Our circle is a very pleasant one, and we are becoming more and more interested in it, and shall soon have plenty of work to do. We do need most deeply the supplications of friends in our behalf, and not the least because we have even here so many earthly props. No conjunction of circumstances, I find, can force a man to become a saint.

Nov. 20.

The most noticeable event in nature lately is the " coming down " of the river. " The river is down " is the common phrase here to denote, not that it is low, but high, and it is a fit word. Day before yesterday, in the bed of this river, half a mile wide, was only a channel of water a rod or two across ; now, the river is full from bank to bank. The late rain (for this is the rainy season) has filled the river in a day and night; not so much, however, the rains here as those up the stream. This is the crowning blessing of the rainy season. All the main tanks are fed by the river, and if these are not supplied, there is no water for the rest of the year, or none of much account. You may readily conceive of what inestimable value the rains are to this people, and it is no wonder that in their worship they make so much of prayer for rain. The tanks are large enclosures, with mud embankments, of various shapes and sizes, some of them two or three miles in diameter. These are supplied by the annual rise of the river, and the water is kept carefully guarded, being wholly under the charge of the several village authorities, who apportion so much time for drawing water to each separate field. The whole system of irrigation is very strictly arranged. Just now the fields of rice look most charmingly. I never saw so rich a green, and you can look in some directions for miles with scarce a break in the soft carpeting.

[TO REV. SIMEON WOODIN, FUH CHAU, CHINA.]

MADURA, Nov. 27, 1861.

. . . . Well, how do the mild-eyed, pig-tailed Chinese suit your notion of the true, beautiful, and good? Is it possible to penetrate behind the skin, and really find a human heart? I always think of a Chinaman as enclosed in a sort of porcelain wrapper, smooth enough, but forbidding any but the most gentle handling. Is there anything to *love* there? or do you have to suppose a substratum really lovable, but imperceptible to mortal ken? The Chinese seem a class thrust aside from other mortals, differing *in toto cœlo* from all others of the human race. Such an uncouth language, such a singular polity, such an unexampled *potpourri* of religious faiths, where one may take his pick or swallow the whole. They certainly are an interesting study. By the way, do you expect to save your shreds of time for study of the people? Some of your celestial missionaries have brought the world under obligation by their labors; shall you join their circle? Which rule of faith appears to you to have strongest hold upon the people? Do Buddhists look toward India with anything of veneration as the birthplace of their faith? Do they hold at all, nowadays, to their old metaphysical dogma of annihilation as the blessed end of all four evils? *Nirvana?* I have looked into Indian Buddhism a little, and have found a good deal to interest; certainly its system of ethics is far beyond anything that Brahmanism has ever been able to propound.

What a beehive must be constantly buzzing about your ears! We have no such swarms of people here, I fancy, as you describe. Indeed, the country does not seem to be over-populated, though hamlets are scattered thickly here and there. I am glad you take so kindly to your adopted tongue. Forgive me my cruel aspersions upon its character. I can hardly believe yet that Hindû children can whisper and laugh and chat as readily in Tamil as I can in English. Are there any such things as native Christian lyrics among you? A great step for Christianity has been taken here by bringing forward native Christian poetry. The people sing native melodies with a will, but foreign importations with difficulty. Do any of your missionaries speak Chinese as fluently as they do English? Such is not an uncommon thing here. I find my previous study of Tamil a solid help. . . . A spirit of benevolence has come upon us, new here, and evidently from above. But the work of conversion is slow in progress, and the people are deplorably low in their state. It is utterly disheartening to labor among them, if one does not look for help beyond himself. The Christianization of a people who for generations upon generations have been descending in the stage of morality and religion, must itself be a work of many generations. God moves slowly, but time is nothing to Him. We can only watch and adore.

[TO REV. CHARLES NEWMAN.]

MADURA, Nov. 27, 1861.

. . . . Put far out of your fancy any notion of tropical luxuriance hereabout. There is no rankness save that of countless goats and sheep too scant to shear. Grass grows in clumps. Blossoms, driven from the bosom of earth, are fain content to show themselves on high trees. Not a bird in these regions is there that could outshine or outsing a home thrush or honest robin. Animals look like scarecrows. Elephants lopped off behind, camels with broken backs, hairless dogs, buffaloes that seem to have been formed from surplus mud, hump-backed cows and oxen, and last and least poor donkeys that hobble about, leading a wretched life between the washer-men who load them down with bundles that turn all their joints out and me who impound them for trespassing on my grass. No, if you want to see Nature in her best attire, don't come out here, at least not if you are to be a dweller on the plains. Give me sturdy New England. An hour's drive in any part will show you more beauty than I have seen thus far here. " Only man is vile," is a vile slander on that abused individual. Man is the only redeeming feature in the scene, and because he can be redeemed.

Now the heathen may set me down as highly magnanimous, for only yesterday, while walking in the temple, one of them took the occasion to break a brickbat over my back, succeeding in his endeavor, but almost breaking me. That temple is a fearful place, the gloomiest, most dread-inspiring of any hole I was ever in. The bats have occupied it before their time; and what with their stench, and the filthy odor from offerings and incense, the pitchy darkness, and the stealthy tread of worshippers coming and going, some parts of it seem to border close upon the lower regions. One can imagine almost any deed of darkness as having been perpetrated there in years past, and, for aught I know, in the *penetralia* where no profane foot may walk such deeds are done now; certainly licentiousness riots there and no one can say nay. Oh, this heathenism is a fearful thing; you dislike to look into it to explore its secrets, for you feel almost certain that there is no wickedness which is undiscoverable there, and that could you fathom all its depths and penetrate all its hidden recesses, forms of crime would meet you that you never dreamed of or thought man capable of committing.

In such a state of society how can we look at once for a pure, spotless church? The family is no longer, or not yet, the sacred spot that it is at home. It is impossible to guard a child from evil as one may at home. As far as we can, we encourage the forming of Christian communities in villages where Christianity has made any progress, though we are glad too to have a genuine Christian testifying for Christ among the heathen where He was found. In certain cases one should abide in the spot as well as in the calling wherein he was called. It is a pleasant thing to find here and there a faithful laborer for Christ, and to hear the testimony of his faithfulness from the heathen. The other day as I was out with a missionary we came across a man and had a long talk with him. He finally said — "Abraham has told us all about this." Abraham was a poor man, an out-caste, not allowed to have his dwelling near the other villagers, but living on a rocky hill with others of his own position. Two years ago he came to Mr. Rendall and asked to be baptized. Mr. Rendall examined him, but to all his questions he got but one reply, "I am a sinner; Jesus died for me." He did not refuse the poor man's request; and from that day Abraham, as he was named, has preached in his poor, but acceptable way, to the people of the village. Thus here and there the gospel penetrates; we sow the seed, it shoots up and runs along, and shoots again, and so it will continue to, we believe.

Our work in form is not materially different from yours, but how widely different are the fields we cultivate. We see, when the truth takes effect, another proof of the mysteriousness of that process by which the soul accepts the truth and is changed by it. It is a process whose nature theology does not teach. How utterly hopeless heathenism is! I was reading the other day, in a book comparing Hindûism and Christianity, of the characteristic traits of the contrasted faiths. The element of the Christian or Biblical religion in all its history was Hope. But of the lack of that in Hindûism I had an instance at sight yesterday. As I was walking through a street I heard a loud, mournful wailing. Looking into the house whence it issued I saw a sight that really touched me. Three elderly women sat on the floor facing each other, with their arms closed round each others' necks; they were swaying to and fro, with their heads bowed, and pouring forth most doleful lamentations. Some one had died in the house, and they were thus giving vent to their grief. In that death there was no hope; no relieving feature in that departure from earth. The people dislike to think of it. Speak to them of their certain death at some future day, and they start back with an involuntary cry, thinking the mere mention of the name of death an ill omen to them.

. . . . Let me sketch a day's life. I rise at six, bathe, order pony, mount and ride two or three miles out, planning to stop in some of the countless mud villages at hand and try my Tamil in preaching a little. A crowd of twenty or more soon collect, I hand them

17

tracts and ask some simple question. There is no lack of answers, for such a people to talk I never did see. I have never met a native yet who, if ordered to preach a sermon on the spot before a large audience, would not do it with the greatest possible ease. After talking awhile, and becoming sufficiently confused by replies and counter-questions, wholly unintelligible to me, I return home to a cup of tea and slice of toast at seven. Then after studying either Genesis or Matthew an hour or so, we sit down to breakfast at nine. After breakfast Tamil prayers with servants, which I am just beginning to lead. Then I study Tamil stories, write on sermons and do like work until four o'clock, dinner-time, the interval being broken by *tiffin* (luncheon) at one. At half-past five we order our American rockaway, and H. and I drive off on some of the numerous hard, broad, pleasant roads, to get a long breath of pure air, and a freshening view of fields and clouds and hills. We can see the towering Pulneys fifty miles westward, and numerous other lesser hills skirt nearly the whole horizon. Then comes tea, if we take any, as we have not to-night, and after tea always letter-writing home. This routine is broken up Thursday evening by a prayer-meeting, occurring alternately at the three houses near each other, and by Sunday. On Sunday I attend Tamil service at church in morning, and did at one time hear some boys recite in Sunday-school. In the afternoon I ride out with Mr. Rendall in his ox-bandy to some village near by, where he has a congregation. He gives the meeting to me, and I then and there expound before a poor set of people who form the congregations. So I stammer along. . . . .

[TO REV. EVARTS SCUDDER.]

MADURA, Dec. 6, 1861.

. . . . To-night I ought to feel in just the mood for talking with home friends, for we are fairly alone in our house, the first time in six weeks. So we are sitting in our hall, all doors open, — no windows in the house you know, — H. by me just beginning to write. S.'s vase is the prominent object on the table, topped as it is by a pyramidal bouquet and set off by a dish full of flowers by its side. "Rivers of France" lies by it, and our book-rack, with "Palfrey's New England," "Oxford Essays," "Irving's Knickerbocker," "Shedd's Augustine," "Lyra Domestica," "Companions of My Solitude," and so on, to set it off, and show our daily reading. Our famous fluid gas-lamp casts a genial glow over the whole, while the old eight-day clock ticks familiarly from the wall. What a good time we would have could S. and you and Charley drop in on us. It is really home within these walls, though the thud! thuddety-thud! of a sorcerer comes to us on the evening breeze, as he beats his drum not far off, and dins heathenism into our ears.

. . . . My reading is not particularly elevating. I translate Todd's stories into Tamil and Tamil stories into English. The latter are generally barren enough. One of the best I met with to-day. Two swans and a turtle wanted to migrate from a tank, but the turtle said he did n't know how to go. So the swans told him to take hold of a stick with his mouth, and they would carry him between them, but they charged him not to talk on the way. As they were flying with him over a village, the people saw them and laughed. The turtle hearing the great noise forgot the charge, and

asked what it was; whereupon, having opened his
mouth to talk, down he dropped and was speedily
extinguished. "So," is the moral, "will it be with
all who do not heed friendly advice."

. . . . I keep a book to note down impressions and
facts, and whenever I put one in, I think to myself
how will this sound twelve years hence in a speech at
home? You see home is not all lost to me. I am as
happy here as I ever could be at home, and if I choose
to avail myself of them there are opportunities for usefulness, equal at least to such as meet you.

[JOURNAL LETTER.]

DEC. 20.

In my last entry I said " news is rare, nowadays."
But times have changed. There is a wee bit of news
which I may communicate to the home public. It is
in the shape of a little girl who has dawned upon our
Indian home during this past week. It is a very awkward position to put a man in, this of chronicler of
such an event. One is in danger of exaggerating the
importance of the occurrence and its destined effect
upon the fortunes of the world, when he is himself an
interested party. Besides, what can one say about such
a small matter as this particular one is. It has of
course been duly weighed and compared with all other
babies, and positively declared to be the crowning baby,
and to resemble remarkably both sides of the house.
But I find some drawbacks to its perfection. It has a
most unaccountable faculty at sleeping, and the utter
coolness with which it drops asleep night and day is to
me perfectly appalling, suggesting most unhappily the
fat boy in Pickwick. Pray, do all babies indulge thus?

and do they think there is nothing better to do? I think this baby takes after its father, who would indulge in the same, if he dared. It is the fashion here to advertise your babies, so the first duty which I had to attend to was to write notes indefinitely, announcing the arrival of a new member in our circle. Replies of congratulation are pouring in, and with them all sorts of knicknacks for baby.

[If the last letter contained the only announcement of the birth of my brother's child, one might be surprised, knowing his temperament, at the matter-of-fact way in which it was made. But this was a letter for general circulation among his friends at home; he had already given vent to his feelings in a previous special letter to his mother, brimful of the most grotesque expressions; in that he capered about the subject with the most amusing mental antics, laughing and half crying by turns; and afterward in private letters he was running over with glee whenever he began to speak of his child, which was not seldom, as may be guessed. Even in his more public letters he had sometimes to say what he wanted to, but generally he practised a reasonable restraint which I follow with some reluctance.

I have not thought it necessary to print the frequent comments upon the progress of the war in America. When the missionaries landed at Madras they were first made aware of the breaking out of hostilities, and with every fresh intelligence they wrote cheerfully or despondently according as affairs looked prosperous or doubtful. They could not help making speculations respecting the issue, immediate or final, but these when they reached America were generally amusing from their remoteness from fact. It was rather disagreeable also to be reminded four months afterward of untoward events which we were all trying to forget. In every letter David wrote earnestly about the war, though visited, every once in a while, by the reflection that his comments must be very odd when read so long after the events commented upon had taken place.]

[JOURNAL LETTER.]

DEC. 24.

. . . . This is delicious weather. I have just looked at the thermometer. It stands at 78° in this room. The mornings are very cool and bracing, and we never think of complaining of heat at all in the day. I never was more comfortable at home, except that I am constantly catching cold. This is Christmas eve. We have no snow or frost here; if we should celebrate the day at all, it would be in honor of the victory which an extra telegram apprises us of to-day — the capture of Beaufort. We have been on tiptoe ever since hearing of the fleet's sailing, and have been looking out for good news. Now it has come, and we take a good long breath. . . . . As soon as a telegram reaches Madura it is copied and sent to every missionary. We are not dead here, I can tell you, and almost every shade of political sentiment at the North, outside of radical pro-slavery views, finds its representative and strenuous advocate amongst us.

DEC. 26.

I must add one sentence, though I have been out to Pasumalie to meeting to-night. Just before starting I caught sight of a donkey trespassing on our grounds. So, as I am a sworn foe to all this kind, I sang out to the gardener to put him in the pound, but instead of saying *kaluthei*, donkey, I said *kalanthei*, baby, and coolly told him to impound the baby. It shows where my mind runs, but the gardener looked dumbfounded, and there was an ominous whispering among the servants near.

This morning we were astounded out of measure by a telegram from Madras : " An unofficial telegram announces that England has declared war with the United States on account of the forcible seizure of the Confederate Commissioners from a West India mail steamer," or something to that effect. It was a bomb thrown into our company, coming right upon the last good news. What can it be? All here pronounce it a hoax, yet the rumor is bad enough. One of the first effects I thought of as following a rupture was, that you might not hear of baby's birth!

. . . . Christmas this year chanced to agree with a heathen feast-day, and there was quite a display by the votaries of the great idol here. A great procession went round the city, accompanying images of the goddess and her spouse. They were borne in two immense bamboo pyramidal pavilions on the shoulders of men. Two elephants with gay trappings stalked along with the crowd, and lots of men bearing umbrellas with immensely long handles, having no apparent use. The feast-day is in connection with some legend of the tutelary deity of Madura, and one of the peculiar features of the show is that bushels of rice are thrown to the ants, in commemoration, they say, of something that the idol did ages back. I saw men bearing rice and scattering it by ant-holes on the road-side. Just at the gate I came upon a crowd surrounding a man who was fitted out in a most comical manner. He was wearing crinoline, but in a way that made him appear as if riding horseback. The crinoline frame was shaped like a horse, with a head projecting forward. It was a droll-looking thing, not exactly a perfect illusion, but enough to puzzle you as to how the thing was fixed. The people here certainly love fun.

DEC. 30.

.... This is weighing day, baby Julia having completed another week of her earthly existence, but we forgot to do our duty. You would laugh to see how reverentially the natives treat her. Every morning regularly the sweeping-woman, when she comes in, marches up to the bed and presents her respects to the miss; and Mrs. Capron's cook coming in to-day called on us, and presented Julia with a posy, making a most profound salaam. All the first class in the girls' school came over on Saturday last to see her, and amused us mightily by measuring where her feet came to, to see how short she was.

JANUARY 1, 1862.

Happy New Year! Well, we renew our journey under a new sky and under different auspices from those which smiled on us one year ago, and as I write the words, " Happy New Year," it is with a sad and heavy heart that has been weighing me down for a fortnight past. Will these words ever reach your ear? .... But I won't write useless words, but be a faithful chronicler, until we hear that further writing is useless. Yesterday we all went out to dine. When we got home, about half-past ten, I found quite a gathering of servants on the back veranda, plotting about something, and guessing what, I drew back and said nothing. All night there was confused talking and all sorts of noises, and lo! on waking and opening the front doors, all the veranda was decorated with plantain-stalks and leaves, festooned gracefully along the whole length, and adorned further by bunches of flowers, hanging from strings. It was quite a pretty sight, and spoke well for the taste of our household. There was to be a meeting at half-past eight, so we breakfasted at seven. After we had done, Savarimuttu asked H. to sit still, and retiring, returned presently heading the whole troop, tailor, washer-man, cook-boy, gardener, horse-keeper, sweeper, and *ayah* (nurse), bearing a big tray covered with golden plantains. Each of the company then presented each of us with a lime and little posy, while two or three hung garlands of flowers round our necks. Baby was summoned, and tailor hung about its precious neck a pure and delicate wreath made of the beautiful pith. It was a really lovely gift. Savarimuttu also presented H. with quite a pretty pith dove perched on wire. We could n't keep our heavy garlands on long, so H. took hers off, and Savarimuttu very gracefully hung it upon father's picture, making a profound salaam; whereupon I, taking the hint, hung mine on H.'s father's picture, and paid my respects likewise. All appeared greatly delighted.

JAN. 4.

Courage revives; details of news by to-day's paper leads me to hope that war will be averted and news of baby reach you! To-night it rains steadily, an immense blessing, if it will but rain enough to fill the tanks. A famine is imminent, and nothing but a plenteous rain at once can avert it. A serious affray occurred at a village not far distant, when two young English officers undertook to force a village, whose tank was full, to allow water to run from it to a tank belonging to a neighboring village. It was against all custom, which is law here, and the consequence of the attempt was that the villagers mustered in force, armed with slings. and a fray ensued ; the Sepoys under the English shot three men ; one of their own number and an Englishman were wounded. My mûnshi tells me that it is a maxim among this people to give their lives for their grain.

. . . . We have a new cook. We had to dismiss our last; he got wind of what we were to do, and accordingly drew up a petition, which I add as a sample of the way things are done here. What lawyer drew it up for him I can't say — not himself.

### " THE HUMBLE PETITION OF MARIANNAN, COOK.

With all marks of respect and submission I beg to state that I was brought up from my boyhood in the business of maty, and was doing the same until the time I was engaged as a cook under you. This I was obliged to do partly for want of demand (!) and partly to maintain myself and family in this time of severe drought. I am not so much experienced in the latter as I am in the former. I hope I could easily and clearly manage the business of the maty, as well as giving to the Mr. and Mrs. satisfaction every way. This you can readily know by perusing my testimonials. I beg to state lastly, that if you please, you could exchange my present duty for that of the maty Savarimuttu, who had been engaged as cook for the space of three years under the Rev. Mr. Chandler. You will be kindly pleased to recommend me to Mr. Yorke, who may, as I hear, require a hand, as his maty is to leave him shortly. I remain, most respected madam, your most obedient servant, MARIANNAN."

Perhaps it was not worth the paper, but it will show how we do things. Every man carries his reputation in his pocket, in papers that he can't read, but which have to him a magic charm. Cook's papers were cautious enough, and would not help him on. He wanted me to give him a character. I declined, telling him that it would do him no good, as I should be obliged to state that he was uniformly dirty, sulky, and inefficient. But if I had given it, I have no doubt that he would have confidentially presented it, with his other musty documents, as a strong and unimpeachable testimony. Even Savarimuttu's father, our new cook *pro tempore*, must show his papers, dating back to primeval days, before he could think himself lawfully engaged.

[SUNDAY-SCHOOL LETTER.]

MADURA, SOUTH INDIA, Jan. 21, 1862.

MY DEAR YOUNG FRIENDS, — I wish you could go with me to church some Sabbath morning. You would see many a strange sight: the rattan-mat on the floor; the windows without any glass in them, and with blinds that you can't open; the people all sitting on the floor; men coming in with bright turbans on their heads, and leaving their shoes outside; the women without shoes, and with their heads covered by the cloth which clothes their bodies; the babies in their mothers' arms, or sprawling about on the floor. But that which you would notice above all things,

I think, would be forty or fifty girls from eight to six-teen years old, sitting together in the middle of the church, and dressed in white clothes. With their black, but bright faces, they look as eagerly as any at the preacher as he tells them of the way of life ; or stand-ing up with the rest, they lead off, with all their might, the singing of their Christian songs, in tones that would sound oddly enough to you. Who are they? They belong to the Madura Girls' Boarding-School, to support which many of you give your pennies ; and if you would like to hear, I will tell you something about them.

These girls are the children of persons who have become Christians. The heathen here, as I once told you, think that no girl is good enough to be taught to read ; and so, in heathen schools, you see only boys. But Christians, you know, say that girls are as good as boys, and that all should learn to read and write ; so the Christians, in the towns about Madura, send their little daughters here to be taught by Miss Ash-ley, who has come from America for this very purpose.

Now let us follow these forty girls as they march, two by two, from the church to the school-room, when meeting is over. But first, while they pass the church-door, each one as she goes by touching her forehead and saying " *Salaâm* " (or " Good-day ") to you, let me tell you some of their names. Well, this one is " Grace." Very good, you say, I know a " Grace." These two, walking side by side, are " Lazarus " and " David." What, these girls! Yes, it is very com-mon to give the same name to both boys and girls, such as " Health " or " Blessing." Here again are " Pearl " and " Good-nature," and " Lamp of Wisdom," and

"Nectar," and "Meekness," and "Peacock," and "Grief," and "Brightness." Here come "Little Thing" and "Good Girl," and last of all "Servant of Jesus" and "Heavenly Light." Children, how would you like to be called "Servant of Jesus," or "Lamp of Wisdom"?

We come to the school-house, a one-storied building, in the middle of a large yard. On one side are two school-rooms; there are no seats, as the girls sit on the floor. Here they study, just as you do, reading, writing, arithmetic, and geography. Nice maps hang on the walls, and black-boards stand in the corners. But instead of writing on paper or slate, as you do, they write also on the leaves of the palm-tree, and the very little ones write with their fingers in the sand. They study the Bible too, much more than I did, when I went to school, and they know it well.

On the other side of this house is a long room with a hard mud floor. As you go in, the first thing you notice is a row of brass pans, stretching from one end of the room to the other; and each one is so bright from scrubbing that you can see your face in it. These are the dishes that the girls eat out of, and each girl has one, and one only. They are very proud of them, and try hard to see whose pan shall look the best. They eat rice four days in the week for breakfast, dinner and supper, and on other days some kind of corn. They have a little meat in their rice; but nine cents a day will buy the meat for forty-four girls, except on Saturday, when they have a better dinner, with twenty-four cents' worth of meat for the whole. The girls take their turn in cooking and helping the others to their rice. On New Year's or some other great day, they have a

sheep killed and have a grand feast.  They sweep out
the yard too, making brooms often out of cocoa-nut
leaves.

They all seem to love the Bible ; and the first thing
they do in the morning is to go to some quiet place,
and read the Bible and pray.  A blessing is always
asked before eating, and after eating thanks are returned to God, each one taking her turn from the oldest
to the youngest.  While at school they see hardly any
one beside themselves, as their home is not in Madura ;
but when vacation comes many of them try to do good
among the heathen.  Just before the last vacation,
Miss Ashley asked each one to try and bring some one
to church who had never been before, when they should
go home, and tell what they had done when school began again.  So they promised, and when they came
back to school, Miss Ashley asked them how they had
succeeded.  "Well," said one little girl, " I got a poor
old woman to go to church ; but she did n't stay
through the meeting, because she said her shoulder
ached, sitting still so long."  Another bright-eyed little
one, whose face is always on a smile, and whose name
is Anthony, said she met a tailor, and said, " You must
go to church."   " But what for ? " said the tailor.
" Oh, come and see," said Anthony.  " But what is
the use of going to an empty church ; there is nothing
to be seen, — no God."  " Oh, yes, there is too," replied
Anthony ; " our God is in church, even if you can't see
him."  But the tailor would n't go : said he, " My God
is on my forehead," pointing to the holy ashes which
he had rubbed there.  But was n't that little Anthony
a brave little missionary ?

These school-girls all seem to love to pray, and they

pray just as children ought to, about all their troubles, no matter how small they seem. One little girl, who finds it not very easy to get her lessons, goes to God, and tells Him how hard her sums are; that she has tried hard, but can't do them, and asks Him to help her; and I have no doubt He does.

These school-girls seem as bright and happy as any I ever saw at home, and most of them grow up to love the Saviour, and live useful lives. But it is n't always so; and I must tell you a story about two girls who had been in the school nearly eight years, but who have now left us altogether. They are children of a man called John, who was a few years ago a Christian teacher, whom all loved. But one day he heard that he could earn a great deal of money by selling rum. The devil tempted him and he fell. He opened a rum-shop, and the next thing he did was to send for his two daughters, who were here at school, to come and help him. What could be done? He was their father and they must obey him. They went, and I'm sorry to tell you that it was n't long before we heard that they were indeed helping their father to sell rum, and thus helping to ruin others, while they themselves had given up Christ, and put on heathen marks! It was a sad, sad fall; but you will be glad to learn that the other girls, who remain in the school, pray to God every day that Mary and her sister may yet again come back and follow Christ. Perhaps you will pray for these two wandering ones this night. Will you not?

This last is a dark picture, but let me show you a bright one. It shall be about that little girl who prayed to God to help her get her lessons. She lives about forty miles from Madura. Her father is a poor man, and he alone, of all the people in his village, is a Christian. There is no minister where he lives; so every Sunday he collects together the heathen and preaches to them. After his little daughter had been here only one term of a few months, she went home to spend vacation. Sabbath-day came, but her father was too sick to talk. The people came to the house for meeting; what could be done? A boy was found who could read. He was a heathen, but he read the Bible to them; several of them could sing; but it was the part of this little girl, not over ten years old, to pray. Yes, she prayed before them all; and I am sure her prayer was heard. But was n't she a brave Christian? Who of you will be like her? It is to send such girls to school that you give your money.

Here I must stop. In a week or two I am to move to a home of my own, where I shall find plenty of work to do. I write these letters to a great many Sunday-school children. If all who hear them offer one prayer to God for me, and the heathen around me, God will surely answer them. Will you join?

Your sincere friend,

DAVID C. SCUDDER.

[JOURNAL LETTER.]

JAN. 19.

Mail leaves in three or four days, and yet I have not written a line. But events worthy of record have passed. I have been examined, approved and stationed. Henceforth address all communications of whatever kind, not to Madura, but to Periakulam. Yes, I have at last a place among men, a local habitation. But let me begin, as far as I can, at the beginning. My examination in Tamil, which was to test my capability in that line, and govern the mission respecting my appointment, took place a week ago yesterday. I went out to Pasumalie with Mr. Rendall to breakfast at eight A. M. After breakfast I was set to work translating Tamil into English and English into Tamil until two P. M., save an hour at noon, when I conducted a weekly prayer-meeting, and talked to the students of the seminary on the words " Grieve not the Holy Spirit." I spoke about half an hour, and succeeded much better than I expected to. Then after dinner, they put me through grammar, reading Gospels and conversation. The last I dreaded, but as it came last, they let me off easily. So I rode home with a light heart, confident that I should be accepted, as the event proved.

I came home from our annual meeting at Melûr this morning at three o'clock. All missionaries attend the regular mission meetings held thrice a year, in January, May, and September. So on Tuesday evening about nine o'clock, Washburn, who had come in from his place, joined me in my bullock-bandy. It was a delightful moonlight night. Indeed you cannot fancy the peculiar brilliancy of the moonlight here. . . . . The distance is eighteen miles, and we reached Melûr about four o'clock. . . . . I awoke to find myself in one of the most beautiful regions about here, the horizon bounded by hills on all sides. All the missionaries were prompt, and we had a jolly time greeting one another. The providing for such a company was no small matter in a place where no tavern is to be had, and where little or no market is to be found. But two or three took to the church and spread their cots there,

18

some in the house, while **Washburn** and I took up our lodgings under a capacious tent which Mr. Burnell, the missionary here, uses on his tours, and which he had pitched on his ground.  How I did luxuriate that night, no rocking bandy, nothing to break in upon the delicious repose but the unmerciful Mr. Burnell, who roused us out of bed by moonlight to give us a bath in his famous swimming-basin.  He has built a big bathing-tub, about a third as large as Braman's,* and has had it filled from the well.  It is a rare treat to plunge about in water, a thing which I have n't done since leaving home.  Such baths are common among the English, but we have only two.

We had our meetings in the church, and they occupied from ten o'clock to dusk, excepting dinner-time.  All scattered to walk by dark.  There is a famous banian-tree here, one of the largest in the country.  It is a splendid thing, fully coming up to my idea of such trees, except that the shoots are clustered nearer to the trunk than I had supposed.  We paced it.  The measurement about the outer circumference was one hundred and eighty paces, the diameter about forty.  The shoots, as soon as they enter the ground, swell at the base so that they grow to look like real, independent trees, and the effect is fine.  The length of the unsupported branches running horizontally outward would astonish you.

The meeting is important, as being the meeting at which the appropriations for the year are made. . . . . But what interested me mostly was my fate.  I was not kept long in suspense, for upon the motion of Mr.

---

* This is a comparison which Boston boys only can be expected to understand.  The basin must have been about fifteen feet square.

Rendall, I was summarily appointed to the station of Periakulam; of the position and character of the station I must speak hereafter. . . . . Thursday evening after meeting, we all went on top the house and sang under the open sky, with the full moon looking benignantly upon us, " The Star-Spangled Banner," with all our might and main. Somebody had given us a miniature "Stars and Stripes," which Mr. Burnell waved over us. It was a stirring time. I tell you, there is no unloyal heart here. . . . . I enjoyed the meeting highly, and came home as I went. So I am stationed. We begin to move next week, and I expect to visit Periakulam with Mr. Noyes, who formerly had the entire field which now is divided. [This visit was immediately made, and occupied a week and a half, but I defer the narrative of it till the next chapter, in order to make the description of the place more connected. He returned to Madura, remaining there only long enough to prepare for removal, and anticipating with eagerness his establishment at a station of his own.]

[TO HORACE E. SCUDDER.]

MADURA, Feb. 6, 1862.

' . . . . How many times lately I have longed to have you or anybody from home along with me. I have been off on a tour and have often been alone. Tossing about in a bandy I have ample time to think, and such jolly times as two in a cart do have. Missionaries here are fresh as boys, and the way we chat about college and seminary life would amuse you. Then there is always a comical side to bandy-travelling; the bandy-man sitting cross-legged on the pole, working the bullocks with his hands, much as an artist might two

pianos at once, thrumming on either at will, with a
querulous expostulation with them for acting badly, —
" Don't I give you your grass and cotton-seed? Why
do you treat me so?" Thus they go on, talking to
them as if they were men. Oh, it's real droll.

I have work enough before me now; a district some
twenty miles in diameter put in my keeping, with the
charge " Till it." I am fruitful in plans, but it is to be
seen how they will result. You at home can have no
conception whatever of the dismal deep into which
portions of the Hindû people have sunk. The sight
shocks me even to-day, and you can find no terms so
expressive of your feelings as the Prophet's " Can
these bones live?" People who gloat over carrion,
feast on rats and vermin, and roll in filth, form the sta-
ple of our congregations, that is, our people come out
of such castes. It is deplorable, and often very de-
pressing. Extremes in society here are far greater than
at home, even bringing into account Romanist Irish.
I mean to aim higher, not indeed ambitiously; but I
question whether we have not confined ourselves too
exclusively to classes who will hear us most readily.
The lowest of the low have least to lose in changing
their faith.

[TO HIS SISTER.]

MADURA, Feb. 13, 1862.

. . . . You may believe that being so soon to have
a station of my own I am full of plans as to how I
shall conduct it. I am reading a little volume of
Dr. Caldwell's on Tinnevelly Missions. He describes
briefly but ably the field, the work, the results. It is
the best description of our way of working that I have

seen. There are lots of suggestions in it. My chief task, aside from preaching to the heathen, will be to instruct the congregations. I want to have a plan by which the life of Christ shall be studied in course by all the congregations simultaneously. I mean to assign Bible lessons to the catechists, which I shall go over at the monthly meetings with them. Then they teach the same to their people. So when I visit them I shall know the lesson for the day and be ready with a talk. Systematic, progressive instruction, line upon line, precept upon precept, is what they need most emphatically. Can't you suggest some method of studying the Bible? Pray for me, that above all things the eternal welfare of the thousands under my care may lie close upon my heart, daily, hourly.

## CHAPTER XIII.

### HOME AT PERIAKULAM.

#### [FEBRUARY–APRIL, 1862.]

[PERIAKULAM is in the Madura District, and distant from the city of Madura about fifty miles, being a little north of west. It is in the valley of the Vaikai River, which rises in Kambam, about forty miles south of Periakulam, flows in a northerly direction between two ranges of mountains for thirty miles, when it bends toward the east, and flowing northeast as far as Battala-gundu changes its course and flows southeast by the city of Madura into the Gulf of Mannar. The valley of the Vaikai is about twenty miles wide at Periakulam. The missionary district under this name had been recently set off from a larger one, and was about twelve miles in diameter. The letters and journal will sufficiently indicate the nature of the country and character of the people. The reader has seen how eagerly David anticipated his work here, an eagerness which was increased by the preliminary visit which he made in January with Mr Noyes, when he made a short tour through the field. His memorandum journal bears record of his earnest spirit in these words written on the day of arrival : — " Here I am at my own station, and in my own house — home. Am pleased with the looks of things, especially these everlasting hills. May the blessing of Almighty God, Father, Son, and Spirit, be with us. How long shall I be here ? " In a little less

than ten months that question was answered. His first
impressions, derived from his visit, are shown at length
in the following extracts.]

PERIAKULAM, Jan. 23, 1862.

Note this, my first letter from my own station, my
house, and to be my home. I have come here to look
around and see what needs to be done before moving
here. Oh! it is a grand, grand spot. Right in front,
as you look off from the veranda, are these towering
Pulneys gazing down upon you in solemn front from a
height of over eight thousand feet. If I had a gifted
pen, I could furnish you with any amount of fine writing on the subject, but must content myself with a
bare description. The house faces the north. The
spur of hills on which is the Sanitarium runs east and
west, and you seem to see each end as you look upon
them here. The eastern end terminates in a singularly
shaped mountain. It tapers up quite to a point, and
from its apex to the base a sharp ridge runs very
straight and very sharp. Toward the west, some ten
miles away, the range takes a turn, and two enormous
hills face you, each having a capacious lap. On all
other sides are mountains also, but at various distances
from you, some in the distant horizon, some little hills
near by. The Pulneys, immediately in front, are only
four miles distant, and you may fancy how imposing
is their appearance with such a uniform elevation extending for miles and miles in unbroken line. It is a
grand site for a house, and these lasting hills will be
lasting friends to us. Their convenience, in case of
sickness, the summit being only five or six hours dis-

tant, will at once be apparent. A large valley is all about us, and the scenery of the valley will compare well with that of New England. I long to bring H. here to enjoy it.

. . . . The church and congregation called on me, " the new man." They came, headed by the pastor, and bearing a basket of plantains, with a paper of sugar, as a token of greeting. The whole congregation could not come, many being away; about twenty presented themselves and sat down before us on the veranda. I must say that their first appearance was not altogether favorable. Half-clad, dirty, and unintellectual, I asked myself could I find sympathy as a Christian here? But as one countenance after another lighted up in the course of the conversation, I felt relieved, and could see in them not a little to please and encourage me. But it is a poor congregation; every member is a Pariah, the lowest caste, and only one or two can read. Deacon Moses cannot read. Moreover this church has for many years been in a most lamentable condition. Two members, and deacons, I think, had a quarrel and drew the whole church after them. The ground of the dispute has only lately been removed, and as the pastor said to me, " the hate still remains."

ANDIPATTI, Jan. 26.

This is one of the villages in my field. As I write, I sit in a comfortable touring-chair, in a thatched-roof church, though rather a modest edifice to be so called. . . . . We left Periakulam, eleven miles distant, this morning at five o'clock, while the moon was shining. . . . . I walked a good share of the way. The road is the most like a New England road of any I have seen

this long while, up hill and down, while most roads
here are on a dead level. I wandered along ahead of
the carts, kicking over ant-hills, from common-sized
ones to mounds three feet high, looking at the beautiful
turtle-doves, and listening to the notes of some unknown songster, picking up a monstrous millipede, and
pocketing it for S., though dropping it as it seemed inclined to crawl upward, mounting big boulders and sur-
veying the country, *my field*, all in high spirits. . . . .
As I walked along I planned all sorts of tours or systems
of touring, so as to reach all the villages. In this station
of only about twelve miles diameter there are many
villages that never saw a missionary. I hope it will
not be so very long. It is an advantage which a small
station has over a large one, that it can be more thoroughly canvassed, and labor be spent more economically. It will be years before I can effectually preach
throughout; but I have good catechists, and I hope
through them to organize a more thorough system
than has been possible hitherto.

. . . . We dined at Andipatti at three o'clock, and
immediately after got into our bandy and started for a
village seven miles distant. I got from the head of
police a list of all the villages in this police station.
You will get some idea of the country when you hear that
within a radius of eight miles there are sixty-eight villages, small and large, varying from five to one hundred
houses. A populous country for work, is it not? We
reached the village about dusk and went to the house
of a rich native who belongs to the congregation. He
is a higher caste man than we usually meet with, and
his influence is worth preserving, but he is not a very
stable believer. He had a long story of grievances

to tell to Mr. Noyes, and as I sat under his portico, on a raised mud seat, looking at the singular group squatted around us, I could not help wishing that some of you could sit by me and see the sight, and look at the man speaking, gesturing with natural grace, loosing first his turban and then his upper cloth, in his eagerness.

After a night's rest in the cart, we drove two miles further the next morning to a village where there is quite a prosperous congregation of one hundred and fifteen souls. Mr. Noyes preached to them, introducing me. Three catechists went with us through the village, which is quite a large one. We stopped at a school where quantities of boys flocked about, and Mr. Noyes talked. Coming away a man came along and said he wanted to join the congregation. We received him gladly I assure you, and were talking about it, when I said, "Here's this man following us." He was a man whom I had noticed as having a most singular countenance. We asked him what he wanted, and he said, "I want to join you." Here were two! a most unusual occurrence. I talked with him. He said that he had given up his idols six months ago, and I was interested too to find that he had heard of the gospel from Ragland and his associates, church missionaries in Tinnevelly, while living there. Thus the word is sown, thus it yields fruit. You can hardly conceive of the very peculiar joy I had in seeing these two coming to us.

[A month later the young missionaries had removed from Madura and were established permanently at their new home, in season to celebrate the anniversary thus pleasantly spoken of.]

[JOURNAL LETTER.]

PERIAKULAM, Feb. 27, 1862.

One year ago there was a wedding in Boston. To-day the bride and groom are comfortably housed in a bungalow in South India, their own house, with a baby to adorn it. Yes, here we are, sixteen miles from our nearest white neighbor, settled at last in a station of our own, as happy, as comfortable, as well as if we were in a country parish at home. . . . . We went first to Battalagundu, where Washburn is stationed, and from there took our own horse-carriage. We had Washburn's horse for the first eight miles, I having posted mine half-way on. A horse here would be pretty well used up if he should go sixteen miles on a stretch. But we did enjoy that drive. I had been counting on driving in our own carriage, and we were well repaid. We started just before sunrise, and had a cool time of it for the first half of the way. Then the road was so like home roads, up hill and down, rocks and roots and ruts, reminding us of an up-country road in New England. The grand Pulneys always in sight and always to be, the cool bracing air, the flocks of new, gay-colored birds outside, and the little bird nestling inside, all helped to make the drive a happy one. Then the house, when within four miles, kept peeping in and out between the trees, as we rounded one hill and another, looking so clean and white in its new dress. All the servants were on the veranda to receive us, and I took H. about to look upon our new possessions. Keeping house here is not exactly what it is at home, there is so much shed-room, and there are so many servants. Thus we have a row of buildings, as long as the house, of *go-downs* as they

call them, the big store-room and the little store-room,
the kitchen, the hen-house and dove-cote, and here the
travellers' go-down ; then the horse and carriage stalls,
and extra shed-room for travellers to the hills.   Everything is on one floor, and all on a large scale, as I shall
show more minutely hereafter.   The house has been
newly whitewashed, outside and in, and all the wood-
work oiled.   We have glass windows, which is quite a
luxury here.   In Madura we had no windows at all, to
say nothing of glass.   You would think these rather
odd.   The lower part is glass doors, the upper Venetian
blinds.   The doors are Venetian for the upper, and
solid for the lower half, while above them again is a
glass window.   In Madura, if you shut the doors you
were in darkness ; here you can still see and tell when
morning breaks.   And oh, when it does break, what
delicious air !   I astonished H. one morning by bringing in the thermometer, and showing her the mercury
shivering at 60°, five degrees lower than Mr. Winslow
said he had ever known it in India.

     . . . . I want to give you a complete survey of our
state and position.   So I will go over the servants,
praying that you may not be appalled by their number.
First is the all-essential Francis Xavier or Savarimuttu,
our maty or chief servant.   Next is Vetham, Sav.'s
father, who is cook.   Next is tailor.   The ayah, who
does well with baby, is black as a coal, wears a jewel
or ornament in her nose, and rivals the " fat boy " at
sleeping.   There is the sweeper-woman who does the
drudgery.   She is here only temporarily.   Horse-keeper,
called Mûmyândi, " Lord of Sages ; " two gardeners,
one, Pearl of Wisdom.   Then there is a watchman
paid by the mission.   We have also a *tap-âl*-man (pro-

nounced tap-paul) who goes once a week to Madura and back with a tin box on his head, keeping us in communication with the metropolis.

Now that we have a station we have catechists under our charge. Here at Periakulam the catechist is Manuel, an Indo-Briton, or East Indian, or Eurasian, or Half-caste, as such are variously termed. He dresses like a European, but looks much like a native. He is a good business-hand, and such a man is much needed here, when people arrive on their way to and from the hills. There is here also a church and a native pastor. His name is Seymour. His church is a mile from here, and he has pretty much the sole care of it. It is in a part of the town called Fort Hill. At Andipatti is Kurubatham, " Teacher's Foot," and at two villages near by, Guandmuttu, " Pearl of Wisdom," and Devanaikam, " Divine Lord," or some such meaning. I shall introduce them to you more formally when I visit their villages.

. . . . I must give you as far as I can a description of our house and surroundings. Before reaching the town, about a mile this side, turn sharp to the left and stand still. At the end of a long, narrow lane, nearly a quarter of a mile long, is a whitewashed gate, between two high whitewashed posts, commanding the entrance to the mission compound; a mud wall, coped with brick and mortar, whitewashed upon the top, surrounds the whole, enclosing a space of about six acres. Looking beyond the gate, through an avenue of rather scant trees, peeps out the house. It is a low, one-storied, flat-roofed house, standing in about the middle of the enclosure. On the left is the modest church. To the left of that, outside the mud wall, are the mud, straw-thatched houses of the catechists and house-servants. A couple of rods back of the wall, running almost round two sides of the house, is the river or branch of the Vaikai River which flows by Madura. Periakulam itself is divided into two parts, called South Branch and North Branch, according as it lies south or north of the stream.

Well, will you walk up to the house? or, as we don't walk much in this country, drive with us in our bandy? Entering the compound, on the left is grass as far as the east wall, scanty enough, and scattered about are young palmyra palms, only about four feet high, with their stiff, fan-shaped leaves. On the right is grass half-way up to the west wall. The other half is taken up with a garden in which are about twenty young cocoa-nut trees, ten feet high, some mango-trees, and a spot for potatoes and any vegetables. To-day the gardeners set out some plantain-roots or bulbs. Driving toward the house, and looking beyond it to the right, you see a little gate which lets you out to the river, a few steps below. Built up level with the compound, outside of the walls, is the brick-and-mortar well, into which the river-water is drawn by a little channel, giving us plenty of water for the garden, and overhanging that is the big well-sweep, like those at home, save that for a stone to balance, a man walks on it back and forth, holding on by a bamboo frame built for the purpose at the side, and another man draws up the bucket. Seen against the sky, the whole affair is quite picturesque. At an equal distance inside the wall, just back of the house is the regular well of pure drink-ing-water, with its channels through which the water runs into the garden below. A garden here is divided off into small beds surrounded with channels, and so fixed that by a stroke of the spade the water can be turned into any at will.

Turning Pegu's head to the left, we dismount and make a low bow. Ascend three steps and you are on a veranda laid with square bricks, covered with mortar rubbed to a polish. Above, you see rafters with slit bamboos laid across, supporting the tiles of the veranda roof. The veranda runs in front and partly round two sides; a post is planted at each end, and you might any morning see Pegu tied, and the horse-keeper grooming him, beginning with pieces of brick. This insures his being well groomed and fed. There are four doors in front and two windows on each end. But we have been outside long enough; walk in. The first thing that strikes you is the height and bareness of the walls. We are in the hall or parlor. The walls of this, as of all the rooms, are fifteen feet high, and all whitewashed exactly as the outside. The hall is twenty-seven feet long and eighteen wide, and the dining-room back is of the same size. You look from either hall-door (there are two opening from the front veranda) right through a doorless doorway to a corresponding door in the dining-room, opening upon the back veranda. . . . . . The floor is covered with a big, rough matting made of slit ratan. The ceiling resembles somewhat that of old-fashioned houses. Two enormous beams run across, and between these and the walls, rafters, oiled well, and giving a pleasing contrast to the white ceiling between the rafters.

The room on the left in front is full of furniture belonging to Mr. Noyes, the former occupant; back of it is our Friends' Room, as it is called here. Dr. Arnold's picture adorns one corner. Back of the hall, and of the same size, as I said, is the dining-room. The legs of our sideboard stand in brass cups of water, to be proof against ants. No article of furniture nor common box can stand on its own bottom here. No, not a tub, for the white ants are sure to eat up everything not on stilts. From the dining-room turn to the right, and you are in our bedroom, corresponding to the Friends' Room. From the window we have a fine view of the hills. Between the pillars opposite, on the veranda, hang two *tatties* or sweet-grass shades to keep off the heat and glare of the sun. They can be rolled up. A bathing-room connects with this room, in the rear. Now come into my study which is in front, on the right of the hall, corresponding to Mr. Noyes's room on the left. Like the other three rooms it is eighteen feet square, the floor covered with common straw mat, the ceiling like that of the hall. My great study-table is in the middle, and maps and pictures hang on the walls. My bookcases are in here and in the hall. . . . .

Done with the inside, pass to the back veranda, which is smaller. On the left is the mûnshi's (teacher's) room, where the tracts are kept, and physic and tools. Opposite is Savarimuttu's go-down or store-room, where the "goodies" are, and on this or on the front veranda sits the tailor on his mat, plying his needle and gossiping as he can well do. From the house on the left stretches a long row of out-houses. First the go-down where all heavy articles, flour, horse-food, boxes, etc., are kept; then the kitchen, in front of which is a covered place for bandies of persons on the hills. Beyond is the chicken-house, and above that a dove-cote for one hundred pigeons. Beyond that, at the end is a small calf-pen. On the back side are four stalls for horses and carriages, all whitewashed and shaded by a *pandâl*, as we call it. The church in the compound is bare and plain enough, — plain inside too ; a little raised platform, like the rest, of mortar, at the end, and a movable stand for pulpit, a Gothic window behind.

If you pass through the house on to the small back veranda, you will be tempted to go on top by the stairway on the left. Everything is whitewashed, so don't rub your garments. But I can't attempt to describe the view from the roof. You could walk about and gaze for a long time without wearying. Face the gate, northward. You appear to be in the centre of a vast amphitheatre of hills that tower nearly eight thousand feet upward, right before you. You are four miles from their base. They hardly form half a circle, and terminate abruptly to your vision on either side : on the left truly ; on the right they still reach on toward the east, but the line is broken for you by a mountain nearer, a little to the right and of very peculiar shape, a sharp ridge running from base to apex, its edge toward you. The next most prominent feature is the road, a quarter of a mile distant, running at right angles with the path to the house, and lined all along on each side by big, ungainly, but thickly leaved banian-trees, full of monkeys. Between the road and the mountain are green rice-fields, with a few small streams, and banians, cork and thorn trees, and bamboo clumps scattered about. To the left, just outside the north-west corner of the compound, is a beautiful grove of tall, graceful cocoa-nuts, with dozens of pendent birds'-

19

nests hanging from their high limbs, while over and beyond them you look into the bosom of the hills, where they sweep around toward the south. Southward, the view is less limited, the hills being miles away, but it is much less interesting. You can see a large tank or two, and one or two low, gravelly hills, covered with scraggly cactus-bushes, not far off, — a noticeable feature in an Indian landscape, where low, small hills, not mountains, are rarely seen. You, with home notions of Oriental vegetation, would be disappointed in the general bleakness and barrenness of the view. Certainly, almost any spot that I have seen at home would excel in beauty a landscape in this country. Everything is dry. Trees are not specially beautiful, and of far less variety than is met with at home. The trees on the road to our house are tulip-trees, a kind that neither of us like, coarse, clumsy, and littering the ground forever with falling leaves.

[TO MRS. CHARLES W. SCUDDER.]

PERIAKULAM, March 19, 1862.

A splendid bouquet of hill-flowers, just sent us, is breathing out fragrance singularly suggestive of home. Roses, geraniums, heliotropes, and verbenas are not every-day sights to mortals here below [on the plains]. Well, what has this to do with writing to me? you will ask. Simply, that somehow flowers suggest you, and your letter comes to mind, which has but lately arrived, fresh from Linden Place. . . . . I wish it were as easy for me to give you a picture of our house and room as for me to keep yours in mind. H. and I are sitting in my study, writing at my big study-table, as we do every evening. Doors and windows are open, and we manage to feel comfortable, at least I do, with the thermometer at 86°. Is that warm at home? I have forgotten. You would find little to attract you in our surroundings, certainly nothing which could steal your affection from the Nature with which you have been familiar. These great hills would be grand anywhere, but they have nothing of the summer dress of New England hills, nor the gorgeousness of autumn. They look brown and bald, though forests cover them through which wild beasts roam unmolested. Indian trees do not compare with home trees for beauty of outline, grace of limb, or richness of verdure. The banian is a great, awkward, ungainly, unsightly production. It is a monster, though not the monster of books. There are not over a dozen such trees as figure in pictures, in all Southern India, I dare say. The banians are very common, almost every public road is lined with them, and they throw out their long, unsightly arms in every direction. They take special delight in shooting forth branches but a little above the ground, and almost perfectly horizontal branches that are as big at one end as at the other and reach out an amazing distance. They ought to be propped up by the shoots; but these shoots rarely reach the ground, except close to the trunk, being nibbled off by cattle. The banians are famous resorts for monkeys.

Cork-trees are rather graceful and have a pretty blossom, like the cypress-vine, hanging from a long stem. Tulip-trees are ugly, coarse, and litter the ground with leaves. Thorn-trees are as unshapely, usually, as they ought to be; but there is one kind of thorn called the umbrella-tree, which has an astonishing likeness to that domestic article, and is so very peculiar in

shape as to form a desirable addition to your garden.
Fruit-trees are not as pretty either, I think, as home
ones, but I fear I am partial, and certainly I am en-
croaching on ground that I don't naturally own.   But
what strikes one most forcibly is the bleakness of the
ground.   Except in the rainy season, when the rice is
exceedingly beautiful, — the richest green I ever saw, —
all fields are bleak, and barren of everything save stub-
ble.   You rarely see a watercourse; we are favored
in being near mountains.   Tanks are usually half dry,
showing the mud, and interesting only as the resort of
flocks of aquatic birds.   Save too occasionally a mountain, all is a dead level; there is hardly such a thing as
a hill anywhere, where I have been.   This of course is
favorable for irrigation, but certainly not for beauty.

But we did not come here attracted by any stories
of the beauties of tropical scenery, or the luxuriance
of vegetation, of which we heard.   We are less interested in the land than the people who inhabit it.   And
if I should write of the natural attractiveness of the
inhabitants, I fear I could not give a very glowing account.   Heber said, "*Only* man is vile."   I should
put a question mark after *only*, — but I am not anxious
to destroy his poetry nor rudely break in upon current
notions.   Certainly the rest is true; man is vile, how
vile I am confident that even you, with all your acquaintance with Brookline Creek, can have but the
very faintest conception.   Not vile only but low, wonderfully low.   My heart sinks within me as I look upon
some of these people, and the best comfort I find is in
the thought that God created them.   Even this, as W.
said to me, one might almost be led to doubt, and take
up with Topsy's theology.   However, they are and

have been reclaimed. You would be interested in the work, I know, and I must not fail to tell you that I love this people very much. I like their affectionate, dependent ways. . . . . It does encourage me to think how many love me and pray for me at home.

[TO HIS SISTER.]

PERIAKULAM, March 24, 1862.

. . . . It does come upon me so once in a while, the thought that home is slipping slowly out of grasp! It is very oppressing to feel the impressions of home becoming gradually more indistinct, the shades of home-life, that render the whole picture so pleasing, growing more shadowy, till the merest outline is lost; the consciousness that all this is actually passing out of my hold and that there is no hope for it is really painful. I find myself already straining my memory to recal the appearance of certain parts of the house, and it makes me feel badly. I ride out on horseback every morning, and home rarely escapes coming up for a theme of thought.

[JOURNAL LETTER.]

MARCH 20.

I go to Andipatti to-morrow morning early. This is my first tour by myself; perhaps you would be interested in the disposal of things. I have had no touring-box made yet, so this time I make use of an old camphor trunk. Into this go the canisters for tea and sugar; a butter-pot, its top secured by a cloth and string; plates, napkin, pepper and salt-box are stowed snugly away. In a tin case are two loaves of bread; a tin washbowl, rice and curry dishes, lamp, sweet potatoes, plantains, and a roast chicken all find accommodation in some corner of this odorous trunk. Pots and kettles go into a separate basket. When the bandy has come I shall see that there is plenty of straw on which to lay the mattress. To the inside somewhere I must tie my touring-cot, and place inside also my camp-chair and table, and after all, myself.

MARCH 27.

. . . . I was only away on my tour a single day, as I had a sore throat and headache, and there was trouble in the household. Our good-natured horse-keeper had met with an accident. . . . . I set my " ticker," that invaluable companion, to wake me up at half-past four in the morning. It was faithful, and by five I was off in the bandy with a good moonlight, and dawn soon breaking. The distance to Andipatti is eleven miles, and the bandy-man, whom you must know as Anikatti, or " Young Elephant," managed to reach Andipatti by 9.30, four hours and a half travel. Vetham the cook, Savarimuttu's father, was on hand ; but when we came to open the camphor trunk, the brass key broke. That was a pretty pickle to be in, for I wanted breakfast, and there was the chicken, the plates, and everything else nicely locked up. However we sent for a blacksmith and I managed to pry the cover up. The natives were coming in to pay their respects, but when the table was ready they disappeared, as they do not consider it polite to look at another eating.

In a few minutes after breakfast and before I was ready for them, the bridal party, of which I had been told, appeared. I had made but little preparation, but put a bold face on and proceeded to business. The

little church was full of spectators, partly heathen partly
Christian. The bride's mother sat next to her, seeing
that her cloth was kept perfectly arranged, and especially so that no part of her face should be visible. She
sat the very impersonation of modesty, giving no one a
chance to pronounce on her beauty, though a glimpse
that I caught of her face made me think that fancy
would pronounce better judgment than actual sight.
She opened her cloth while the ceremony was performing. The most noticeable feature of her countenance
was a deep blood-red dash of dye along each cheek-
bone, making her look as though her throat were cut.
I can't tell you how her hair was dressed, as it was
never visible, — a fortunate thing for me. The groom
had no modesty to boast of, but sat with a big wreath
of white flowers round his neck and a cloth thrown
over his shoulders loosely. The company were all behind, an arrangement which I commend to bashful
young men and women at home. We have a marriage
formula here, not uniform, but each missionary adapts
what appears to himself suitable. The native style of
wedding is by what is called a *Táli*. It is a small ornament hung by a cord around the woman's neck, tied
there by the husband. I believe it is never taken off.
The man ties it at the time. We have lately adopted
the open Bible as a suitable emblem for our Christians.
I read Ephesians on marriage to them, married them,
prayed a very short prayer, and pronounced the benediction. A hymn followed to the tune of " Old Hundred." Then the father of the bride brought forward
the fee, — for bride and groom each, three annas and
four pice, — ten cents. Which twenty cents I duly deposited in H.'s keeping as her first pin-money. After

the hymn I wished them both joy and supposed we were well through. But no: the catechist asked me to talk to them. I declined, and he receiving permission, preached to them nearly half an hour, on various topics more or less relevant to the matter in hand. Then another hymn and prayer, and another benediction by the catechist, a layman, in which the whole company joined, as is the custom here. The crowd then left, after the groom had received a copy of the New Testament from me, as he could read. I suppose the groom was in clover, but I was rather surprised to see him come to the church before meeting, seeming to have nothing special to do, and again in the evening to find him at the catechist's house, calling. Not a very faithful spouse.

We had a meeting in the afternoon, in which I talked in a familiar way to the church-members, urging them to learn to read. A man has just moved in with his old mother from a place in Mr. Herrick's field, and he came asking to be received to communion. Such requests are rare and I was glad to hear it. The old woman also wished the same. I shall write to Mr. Herrick about them, and examine them the next time I visit Andipatti.

I decided to visit the church at a place two miles south called Maniakarampatti. *Patti* is a common termination, meaning village. Here is my largest congregation, numbering one hundred and five. I expected to hold a meeting, but the first news that greeted me on reaching the church was that my people were in great tribulation. There is a good deal of young grain growing now, and while young it is almost sure death to cattle who eat it. They die, the natives say, from a

little insect that is in the grain, which chokes them.
How true the explanation is I cannot say, but that day
five or six cows had strayed into a field, eaten and died.
Our people are poor enough, and they can ill afford to
lose them. The cows were all together, and the people
with them, so I went to see them. It was a doleful
sight indeed. Five nice-looking cows lay stretched out
dead, and the women were sitting around them, or
walking about, uttering most pitiful lamentations over
their loss. One cow was just dying, and a crowd was
standing round it mourning every fresh indication of
coming death. I could say but little and do less. They
had poured water down with no avail, and asked me if
I had not some medicine. I got my catechist, or teacher,
who was with me to tell the people, many of whom
were heathen, of Job, how he suffered, and how he
bore it. They appeared somewhat interested in the
tale. But it was really a mournful sight to see the
affection manifested toward the animals. "They were
Christian cows," they said. I left them finally and
walked back toward Andipatti. A few accompanied
me on the way, some distance, till I gave them leave to
return.

I was pleased to witness the anxiety manifested to
have the Lord's Supper administered there, which they
had not had, they said, for a long time. Walking
home by starlight I had ample time to meditate on the
work before me, its extent and its character. I felt a
quiet exultation at the thought of having so much to
do, and I longed to be able to speak readily, that I
might carry out a plan of touring among heathen villages that I have been concocting. Reaching the
church I had tea, and then walking over to the cate-

chist's house, I brought him back with me, and we two
spent a pleasant hour, in talking and praying together
about our work, and the Lord's work around Andipatti. It was the pleasantest hour I had yet passed in
India. Do you remember my describing a singular-
looking man as having presented himself to Mr. Noyes
and me, when we were there before ? Kurubatham
had not seen him for some time, as the man had been
south, but he came to see me and said he had been
sick. He was really very earnest and seemed sincere,
and I am quite interested in him. I made too strong a
cup of tea for my benefit, slept but little, rose at half-
past two, got the bandy, started off and came in upon
H. much to her relief about seven. We soon after
sent the horse-keeper off in the same bandy to Madura.

. . . . It is thundering above, — an unusual but
very welcome sound in these parts. A cool breeze
blows upon me, refreshing after the hot day. I did not
test it, but I am safe in saying that the thermometer
has been over 100° a good part of the day. Hot
weather is rushing upon us like fire on a prairie, and
we shall soon hear the roar and feel the blast. We
have decided to go to the Hills if possible in two weeks,
and then what a jovial time we shall have. Were it
not for H. I hardly think I should go myself, as I am
able to endure ; still to-day I have had a dull, head-
achy feeling, rather disagreeable, though I am in
decent condition otherwise. The whole mission is on
the move, making its annual pilgrimage to the Hills.
The Tracys' goods, cows, sheep, and hens came to-day.
When a family takes a vacation here, the whole concern has to move. They go up on Tuesday morning. Wednesday the Burnells spend with us, going up

Thursday morning. Friday morning Miss Ashley ascends. Then the Hunts are also coming this year for the first time. They will be here in a week; so that if we are fifty miles from Madura we shall see plenty of visitors for a while.

MARCH 28.

We had a tornado at noon to-day. Thunder roared among the hills, the dust flew up in spouts, the rain descended, and the floods came. It was deliciously refreshing. We had been resting, with the thermometer at 98°, a cloudy day too, when of a sudden the breezes came, and the mercury ran into its bulb, stopping at 76°, a very remarkable fall for this country. H. was in ecstasies, ran to the door, drank in the cool air by the throatful, and we had doors open and enjoyed ourselves mightily, for the hour or more that the storm lasted. The wind cut up all sorts of antics, whipping our grass lattice into shreds. The rain, too, was by no means unwelcome, laying dust and coloring the leaves. This evening H. and I took our first walk out. Pony had gone to be shod, gone to Dindigal — thirty-six miles off — just to get a set of new shoes! We went to Lotus-tank back of the house, the gardeners carrying H. over the river in a chair.

. . . . I am about starting a school in Seymour's church, where there has been none for some time. Seymour came yesterday and said that a Roman Catholic, who had been a sort of catechist, wished to join our congregation, and suggested him for a teacher, at one dollar and a half a month! I told him to bring him here to-day. He came, and I thought I would examine him a little; so I asked him to read. He read passably well; then I took up geography. To be safe, I started with fundamentals, and asked the shape of the earth. His reply was, " I have not read the Gospels." A hopeful case for a teacher, is he not? However, I think I shall try him at least, keeping him a little ahead of his classes. He is a clever fellow, and will get pupils, they say.

APRIL 5.

We have had a busy week of it. Saturday eve, a week ago, the Tracys came in upon us, on their way to the Hills. They stayed until Tuesday, leaving at two in the morning. Tuesday evening the Burnells and Miss Ashley came, leaving Thursday morning at the same hour. Thursday the Hunts came, and left this morning at two. Quite a run of company for us, fifty miles from the metropolis. While the Burnells were here, we had the nicest time ; for as we were all seated at the dinner-table, in walked our tapâl-man, box on head, and immediately delivered himself of what had been on his mind a long time, foreign letters. Hurrah, what a jumping and running ! I got the letter-basket and dealt out. The Burnells had a few, Miss Ashley some, and I eleven letters ! Such an astounding batch, perfectly overwhelming. I did n't get through reading them that night, but kept J.'s for morning. Such letters too ! I read aloud to H. till I was hoarse, and we shouted and laughed, till the other folks began to grow jealous. We were all in capital humor, for only the day before we had received the telegram telling us of the capture of Forts Henry and Donelson, and the retreat of the Rebels from Bowling-Green and Nashville.

APRIL 7.

Yesterday the church-members from the village

came up to our church here, and we partook of the Lord's Supper together. It was my first service, and I enjoyed it, though embarrassed by the language. The little church was about full of people. A poor-looking congregation, you would have thought, could you have seen it, and so in truth it was; but I hope that some of those present were true believers. Before service, Seymour said to me that there were three persons who had been suspended from coming to communion for about a year, on account of their having been foremost in the quarrel which divided the church, who wished to be received back, acknowledging their fault, and desiring to be at peace again with the others. The question of receiving them was put on the spot, and they came once more as Christians to the table of the Lord. I looked upon it as an omen of good, an indication of the return of better feeling. Nothing but the existence of this estrangement between members of the church prevents its growth. After service, the women came forward to salaam H., whom they had not seen before, and followed us then to the house, some of them asking for medicine for themselves and babies.

To-day, at eleven o'clock, I had a little prayer-meeting with Seymour, Manuel, my station catechist, and Breckenridge, mûnshi. I propose to hold these meetings monthly, when we shall study together some portion of the Scripture, beginning with First Thessalonians, and talk about matters of interest here. It will be a good thing to inspirit the pastor, who has been somewhat disheartened by the state of things. I proposed to-day, too, to start monthly, or perhaps bi-monthly, concerts of prayer for missions. There are none in the station now. So I shall have Breckenridge study up a set topic, and tell what he knows at the catechists' meetings, and they will rehearse this to their several congregations.   Moreover, I mean to have the pastor and others write letters to some mission, in hope of receiving replies from native Christians abroad.

[Here closes the journal before the vacation on the Pulney Hills.   They had remained on the Plains until late in the season, and the letters written at this time showed evident signs of exhaustion from the prostrating heat.   But shortly after this last date, they followed the other missionaries who had severally halted at Periakulam before ascending the mountain, and joined them on the summit.]

## CHAPTER XIV.

### ON THE PULNEY HILLS.

#### [16 APRIL–14 JUNE, 1862.]

[IT is a happy society that collects during the summer months at the health-retreat of the mission upon the Pulneys. All care is cast aside, and for a few weeks India heat and enervation are forgotten in the enjoyment of a northern climate. There are not enough houses in the settlement for all the mission at once, so that an arrangement is made by which the families spend the former or latter half of the hot season upon the Hills, alternating with each other. The society which can be had only rarely below is here thoroughly enjoyed, and the coolness of the air permits a kind of life which had been wholly laid aside since leaving America. Beside the mission families, English officers, civil or army, also resort to the health-retreat, so that quite a little colony is maintained. How pleasant this change was will be learned from the animated account which David gives of the ascent and sojourn. His letters will indicate also how a period of cessation from work gave an opportunity for more reflection, which was attended by something of his old self-reproachful moods.]

#### [JOURNAL LETTER.]

KODI KÂNAL, PULNEY HILLS, April 18, 1862.

"Praise the Mount; I 'm fixed upon it!" has been not irreverently running in my head ever since we crossed the brow of Nebo. Yes, we are actually up on the Hills. Like the brave captain who stood by his ship till he saw all safe out of her, and then put himself into the boat, we have seen everybody else safe off the burning plains, and have now left ourselves. The clouds are sweeping up over the hills, and big birds are sweeping by our window, as we sit in our cottage. I am too full of business and feeling to write coherently, I fear, but this incorrigible mail-day is hard by, and I must not let one mail pass without writing.

But what a spot this is! Night before last we could hardly breathe, it was so stifling and hot; last night I could with difficulty breathe, the air was so rare. We have left our spacious mansion below, sweltering under a temperature of 100°, and to-day sit in our snuggery, with a fire in the air-tight stove. Night before last the thinnest sheet was oppressive; last night we were comfortable with two thick blankets. . . . . Mr. Hunt and I went out this morning to watch for Mr. Yorke. We missed him, but planting the Stars and Stripes on the high peak overlooking the plains and my house away below, we amused ourselves with plunging rocks over a big precipice, and seeing them go crashing, tearing down for a mile or more. This afternoon we went into the woods, plucked violets, Solomon's seal, eat raspberries, sat and chatted, cut grass for the horse, and did everything that you at home do in the country, but that dwellers on the plain can't do. I raced after the boys, seized our United States flag, shouted out " Long may it wave!" when our anti-North English doctor was near, waved it at the English collector, as he came up the hills just from Madura, and did other uncouth things that I am capable of doing up here — not down there.

But I suppose I must give you for once an orderly account of how we got up to this height of joy. We finished packing on Wednesday; we had crockery to pack, books, of course, mattresses, etc. Then our matting must be rolled up and put out of reach of white ants; picture-backs daubed with solution of corrosive sublimate, to keep off book-worms; loose articles put away. All the packages had to be weighed. Fifty pounds is a Coolie load; if a box weighs over that the contents must be reduced. All was done by nine o'clock, and we lay down on the mattress after setting the invaluable " ticker " at two o'clock. I had a restless nap, dreaming of Coolies and boxes and hills until " rattle, rattle! " went the ticker, and we were on our feet in a jiffy. I went out and roused the Coolie master, and sent for Savarimuttu. Dressing for the trip was a queer thing. There were we sweltering, thermometer at 90°, and I proceeded to wrap up my poor body in home fall-clothing. Boots that had slept eight months were hauled out and pulled on, and a cloth coat must come out of its hiding-place. Then the ayah must put on more clothing than ever she had before. Manuel, the catechist, was on hand to help us off. The Coolies, about a dozen, and mostly women, were ready, and, lifting the loads on to each others' heads, took up their march. Three pack-horses jogged off, each with a double load. Then our bullock-bandy was brought out and bullocks attached. Baby was waked up, and evidently was amazed at the stir. Then leaving our last orders and the keys with Manuel, the ayah, baby, H., and I tumbled into the bandy, Miss Julia staring with all her eyes. The Coolies led the march, then followed the bandy, the sweeper-woman's little boy running after with a big bottle in his hand, then the sweeper, and Savarimuttu leading his dog.

It is a good four miles to the *tope* (grove) at the base of the hills. It was three o'clock, and the moon was shining brightly, just past the full. The road was familiar, but the drive delightful. We passed lots of donkeys loaded with produce, bound for the hills, and reached the tope about half-past four. There the *dhooly* was awaiting us. This is a hill contrivance, you must know. It is a small palanquin, *very* small, with a cloth covering arched over the box. H. and baby were soon stowed in, and my *tats* were in readiness. A *tat* is a native pony, about as large as a big Shetland, very hardy, used mainly as a pack-horse. To go up the hills we hire two for fifty cents. The saddle was a native one, a cushion-like thing, and for bridle I had a rope tied round his neck. Armed with my cowhide, I mounted and sent the dhooly on ahead. All the rest must walk. H. had four bearers, who started off on a grunt. I made effort to keep up on my beast, but did not learn the ways at first. I found the only way to spur up was to get near enough to the other horse that always kept in front, to slash him. He would run and mine would follow. Just as we started, the east was catching its first tint of red and the birds were beginning their songs. A few rods on, as we entered the gorge, the unwonted sound of running water greeted us. The dim moonlight cast a sombreness over all that was very pleasing. The hills on each side rose rapidly, and in front a great mountain closed the ravine.

As day broke, the outlines of the hills grew more distinct, and we began to see flowers on the trees and

shrubs on every side. By seven o'clock we had reached
the first stopping-place, about a third of the way up.
There was a brook, and we got some tolerably good
water. The Coolies took their breakfast, and rested
about half an hour, and all sorts of people, Coolies,
donkeys, horses gathered about, stopping, too, to get a
peep at baby. Just beyond we met our cows and pony
that had been sent on the day previous. The horse-
keeper had an exciting story to tell about a tiger that
had scared pony so that he broke loose. The fact was,
that the man had felt rather reluctant to spend the
night on the road, as a tiger had killed some cows only
a day or two ago. They saw one, and were of course
frightened, but so was his highness. There is one
prowling about here ; an Englishman saw him a week
ago. After leaving the half-way place, the road leads
right up the face of the mountain that has been facing
you. So steep is the hill that the zigzags seem almost
parallel lines. I walked a good deal to spare pony,
which I had now taken, running after flowers for H. ;
getting out of breath in cutting across, but catching
good long whiffs of the delicious air that now and then
would steal over us. From the hill-side we could look
back on the plains beyond the gorge, from constantly
higher positions, and we made free use of interjections.

At last the tiresome zigzag was over, we shot round
the shoulder of this hill, and came in full view of the
range on which the houses are. Here Mr. Hunt's
horse came in sight. He had sent it to relieve mine.
Looking up way above, I could see two white-covered
umbrellas, and the horse-keeper said these were Mr.
Burnell and Mr. Taylor. I pushed ahead, and in
quarter of an hour I came up with them in a beautiful

grove. Shaking hands over, Mr Burnell gave me a cup of water that made my teeth ache from the cold. Then Mr. Taylor coolly handed me a ripe peach! Oh, what a sight, what a taste! H. soon came up, and Mr. Taylor had another for her. This was one mile from the top, and the hardest pull was yet to come. The Coolies take one path and horses another; so leaving H., I pushed ahead, walking and riding with the two gentlemen. Half-way up, lots of boys came racing to meet us, and at last turning a corner, we came in sight first of the little church, then of one house and of another, until the whole collection burst upon us, nestling among the swelling hills that stretch away to the west. On top of the hill we rounded is Mr. Noyes's house. Across a deep valley from that are two other houses besides this, and still further on, hugging a forest, are two others and the church.

The whole top of this range is formed of beautifully rounded knolls, with valleys between, bare of trees save now and then a clump, but clothed with grass. Their smooth slopes form a most pleasing contrast to the sharp ridges of the peaks seen from the plain. As we came to Mr. Noyes's house, we were met by another squad of still younger ones. A few moments after I reached the top, H. appeared by another road. I galloped across the valley to see Mr Hunt, who was hallooing at me, and H. soon followed. The first good breath of cold air that baby caught scared her so that she screeched and screamed and sobbed most fearfully. She became still after a while, but it took a day fairly to reconcile her to her new home.

Well, we are fairly here, and have a snug jug of a house to ourselves. It is a little place, indeed, this

Rock Cottage. It is actually on a big flat rock, and under a hill or slope. But there is no prospect from it, except the uninteresting valley, beyond which is Mr. Noyes's house. We are writing this Saturday evening in our parlor. This room, as indeed the bedroom next it, looks like a big omnibus. The roof is tiled, but the tiles are hidden by a whitewashed cloth, fastened so as to look like the top of an omnibus. I can touch it with my hand. There are two windows opposite each other, one three feet high, the other two feet and a half. The bedroom joins it at the end, and is a trifle smaller, with one window a foot square. At the end of this is the dining-room, big enough to hold a table and chair in length, and a little less wide. So we are cribbed, cabined, and confined; quite a descent from our palace on the plains. But what of that? we have a home climate, and any quarters would be acceptable. Oh, how cold the water is! And how I have tramped to-day. Out at six this morning with H., Mrs. Hunt, and Miss A. on horses, Mr. Hunt, Mr. Tracy, and the boys on foot. We sent the ladies home and then wandered about, rolling rocks down precipices, and gambolling as the freak took us. But the best of it was that we saw two ibexes, beautiful creatures, bigger than goats, skipping along on a slope away below us. We don't see them every day here.

Then after breakfast I went to get some wood. Each one has to go into the woods, find a dead log, sit on it, claim it, and have it hauled out. When out in the woods, Mr. Yorke came here to find me. Hearing of it, I raced back. He had come for me to go in bathing; so we roused up Mr. Hunt and the Tracys, then took in Mr. Burnell and Mr. Taylor, and started off, Mr. Hunt on horseback. It was about eleven o'clock, — think of trudging off at such an hour in India, almost sure death below! We walked and walked, up hill and down, for over an hour, coming upon a beautiful trout-like stream, and following it up till we came to a fine waterfall of perhaps forty feet, at the base of which lay a delicious pool of most inviting look. Off and in, but whew, how cold! I hardly ever bathed in such apparently cold water at home. We swam and frolicked like boys, as boys we were, and then sunned ourselves and started back. Mr. Yorke and I lingered behind and clambered over the hills by a new way home, getting back by a little after two.

One day has been the over-making of me, all my old life has come back, and I mean to enjoy myself here to the full. So like home : anemones and Solomon's seal, violets and lots of little familiar flowers laugh at you and drive away the gloom. Think of having a cane made of geranium-stalk! Rhododendrons grow on trees as large as apple-trees. I have set the boys to work catching butterflies for S. They are not very plenty, but now that I hear of the safe arrival of my first despatches to S. I shall repeat the experiment often. It hailed here yesterday, and we frightened the ayah by putting a hailstone in her hands. She dropped it as if it had been a coal.

APRIL 24.

As I write there is a fearful storm of rain, thunder, and lightning raging outside. The rain penetrates the roof too; it is an awful storm, hardly a dry spot in the house. The ayah, who sleeps in the dining-room, has come in here to get comfort; she is scared. I had

a nice ramble with pony this morning. The top of
these hills is most singular. All the eminences are of
a like height and contour. Each one has a rounded
head and slopes gradually down till it reaches a stream
below. It is hard, for this reason, to cross from one to
another, as a deep ravine divides and a grove skirts
one side or the other. There seems to be no end to
these hills. We had a grand sight from Nebo, a peak
near by the house and a favorite resort, a morning
or two since: clouds covered the whole plain so that
nothing beyond us was visible, except now and then a
hill - top, looking like an island in the ocean. The
clouds were away below, but I presume looked from
below as clouds usually do; from above there was
much the appearance of a broken sea of ice, covered
with snow, the cakes tossed up in the wildest confusion.
By-and-by the cloud-sea broke up and the plain once
more appeared. I saw a similar sight once from the
Catskill, when we were there together, you remember,
but it did not compare with this for grandeur. . . . .

Another fine excursion was to a spot about three
miles off, where we looked down upon Bow Village.
Whether the people are archers or not I cannot say,
but they certainly have chosen a most romantic spot
for a home. Down deep in a valley they can cultivate only by raising terraces, which, looked at from
the height where we were, presented a very pretty appearance. The whole view would furnish a taking
theme for an artist's pencil. On the way we scared
two deer which soon fled into the jungle.

APRIL 28.

We have a tiger here! This afternoon I went over

to the lower houses to see the people, and was told on
entering that they were looking after a leopard. That
was game somewhat novel, so I started off in pursuit.
Some wood-cutters told me where the gentlemen were,
and I soon met them coming back without the game.
We came up to the wood-cutters, and found that one
of them knew about the beast, that a horse had been
killed by it, and he could show the spot. So back we
went, some on horse and some on foot. About a quarter of a mile beyond the houses is a deserted spot which
goes by the name of the Bombay *dhorie's* house. *Dhorie* is " gentleman." It is a beautiful spot, deserted
six years since, and now rankly overgrown with thistles,
roses, geraniums, peas, and honeysuckles. Friday last
H. and I had wandered through the woods to the spot,
and enjoyed ourselves, all unconscious of our probable
proximity to the beasts of the wood. A long avenue
of tall geraniums leads to the house. To this place,
in the open field, the guide took us and pointed to a
spot in the grass where there had evidently been a tus-
sle. He then followed along by the wood, showing
where the beast had dragged his prey. A little further
on a large round stone, which had been sunk quite
deep in the earth, had been pulled out, and upon it
were horse-hairs. We began to comment on the
strength of the animal that could lug a horse in such
style. Now the trail entered the wood and we followed,
having hard work to make our way through the thicket.
We came to a pool of blood, and a few rods further on
came upon a sight that looked indeed like murder.
The entrails were lying spread out entire, while a few
steps beyond was the head of a horse, with the legs
and ribs, a startling proof that this was no hoax as

some had averred. The head was untouched, but underneath we could see the hole that the animal had made in the neck, evidently when springing upon him. Well, we had the facts, and now what did the deed? Certainly it must have been a powerful brute that could have dragged a horse so far, through the jungle and up-hill too. No chetah did that, we all said; it was a tiger. To-night our opinion is confirmed. There is an old sportsman on the hills who went to look at the spot. He says that nothing but a tiger, and a large one at that, did the deed; that he has been twice to the spot and is in the wood now. So there is a story for you.

It is a little exciting I assure you to think that a Royal Bengal is actually about in such close neighborhood. When the Deputation was here, a tiger broke into Mr. Taylor's cow-house and carried off an ox, actually having to break away the gate-posts in the attempt to get him out. There are two chetahs just over a hill near by. In this wood there are two troops of very singular-looking black monkeys. They are as big as ordinary sheep, and leap immense distances. It is really frightful to come across them. They have an astonishing roar, a most unearthly sound, a hoo! hoo! with an awful gurgling-like sound following it. Mr. Yorke shot one on Saturday; it fell dead from the top of a high tree, and instantly after, down came another like a flash. He thought he had killed two, but to his astonishment the last jumped off and away before he could get his gun to his shoulder.

. . . . A few days ago a party of us went on horseback to Glen Falls, a place close by Bow Village. Coming home we struck off to view an ancient fortification. On the top of low hills we not unfrequently find circular enclosures surrounded with a stone-wall, and below, a range of terraces. They appear to be the sites of ancient villages, with these enclosures for the protection of cattle against wild beasts. As we were riding toward one, Mr. Taylor spied a herd of bison, and at once gave the shout, for it is a rare sight here nowadays. They were on a slope about two miles off, but our glasses brought them near enough for us to make out some twenty-five with calves, grazing wholly unconscious of being ogled by a lot of white folk. It would have been a rich haul for a huntsman. Formerly they used to be in this wood where the tiger is, but they have been gradually driven away. Mr. Burnell has been up here eight times and has never before seen a bison, so you see I seem to be having all the sights on my first visit. A gentleman told me that on the mountains bounding the Kambam valley, on the south, is a vast tract of unexplored land; that, travelling once across it, he came upon a heathen temple, either built of or covered with brass, a resort of pilgrims; that so wild was the spot that elephants wandered into the temple enclosure and actually slept in the temple itself. You see I am full of tiger to-night, and so tell you all the wild stories I can muster.

MAY 3.

All excitement to-day again, not from the tiger however, but from a more harmless thing, — a box. The box has not come yet, but it is coming and within friendly hail. The expectation of its arrival has kept us on the alert all day. The washer-man, who brought up the clothes to-day, said that he saw a box on the way, which I thought would pass for the long-looked-for box, so I seized the spy-glass and ran to a hill about a quarter of a mile off, which commanded the road for a long distance. Nothing to be seen. In the evening a tapâl-man was to be in, so I waited anxiously for that arrival, expecting also a telegram. He came at last, bringing no news except that England was to reconstruct her navy, from the result of the engagement between the Merrimac and Monitor. But the man said he had seen no box. Soon after Mrs. Noyes rode over with a letter from Mr. Noyes, at Periakulam, which settled matters. We had the contents of the box, with the intelligence that they should be sent up on Monday morning, — to-day is Saturday. On the list was a bundle of books weighing fifteen pounds. What it can be I can't guess. However we shall rest over Sunday. But all this fuss and fume would n't have been, if I had not been disappointed before, and of this I must needs tell you, as a faithful chronicler.

My catechists were to meet me below on the 30th, Wednesday. We had calculated also that our flour and boxes would reach Periakulam by the same date. So it was arranged that I should go down and take Sav. with me to put the flour into tins at once. Sav. started off Tuesday morning before sunrise. At two o'clock precisely I started, proposing to foot it down half-way and ride on a tat from there to the base, meeting my bandy there. I trudged off manfully and reached the half-way place in just two hours. There I found my tat and mounted him. He was a raw beast, but I kept my temper for a while. Before long, however, the clouds began to blacken, and the muttering among the hills told me to prepare for a mountain-storm. We have one almost daily toward night. I hurried the

nag as well as I could for half the distance, when the
drops began to fall.   Then I got off and hurried on,
on foot.   A brisk walk would, I hoped, carry me safe
through ; but a whiff behind made me turn round, when
I saw the wind come tearing down the valley behind.
I started on a trot, but the wind gave chase, tossing the
water of the little stream away below me into foam,
and whirling the leaves and dust about me.   I saw I
was in for a run, so in the hope of outstripping the
rain and reaching my bandy, I put in and tore down
the path in a real old-fashioned Williams-College gait.
But it was no use.   Pat came the big drops, faster and
faster, and soon sharp lightning, and peals of thunder joined in, till I was in the midst of a storm that
for wild fury beat any storm that I ever was in.   It
was from behind and the wind blew me along, while
the big drops of rain and the hail pelted me most un-
mercifully.   In five minutes I was wet to the skin,
and concluding that running down below would not
keep me dry, I held up and trudged philosophically
along, as well as my water-logged boots would let me.
The storm was soon spent of its force, and when at last
I reached the bandy it was quiet.   I got in, hauled off
my boots, wrapped myself in the dusty bandy-covering
and felt comfortable.   But I was not to be left so long.
The bullocks went slowly and I tried to hurry the man,
as we had four miles more to the house.   He said that
one bullock was sick, and the bullock soon showed his
indisposition by quietly lying down.   There he lay.
The driver pulled and tugged and coaxed, twisted his
tail, tied his nostrils up so that he could not breathe,
and resorted to all the ordinary and extraordinary ex-
pedients familiar to bandy-men, but in vain.   So I,

disgusted, pulled on my boots, after a deal of labor, and set out on foot again. But my heels were sore, and I spied my tat hobbling along in the rear. I waited and tried him for about half a mile, but he was too slow, absolutely ; so I dismounted and stood it out to the house, which I reached at exactly six, a remarkably good go for this country. I had a good bath and rub and was as well as ever ; a little better too, for our tapâl-man came from Madura bringing the first instalment of home goods in the shape of two " Bibliotheca Sacras " containing my article. I was quite interested in looking over the articles, reminding me as they did of the acquaintance who got them up. I was better still when nine o'clock brought Mr. Rendall along on his way to the hills, and having in charge all the overlands.

Wednesday the catechists came and I spent a good part of the day with them, hearing reports and lessons. They have lessons in the Bible, Church History, Theology, Catechism, etc., to recite. No bandies came, and on Thursday I again had the catechists, and a very pleasant meeting it was too. One of the subjects up for discussion was Self-Denial, and we had quite an animated time over it. Pastor Seymour told a curious story of a man in Periakulam, whom he had lately seen, who for one whole year had gone without speaking a word, and for another year without asking a question. He told Seymour that he did it to " subdue himself." I am getting the catechists to learn about missions, and had Breckenridge give an account of the Nestorians. I shall have Seymour write a letter to them, perhaps to Mar Yohannan, and hope thus to put the people in communication. I shall try the same thing with other missions.

Still the bandies did not come, and in despair I determined to go up the hills again in the morning, and by eleven o'clock I was again at the top. By next morning I learned that the goods reached Periakulam the evening of the day I left. But Monday noon will bring them doubtless, and then what a time we will have.

[The box which causes such excitement, is one which friends at home find opportunity to send by ship every few months, and which contains beside flour and other necessaries, the numerous tokens of home remembrance, and the papers, books, and periodicals which cannot be sent by mail. One can guess the twofold pleasure which a box would create, in the sending and the receiving.]

[JOURNAL LETTER.]

MAY 9.

The box has come! after plenty of delays it has come. Monday morn I went out with my marine glass on to Mount Nebo, which overlooks the plain, and tried to spy out the long-looked-for box, which was to come up that morning. And not in vain, for away below I could just descry two men lugging some big thing swung on a pole. I watched them till they came tolerably near, and then ran back to tell H. The box very provokingly stopped to rest on the hill just opposite, close by, in full sight; but though I got all the coolies to shout after it, it would not budge for half an hour. At last it came, and I triumphantly led it into our little room and attacked it with hammer instantly. We made as long a job of it as possible, making a rule to open only one package at a time. One of the first things that turned up was a serious-looking bundle, promising something extensive, and which set us agog as we read on a slip of paper outside, "Here's fun." Unwrapping it, another slip disclosed itself with "Must be something patriotic; see the red, white, and blue," and a flag appeared of dimensions small. I began to suspect somebody and that somebody S. The fellow was at his old pranks, and I made preparations for storing a supply of string. I was not wrong, but did n't obey one slip's injunction, "Cut the string," and was bound to see the fun through. So, after patiently unknotting twelve successive snarls, the bundle rapidly diminishing, we came at last as our reward to a stereogram of a soldier's tent. We used ourselves up laughing over that. Then came a book. . . . . . "Littell's," etc., came out, all in due time, until finally the whole box was emptied, when I got into it to find a clear place in the room to stand in. Such a litter as this room has been in since!

[TO HORACE E. SCUDDER.]

PULNEY HILLS, May 16, 1862.

. . . . I often picture our meeting years hence. The circle of acquaintance is already changing. Two uncles and a cousin have passed from the world and will soon from mind, and no year probably will go by without witnessing similar changes. Then we who live shall change, and not having been with you I shall be startled at your appearance, and you at mine, for I have no doubt that in many things our sympathies will have become estranged, which would not have been the case had I remained in America. Already I have changed. I have a baby, and I sit and rock her to

sleep or carry her about in my arms, as if I never had
been a stranger to the little thing. I fear my years do
not add worth to my character. Whether it be the
climate or not, I am not sure, but certainly I am not
the systematic, plodding hand that I once was. I shirk
work with fewer stings from conscience than once was
true. I see many opportunities for at least fancied
good, which I do not improve; duties plainly imperative I lay aside for engagements more consonant with
taste. How difficult it is to reform, to change old habits. . . . . But how I have been running on about my
poor self, forever making resolutions, forever breaking
them.

Oh, H., you don't know how I want to go home
sometimes. I fear I am a poor missionary in spirit,
not that homesickness is a sin, — but a feeling of selfish-
ness comes over me. It is easier to live a Christian
life at home. Extraneous promptings to labor are
plenty there, here very few. Here am I set down
twenty miles from any white body, with an illimitable
work to do, a work which will more than meet my
ability to labor, a field where the best powers could
work freely, and nothing to prompt me to work, save
my own spirit. Little or no adequate sympathy will
you find among the natives, little or no opportunity for
displaying yourself. There is no approved model or
method of working, at least none so binding as you find
in a home pastorate. The people are not at all solicitous for your services, and you have no invitation in the
character of your audiences to display your talents.
Your work is to impress upon most unimpressible material the pure truth of the Word. You ought to go
and talk to a people day after day, who don't want to

hear you, about things wholly repugnant to them, and which find little response in their consciences. Our religion is not popular or even respectable, as it is at home, and the coarsest minds shrink from appearing before a crowd, only to be laughed at.

And then the quiet pleasures of a home pastorate come before me. Here our best energies are expended in making the mere tools for our work, — bare words. All the time thus employed here — in itself of no value scarcely — is gained at home where your tools are at hand, for other work. So that the actual amount of labor put forth by a missionary in preaching is much less than that of a home pastor in the same time, a point not to be forgotten. Yes, I do want to go home sometimes, and like E. run down to old Boston. I suppose it is human nature to think and feel so, but I do want to have such thoughts swallowed up in brighter and truer, nobler ones. Life is quickly over, and I sometimes picture the good time we shall have in another world in talking together about things that have happened since we parted. Could you come with me to Nebo and look down on my wide field with me, you would say, — "What an inspiring view!" It is, and there is everything in it to nerve a real Christian to jubilant labor. Here is where I want your help and that of all at home. Help me to labor in courage and in faith.

[TO HIS SISTER.]

KODI KÂNAL, May 20, 1862.

We are on the Pulneys, of whose fame you have heard so much. You would relish racing about on these hills, especially after having been in the furnace below for a twelvemonth. The country is very, very

21

different from mountain country at home. If you go
to the White Hills, you have to go up and up a long
way before you come to the genuine Washington.
Here you ride along on the dead level, till you come
plump abut a range of mountains. The effect of this
from the summit is peculiar ; for so close to you do the
plains seem, that you fancy you could jump off on to
them. Then again, if you go up Mount Washington,
you find about room enough to turn round on tiptoe
in ; here, the top of the hills is much like the second
story in the old Chatham House, quite as spacious as
the lower, only a little more wavy. You can go an indefinite distance, all the while eight thousand feet above
the plains. It is exactly a second story, only instead
of being level, like an Indian plain, it is diversified, like
Berkshire County.

We have three weeks more of leave, and then return
to our Plain life. It will be to me much like beginning
life here, for I shall have a full year in view, as I have
not had before. It will be an interesting and test year
with me. It will prove either my worthiness or in-
capacity, and I do dread it not a little. Any amount
of work is possible ; a broad field and plenty of ways
of doing good, in any one of which I shall have occasion to try my best powers. Shall I have the spirit to
meet all cases ? Shall I conquer indolence, worldliness,
false ambition, personal preferences, and set myself with
a hearty will to battle against this gigantic heathenism ?
I tell you, J., I dread the encounter, for I do feel my
weakness. Yet the work to be done is plainly before
me, and if I fail, I foresee that upon myself the blame
will fall. It is a hard field, yet not by any means a
discouraging one, for if one choose he can succeed in

throwing a better spirit into the community where he
labors. But this can be done only by being possessed
entirely with the Spirit of God. Our power, our courage is from Him only, and we can't help seeing this in
India.

[TO A NEPHEW, H. B. S.]

KODI KÂNAL, May 27, 1862.

Don't think from the heading of this letter that I
am an amphibious dog, spending a part of my life in a
canal, or acting the part of the individual whose business it is to sing out, " Bridge ! heads, gemmen ! "
*Kânal* is " grove," which alters the picture at once, and
places me in a more romantic situation, one corresponding better with fact.

Your letter was welcome enough, showing me that I
had not lost my uncleship by exiling myself out of all
reach of you. . . . . It was a regular vacation epistle,
a lazy, meandering, sunshiny, clever thing, but did not
smack of the days when Virgil or Horace or Day must
be whipped off, and room made for stationery. Send
me another, clear from Berkshire, that shall be redo-
lent of Flora's Glen, New (Boot-jack) Street, College
Hydrant, and West College, if you want to stir the
deeps in an old collegian's heart. Could n't you let out
whether you are 'Logian or — what was the name of
that other across the way ? But perhaps the old halls
are deserted, and young Williams enjoys better accom-
modations.

. . . . You know, Harry, an old dog always talks or
barks sagely, an old crab is forever telling his children
crabs not to crawl so one-sidedly ; so I, looking back
over my sprawling and hobbling career through college,
feel terribly like taking you by the button, and reading

a little lesson to your innocence. But I suppose you will be a Soph by the time this reaches you, and be important enough in your own eyes at least not to need lecturing. However, take a leaf or two from my experience. Don't be afraid of fresh air and out-door work. Gymnasium is good, but Northwest Hill is better. Don't think because you don't expect to be Astronomer Royal that calculus is of no use to you, or give up trying to be a good scholar because you did not have as good a " fit " in one thing as another. Don't lie by lazily because you don't need to study hard to get the lessons; the tortoise will be clawing your back if you don't persist in keeping ahead. Don't go fish-ing always inside the breakwater of tasks assigned, but go outside in rough sailing and look out for other fish. Take up some subject that you like and follow it up, finding out all you can about it — let it be the history of the Aztecs or the Pottawatomies. (I wish you would write me a treatise on Cromlechs, who built them, etc.) Read a little and eat the words; read not for quantity, but for quality. (A groan — " Oh that I had done so!" D. C. S.) Don't (What! another " don't?") think that I mean to bother you any more. Let me wind up with one good *do*. Maintain the reputation, not of a race of Scudders, but of your heavenly Master. Guide your course in college by that thought, and you can't go far wrong. . . . . .

[TO HIS FATHER.]

KODI KÂNAL, June 5, 1862.

Your abundant and always most excellent journals deserve more than a general journal reply, but I am unable to find time enough to answer as amply as I

could wish. To-day, though, you must of course have
a letter all to yourself, for if I write common folk upon
their birthdays, above all should I write you. It is a
subject of personal rejoicing to me that you have fairly
arrived at this landmark. As far back as I can remember, I have given as answer to persons who,
wondering at your activity, have asked your age,
seventy-three. To me you have stood stock-still for I
don't know how long a time; if I could hope that it
would be in future as in past, I should be glad to hold
you still, but I fear that is impossible, so I rejoice
that hereafter I shall have some confidence in pro-
nouncing you seventy-three. It is a real pleasure to
me to know that how many soever years you mark
upon your calendar, you will to me continue where you
were when I saw you last, and I can, must always
think of you as the kind, cheerful father that I knew
then.

This is a blue day to me ; various circumstances
have made me feel unhappy. . . . . I don't see, and
never did see, where my gloominess and sulkiness and
down-heartedness came from. Certainly not from
either of you, and yet there is nothing that causes me
so much grief. . . . . Dear father, a man whose heart
was the abode of no one but the Holy Spirit, would be
full of joy at the prospect before him in such a field as
mine. Here are countless numbers who know nothing
of the gospel, to whom the gospel is capable of imparting infinite good. It is in my power to give it to them,
— nothing whatever hinders but time. I ought to leap
at the thought of the opportunity, while, in fact, it is
usually a hard trial for me to preach to the heathen.
In our weekly prayer-meeting up here, which fell to

my charge this afternoon, I remarked on these words of
Paul, " We also believe and therefore speak," and the
others followed in the same strain. Belief is requisite
to preaching, and according to the depth and firmness
of our belief will be the fervency of our labors. Abundance to do, and nothing in the way but an unbelieving
heart. In one week we go to the Plains again, and my
prayer is, that I may have grace to overcome my
natural diffidence, fear of man, and love of quiet ease,
and be bold and untiring in preaching the truth.

To do what I ought, I must be away from home a
great deal, in fact more than half the time. This in
itself is hard for me and hard for H. She is alone then,
sixteen miles from any one, and I am constantly solicitous lest some evil shall occur in my absence. I grow
weary of being away in uncomfortable places, seeing
nobody but poor heathen, and as I cannot be out in the
daytime much, I have abundance of time for reverie.
I must make some arrangement by which I can carry
on my studies in my absence from home, and occupy
my time fully. As mother knows, I am sure to be out
of sorts if I am out of work. I do easily get tired of
talking. I don't think that naturally I like to talk,
except to boon companions on pet topics, and I need to
rouse myself to converse on religion with everybody I
meet. But all these difficulties may in time be overcome, if God's grace be but granted, and that is always
procurable. I certainly am deeply interested in my
work, and feel at times enthusiastic enough. I look
forward to entering anew upon it, with really pleasurable anticipation. I am still tempted, however, to turn
aside from legitimate labor to work at topics always
interesting to me now, as they were at home, but

which are not of direct bearing upon my missionary work.

. . . . We have a pleasant household. Our head-servant Savarimuttu is invaluable. His own father is cook. The two gardeners and the horse-keeper are all good friends of these two, and all moves on harmoniously. It seems a great number, but were you here, you would see the necessity. A common Yankee is worth three or four Hindûs. . . . . I don't wonder that you are happy in your old days in looking at what we purpose to be. What a singular feeling this of paternity is. How I look at little Julia and ponder over the subtle way in which her immortality is locked in with mine. I believe I have given her to the Lord, but there remains so much to do; the giving does not release me from responsibility, but binds me in it the more strongly. How you would delight to have another little grand-daughter to play with. She is. full of smiles, and as good as a child knows how to be. Oh, how I hope she will be a good girl!

[TO GEO. D. DUTTON, ESQ.]

KODI KÀNAL, June 12, 1862.

. . . . I trust that the good people at home will not contract any extravagant notions as to the barbarousness of our surroundings. We are amongst heathen truly, and bad enough ones, still we are not outlawed from all comforts and conveniences. As we did not come out with the intention of making ourselves as uncomfortable as possible, we do not deem it out of place to take in a comfort when one happens along. I take it that the principle upon which a Christian missionary, as every Christian man, should act in life, is to place himself, as far as is in his power, in just such a position as shall insure the best possible use of his faculties. We need comforts for the flesh in India more than you at home; that is, we take from the list of luxuries, as you deem them, and label them necessaries. Missionaries here are not extravagant at all; indeed, they cannot well be on their salaries. At first sight, one fancies that money goes farther in India than in America, since labor is so much cheaper and food simpler; but in truth many things unite to raise living to about the same notch in expense that one reaches at home. Wages of one man are low, but a man here is not worth one fifth as much as a man at home, as respects the amount of work you can get from him. The people are not exactly lazy, but *work* is not in them. Then it is impossible wholly to ignore the customs of the country; in India we must do as the Hindûs do. . . . . .

[JOURNAL LETTER.]

JUNE 13.

I begin my journal on the Hills, the evening before moving down. Our boxes are pretty much all packed, ready for the heads of Coolies to carry them. Pony is to go half-way, early in the forenoon, and a little afterward we shall follow: H. in the dhooly, as she came up, and I on foot, till I catch up with pony. I am bound not to put up with tats, the wretched beasts that I rode up. . . . . Well, we have done with the Hills for one year. We certainly have been bettered physically by our stay. I feel much less of the lassitude and reluctance to work that had crept upon me on the Plains, and go down with spirits a little more alive for work. There will be plenty to do, I assure you. A catechists' meeting comes in a few days. Then I must put the whole station into better working order, visit the congregations at once, and prepare for an early tour of exploration through my whole field. . . . . The southwest monsoon has set in. It blows most furiously, and brings clouds of dust, but it generally cools the atmosphere. It has been intensely hot below for a few days past, thermometer over 90° at 5 P. M.; but I hope the winds have moderated the temperature, so that it may be a little more endurable for us. But we must put a bold face upon it. At the best it will be hot.

## CHAPTER XV.

### RETURN TO THE PLAINS — TOURING.

#### [JUNE–OCTOBER, 1862.]

[THE vacation of eight weeks over, the missionaries returned to their work on the hot plains. The rest had refreshed David; he had also gained, I think, new and more quiet resolution. He saw before him a year of toil, the character of which had been made known by his short experience, and he looked fully in the face the discouragements that awaited him. He retained his old buoyancy, but he was growing more constantly thoughtful: not care-worn, but care-sobered. I cannot forbear reminding the reader how, in the midst of his sorrowful self-reproach at opportunities of good lost or thrown away, we see him turning again to work with unceasing energy, confirmed in his habits of devout confidence in God, and inquiring diligently the will of his Master. " Nothing," writes an associate, Mr. Washburn, " could deter him, whether he was at home or on journeys, as I have often seen him, from protracted philological and devotional study of the Bible in the morning, and in the evening from private meditation and prayer. I have been astonished at the jealousy with which he regarded these habits. It was his wont to walk on the veranda in the dusk of eve and review the day. If he was occupied with company or other disturbance, he retired to the roof, and there, beyond the reach of any who knew his habits, he communed

with himself and his God.   If it could be said that no
one was so enamored of philosophical and antiquarian pursuits, it could also be said that no one among
us had studied the sense and language of the Bible
more thoroughly or sought more devoutly its spir "

It was in this temper of loyalty to his Master that
he worked patiently, cheerfully, and with the enthusiasm which so often thrilled him.   He gave himself no
time for reluctant thoughts or unwise expectations;
backward he did look, often, to the group of friends
whom he had left in America.   Before leaving home, a
stereograph had been taken of the family in the house
where he had lived; regularly each Sunday morning,
when not touring, did David sit over his stereoscope, his
eye riveted on this group, seizing hold by his memory
of every line in the faces, every attitude and expression.   But he turned away from this sad pleasure
doubtless with more earnest purpose to the work at
hand, looking, how wistfully his letters sometimes show,
to a more perfect union in a better world.   His own
removal was nearer than he knew; but the faith which
bade him look to that coming day, inspired him also
with more ceaseless daily diligence.]

[JOURNAL LETTER.]

PERIAKULAM, June 27, 1862.

Yesterday one year ago was a day to be remembered, when we first saw Madras, and first touched
Indian soil, and first breathed Indian air.   We shall not
soon forget it.   I can see the first footprint I made on
the beach; I can breathe over again that first breath,
the like of which I have not known since, — all the
impression of that first stifling evening and the next

morning. One year has gone; two years it seems to me at least. Certainly but one year in my life has been of like interest or importance to me. Now just about one year from my landing, we begin life fairly, for now we are down from the hills, and have a full year clearly in view. I cannot feel wholly despondent upon looking at my position. I certainly am better off in the language than most at a year's distance from their starting-point, which is due of course to my having studied at home; but I am equally and more sure that it is owing to culpable negligence that I am not much farther on. The coming year will, I think, witness more satisfactory progress.

[TO SAMUEL H. SCUDDER.]

PERIAKULAM, July 1, 1862.

I have been wishing I were at home to-day. I do sometimes. I often think of home, you may believe, but now and then I have a crying after it. It is almost always associated with a sense of my unfitness for the place I occupy. This day sadness arose from a failure in duty yesterday morning. Early in the morning I took a handful of tracts and started off to preach in the village alone. I thought I should succeed, but when I reached the village my fancied courage fled; and after walking about, where was any amount of people ready to listen, I turned and came back, my conscience all the while hammering at me, and I virtually saying, "I know it, but I won't." That it is a severe cross to me is true, but no excuse for actual dereliction. It is very hard for me to go into a crowd whose language I can't understand to a tenth part, and stammer out facts that they don't want to hear, and I feel that the simple secret of it all is that my love is not strong enough to bear up against the pressure of disinclination. But if I cannot do this, what am I staying about here for? To many persons this work is scarcely at all trying; it always was to me at home, and it is here. The circumstances are more favorable here, save that we know the language so poorly. The people are seldom disrespectful, and always fear you in a measure. But next week I am going upon an extended tour through my field and must preach.

. . . . As we were driving this afternoon I met a Brahman with a native book in his hand. I stopped and asked him what it was, and he said " the Veda." It was a large palm-leaf book, and was only a tenth of the whole. He was rather scared at my talk, but gradually became more communicative, and engaged to come to the house next Monday and bring me some books. It was just the thing I wanted to see. Precious little learning have these people, and miserable beings they truly are. Yet it is not an improbable supposition which has been broached to account for the fact that so few Brahmans have received the truth, that they are sunk more deeply in sin, moral pollution, than the common people. I believe they are.

[TO HORACE E. SCUDDER.]

PERIAKULAM, July, 1862.

I have had in mind for a long while to write you a letter in answer to your request, giving you a minute (accent on the first syllable) account of the daily life of your exiled brother. I fear that the most finely drawn-out story will fail to give any adequate picture of life here, where all the surroundings are so utterly antipodal to yours, — trees and ground and sounds and moving creatures of every grade so different. But such as it is I will give.

The sun rises in May at 5.36, in January at 6.30; and these are the extremes in the year. This morning it rose at 5.47. It is not light before five. I mean to get up by five, but resolves in India are as apt to be broken as in America, especially when you sleep in the same room with a baby, who pays no sort of regard to the ordinary laws of man. I am usually, when at home, awakened by somebody, gardener and nurse perhaps, talking on the veranda. I retire to the room close by, rubbing my eyes and peering somewhat cautiously about lest there be a cobra in the bathing-tub, as there was one morning. Then I bathe, usually in the style peculiar to this country, by pouring water over me, for which operation a place is sunk in the floor. During this process I muse upon my somnolency, and solemnly affirm that next morning shall see me prevent the dawn. Appearing outside I usually find all doors open, the ayah sitting on the floor, doing her hair, — the amount of her or any native lady's toilet; the sweeper-woman sweeping the hall with her little wisp-broom, stooping till you begin to think her back will break; and lastly Savarimuttu, who touches his hand to his head and says, "Good morning." His first business is to provide a cup of tea and a couple of slices of toast. This answers until nine o'clock, the break-fast-hour.

Two courses are now open. If I am to preach, I summon Manuel Sylvester, and together we trudge off for some mud village, within three miles, and preach for half an hour; or I go to the town alone and meet the pastor. My habits are not thoroughly settled yet. This morning, as Manuel is not at home and I do not think it advisable to go without a catechist, I stayed at home and tried to put in order my grindstone which has lain unused thus long. In the mean time everybody has waked up. H. appears and baby. We call the horse-keeper and tell him to " tie Mistress's saddle," and forthwith pony appears with a saddle that looks on him like a howdah on an elephant. H. mounts and is off for an hour's ride before the sun is out brightly. The hen-house and dove-cote are opened, the hundred white and speckled pigeons come fluttering along, the hens follow, and our three ducks solemnly quack their contented salaam. The two gardeners, one of whom lives here in the servants' houses, one in town, take their little short-handled hoes, their solitary implement, and go to work in their lazy way, or they draw water to water the parched ground, one man walking the long sweep, holding on by a tree growing beside it, the other straddling the well and pulling up the bucket and emptying, while the old watchman, who has slept soundly all night, turns the water by his hoe into one bed and shuts it out of another. Then our dapper-looking tailor comes from the village and seats himself on his mat upon the back veranda, and invites anybody to come and have a chat. Add to these the cook and cook-boy whom we have just added to our attendants, and you have our domestic establishment *in extenso*.

Until 7.30 all hands busy themselves, baby among the rest. At that hour the big bell bangs, and summons us all to prayers. Then, beside the above, we have the wives and children of catechist and servants, forming quite a little congregation. We read a chapter, and Manuel asks questions upon it. We sing a Tamil hymn, during which time the gardener's daughter makes a fearful rumpus, and then close with prayer from Manuel or myself. The whole exercise occupies half an hour. We disperse. The ayah scampers to get hot water for baby, whom mamma is probably trying to keep good-humored until bathing and eating-time. Horse-keeper brings pony round and ties him near my door, so that I may see him groomed and fed, else he would not groom him and would himself eat the food; and I take my Hebrew in Genesis or my Greek in the " Life of Christ," and study half an hour, enjoying the task greatly. I have commenced the Bible and also " Life of Christ," following Ellicott's plan.

At nine comes breakfast, when I begin to feel a little cross; but chicken cutlet and fried plantains and waffles give me better spirit. After breakfast come English prayers, and then the day begins with a sweep from ten to four. First I must perhaps give directions about the carpenter's work, who is mending some church-windows or what not, or I must nudge the gardeners. For Tamil I read a Tamil story, then Henry Scudder's tract, then a Psalm. In the mean while my mûnshi comes and sits by my side upon the floor, adjusts his spectacles, fans himself with his handkerchief, and goes to work at collecting synonyms or vulgarisms, which latter it is well to know, if not to use. I read to him what I have studied. Then I translate an English tract into Tamil and English Bible into Tamil, with the mûnshi and three separate versions, a first-rate exercise. To-morrow I shall study up a sermon on miracles, an introduction to a series that I propose preaching

upon Christ's miracles. H. sits in the next room, poring over her Tamil exercises until one o'clock, when
we have " tiffin," consisting of cold yesterday's pudding,
cake, plantains, custard-apples, or what not. Then H.
recites. At three o'clock, I throw aside my special
Tamil studies and take up some different task. Just
now I am studying "Renan on the Semitic Languages."

At four o'clock comes the ever-welcome dinner. I
must not forget to state though that little Miss Julia
makes herself a conspicuous actor in the forenoon scenes.
When awake she sits in her mother's room, talking
most assiduously over her simple toys, or visiting me
now and then and making fun with the mûnshi. We
dine on chickens, on rice and curry, now and then on
mutton : to-day, note it, on partridges ! After dinner
I go about generally, perhaps doing a little fixing-up,
usually overseeing the gardeners, to-day showing them
how to lay out the flower-garden. At half-past five
H., baby, and I are off in our nice little rockaway for
a drive. Baby talks half the way, then cries and goes
to sleep. We have various drives about, and always
come home refreshed by the cool breezes. Next comes
tea, right after tea prayers and a fuss with Julia, who
won't go to sleep, do what we will. And then, — the
inevitable letter-writing in my study, H. sitting opposite to me. Thus we are now, various insects fluttering or crawling about or banging against the wall, bats
stealthily whisking back and forth through the rooms,
frogs croaking, crickets chirping, and a pleasant breeze
coming through the open Venetians. Baby usually
gives us a tune or two in the evening, but has been
quite unmusical to-night. "What time !" just now
says H. "Half-past nine." "Oh, I must go right to

22

bed." And so we must, for ten o'clock is late sitting up for us here. We seem to need more sleep.

So, my boy, I have given you a day, and very much in this way does each one pass. Sunday varies by necessity. We have two services here, and in the afternoon I go to the town church. On Tuesday evening the weekly tapâl from Madura comes in, putting us in connection with the outward world. Monday morning I have a meeting with helpers here, studying Paul's Epistles with them. Once a month they all come to be examined and to report. Every fourth week I propose to tour.

[JOURNAL LETTER.]

ANDIPATTI, July 13.

It is Sunday, the day's work is done and, while waiting for Kurubatham, the catechist, to come and have a little prayer-meeting with me, I will commence my journal, on themes as appropriate for Sunday as any other day. Vetham the cook and my bandy-man are sitting talking in rather loud tones upon subjects somewhat abstruse for them. Bandy-man asked me about our country and the ocean, and the few things I told him have greatly excited him, so that he asks me if white men can sail to the sun. This day has been a most interesting one to me. I came here Friday night, and yesterday morning early walked to Maniakaram-patti, to examine the school. On my return I went on top of a high hill, and had a good view of my field, and laid out my work: you see I have come now for a week's stay. After breakfasting at half-past nine, I studied some, and at two o'clock examined two persons who wished to join the church; they were man and wife, the woman rather an intelligent person, but fond of trifling, and I did not feel so confident as to her piety. The man was less intelligent, but gave better evidence of being a humble Christian. I was really pleased with him. Immediately after dinner I went to M. again, and held lecture preparatory to Communion, talking about the persons who were refused admittance to heaven, although familiar with the Lord. One often questions whether the same end does not await many of those who have nominally renounced heathenism. Coming back, I had the same talk here and went to bed. To-day I woke with the feeling of a burden upon me, from the recollection of what was before me. I was to perform offices which were wholly new to me, — to receive persons for the Communion, to baptize old men and children, and administer the Supper for the second or third time. At ten o'clock another man came to be examined. I had seen him when here last and knew about him; he is of higher caste than our people generally, has long been familiar with this way in Mr. Herrick's field, and has for some time been desirous of joining the church. He has an old mother already a communicant, but not over-faithful to the spirit of her persuasion; he has no wife, but three children. I had quite a conversation with him. He spoke well and easily and familiarly on the topic in hand, and when speaking of his duty as a church-member, took off a silver ring and threw it down, as a signal, he said, of having renounced earthly pomp. I did not feel wholly satisfied with his spirit, but could not feel that I should do right in refusing his request. He is punctilious in religious duties, praying when he goes to his field to work, and when he begins to draw water from the well, etc., and has, according to the catechist's testimony, been striving to overcome a somewhat hasty temper.

MONDAY MORNING.

At twelve yesterday the church-members from the two villages assembled here for service. We decided to alternate in holding the Communion, first in Andipatti, next in Maniakarampatti. I was sorry to notice evidences of caste feeling. The mother of the man last-mentioned was at considerable pains to secure a seat where she should not be polluted by the Pariahs in the house. The M. people are all Pariahs, Andipatti people are Shanars, a little higher, and the old woman higher still. Last Communion season this woman refused to be present, because it was held in M. church, and she could not avoid contamination. Her son, I am glad to say, is quite indifferent. We had quite a good congregation, and I talked about this feast which the Lord had spread for us; after a short sermon I baptized the two adults — men — and two children. The woman who was to join the church had been baptized when a child. I made the three candidates stand up, while I read to them the Apostles' Creed, to which they assented, and also a short promise which I had drawn out, to the intent that they were hereafter to renounce the devil and his works, and all earthly aims, — to seek to build up the church, and live according to the commandments of God. It was as simple as I could make it, and I think it was intelligible to the people.

But in spite of all my anxiety I enjoyed the service, particularly the baptismal rite, and felt unusually the solemnity of my office, which authorized me to pronounce over my fellow-man the name of Jehovah:

those who decline to administer the rite, shut themselves out from a peculiar blessing, I think. In the afternoon we had another meeting of this congregation, and examined all in New and in Old Testament history. You can have no conception of this "windy season." It blows a perfect gale for two months from the southwest, for the most part unremittingly, night and day; it reminds me constantly of a gale at sea. I speak of it, because it confused me greatly yesterday. It blows the dust furiously, too, so that you can keep nothing clean, — books, plates, bed, person, are all covered with it, and there is no keeping it off.

After meeting, yesterday evening, I went out for a walk and a talk with Kurubatham, but was met at the door by a party of Brahmans and others, who had come to pay their respects to me. Intelligent men they were, and one can't help longing for the day when such persons shall be numbered among our church-members. I must say, however, that the day does seem nearer than it did. One year ago, when this church was built, these very men were mad against Mr. Noyes, and cursed him bitterly, utterly refusing to have anything to do either with him or with his books. Yesterday they were as civil and courteous as my best friends, and received tracts and gospels gladly, and talked freely about our religion, while the head man, a Brahman, asked me to send him a New Testament, promising to pay for it. The rest of yesterday's doings you know.

This morning I rose at five, and after a cup of tea as usual, Kurubatham joined me, and we set out to visit some neighboring villages. The first one we went to, about a mile distant, was the "outside" of a larger village, — the shoemakers' quarter, it being custom-

ary for this lowest caste of all to live by themselves,
outside the village limits. There we talked, for about
three quarters of an hour, to a dozen men, beside
women, children, and dogs. I noticed on the wall of
the house where we stood a number of white dots,
and found they were put on when the house was first
built, " to keep the house from falling down." I said
only a few words, explaining to them why I had come
to the country, to tell them good news which I had
heard, and therefore wished to make others know.

We then went to the larger village, and had another
long and very interesting talk. There are always one
or two persons who take the lead in the conversation,
and the others listen. Kurubatham said to the crowd
that soon gathered, " I will read a proclamation, and
then the ' gentleman ' will talk ; " so he read Mr Taylor's simple tract, " A Brief Statement of Bible Truth,
of Man's Fall and Recovery," and then I began by
saying pretty much what I had said before, how there
was a difference between them and my countrymen,
in color and dress and worship, but that formerly my
forefathers also worshipped idols, and that having heard
of the Christian way they had left off their old customs,
and worshipped the one true God ; and that now I had
come to give them the same message we had heard,
that they too might believe. The chief speaker was a
very pleasant fellow, about my age, and spoke without any bitterness or ridicule, but apparently in sober
earnest. I cannot remember, nor did I fully understand enough, to give you the conversation as it occurred ; it turned mostly upon an expression in Mr.
Taylor's tract, which I had repeated, that " the former
time was a time of darkness, but the light had at last

come." The man asked what had become of all my forefathers and all his forefathers; was their time, in truth, only a time of darkness? Others believe differently, saying there are many gods, etc., how can we tell which is the truth? I told him that persons living and working in mines might as well say, " There is no such thing as one great light, the sun ; all we know about is the lamp or torches we carry." Kurubatham explained how Jesus Christ was come as the true Light, now for the first time shining. We talked a long time on this, a large crowd listening attentively. Of course, Kurubatham bore the brunt of the conversation, I putting in a word now and then, as I understood an objection, and felt able to meet it, with my scant stock of Tamil. Toward the end, the man said there was a great deal of evil in the world, and that we needed weapons to contend against it with. " Yes," Kurubatham said, " and we have them in these verses which we must place in our hearts where the enemy is ; " and I added that God, who had made our souls, had promised to give His own power to any one who, storing these verses within, should sincerely strive to fight against sin. Then we left after distributing some tracts. I do feel encouraged to labor here. People do not oppose us with anything but argument, at least, not with ridicule or abuse, and they are not indifferent, but listen and talk, which is a step in advance of past days.

To-day is the Fair Day in Andipatti, when all the villagers from towns about bring in their produce to sell ; it is now ten o'clock, and the crowd is gathering fast. Hundreds come, and we shall have abundant opportunity to preach; so I stay in the village, and will write as to our success.

Well, the day has passed, and it has been a day of work, and the work has come nearer my ideas of missionary labor than any I have spent in India thus far. I had a short nap, and read a little in Littell, after breakfast, and at eleven went to see the fair. About seven hundred people had come together, and were squatted by their goods, in the middle of the open space by the church, and through the bazaar street. I stopped at a trinket stall, and bought a wooden rattle for baby, and several curiosities to send to you when time offers. I then went back to the church, and leaving my purchases, went with Kurubatham to a temple where the people were squatted about; we had been there just before, and seen a cow-doctor extract a thorn from each of the eyes of a poor cow, and then squirt into them tobacco-juice; he appeared to suck the thorns out, but I am not sure that the whole thing was not a hoax.

I sat down on a round seat, and we chatted with a very large crowd for nearly an hour. I talked considerably. Then a head man, or one of the chief men of the villages here, came and asked us to see the school, which was in the temple. We went into the inner court, and sitting on the ground, just at the door of the temple, my back very disrespectfully placed toward the idol, I examined the boys in reading, etc.; but the man was anxious to examine me, and he asked a number of pertinent questions about my country, as to the weather, the people; whether any black men were there; who did the work for us; whether Government owned any lands, and how they were taxed; and whether we had a queen: all which I endeavored to answer, and upon his finally passing a high eulogium upon our country, found a fitting opportunity to explain to him that it was nothing but Christianity that had made England and America what they were. He was very friendly, and I parted with him much pleased.

. . . . I have returned home from my tour [of a week] having visited twenty - five villages; I must have preached to twenty-five hundred people.

[TO HORACE E. SCUDDER.]

PERIAKULAM, July 23, 1862.

. . . . The last tour that I took has given me good spirits. It is pleasant to be brought fairly face to face with your work and not flinch. I was forced to talk and did talk, and found to my delight that common folk understood me well, and that I had the command of a serviceable though limited vocabulary. I felt specially delighted because, from the nature of my field, such must be my work. Some of the missionaries seldom visit a heathen village or address a purely heathen crowd, their Christian congregations being so numerous as to demand all their time. My case is different. Then you know the native reluctance to speak or talk to strangers about religion that I have always felt; how discouraging to me my Bible agency and my tract-distributing work were. In spite of all my fears, I have succeeded, and take pleasure in what before was a cross. I trust God will enable me to go on steadily in this work. I foresee that it will inevitably conflict with study and research, which I take pleasure in also. A man in the field literally half the time is not the one to push investigations very far, and I fear that I shall not. However, I do not mean to let it trouble me;

my duty in the one case is plain; if I can find the way to connect the two I shall try. I·have been studying Sanskrit grammar a little, and look wistfully at a class of works hitherto untranslated and almost unknown. I am feeling about here in hopes of getting some. They are Sanskrit philosophical works, from which translations have been partially made, and serve as the great authorities in Tamil. Mr. Hoisington translated the books. If one could bring out the original Sanskrit works, he would do a good service to literature. Dr. Caldwell wrote a little while since, urging me to undertake it; but I must first get the books, to deliver which to any uncaste man the Brahmans deem a mortal sin; secondly I must master a language and an abstruse terminology. I have little expectation of doing this.

In going among the villagers one may, I fancy, learn not a little about popular notions and customs that may throw light upon some questions of ethnology. The popular religion is a very mixed-up affair, and I have always had a passion for searching for the original fabric of common faith upon which Brahmans have woven their own belief. If one could put together common superstitions into a system, he would contribute something towards settling a vexed question of races here. But all these questions are subordinate in interest to me just now to the purely missionary question, how can we most economically evangelize these heathen and best build up these churches? My head is full of projects. . . . .

I am going to set apart Saturdays as holidays, and I have now by me the early volumes of the " Missionary Herald," containing the origin of this mission, from which I hope to extract material for a project of which

I must have spoken. I have also a large Tamil MS. autobiography of a famous old catechist, and may make something out of that. I try to keep the children in mind, and work for them. It is splendid to plan, is n't it? but one needs patience to bide his time and not be in a hurry for fruits. I sometimes think I see Christian congregations springing up all around, but I fear that many years must pass away ere it be anything more than picture, or prophecy at best.

[TO HIS MOTHER.]

PERIAKULAM, July 28, 1862.

. . . . Time flies faster than it ever did in Myrtle Street, and I think more happily too. I have plenty of work to do and it is growing fast upon me. My young head is full of all sorts of projects for touring and laboring here, some crude enough, and all tumbling helter-skelter over each other in my brain. . . . . The care of all the churches weighs upon me. How can I get more than fifty persons out of a church of one hundred and fifty to come to meeting on Sunday? How can I get the people to give contributions regularly? How can I induce one solitary girl to learn to read? How can I get more than ten boys from this church to attend school? How can I start an evening-school? How can I, with a force of four catechists, preach the gospel effectually to a thousand villages? Such questions and many more are in my mind the whole time. . . . . But in spite of all, or perhaps more truly on account of all this, I am happy and becoming more and more interested in the work. If one only goes to work the right way here, he will certainly see the fruits soon. . . . .

AUG. 2.

. . . . Last week I was obliged to go to Madura.
We passed through Devadanapatti, half-way to Battalagundu, where Washburn met me as agreed.   A great
bazaar was holding here. . . . . After our lunch we
came out of the bandy and sat on a log, when I took a
tract called " The Bible Proclamation " and called out
that I had a proclamation to read.   It was in the thick
of the bazaar, and two thousand people kept up a constant jabbering, so that I had to cry out the proclamation pretty loudly for the fifty or more crowding about
to hear.   Then I expatiated a little on some points in
it, and in the midst of my speech was interrupted by a
Mohammedan, who asked about Jesus Christ.

" Who was he ? "

" The Son of God."

" Who was his mother ? "

" Mary."

" Who was his father ? "

" God."

" Take care," said Washburn at my side ; " he 'll
have you."

I knew of course what he was after, but did the best
I could in replying that God had made creatures who
had sinned against Him ; that in spite of all He wished
to save them ; that in order to save them He had sent
His Son to be born as a man and die for them, and it
was not for them to criticise his plan for their recovery.
I had never met a Mohammedan before.   W. had, and
he said that he always represented that God himself
had come upon earth as man, not bringing prominently
forward the fact of the Sonship.   The man evidently

intended to puzzle us, and yet he was not obtrusive or violent. We had a long talk, W. coming to my aid, and gradually taking the talk from me, so I turned about and soon had a separate audience. One boy seemed to get my meaning, and, as is very commonly done, took up my words and explained them to the crowd. One man apparently had not heard the gospel before, — probably the majority had not, — and I was pleased with the eagerness of his inquiries and the manner in which he received the news that it was no longer necessary to go on pilgrimages or do penance to get to heaven. Who knows but what this news comes as good tidings now and then to some poor soul? The people crowded about to get tracts, and telling them that it would do a sick man no good to hold medicine in his hand and not eat it, applying to them the moral, we beat a retreat, having given away all our tracts, and I so hoarse that I could hardly talk.

PERIAKULAM, Aug. 12.

Another batch of letters came to us on Saturday. . . . . The special matter of interest was the news that you were going to send us a magic lantern. It will be invaluable for this people, to amuse and instruct. It is hard to find anything that they can appreciate, — this they will. To-day we had the monthly meeting of school-children at the house, when I showed them " Harper's Weekly " and the stereoscope, had them sing, and wound up by playing blind-man's-buff, a new game to them, which they enjoyed hugely.

. . . . I am studying up a talk for the heathen, to be in readiness for my tour next week. I propose to take different topics of importance and dwell separately

upon each, until I have a stock of themes well di-
gested and in shape for delivery. I begin with Sin,
and my method thus far developed is as follows: —
" Many of you do various acts of penance; (here I
enumerate, which always interests;) what is your
object? There must be a purpose to gain something
not before in your possession. A man does not go to
the jungle in search of a sheep in his pen. That
object, as you say, is to get merit, and to remove sin.
Therefore you admit that you are destitute of something, and that you are sinners. Yes, we are all sinners; but what is sin? Can a tree sin? or does your
mouth or hand sin? No, the spirit. (Then I enumerate sins that are especially common here, as perjury,
slander, theft.) To remove these sins you attempt a
great deal and your intention is good, but the way in
which you make the attempt is faulty. If you white-
wash a black man, he does not become a white man.
If you visit the Ganges to bathe, your heart cannot be
cleansed. Sin is within, and your own poets say, —
' Though you travel to Benares with aching feet, black
will not become white.' I will show you a more excellent way," and so on to the gospel. By taking one
theme at a time, I think I can supply myself with appo-
site illustrations and learn proverbs, so as to have in
time a valuable stock at command. You see I have to
make the talks as plain as possible, and on sin even it is
necessary to be very explicit and circumstantial. The
people have very little consciousness of sin, their conscience is so seared and perverted; to neglect feeding
a Brahman is as heinous a crime as theft, and perhaps
more heinous.

[TO REV. GEORGE F. HERRICK.]

PERIAKULAM, Sept. 3, 1862.

. . . . Since getting into my work I have found but little leisure and I may add desire for other pursuits. I have not lost my interest in topics that formerly claimed a share of my attention, but a growing interest in special duty as missionary has cast into the shade desire after literary pursuits.  I find that the only people we have to do with know precious little, as they themselves often say to us, but how to plant and reap. The higher classes are also ignorant enough.  It is almost exclusively in Upper India, I fancy, that philosophy is studied with any zest or success.  There is however a wide field of investigation for one who likes such work, in current and popular superstitions and worship.  The mythology of the lower classes of India is not known at all, and it is this that practically concerns us much more than the Hindû Pantheon which we learn in books.  I hope, after becoming familiar with the dialect of the people, to be able to pick up some things which may be valuable.  I have just now come across a book of "Dialogues on Hindû Philosophy," by a converted Brahman of Calcutta.  It is the best contribution to our knowledge upon the subject that I know of, outside of translations.  It is a dialogue in which the principal speaker is a Brahman who has been led to adopt Christianity, after a full study of the several systems, and is an admirable exposition of the characteristic traits of each.  As an argument for Christianity, it is very fine.  It has upset many theories that I was led to adopt respecting the history of Hindû Philosophy, and certain criticisms on special systems. All the better, as it certainly has made an advance in the discussion of the subject.

. . . . What sort of a literature have your Christians in Turkey? the Armenians for instance. Have they any native literature that you can avail yourself of? any ancient religious works? The English have done a good deal for Christianity here in this way, and the Christian Vernacular Education Society are publishing many valuable works, so that we are gradually getting up a literature, but must yet have many new books. Books already published have not reached a very wide circulation, chiefly because the people are so extremely poor. I think of starting a sort of circulating-library here at my station centre, for the use of the catechists. They are fond of reading and would profit by it, I think.

[TO HENRY BUCK, WETHERSFIELD, CONN.]

PERIAKULAM, Oct. 25, 1862.

. . . . You are a farmer, and I suppose if you should take a trip to India you would look upon all things with a farmer's eye, and judge of the land from its capacity to produce onions and corn, horses and cows, barley and buckwheat. Now I feel quite happy in having a farmer among my acquaintances, for I can vary my tune and write upon fresh topics. I don't know how many times I have said to my wife, "I wish Henry Buck were here, he would enjoy this so much." You would go home with ideas of the variety in modes of agriculture that would astonish home folks. A missionary once introduced among his people some wheelbarrows. The custom is to carry everything under a cart-load on the head, and you wonder that the necks of the people don't snap under the extraordinary bundles that they stagger with. The people thought

the wheelbarrow an excellent thing, but the missionary,
happening among them one day, found some men carrying bundles, barrow, and all on their heads. It is
a good illustration of the way that Hindûs do things.
You have your spades and shovels, common hoe and
potatoe-hoe, rake, sub-soil plough and side-hill plough,
harrow and cultivator, patent seed-planters, and what
not. All that the Hindû has to do the work of these
is the plough, the hoe, and his toes and fingers. Such
a plough! it is of wood, two sticks, one the beam, and
the other the handle and share; there is a bit of iron
fastened to the end which is about two inches broad.
The bullocks draw this machine over the land, and it
makes a scratch of perhaps three inches deep at the
most. They will have eight or ten yoke of oxen
ploughing together, a little to one side of each other,
and it was doubtless while ploughing in this style that
the prophet Elisha was called. They plough twice a
year, in spring and in fall, just after enough rain has
fallen to soften the ground a little. If they have what
is called "wet cultivation" rice-fields, they plough
when the water is so deep as to hide the ground, and
they go plashing through, up to their knees in mud.
But the hoe is the most striking example of the civilization of the people. It is not such a hoe as you know.
It is called a dirt-digger, and the iron is more like a
spade in size. The handle again is not like that of a
hoe, except in the way it is inserted. It is about three
feet long, and I have seen them not over a foot in
length, and nearly parallel with the iron. You wonder
that the backbone does n't crack, they have to bend it
so. A spade would not do for bare feet, and this
really seems to be an admirable instrument. The

23

people are quite handy in the use of it. It is used just
as much for digging the foundation of a house, or preparing the ground for planting, as it is for the cutting
of weeds or working after a plough. It goes much
deeper than a plough.

The cattle they have would hardly draw a little
horse-plough. They are quite small and very different
looking from home cattle. But the cows — they are the
breed to draw the prize for milkers. Some of the families here keep half a dozen, with as many calves, and
you would think at first sight that they were going
into the dairy business ; but when I tell you that the
best milkers don't give over a quart and a half at a
milking, you will see that a family of babies will need
a family of cows. The cows here have a way, too, of
not giving milk unless they have their calves by them.
The people never kill a calf ; it stays by its mother till
she dries up. Our cow's calf died, and the cow-man,
to insure the milk, skinned the calf and stuffed it.
This was presented to the cow at each milking, and
duly licked by the mother. When we went to the
Hills for our health, the cow was taken also, but the
man thought it hardly worth while to take the stuffing.
But he took the skin, and daily it had to be licked, or
the cow would not give down the milk. The people
here milk a cow on the left side.

The grains that are raised here are numerous enough,
but hardly one is known at home. Wheat of an inferior kind is raised upon the Hills, where it is cooler.
They raise a kind of maize, but it is poor. Some
vegetables have been imported and grow tolerably well.
We have tried gardening, and have new tomatoes,
cucumbers, squashes, and melons. Pease, beans, turnips,

cabbage, lettuce, celery, beets, have also been planted. Some have come up, but whether they do well or not remains to be seen. The chief difficulty is in getting good seed.

. . . . Well, after going into agriculture, I have space left to say " How do you do?" to one and all. . . . . I need no fancy or stereoscopic view to tell me how things look at Uncle W.'s. I can see the old Maltese as she dives into that square hole in the back porch. I can see the shiny, creamy pan of milk in that pantry, and my! does n't it smell tip-top? I can see the keys hanging on the nails in the kitchen, the ostrich eggs, the supplement to the " Courant." I can hear the chair crush up the wall, —— pounding the clothes as if bound to give them a good pinching for getting dirty. . . . . I might go on to specify the several smells, good, bad, and indifferent, that even now salute me, as memory runs over the days gone by, spent in that blessed spot hard by the Folly. I tell you, H., those were glorious days for me, and there are none that I look back upon with such un-mingled satisfaction.

## CHAPTER XVI.

### SEARCH AMONG CROMLECHS.

[1862.]

[WHILE on the Pulney Hills, David's interest was excited by the report that there were in the neighborhood monumental remains, which might throw some light upon the investigations which he had been making concerning the earlier inhabitants of India. He made an excursion to the place, and afterward, discovering similar remains in the valley, he entered upon an enthusiastic exploration which was promising valuable results when it was brought to an end by his death. I have collected into one narrative the accounts of the various excursions which he made, the last occurring but a few days before his death.]

[JOURNAL LETTER.]

PULNEY HILLS, May 22, 1862.

. . . . I had what might fairly be termed a tramp, and with rather an unusual object in view. You know I have always been interested in the antiquities of India, and especially in matters pertaining to the hill tribes. I had read often of the relics found on the Nilagiris, but did not know until recently that similar remains were to be found on these Pulney Hills. A few weeks ago I heard from Mr. Taylor that such remains were upon the hills and accessible, so I at once proposed an excursion in search. Yesterday we started

off, Mr. Taylor, Mr. Burnell, Mr. Hunt, and I. A
Coolie went with us carrying provisions for the day, and
my gardener carried a crowbar and hoe. We had a
cup of tea early, and were off by half-past six. We
went down the mountain to the first landing-place on
the way to Periakulam. But then, instead of descending the mountain, we went up in another direction, by
a decidedly rough specimen of a path, often having to
dismount and pull our horses along. After a toilsome
ride we arrived, at half-past nine, at the ruins of an old
house, occupied by a former collector of this district.
It is called Blackburn's bungalow. Here we stopped,
opened our box and breakfasted. We were greatly
annoyed by flies, that reminded us of Livingstone's famous tsetze-fly, they tormented us and the horses so.
We left our horses here in charge of our Coolie, and
then set out for the supposed site of the cromlechs.
The foot-path was a most romantic one. It skirted the
side of a high mountain, looking down into a beautifully
wooded stream away below, from which we heard a
perfect orchestra of insects. It wound along, descending gradually until it brought us to a brook, a good
way down the hill. We left our coats by the side of
the path, for tramping was hard work, and the sun was
hot, even under umbrellas. Crossing the brook, we
scoured along by the side of another hill and down over
another brook. Here the recent footprints of elk were
clearly seen and the hollows where they wallow.

We had travelled so far, a little over an hour, when
Mr. Taylor, who always keeps his eyes open, shouted,
"There they are! Cromlechs! Hurrah!" and away
we rushed pell-mell at what he pointed out. Sure
enough, here was the veritable thing, not to be mis-

taken a moment. It was upon the nose of a ridge, running out from the mountain and overlooking a long and beautiful valley below it, — a most picturesque spot. The first that we came upon were placed within a raised place twenty-four feet square, facing east and west. In or on this platform were a dozen and more of these structures. They were much broken up and falling to decay. As originally built, they consisted of slabs of unhewn stone, three placed on end, and another immense one laid across them, giving an opening at one end, and making a nice " cubby-house," — one large one measured eight feet in length and four in breadth. We crawled under this, though the slab was partly fallen down, and calling for the hoe, I scratched away the soil that was below, in hopes of finding flooring. I think I was not mistaken, for I found a flat stone wherever I dug, and it sounded hollow. I did not scratch away all the mould, as it was not easy work, and it was a sheer impossibility to attempt to move the slab, in hope of finding anything beneath. There were six of these cromlechs in a row, and we made out three rows pretty clearly.

The platform itself was neatly walled up with square unhewn stones, and raised about three feet above the ground. A couple of rods down the hill were several others of the same style, but not enclosed with any wall, or, at least, with none well preserved. We pried open one that seemed closed, but found only a heap of cobble-stones. We needed a force of men to make proper investigation, and had to leave such further and more thorough search for another time. Leaving Mr. Burnell here, Mr. Taylor and I walked on for about half a mile, in hope of finding others on the side of a knoll. But none were visible, and after a rest we returned.

PULNEY HILLS, May 31, 1862.

Yesterday I had a tramp indeed. A little after six I was off on pony with the horse-keeper and a Coolie who carried my lunch and a hoe. By nine o'clock I reached a river not far from the first-seen cromlechs. There, seated on a flat rock, the water foaming all about me, I ate my cold eggs and biscuit, and then went on to the old spot. I set the boy at work digging in one to see if he could find a slab below, corresponding to the slab above. He soon came to one, though it was well covered with rocks and loam. At the end of this cromlech was another apartment of about like size, full of cobble-stones. To get at this end of the slab, I must remove part of the pile. It was hard work in the hot sun, but we finally succeeded in uncovering both ends. The slab was very heavy, a foot thick, three feet wide, and five feet long; it was impossible to lift it. All I could do was to feel underneath. There was clearly a hollow, but whether anything was in it I could not tell, though I pulled out a handful of damp leaves. After digging awhile I pushed further on in search of new cromlechs. After riding two miles along a mountain-slope I came to another spur of the mountain, jutting out into the valley. . . . . Of a sudden, looking about me I espied what I most wanted to see, — cromlechs. They were on the brow of the hill, in exactly similar position to that of the old ones. But they were much finer, in a better state of preservation and larger. One slab was enormous. It was full eight feet high, six feet long, and a foot and a half thick, standing perfectly perpendicular on edge. This

had nothing to correspond with it, but abreast of it
and in perfect line were two well-shaped apartments
measuring each about six feet in length and three in
width, about four or five feet high, three-sided, with
no slab on top.   Then, on what would answer as the
opposite side of the street, was another row, but in a
very tumbled-down condition, and at one end of the
street was another smaller one, facing in the opposite
direction.   They all face either east or north.

It was very evident where the slabs came from, for
the brow of the hill was a bare, stratified gneiss rock,
easily peeling off into thick slabs, and the places from
which they were taken were plainly marked.   Some of
these cromlechs also were wholly shut up, and I should
like to look beneath.   I dug again here in search of a
lower slab, and after digging over a foot, came to one.
So all, thus far examined, have slabs below.   Now the
question is, have these cromlechs relics of any kind beneath?   The slabs are so heavy that it would require a
strong force of natives to lift them, and I want to get up
an expedition that shall do up the thing thoroughly.
When you remember that these have an antiquity probably equal to that of Celtic remains in Britain, that
the most primitive of the inhabitants here have not a
whisper of tradition about them, you will admit that
they possess an interest of no common kind.   But they
are hard to get at in one day, and there is no village
handy.   There are villages below you, and most lovely
spots are they in; I think I shall try to reach one and
stay there a day or two, making explorations.

Another trouble is the rain, as I can testify.   I got
back for dinner at the brook by two o'clock, and at
three I was ready to start, but already the drops had

begun to fall, and I was a hard five miles from home.
But I buttoned up my coat, spread my umbrella and
started on. First came an awful tug on foot up a high
hill for nearly a mile. The grass was so tall that you
could often find the path only by shuffling with your
feet. Coming down the soft grass felt nicely, but now
it needed but a few wisps to put you into a pleasant
state of wetness. Pony and the men followed dolefully
on, and before we had reached the summit, we had it
in fuss and fury. Once a year we have such rains at
home, but not oftener. Here among the mountains
they are truly fearful. The little bridle-paths were
full of water rushing along, and as we turned one
corner of a hill and another, the rising wind came
swooping upon us from one quarter or another, till it
seemed as if old Boreas would split his cheeks. Finally
it came with such a burst, that I burst out laughing
and struck up Yankee Doodle and Star-Spangled
Banner. It was a ride worth riding. The road was
bad, and I had every now and then to get off and lead
pony, not risking my neck on him, and it was impossible to get out of a walk. So we had to grin and bear
it, plunging along through the swash for two hours and
a half, till within half a mile of home.

[A few days after this David was obliged to leave
the Hills, without an opportunity for further search;
but several weeks later he made an excursion with Mr.
Washburn and Mr. Capron to Mânâ Madura, to examine some remains which had been discovered by
Mr. Capron while engaged in building a house at this
place.]

TIRUPUVANAM, Sept. 20, 1862.

We have come back from our tour of scientific research in the vicinity of Mânâ Madura. We reached
the village near which the relics are at dusk, and passed
the night. . . . . Before five in the morning we set
out for the remains, about half a mile off. All that is
seen above the surface is the rim of an earthen pot,
about a foot and a half or two feet in diameter. There
were some dozen or more to be seen. So we set to
work to dig one up. It was about two feet deep, without a cover and filled tight with gravel. We dug out
the gravel and at the bottom found two little pots, of
such pottery as all vessels are made of in this country.
Their shape, however, differs from the one common
now, and in one we found about half a skull, much
worn and its form preserved only by being imbedded
in earth. Several teeth and remains of other bones
were also discovered. We had two or three Coolies to
work for us, and opened four more. On the outside
of one we found a lot of vessels, broken and whole, of
various forms, one kind a very graceful cup, not unlike
a finger-bowl. In each jar we found several vessels,
and always remains of bones, though almost all were
undistinguishable for rottenness. The object of the jars
however was clear; the place was a burial-ground and
a very ancient one too. No one now can tell anything
of the origin of the jars. The people say that formerly
there was a caste that did not die, and that such people
were placed alive in these jars, with a little rice and
water in the cups. Thirty years ago there was a forest over this spot, of large trees. Whose are these
remains? I suppose they are allied to old relics found

in various parts of the Peninsula, which are considered
to be Buddhistic remains. But that is all I can say.
The Buddhists were expelled from the country a thousand years ago or so.

[These explorations were continued in various quarters, and a general interest excited among the missionaries, when suddenly, to David's delight, a new field of
exploration came into knowledge in his own station.]

[JOURNAL LETTER.]

PERIAKULAM, Nov. 3, 1862.

I have been quite excited to-day and may be more so
to-morrow. You know that I have been a good deal
interested in old stones and mud, and have been making explorations in different quarters. Mr. Webb is to
excavate in Dindigal, and Washburn writes that old
cairns have turned up somewhere in his station. But
I have them nearer home, and shall not have to go
to Dindigal or Mânâ Madura to pursue antiquarian
researches. The other day I found an old mud fort,
and near it a lot of circles of rough stones corresponding precisely to those found in Dindigal. I inquired
about them, and found the people had all sorts of notions as to what they were. I inquired of Pastor Seymour, and he knew of others, and told me what the
people thought of them. We are eighty miles from
Mânâ Madura, yet the same stories are current here
that we heard there: that formerly the people lived to
a great age, and had to be buried alive in these big
pots. They were giants too. Well, I sent Seymour
to explore this morning in a place where there were
said to be some of these pots. He came back about

two o'clock, bringing me a piece of iron looking much like a cleaver, only very much rust-eaten. He said he had found pots as tall as his head, and that one of our church-members had ploughed up this year a piece of iron like a sword, and had seen many of these big pots, but they were broken now. He said too that circles of stones similar to those found near here were there; that there were cromlechs like those on the hills; and that in a small stone house the man had found a pottery horse of very neat pattern, much above the style common now. The whole story has quite woke me up; so to-morrow morning early I propose to go to the spot, close to the foot of the hills, on the road to the tope, and see for myself. They say that they find the skull in a basin and the bones arranged around it. Is it not singular that all throughout this district such remains should be found, telling us of a race inhabiting the country differing totally in their modes of sepulture from any now existing? The iron instrument which was brought me is the first thing of the kind found, and I hope may add something to what we know of such matters.

Nov. 7.

I have spent the day in a cromlech! So you must have some account of it. Some days ago I was attracted by the sight of some circles of stone along the side of a road which we frequently travel upon. I suspected there was something within and had our gardener dig in the centre. He soon struck upon a slab. I left it a day or two, but yesterday had him try it again. We had other help, and soon found that it was hollow below. But we could only pry off a small piece of a slab large enough to let me in. I got in and found myself in a regular cromlech about six feet long and three wide, but quite choked up with dirt. We could not lift up the larger piece, and had to leave and come again at night with two big levers and ropes. This was last night while I had my catechists here, and they helped me. We dug some and found in one corner a potter's vessel, and on the side four. It was almost dark, so we covered the vessel with dirt and came home. The meeting closed yesterday. So today I set out with the determination of giving up one day to antiquities. I went out about six with a gardener and we went to work. The first thing we came to of interest was a doorway in one end, that is a round hole, with a stone set up against it outside. I hurrahed internally, for this was a discovery. It corresponds precisely with cromlechs found upon the Nilagiris, and which I have never seen here. It is supposed, and I think with good reason, that these are tombs, and that the hole was made for a person to enter and deposit the bodies for sepulture. In proof of this are the contents of the tomb. One thing after another turned up, but I will simply state what, not detailing the individual things. We found a pot on four legs, a remarkable affair. The chief things were two big pots, such as I described before as containing smaller vessels, lying on their sides facing the door. In the rest of the room were fragments of pots and vessels of all sorts, heaps upon heaps. We hardly found a whole one there. We did however secure some, and of different patterns from any I have seen before, and among other things some covers to pots, — rare things. I found also several iron instruments, but they were too far gone by rust to make them out. Lastly some bones made their appearance. I think there were bones all through the soil, but crumbled so as to leave only a white powder. We got out one of the big pots, and tying it to two beams, the men, some half dozen, brought it home. I came home late to breakfast, and returned immediately after, having a shady place under ground. I stayed until four, eating lunch in the cromlech, and then went home to dinner. I worked hard all day and am pretty decidedly tired to-night, so you will give me credit for writing at once. I think the broken pots, etc., are evidences that the place is a family tomb, or was, and that pots were broken or disarranged by persons entering to make fresh deposits. But such enormous slabs of stone! The room faces exactly east, and the slabs are six feet thick by seven or eight high; the end ones three feet wide by seven high. There is no place short of a mile whence they could have been brought.

# CHAPTER XVII.

## LAST LABORS — DEATH AND BURIAL.

[OCTOBER–NOVEMBER, 1862.]

[TO HORACE E. SCUDDER.]

PERIAKULAM, Oct. 16, 1862.

. . . . I FIND that it won't do to be in too great a hurry. As I was feverish with haste this morning, I took up a little pocket Proverbs and read, "Commit thy works unto the Lord, and thy thoughts shall be established." It was just the verse for me. I need to cast my care upon Him and be quiet. But you have no idea of the multifarious vexations in this life, and the trouble is that the whole matter rests upon you, — everybody looks to you for what they shall do, and your spirit will almost necessarily infuse itself throughout. One requires a cheerful piety to work steadily among this people, much patience to wait for good, forbearance with individuals, and a general purpose to take things happily, no matter how perverse they may appear.

[JOURNAL LETTER.]

PERIAKULAM, Oct. 14.

[Returning from a tour he passed the night at Andipatti.] I woke rather later than I meant to be, took my tea and toast, and was off on Burnside for home just as the sun rose. Now you must know that the rainy season has fairly set in and our rivers rise and fall without warning. I left home Saturday afternoon; in crossing the river by our house I got my feet wet, the water being up to the horse's girths. Had I been half an hour later I could not have gone. H. tells me that the workmen, who were ploughing our ground, could not cross to go to the village. But this river is a small branch only of the Vaikai River, which has its chief source way down in Kambam valley, and passes between Andipatti and Periakulam. On Saturday I had sent the bandy ahead in the morning, with orders to return and wait at the river to help me over. I met it however only two miles from home, but was reassured when the man told me that there was only a little water. I found enough however to wet my feet again. The Vaikai River is three times as wide as ours. This morning I felt a little misgiving as to how I should find the river, but pushed ahead, telling the bandy to come as soon as it could. Half a mile from it, I met an old man, who did not comfort me any by saying that there was a lot of water in the river. As soon as I caught sight of it I saw it was true. The water was red with mud and tore along at a furious rate. Moreover there was a bandy with no bullocks by the side, and it did not need the word of two or three men sitting by it to assure me that it was " no go." But I put on a bold face and drove Burnside in. Down he went over my shoes at the first step. That would not do, so I backed out.

I called a council of war, — I was almost half-way home; the sun was growing hot; I could not wait for my bandy, and if I did it would not help me much. If I waited two days, possibly the water would not fall; so in less time than I have taken to say so, I decided that there was only one thing to be done. I stripped, and chirruping to Burnside, stepped in. He did n't want to go, but after drinking a little, seemed more favorably disposed, and in we went. I never was in a stronger current, and the water up to my chest. But after a few rods the water was lower, and we stopped to rest. The bottom was very soft, and I went floundering along, sticking my toes into the mud to keep a footing. But I had n't gone far again before it grew deeper, and almost before I knew it I was rushing along down-stream at a jolly rate, old Burnside snorting, but sticking to me. A dozen or two of hard strokes gave me a footing again, and after another stretch of wading we reached the shore. I tied Burnside to a tree and went back for my clothes. I had to make two bundles of them, to tie on to my head, and so had to cross twice to get them. The last time I crossed for them, I was pretty thoroughly used up and excited the sympathy of the natives, several of whom had collected to see the performance. I should have been pushed to have gone over again. The current was very strong indeed, but had I not been in India a twelvemonth it would not have been a tough thing at all. Here, however, we have no extra strength of muscle for extraordinary occasions. I did not succeed in keeping my clothes wholly dry, though the men tied my bundle on my head quite artistically, but a little water was no harm on a hot morning. Mounting, I urged Burnside on as rapidly as possible, as the sun was becoming decidedly uncomfortable, and I had seven more miles to go. I had a pleasant ride until within half a mile of home, when the roar of a tank-dam, or rather the waterfall, told me that I might have trouble

24

in getting over our river. Sure enough, it was as high
as it well could be. I called to the horse-keeper and
the servants, and then Mr. Noyes and H. came down,
but they could not help me a bit; so not caring, as I
was at home, about apparel, I let Burnside graze and
jumped in as I was, much to the concern of our worthy
gardener. The river, though narrower, proved to be
deeper than the other, and I had to swim fully as much.
Mr. Noyes's horse-keeper could swim, the only one on
the ground, and he took a rope and made out to get
Burnside over. So we have had a bit of excitement
without any harm to anybody. H. says the storm here
last night exceeded in severity any that we have had
before. One consequence is that a big tank above
broke loose, and it is this that has forced the river so
full. Communication with the hills is broken off, and
the road is flooded.

[Some idea of the suddenness and violence of this
rise in the river may be formed from the fact that
frequently of two bandies attempting to cross, one
would get safely across and the other have to wait,
and that cattle, and often people are swept away by the
violence of the flood. What was before but the bed
of a stream with a narrow, sluggish current, becomes
in a few hours a wild, roaring river, impassable except
for the most venturesome. So sudden is the descent
of an increased volume of water that it can be likened
to nothing but another river precipitated over the previous stream. To resume the journal.]

OCT. 17.

The river is down again. It has been raining on

the mountains west of us all day, and their summits
have been as dark as night. About dinner-time the
flood came. I ran out to see it, and H., baby, and I
had a nice time walking along the bank, seeing the
water rush by, and watching the servants catch the
wood that floated down. They picked up enough fire-
wood to last a couple of months. It is astonishing how
quickly the torrent comes, we are so close to the mountains. The flood has brought something else than tim-
ber to us. While I write, Manuel the catechist is on
the veranda preaching to one hundred people, sitting
on it, who have been caught by the river and forced to
spend the night here. They belong two miles away,
and came this morning to their work at the base of the
mountains. Quite an unexpected audience for us.
You can judge of the capacity of our veranda, when
I tell you that it is not a quarter full.

OCT. 22.

I came home last night from a visit to Dindigal,
where I assisted at the dedication of Mr. Webb's new
church. . . . . When I came to the river, there was a
scene: one bandy was capsized in the middle of the
rushing stream, and the men were tugging away to get
it out. The swimmers were reaping a harvest by taking over bundles, and persons too, for a cent apiece.
On the opposite bank was Mr. White's empty bandy
coming from our house to Pulney, and I watched to
see how it would come over. They took out the bullocks and then pushed the bandy over. It came out
full of water and I began to make up my mind for a
ducking and possible upset. So I took out the mattress and valise and stuck my shoes out of water's

reach. Then straddling, standing upright, I gave the word and in we went, a dozen men hauling and shoving, calling on their gods and laboring as if it were a case of life and death. Half the number would have done as well. The water came high enough to wet my feet and lift up the straw; but beyond that no harm was done, and after giving the men a cent apiece we drove on.

. . . . On the way home I saw a temple on the road-side, and opposite it a stone. A man said that long ago for some reason a man and his wife died together. Now the people worship them; the stone was the man, the image in the temple the woman. This custom is confined to one caste. . . . .

[TO CHARLES W. SCUDDER.]

PERIAKULAM, Oct. 29, 1862.

. . . . Within these few days I have been very much depressed about this people. Oh, my dear brother, if you could come here and see one woman, — any one, and see in her the picture of the condition of this people! It is awful, awful. The mass of the people live and die like swine, and the higher classes are utterly sealed against the truth. What power can break through? As soon as the rains are over I hope to organize a system of preaching, but oh for piety! love to Jesus! the only thing that can give me courage to face a sneering crowd, a callous crowd. Pray much for me.

[JOURNAL LETTER.]

Nov. 3.

. . . . Our days pass very uniformly now. We are in the rainy season, and consequently somewhat con-

fined. I cannot easily tour, and even going to the
town is a matter of no little trouble, as I have two
streams to cross, each of which is up to the saddle-
girths. I have not really preached but once or twice
in the town since I have lived here. I am to blame.
A feeling of dread has prevented me, knowing that the
people are less ignorant, and consequently more rude,
than in the villages. Most of my preaching here has
been in the various hamlets about. But I hope by
God's grace to do differently, and, as soon as the
weather moderates, to set going a systematic mode of
operation, by which the town and neighboring villages
shall be effectually reached. I am quite busy now over
an enlargement of the government map that used to
hang in my room at home. How I should have studied my field then, could I have foreseen what it was to
be. I am enlarging it fourfold, making it on the scale
of a mile to an inch, so that every little village can be
down and named. It will be a capital thing for me,
and for any who may come after me. Oh, for help to
be faithful the little while that I shall be here. I was
thinking yesterday evening, while walking on top of
the house, of the kind of preaching that was required
here, and it occurred to me that I had not given God's
truth the credit of being mighty enough to pull down
these strongholds. I have thought of the doctrine of
the cross as foolishness to this proud people, and have
perhaps unconsciously wished to gloss it over with soft
words that it might not offend. But I begin to see that
I ought to be willing to trust the bare, strong truth to
make its own way, — the naked truth that all have
sinned and come short of the glory of God, and that
there is salvation in none other than Christ Jesus: this

it is which is mighty through God. I think I see now
that my duty is to preach the doctrine boldly to all,
and leave it to work its own fruit through the Spirit
of God. A missionary, if he *believes*, will feel himself
on a platform so infinitely above all cavilling that the
reproach or ridicule or indifference of men to whom
he proclaims his message will excite only compassion,
never shame. Yes, we need to believe more in the
power of the gospel.

PERIAKULAM, Nov. 11.

You will want to know the dark as well as the bright
sides of my life, that you may sympathize with me in
all things. I have been feeling very sadly for a few
days past about my congregation, and I must tell you
why. Last Sunday we had communion in the village
church. The river had been down in the night, but
there was not too much water to prevent my riding
through. I went down with a heavy heart, for it had
been decided that one of the deacons should be suspended if he would not acknowledge his fault. He was
not at church. Only a few persons were there when I
reached the church, and I sat down waiting for them
to come. One man came to the door, and then stopped
and turned round to talk very loudly with some
heathen outside. He was with difficulty induced to
be quiet, but came in, sat down, prayed as usual, and
afterward received the Sacrament. While waiting, my
mûnshi came up to me, and said that there had been a
fearful quarrel there the night before, on account of
which many had gone to court.

My heart sank within me, and as I looked around
upon the little congregation and felt how very, very

low the people were, I wondered when their day of regeneration would come. But even then the thought came into my mind that Christ had some souls there true to Him, and that He had undoubtedly had to bear with me on account of failings of far greater moment than those that caused me anxiety here. But the people had mostly come, and after opening the service, the pastor briefly stated the case of the deacon as known to them, and said that it seemed necessary to suspend him, asking what they had to say. One man only spoke, saying simply that they must do as I said, but I believe he did not speak complainingly. I then read a part of the first two chapters of First Peter, and showed what the people of God should be, holy; but that we must not judge that he who was to be suspended was the greatest sinner amongst us. You know that the old feud was between the two deacons. . . . . I have no doubt that the remaining deacon ought to be suspended also, and I fear excommunicated, but there is nothing upon which I can lay my hand as punishable. But what a state of things! The quarrel that I referred to was between a member of the congregation and his wife. He dragged her about by her hair and beat her. Her father took her part, a crowd gathered and an officer was called. I believe he will be fined by the church. . . . . The affair has been settled, and to-day his wife has returned to his house, having been absent nearly a month from his ill-usage of her. Her father is a church-member and the head man of the church, and Sunday he would not come to communion because he said he was angry. My poor people! I would do anything for them, but oh, what can I do? . . . . I was going to Andipatti to-morrow, but I learn that the river is down, and I don't want to have another swim just now.

---

With these words his journal ends. The narrative of my brother's life, which I have gladly given through his own words since his arrival in India, returns to me; a few pages only remain, and the reader will pardon me if I assume in one who has read thus far an interest which will linger over the last days of one of the noblest of men, the best of brothers. For what follows I am chiefly indebted to Mr. Washburn, who collected the facts with care; other letters also and the simple words of David's native helpers serve to complete the account.

On Sunday the 16th of November he preached in the village church, and after service began to visit all the Christian families, in accordance with a plan previously proposed, calling at four houses and praying with the inmates; in the afternoon he visited also the Sunday-school in the mission compound. He had been intending the previous week to visit Andipatti, but the swollen rivers had decided him to postpone the tour. It was now, however, quite imperative that he should not longer defer it. He was about preparing his annual report of the station, and wished to secure further details respecting the state of schools and congregations; moreover the wife of one of his catechists was dangerously ill, and he wished to see her. So, though reluctant to go, he decided it to be his duty, and prepared to leave on Monday, expecting to return on Wednesday. He rode early in the morning to the village to do what he could in settling the quarrel which has been mentioned in his journal. He was occupied a long time, and came home not far from ten o'clock to breakfast. He was busy packing for the journey, expecting to leave by two o'clock in the afternoon; but the bullocks did not come until four o'clock, when he set out. It will be remembered that a little stream runs back of the house; the bandy in which he was to travel could not cross here owing to the steepness of the opposite bank; it was sent round by another way, and David was carried across the stream by the two gardeners. His wife, bearing the little child in her arms, came to the bank and waited for ten minutes until the bandy should arrive, when both bade him good-bye, watched the bandy till it was out of sight, and returned to the house.

David proceeded to Andipatti, ten miles distant, crossing the intervening Vaikai River, and reaching the town at nine o'clock in the evening; after tea and prayer with the catechist he went to sleep. Early on Tuesday morning he went out to a village with the catechist to preach, and after breakfast examined the school, when he made the children, who met him with great affection, run round him in a circle for a frolic, giving plantains to those who did it well. He held no other meetings during the day, and his attention was given to his cook-boy, who had been taken ill. As evening came on two or three catechists and teachers came into the church where he was staying, and he spent the time in conversation with them. He had been visiting and conversing during the day with the catechist's wife who was very sick, and the conversation naturally turned upon death, and he asked the catechist what were his feelings, now that he was brought face to face with death and compelled to contemplate it every day. From this their talk turned upon the resurrection and immortality, as set forth in the first epistles to the Corinthians and to the Thessalonians.

The catechist, in his narration of these scenes afterward, dwelt with a fond interest upon each little point. He told how, in attempting to flatten a large Scripture placard, David laid it down and put his foot on it, when the scrupulous teacher reproved him with the question, " Sir, may one put his foot upon the word of God?" and "then," said the catechist, "we talked much, and he thought much within himself, for past one o'clock he called out to the teacher sleeping near, ' You say it is not right to put your foot on that placard, but you have got the Bible there for your pillow,' showing that he had been thinking much about what we had been talking of."

He rose early on Wednesday morning and proceeded to Maniakarampatti, a village a mile and a half distant, where was a congregation. Here he preached upon the healing of the nobleman's son, the same sermon which he had preached the Sabbath before in the village church. He breakfasted, collected the statistics for which he had visited the place, and then hurried his things into the bandy, wishing to cross the river and return to Periakulam without further delay; no doubt he had some anxiety about the river, as the weather during his absence had been of the most comfortless sort; rain had fallen on the hills, and Tuesday night it had rained uninterruptedly. No wonder he made haste, since the delay of an hour or two might prevent him from crossing the river, and keep him in restless inactivity at Andipatti. The catechists endeavored to dissuade him from setting out, telling him that they had heard from many persons that there was much water in the river, but David knew that the difficulty of the passage would seem more formidable to the natives than to him; he finally said, "If there really is a heavy flood, as you say, I will return to Andipatti."

Leaving the bandy to follow, he set out on foot; one of the catechists and a church-member accompanied him, and they reached the river about one o'clock. His plan was to do as he had several times lately done, to swim the river, trusting to meet his horse on the other side, which indeed was sent, as it proved, and at any rate to be able to reach Periakulam, only five or six miles distant, long before his bandy, which would have to wait. He rested until the bandy came up, and lunched, for he had a somewhat arduous walk before him. The river was rising, and indeed was higher than he had known it. The catechist begged him not to go, but he remembered that he had often crossed when it was called impassable, and had not long before made three transits, when he led his horse and carried his clothes. Time was precious to him, and if he waited at all it would likely enough be for two or three days, making him miss the mail and deranging his plans greatly. He felt no misgivings, saying to the catechist, "I have swum two miles in the ocean and I will try." But he must have his clothes and his papers, as he would have to walk home, or till he met his horse, and the bandy might not reach him for several days. So he removed and adjusted his clothes, untying and tying them again until he had arranged them so as least to impede the movement of his arms. He placed the papers in his hat and secured it to his head.

He went a little above the regular ford, to a place where a brook makes into the river, in order to take advantage of the current, waded out some distance into the stream, and struck out boldly. The river is about a hundred yards wide at this place, and he had swum easily about half the distance, when suddenly the bystanders on the bank saw, as it were, a new river upon the top of this swift current come down like a wall, overwhelming him; a tank above had given way, and the volume of water to the depth of several feet had rushed vehemently down the stream, carrying everything with it. No strength of man could withstand the force, and the swimmer was carried under. He rose again, freed from encumbrance, but there was no exertion. He floated swiftly down the stream, his upturned face alone visible; soon nothing was to be seen but the turbid water.

The catechist, servant, and other bystanders stood for the first moment terrified on the shore, then rushed along the bank beyond where anything was visible, yet hoping that the flood would throw him on shore at a bend in the river, thirty or forty rods below. They were suddenly arrested by one of the hill torrents created by the sudden rains. They had already passed through a village in their pursuit, and were joined by the villagers, who were aroused by the tidings that a white man had gone down the stream. The Christians turned back with heavy hearts; they could not cross to carry tidings to Periakulam and they went back to Andipatti, to resume the search immediately, following the river down for thirty miles.

It was on the day following only that word could be got to Periakulam. Mrs. Scudder had twice sent the

horse-keeper with the horse in expectation of her husband's return, and had waited breakfast. About one
o'clock there was a hurried passing to and fro among
the servants. She went to the veranda and saw by
their faces that something was wrong. She asked the
matter, and, dumb at first, one at last said, " Master
has gone down the river," and that a note was waiting
for her at the police station. She said aloud that it
could not be, and sent the servants away, one for the
note, another for the Madura collector who was in
town, with the word that " Master must be brought
back if he could not come." Two hours of suspense
and the note came, a Tamil one, which the mûnshi with
great difficulty read aloud into English. All doubt was
gone; it must be so. She despatched notes to Mr.
Noyes, who was on the Hills, to come to her, to Mr.
Washburn, at Battalagundu, and to Mr. Rendall, at
Madura, to do what was possible.

Thursday night passed, and on the afternoon following Mr. Noyes reached Periakulam, and was followed
by Mr. and Mrs. Washburn a few hours later. The
collector had given orders that a watch should be kept,
and a search made for forty miles down the river. The
members of the church with their pastor also volun-
teered to go, and the catechists and Christians upon
the other bank were equally zealous. The news passed
through the district very rapidly, reaching at once the
various mission stations. Yet all this was with little
hope of recovering the remains. The flood that over-
whelmed him had brought down vast quantities of
sand, and given reason to believe that even in the moment of his death God had buried him.

The days wore away. On the Sabbath the mission-

aries and the native Christians assembled in the compound church and listened to words of comfort and
exhortation, comfort to all, though spoken in a language
unknown to the chief mourner. On Monday before
light came Mrs. Webb from Dindigal, having set out
on receiving the news. The morning passed; at one
o'clock came a note from the Battalagundu catechist,
saying " Mr. Scudder's body just now came from Solavanthan. I hired two bullocks and sent it this morning at nine o'clock. I think they will make some
delay on the road. It is better, I think, if you please,
to send two pairs of bullocks from Periakulam. The
head-constable of Solavanthan and a catechist came
along with the bandy." There could be no doubt about
this, though many false reports had repeatedly come.
Solavanthan was forty miles from Periakulam, and the
turbulent river had carried the body there, where it
was discovered on Sunday morning, floating in the
stream, and taken in charge by the police stationed at
the spot, who took measures to bring it ashore and convey it to his home.

At five o'clock the bandy drove into the gate, but
though the form could be distinguished beneath the
white cloth, there could be no sight of the face.
Preparations were concluded for burial, and on Tuesday morning early, the company gathered upon the
veranda, the burial-service was read, and the Divine
assistance was invoked upon the burial, which was to
be upon the summit of the Pulneys. " The sun was
just rising," writes Mr. Washburn, " when we mounted
our horses and started forth. I need not linger by the
way. Yet I seemed, as I rode up that zigzag path, to
hear the voice that shouted welcome to me when I

last ascended, but now it came not from Pilliyar Sûttû, but from heights which foot of flesh and blood had never trod, and the voice was not now one of welcome, but those apostolic words, — ' Seeing therefore we are surrounded by so great a cloud of witnesses, let us lay aside every weight and the sin that doth so easily beset us, and let us run with patience the race that is set before us.'

" We reached Kodi Kânal at two o'clock ; we were our own heralds, but our coming at once announced our errand. We rode by the east house, past Nebo, past Rock Cottage of pleasant memories, and down the woody pathway to the church, and across the churchyard to its western side. There, within the churchyard, just behind the church, is a warm living hill-side of yellow mould ; a pleasant path bordered by a hedge of roses separates the church-yard from the overhanging woods. A beautiful rhododendron stands there, leaning to the east, and beneath its shade was without doubt the place for the grave of our most precious one, — far enough from the main path to the church to be beyond intrusion or common gaze, yet near enough for those who wish to frequent it, to be reminded of him and to blend his memory with the worship of the place.

" It was nearly five o'clock in the afternoon before the bearers were announced as up the Hill. As I again returned from the east house, I stopped and looked down upon the plain below. The rain had passed, the sun was shining mellow and invitingly upon the bungalow and all that region. It was all beautiful beyond description. It seemed to me a token that comfort, not to say joy, had again visited those

stricken ones.    I had not been long in the church-
yard, whither I had gone to attend to the last details,
when sounds announced the approach of the Coolies,
but they were not the chant of the bearers.    It was
the sound of continued music, as the people came down
the hill-side, through the grove, over the knoll, — now
swelling out, now dying away, and again breaking
forth into the words of Christian song as they approached.    A bend in the path discovered the catechist, servants, and Christians in decent procession
before the bearers, singing.

"It was a spontaneous outflowing of all that was
Christian in them, the song of victory which Christianity alone can inspire.    Such a triumphal procession
through the long ages those hills had never witnessed.
Alas! India raises only wails and clamor alike around
the funeral pile of the twice-born and the grave of the
Pariah.

"Mr. White, who had just arrived on the Hills in
anticipation of our coming, Mr. Noyes and his son,
two English gentlemen residing there, myself, and a
large company of natives gathered around the sacred
spot and under the sound of the church-bell; with the
decencies of burial in our own native land, and with
the words with which millions have been laid to sleep,
we consigned dust to dust and ashes to ashes, in sure
hope of the resurrection to eternal life through Jesus
Christ our Lord.    And so our precious, cherished work
was done.

"The next morning very early I returned to take
another look at that spot and to gather a few flowers
as mementos for those who were not there.    The old
rhododendron-tree seemed to me to have accepted the

guardianship of the spot, and had already begun to shed its wreath of gorgeous flaming flowers around and upon the grave. I gathered a few flowers and came away, not to leave it alone, but in charge of Him who shall change our vile bodies that they may be fashioned like unto His glorious body."

Over that quiet grave stands now a memorial stone, bearing upon its face this inscription, —

### DAVID COIT SCUDDER.

"HE LEADETH ME BESIDE THE STILL WATERS."

and on the reverse, his office, the dates of his birth, landing at Madras, and death.

25

# CHAPTER XVIII.

### CONCLUSION.

As soon as the necessary arrangements could be made, Mrs. Scudder and her child left Periakulam for Madras, on their way to America, taking ship to England and reaching Boston in May. It need not be told with what affectionate care they were sent on their way and accompanied by the various members of the Madura Mission. That little community, separated from other society, was united by the closest ties, and when one member suffered, all the members suffered. It was with sad hearts that they returned to their appointed work, leaving one whom they had so lately and with such fond expectation welcomed to their number in his grave on the Pulneys, and bidding farewell to another, more closely joined to them now by this recent sorrow. It may be judged how these missionaries, with their strong desire for the salvation of India, would mourn the loss of one possessed of such ability, and giving promise of so great usefulness. From every one came the sorrowful word — why was it he? One after another bore testimony spontaneously to his worth and attainments. One, out of the mission, who is recognized as the leading scholar of Southern India, wrote to a friend: " I met him twice in the beginning of the year, and corresponded with him a little, and it was my impression that he was the best prepared and most learned young missionary that had ever come out to Southern India; but it is delightful to perceive, from the manner in which his missionary colleagues write of him, that those who knew him best entertained as high an opinion of his Christian simplicity and missionary zeal as I, who had but slight acquaintance with him, entertained of his scholarship." And another, also out of the Madura circle, who occupies perhaps the foremost place among American missionaries in India, by his learning, his eloquence, and his missionary ardor, wrote, on hearing of the death, "Kneeling down I have prayed that his mantle may fall upon me."

David loved the native Christians; he took a very favorable view of Hindû character, and declared that he enjoyed Christian intercourse with his catechists as much as he had with friends at home. His ardent and affectionate concern for those about him could not fail to impress them, and children especially reciprocated his affection. He lived long enough with a few Hindûs to become intimately acquainted with them and to leave a strong impression of his own character upon them. The pastor of the church at Periakulam, the catechists of the villages in his district, and his mûnshi, all bore testimony in their simple manner to his worth. The last-named wrote as follows to David's father not long after the death of his pupil. I make no apology for inserting the letter without any alteration of the phraseology.

[TO CHARLES SCUDDER, ESQ.]

MOST VENERABLE SIR, — With due submission and unutterable grief, I beg to bring to your notice the very painful news concerning my valuable and most beloved master, the Rev. D. C. Scudder, your affectionate son, whom we all expected to be the first-rate literary spiritual guide in our country. No sooner he arrived at Madura, I had the privilege of being taken by him as his Tamil mûnshi and mission helper. Indeed I was very glad to place myself under the care of a worthy, good master and mistress. While in Madura he not only devoted his time to his Tamil studies, but also was very particular in examining the histories of the former Tamil kings and taking a clear view of the celebrated Meenāchee's temple of Madura, and began at once in his daily ridings to converse with the Brahmans and visit the Tamil heathen schools, while he was yet unable to speak Tamil well. The Brahmans were quite astonished at his deep knowledge in their shastras, while most of them were ignorant of their own. He expected to study Sanskrit next year.

Last February he removed with his family to his new field, which lies close to the mountains and rivers, where he at once adopted suitable plans to accomplish the great object for which he came, and at the same time paid especial attention to his Tamil studies, in which he made wonderful progress. He commenced to translate English and Tamil into one another, and recently preached two Tamil sermons on the first two miracles of Christ. He was much beloved by the people for his good disposition and fluent talk of the Tamil language. He and his admirable lady were very kind to their servants as well as to others. His brain was full of thoughts, that he was ever industrious. Since September last his mind was turned to discover some ancient curiosities, which he was told to be deposited into the ground. Accordingly he set out to work, dug

out several places on the ground, and found out some
mud vessels, &c., that the people, to whom it was very
curious, created a false name everywhere that a white
man had dug out sufficient wealth from the ground,
through the means of an enchanting glass, — referring
to his telescope.

My master has begun everything that should be
done in future, and it is a sad thing that he disappeared before his works were manifested, both among
his countrymen and Hindûs. We were glad that a
new star appeared in a region of shadow of death, but
to our loss and misfortune it disappeared so soon and
so unexpectedly. No doubt, sir, if our master had
lived, you will be glad to hear that great and remarkable things were done by him. It is no small thing
to lose such a beautiful, young, scientific, bold, and
good-natured gentleman for us all, especially for his
dear consort and child, whom he loved most tenderly.

We all, the native Christians as well as the American gentlemen and ladies, feel very sorry indeed for the
loss of our able minister. I pray that Lord of Mercy
to give consolation to the discomforted hearts of my
master's parents and friends, especially my kind mistress, who is left to lament after her dear husband.

With my humble salaams to you all,

 I remain, most venerable sir,

  Your very obedient and humble servant,

   J. H. BRECKENRIDGE.

Our father had already of his own accord written
the following affectionate letter to the mûnshi, which I
did not discover until it was too late to insert it in its
order: —

[TO J. H. BRECKENRIDGE.]

I notice that in very many of the letters which my beloved son sends to me from India, informing me of what he is endeavoring to do to benefit the people, he often mentions you as one of his best helpers in his work, and as I read these words respecting you, my heart is drawn out toward you in Christian love, and I feel very much like writing you a short letter.

My son left a pleasant home, loving parents, brothers and sister, and everything to make life desirable and happy, that he might go to India and tell the people there of the preciousness of Christ and his salvation. He had for many years thought a great deal about India, and I believe was moved by the Holy Spirit to devote his life to laboring among your people for their good, expecting no reward but to win the approbation of his Saviour and yours, in that great day when we shall all render up our account to the judge of the quick and the dead.

We, his parents, freely let him go, for we also have strong desires that the people of India may hear the message of Christ's love, and were willing that our son should obey the command of our Saviour to go "into all the world and preach the gospel to every creature." And now he is in his chosen field of labor, having spent years in qualifying himself for the work, and you are with him and know him, and already I do not doubt love him as a brother; and he is worthy of your love, for you will ever find him a fast friend, as will every soul that shall listen to the message he brings, and shall come to Christ with all their heart.

It rejoices me much to know that he has so kind a friend and helper as he has in you, and I pray you to confide in him in all things, for he will never disappoint you; and with your aid and sympathy and God's blessing, I have strong hopes that he will persuade many to renounce all superstition and idolatry, and to receive the Lord Jesus Christ as their only Saviour.

My dear Mr. Breckenridge, I am an old man, past threescore years and ten, and never expect to see again my son in the flesh, or to behold your countenance in this world. But if we bear the image of Christ on earth, we may with confidence look forward to the time when we shall bear his heavenly image in that better world to which we go. There I shall know you and you will know me, and we will sing together the song of redeeming love.

I am your brother in Christ,

CHARLES SCUDDER.

David's catechists each wrote to Mr. Capron, giving some particulars of his life and death, the most noticeable of which have already been used in these pages. Their letters are couched in the flowing terms of an Oriental speech, but display the simplicity of their feelings and sincerity of their grief. "As I think about his death and his life," writes one, "it is a great sadness to me. If he were living I should have many blessings." Next to his mûnshi, probably Pastor Seymour, of the town church at Periakulam, had the closest intercourse with David, and from his letter, addressed to Mr. Capron, I make the following extract: —

"To your loving presence, my much honored and most excellent father, your servant Seymour, making salaam with much reverence, writes as follows: According to the request of the honored Mr. Noyes I was strongly desirous to write you the brief history which follows of my dear and most excellent father, the honored Mr. Scudder. Therefore to whomever you desire to write and make known these facts, I earnestly beg you to do me the favor to write and make them known in my name.

" Those who knew and those who did not know our dear and excellent teacher and father, will desire to hear about the good disposition and wisdom well befitting a Christian teacher which were his, and about the way in which he performed the splendid labor of his service during the ten months that he came and lived among us. At the time he came here and began his great work, as all knew that he was recently from America, it was to be expected that both the Christians and the heathen should fasten their eyes on his disposition and his daily life. When he came he had learned to speak the Tamil somewhat; he conversed with much eagerness and benevolence, and with exceeding kindness, with the Christians and the heathen who came to see him, speaking with the hesitancy of a child, and in brief sentences, but striving to remove the errors of heathenism, and to impress upon the mind the truth of the Christian religion. Besides, in order to give instruction to the heathen, and to the members of the congregation, he used to come to Periakulam morning and evening, taking a few religious tracts in his hand, and having first seen and spoken with those of my congregation in a quarter of Periakulam, who met him, he would call me, and going into the village and seeing men of various sects, and speaking wisdom with earnestness and patience, would distribute his books and return. When, as sometimes happened, a dispute arose, he would reply with much love, and if he saw that what he said was not understood by those who listened, he would look at me with a smile, which indicated his feelings. It was on this account, from the eagerness he felt to be able to speak Tamil clearly, that he learned so rapidly. . . . .

" Once when he came by the way of Tenkarai to hold a meeting in my congregation, he saw a few heathen standing together. Although he desired to make known our Saviour to them, he was afraid that they would make a disturbance, and did not speak to them ; this he not only mentioned to me and to the members of the congregation, but thinking that he had denied the Saviour, he earnestly begged forgiveness for this fault in prayer.

" . . . . Moreover, among Christians also he exhibited an amiable disposition and a bright example. Although there were some well-known faults in the congregation, he did not despise the people on account of their faults, but was constantly putting forth efforts that they might, by whatever means, become true Christians. If you told him about a weak Christian, he longed to reconcile him and to establish him again in the Lord. He would see him often and question him, and advise him with patience, with thought of the Saviour, and with tears, leading him to reflect upon his fault, and not giving up till he had established him. Although a few of the members of the congregation spoke roughly to him, he would listen to them cheerfully and advise them with much tenderness. There is no one of my congregation whom he had not seen and conversed with. Besides every week, on the Sabbath, after the

afternoon service he went regularly to three houses for
the purpose of having prayer with the people. . . . .

"There are facts which show that he was prepared
for death. For once reflecting about himself, he said
to me many times that he was a great sinner. That
he should speak in this way was very surprising to me,
for while I could not but believe that he was, as far as
I knew, a teacher who possessed the spirit of our
Saviour, the surprise was that he had such little
thought of himself as to say in this way that he was
a sinner. At another time, he began to converse with
me about true faith, and asked me to describe briefly
and accurately the faith which is necessary to salvation. To this I replied : ' The faith which is necessary
to salvation is an eye which is always turned to Jesus
hanging upon the cross; it is an empty hand which is
always stretched out to receive the forgiveness, righteousness, wisdom, and other blessings which He gra-
ciously gives. A person of such faith that he may
win Christ and the righteousness which comes by Him,
will count all things else but dung. Besides this faith
is not dead but living. It works by love, it purifies
the heart. This is the victory which overcomes the
world. It is by such marks as these that the faith
which we have will be found to be the true faith.'
' Is this so ? ' he asked ; ' then,' he asked himself,
' have I such faith ? '

"At another time he spoke about death. That one
who spoke thus about death had premonitions of his
own death there is evidence from his own words. For
when paying forty rupees, advance money, to a man
to get a touring-cart made for him, he looked at the
man and said, ' If I die, you must give this money

without the least trouble to Mrs. Scudder.' Finally, a few days before he died, when he was questioning me about the bliss of heaven, he enlarged upon the brief reply which I made, and closed by saying, ' Oh, that will be joyful, joyful.'

"Alas! that one of such benevolence of heart, quick perception, love for souls, delight in prayer, true godliness, self-abhorrence, unfailing perseverance, and other noble qualities, who also had much learning, a keen intellect, humility of opinion, so patient a disposition, such vigor of body and youth, should die so suddenly, is certainly to us a great loss."

To his former comrades, both in college and in the theological seminary, the news of David's death brought personal sorrow; they had not thought of death in connection with one so flushed with life, so full of great capacities of labor. At Andover the Senior Professor, when the intelligence came, met his class in the lecture-room and spent an hour in a heartfelt tribute to the memory of one who had left upon the seminary the stamp of his individual power. " You could trace his course through this seminary," said he, " as a river through a meadow, by the greenness of its banks. If he had died immediately upon leaving us, he would have done a life's work."

It needs not that mention should be made of the sorrow which this death brought upon the household which it entered. But the love of the father for his son, which I have not set forth as I ought, strong in the child's infancy, growing with his growth, sanctified by the sacrifice which it made in the world-wide separation, deepened by the unceasing interchange of thought and words of affection, — this love, answered by the steadfast, tender feeling of the son, was permitted its fullest joy in the quick union of souls above. The father, growing in years, had not thought to be the one left behind. Nor was he long detained. The first intelligence of the death, travelling for six weeks, came in one short sentence upon the envelope of a letter from Madras to the Missionary House. On Friday, the 16th of January, 1863, came this message. On the Wednesday following, our father, going out in the morning through the city, felt weary and entered an office to rest, where suddenly, without pain, without the hour of trouble, he died.

It will not be thought strange that these two souls, so joined in life, should be reunited also at death. To our minds who knew them both they ever dwell together; and if it shall seem to any one reading this memorial of a brother that it was not necessary to record so uneventful a life, or that my partiality has magnified the worth of one little known to the world, let me answer that I have obeyed the request of my father, uttered the night before his death, with no thought that it would be his final charge to me. "It is not," said he, " because I love my son that I think his life worthy to be published, but because I think that Christ will be honored and His cause advanced." In the spirit which led him to ask me to prepare this work, I have sought to perform it, and now offer it reverently to Christ and the Church.

*LAUS DEO.*

# INDEX.